THE
TEN
THOUSAND
DOORS
OF
JANUARY

ALIX E. HARROW

REDHOOK

Copyright © 2019 by Alix E. Harrow
Cover design by Lisa Marie Pompilio
Cover illustrations by Shutterstock
Cover copyright © 2019 by Hachette Book Group, Inc.

Redhook Books/Orbit
Hachette Book Group
1290 Avenue of the Americas
New York, NY 10104
hachettebookgroup.com

Simultaneously published in Great Britain by Orbit and in the U.S. by Redhook in 2019

First Edition: September 2019

Redhook is an imprint of Orbit, a division of Hachette Book Group.
The Redhook name and logo are trademarks of Hachette Book Group, Inc.

The publisher is not responsible for websites (or their content) that are not owned by the publisher.

The Hachette Speakers Bureau provides a wide range of authors for speaking events. To find out more, go to www.hachettespeakersbureau.com or call (866) 376-6591.

Library of Congress Cataloging-in-Publication Data
Names: Harrow, Alix E., author.
Title: The ten thousand doors of January / Alix E. Harrow.
Description: First edition. | New York, NY: Redhook Books/Orbit, 2019.
Identifiers: LCCN 2018049178| ISBN 9780316421997 (hardcover) |
    ISBN 9780316422000 (library ebook)
Subjects: | GSAFD: Fantasy fiction.
Classification: LCC PS3608.A783854 T46 2019 | DDC 813/.6—dc23
LC record available at https://lccn.loc.gov/2018049178

ISBNs: 978-0-316-42199-7 (hardcover), 978-0-316-42198-0 (ebook)

Printed in the United States of America

LSC-C

10 9 8 7 6 5 4 3 2 1

For Nick, my comrade and compass

THE
TEN
THOUSAND
DOORS
OF
JANUARY

The Blue Door

When I was seven, I found a door. I suspect I should capitalize that word, so you understand I'm not talking about your garden- or common-variety door that leads reliably to a white-tiled kitchen or a bedroom closet.

When I was seven, I found a Door. There—look how tall and proud the word stands on the page now, the belly of that *D* like a black archway leading into white nothing. When you see that word, I imagine a little prickle of familiarity makes the hairs on the back of your neck stand up. You don't know a thing about me; you can't see me sitting at this yellow-wood desk, the salt-sweet breeze riffling these pages like a reader looking for her bookmark. You can't see the scars that twist and knot across my skin. You don't even know my name (it's January Scaller;

so now I suppose you do know a little something about me and I've ruined my point).

But you know what it means when you see the word *Door*. Maybe you've even seen one for yourself, standing half-ajar and rotted in an old church, or oiled and shining in a brick wall. Maybe, if you're one of those fanciful persons who find their feet running toward unexpected places, you've even walked through one and found yourself in a very unexpected place indeed.

Or maybe you've never so much as glimpsed a Door in your life. There aren't as many of them as there used to be.

But you still know about Doors, don't you? Because there are ten thousand stories about ten thousand Doors, and we know them as well as we know our names. They lead to Faerie, to Valhalla, Atlantis and Lemuria, Heaven and Hell, to all the directions a compass could never take you, to *elsewhere*. My father—who is a true scholar and not just a young lady with an ink pen and a series of things she has to say—puts it much better: "If we address stories as archaeological sites, and dust through their layers with meticulous care, we find at some level there is always a doorway. A dividing point between *here* and *there*, us and them, mundane and magical. It is at the moments when the doors open, when things flow between the worlds, that stories happen."

He never capitalized doors. But perhaps scholars don't capitalize words just because of the shapes they make on the page.

It was the summer of 1901, although the arrangement of four numbers on a page didn't mean much to me then. I think of it now as a swaggering, full-of-itself sort of year, shining with the gold-plated promises of a new century. It had shed all the mess and fuss of the nineteenth century—all those wars and revolutions and uncertainties, all those imperial growing pains—and now there was nothing but peace and prosperity

2

wherever one looked. Mr. J. P. Morgan had recently become the richest man in the entire history of the world; Queen Victoria had finally expired and left her vast empire to her kingly-looking son; those unruly Boxers had been subdued in China; and Cuba had been tucked neatly beneath America's civilized wing. Reason and rationality reigned supreme, and there was no room for magic or mystery.

There was no room, it turned out, for little girls who wandered off the edge of the map and told the truth about the mad, impossible things they found there.

I found it on the raggedy western edge of Kentucky, right where the state dips its toe into the Mississippi. It's not the kind of place you'd expect to find anything mysterious or even mildly interesting: it's flat and scrubby-looking, populated by flat, scrubby-looking people. The sun hangs twice as hot and three times as bright as it does in the rest of the country, even at the very end of August, and everything feels damp and sticky, like the soap scum left on your skin when you're the last one to use the bath.

But Doors, like murder suspects in cheap mysteries, are often where you least expect them.

I was only in Kentucky at all because Mr. Locke had taken me along on one of his business trips. He said it was a "real treat" and a "chance to see how things are done," but really it was because my nursemaid was teetering on the edge of hysteria and had threatened to quit at least four times in the last month. I was a difficult child, back then.

Or maybe it was because Mr. Locke was trying to cheer me up. A postcard had arrived last week from my father. It had a picture of a brown girl wearing a pointy gold hat and a resentful expression, with the words *AUTHENTIC BUR-MESE COSTUME* stamped alongside her. On the back were three lines in tidy brown ink: *Extending my stay, back in October. Thinking of you. JS.* Mr. Locke had read it over my shoulder and patted my arm in a clumsy, keep-your-chin-up sort of way.

A week later I was stuffed in the velvet and wood-paneled coffin of a Pullman sleeper car reading *The Rover Boys in the Jungle* while Mr. Locke read the business section of the *Times* and Mr. Stirling stared into space with a valet's professional blankness.

I ought to introduce Mr. Locke properly; he'd hate to wander into the story in such a casual, slantwise way. Allow me to present Mr. William Cornelius Locke, self-made not-quite-billionaire, head of W. C. Locke & Co., owner of no less than three stately homes along the Eastern Seaboard, proponent of the virtues of Order and Propriety (words that he certainly would prefer to see capitalized—see that *P*, like a woman with her hand on her hip?), and chairman of the New England Archaeological Society, a sort of social club for rich, powerful men who were also amateur collectors. I say "amateur" only because it was fashionable for wealthy men to refer to their passions in this dismissive way, with a little flick of their fingers, as if admitting to a profession other than moneymaking might sully their reputations.

In truth, I sometimes suspected that all Locke's moneymaking was specifically designed to fuel his collecting hobby. His home in Vermont—the one we actually lived in, as opposed to the two other pristine structures intended mainly to impress his significance upon the world—was a vast, private Smithsonian packed so tightly it seemed to be constructed of artifacts rather than mortar and stones. There was little organization: limestone figures of wide-hipped women kept company with Indonesian screens carved like lace, and obsidian arrowheads shared a glass case with the taxidermied arm of an Edo warrior (I hated that arm but couldn't stop looking at it, wondering what it had looked like alive and muscled, how its owner would have felt about a little girl in America looking at his paper-dry flesh without even knowing his name).

My father was one of Mr. Locke's field agents, hired when I was nothing but an eggplant-sized bundle wrapped in an old traveling coat. "Your mother had just died, you know, very sad case," Mr. Locke liked to recite to me, "and there was your father—this odd-colored, scarecrow-looking fellow with God-help-him *tattoos* up and down his arms—in the absolute middle of nowhere with a baby. I said to myself: Cornelius, there's a man in need of a little charity!"

Father was hired before dusk. Now he gallivants around the world collecting objects "of particular unique value" and mailing them to Mr. Locke so he can put them in glass cases with brass plaques and shout at me when I touch them or play with them or steal the Aztec coins to re-create scenes from *Treasure Island*. And I stay in my little gray room in Locke House and harass the nursemaids Locke hires to civilize me and wait for Father to come home.

At seven, I'd spent considerably more time with Mr. Locke than with my own biological father, and insofar as it was possible to love someone so naturally comfortable in three-piece suits, I loved him.

As was his custom, Mr. Locke had taken rooms for us in the nicest establishment available; in Kentucky, that translated to a sprawling pinewood hotel on the edge of the Mississippi, clearly built by someone who wanted to open a grand hotel but hadn't ever met one in real life. There were candy-striped wallpaper and electric chandeliers, but a sour catfish smell seeped up from the floorboards.

Mr. Locke waved past the manager with a fly-swatting gesture, told him to "Keep an eye on the girl, that's a good fellow," and swept into the lobby with Mr. Stirling trailing like a man-shaped dog at his heels. Locke greeted a bow-tied man waiting on one of the flowery couches. "Governor Dockery, a pleasure! I read your last missive with greatest attention, I assure you—and how is your cranium collection coming?"

Ah. So that was why we came: Mr. Locke was meeting one of his Archaeological Society pals for an evening of drinking, cigar smoking, and boasting. They had an annual Society meeting every summer at Locke House—a fancy party followed by a stuffy, members-only affair that neither I nor my father was permitted to attend—but some of the real enthusiasts couldn't wait the full year and sought one another out wherever they could.

The manager smiled at me in that forced, panicky way of childless adults, and I smiled toothily back. "I'm going out," I told him confidently. He smiled a little harder, blinking with uncertainty. People are always uncertain about me: my skin is sort of coppery-red, as if it's covered all over with cedar sawdust, but my eyes are round and light and my clothes are expensive. Was I a pampered pet or a serving girl? Should the poor manager serve me tea or toss me in the kitchens with the maids? I was what Mr. Locke called "an in-between sort of thing."

I tipped over a tall vase of flowers, gasped an insincere "oh *dear,*" and slunk away while the manager swore and mopped at the mess with his coat. I escaped outdoors (see how that word slips into even the most mundane of stories? Sometimes I feel there are doors lurking in the creases of every sentence, with periods for knobs and verbs for hinges).

The streets were nothing but sunbaked stripes crisscrossing themselves before they ended in the muddy river, but the people of Ninley, Kentucky, seemed inclined to stroll along them as if they were proper city streets. They stared and muttered as I went by.

An idle dockworker pointed and nudged his companion.

"That's a little Chickasaw girl, I'll bet you." His workmate shook his head, citing his extensive personal experience with Indian girls, and speculated, "West Indian, maybe. Or a half-breed."

I kept walking. People were always guessing like that, categorizing me as one thing or another, but Mr. Locke assured me they were all equally incorrect. "A perfectly unique specimen," he called me. Once after a comment from one of the maids I'd asked him if I was colored and he'd snorted. "Odd-colored, perhaps, but hardly *colored*." I didn't really know what made a person colored or not, but the way he said it made me glad I wasn't.

The speculating was worse when my father was with me. His skin is darker than mine, a lustrous red-black, and his eyes are so black even the whites are threaded with brown. Once you factor in the tattoos—ink spirals twisting up both wrists—and the shabby suit and the spectacles and the muddled-up accent and—well. People stared.

I still wished he were with me.

I was so busy walking and not looking back at all those white faces that I thudded into someone. "Sorry, ma'am, I—" An old woman, hunched and seamed like a pale walnut, glared down at me. It was a practiced, grandmotherly glare, especially made for children who moved too fast and knocked into her. "Sorry," I said again.

She didn't answer, but something shifted in her eyes like a chasm cleaving open. Her mouth hung open, and her filmy eyes went wide as shutters. "Who—just who the hell are you?" she hissed at me. People don't like in-between things, I suppose.

I should have scurried back to the catfish-smelling hotel and huddled in Mr. Locke's safe, moneyed shadow, where none of these damn people could reach me; it would have been the proper thing to do. But, as Mr. Locke so often complained, I could sometimes be quite improper, willful, and temerarious (a word I assumed was unflattering from the company it kept).

So I ran away.

I ran until my stick-thin legs shook and my chest heaved against the fine seams of my dress. I ran until the street turned to a winding lane and the buildings behind me were swallowed up by wisteria and honeysuckle. I ran and tried not to think about the old woman's eyes on my face, or how much trouble I would be in for disappearing.

My feet stopped their churning only once they realized the dirt beneath them had turned to laid-over grasses. I found myself in a lonely, overgrown field beneath a sky so blue it reminded me of the tiles my father brought back from Persia: a majestic, world-swallowing blue you could fall into. Tall, rust-colored grasses rolled beneath it, and a few scattered cedars spiraled up toward it.

Something in the shape of the scene—the rich smell of dry cedar in the sun, the grass swaying against the sky like a tigress in orange and blue—made me want to curl into the dry stems like a fawn waiting for her mother. I waded deeper, wandering, letting my hands trail through the frilled tops of wild grains.

I almost didn't notice the Door at all. All Doors are like that, half-shadowed and sideways until someone looks at them in just the right way.

This one was nothing but an old timber frame arranged in a shape like the start of a house of cards. Rust stains spotted the wood where hinges and nails had bled into nothing, and only a few brave planks remained of the door itself. Flaking paint still clung to it, the same royal blue as the sky.

Now, I didn't know about Doors at the time, and wouldn't have believed you even if you'd handed me an annotated three-volume collection of eyewitness reports. But when I saw that raggedy blue door standing so lonesome in the field, I wanted it to lead someplace else. Someplace other than Ninley, Kentucky, someplace new and unseen and so vast I would never come to the end of it.

I pushed my palm against the blue paint. The hinges groaned, just like the doors to haunted houses in all my penny papers and adventure stories. My heart *pat-pat*ted in my chest, and some naive corner of my soul was holding its breath in expectation, waiting for something magical to happen.

There was nothing on the other side of the Door, of course: just the cobalt and cinnamon colors of my own world, sky and field. And—God knows why—the sight of it broke my heart. I sat down in my nice linen dress and wept with the loss of it. What had I expected? One of those magical passages children are always stumbling across in my books?

If Samuel had been there, we could've at least played pretend. Samuel Zappia was my only nonfictional friend: a dark-eyed boy with a clinical addiction to pulpy story papers and the faraway expression of a sailor watching the horizon. He visited Locke House twice a week in a red wagon with *ZAPPIA FAMILY GROCERIES, INC.* painted on the side in curlicued gold lettering, and usually contrived to sneak me the latest issue of *The Argosy All-Story Weekly* or *The Halfpenny Marvel* along with the flour and onions. On weekends he escaped his family's shop to join me in elaborate games of make-believe involving ghosts and dragons on the lakeshore. *Sognatore*, his mother called him, which Samuel said was Italian for good-for-nothing-boy-who-breaks-his-mother's-heart-by-dreaming-all-the-time.

But Samuel wasn't with me that day in the field. So I pulled out my little pocket diary and wrote a story instead.

When I was seven, that diary was the most precious thing I had ever owned, although whether I technically owned it is legally questionable. I hadn't bought it, and no one had given it to me—I'd found it. I was playing in the Pharaoh Room just before I turned seven, opening and closing all the urns and trying on the jewelry, and I happened to open a pretty blue treasure chest (*Box with vaulted lid, decorated with ivory, ebony, blue faience, Egypt; originally matched pair*). And in the bottom of the chest was this diary: leather the color of burnt butter, creamy cotton pages as blank and inviting as fresh snow.

It seemed likely that Mr. Locke had left it for me to find, a secret gift he was too gruff to give directly, so I took it without hesitation. I wrote in it whenever I was lonely or lost-feeling, or when my father was away and Mr. Locke was busy and the nursemaid was being horrible. I wrote a lot.

Mostly I wrote stories like the ones I read in Samuel's copies of *The Argosy*, about brave little boys with blond hair and names like Jack or Dick or Buddy. I spent a lot of time thinking of bloodcurdling titles and copying them out with extra-swirly lines ("The Mystery of the Skeleton Key"; "The Golden Dagger Society"; "The Flying Orphan Girl"), and no time at all worrying about plot. That afternoon, sitting in that lonely field beside the Door that didn't lead anywhere, I wanted to write a different kind of story. A true kind of story, something I could crawl into if only I believed it hard enough.

Once there was a brave and temeraryous (sp?) girl who found a Door. It was a magic Door that's why it has a capital D. She opened the Door.

For a single second—a stretched-out slice of time that began on the sinuous curve of the *S* and ended when my pencil made its final swirl around the period—I believed it. Not in the half-pretending way that children believe in Santa Claus or fairies, but in the marrow-deep way you believe in gravity or rain.

Something in the world shifted. I know that's a shit description, pardon my unladylike language, but I don't know how else to say it. It was like an earthquake that didn't disturb a single blade of grass, an eclipse that didn't cast a single shadow, a vast but invisible change. A sudden breeze plucked the edge of the diary. It smelled of salt and warm stone and a dozen faraway scents that did not belong in a scrubby field beside the Mississippi.

I tucked my diary back in my skirts and stood. My legs shivered beneath me like birch trees in the wind, shaking with exhaustion, but I ignored them because the Door seemed to be murmuring in a soft, clattering language made of wood rot and peeling paint. I reached toward it again, hesitated, and then—

I opened the Door, and stepped through.

I wasn't anywhere at all. An echoing in-betweenness pressed against my eardrums, as if I'd swum to the bottom of a vast lake. My reaching hand disappeared into the emptiness; my boot swung in an arc that never ended.

I call that in-between place the threshold now (Threshold, the line of the *T* splitting two empty spaces). Thresholds are dangerous places, neither here nor there, and walking across one is like stepping off the edge of a cliff in the naive faith that you'll sprout wings halfway down. You can't hesitate, or doubt. You can't fear the in-between.

My foot landed on the other side of the door. The cedar and sunlight smell was replaced by a coppery taste in my mouth. I opened my eyes.

It was a world made of salt water and stone. I stood on a high bluff surrounded on all sides by an endless silver sea. Far below me, cupped by the curving shore of the island like a pebble in a palm, was a city.

At least, I supposed it was a city. It didn't have any of the usual trappings of one: no streetcars hummed and buzzed through it, and no haze of coal smoke curtained above it. Instead, there were whitewashed stone buildings arranged in artful spirals, dotted with open windows like black eyes. A few towers raised their heads above the crowd and the masts of small ships made a tiny forest along the coast.

11

I was crying again. Without theater or flair, just—crying, as if there were something I badly wanted and couldn't have. As my father did sometimes when he thought he was alone.

"January! *January!*" My name sounded like it was coming from a cheap gramophone several miles away, but I recognized Mr. Locke's voice echoing after me through the doorway. I didn't know how he'd found me, but I knew I was in trouble.

Oh, I can't tell you how much I didn't want to go back. How the sea smelled so full of promise, how the coiling streets in the city below seemed to make a kind of script. If it hadn't been Mr. Locke calling me—the man who let me ride in fancy train cars and bought me nice linen dresses, the man who patted my arm when my father disappointed me and left pocket diaries for me to find—I might have stayed.

But I turned back to the Door. It looked different on this side, a tumbled-down arch of weathered basalt, without even the dignity of wooden planks to serve as a door. A gray curtain fluttered in the opening instead. I drew it aside.

Just before I stepped back through the arch, a glint of silver shimmered at my feet: a round coin lay half-buried in the soil, stamped with several words in a foreign language and the profile of a crowned woman. It felt warm in my palm. I slipped it into my dress pocket.

This time the threshold passed over me like the brief shadow of a bird's wing. The dry smell of grass and sun returned.

"Janua—oh, there you are." Mr. Locke stood in his shirtsleeves and vest, huffing a little, his mustache bristling like the tail of a recently offended cat. "Where were you? Been out here shouting myself hoarse, had to interrupt my meeting with Alexander—what's this?" He was staring at the blue-flecked Door, his face gone slack.

"Nothing, sir."

His eyes snapped away from the Door and onto me, ice-sharp. "January. Tell me what you've been doing."

I should've lied. It would have saved so much heartache. But you have to understand: when Mr. Locke looks at you in this particular way of his, with his moon-pale eyes, you mostly end up doing what he wants you to. I suspect it's the reason W. C. Locke & Co. is so profitable.

I swallowed. "I—I was just playing and I went through this door, see, and it leads to someplace else. There was a white city by the sea." If I'd been older, I might've said: *It smelled of salt and age and adventure. It smelled like another world, and I want to return right this minute and walk those strange streets.* Instead, I added articulately, "I liked it."

"Tell the *truth*." His eyes pressed me flat.

"I am, I swear!"

He stared for another long moment. I watched the muscles of his jaw roll and unroll. "And where did this door come from? Did you—did you build it? Stick it together out of this rubbish?" He gestured and I noticed the overgrown pile of rotted lumber behind the Door, the scattered bones of a house.

"No, sir. I just found it. And wrote a story about it."

"A story?" I could see him stumbling over each unlikely twist in our conversation and hating it; he liked to be in control of any given exchange.

I fumbled for my pocket diary and pressed it into his hands. "Look right there, see? I wrote a little story, and then the door was, was sort of open. It's true, I swear it's true."

His eyes flicked over the page many more times than was necessary to read a three-sentence story. Then he removed a cigar stub from his coat pocket and struck a match, puffing until the end glowed at me like the hot orange eye of a dragon.

He sighed, the way he sighed when he was forced to deliver some bad news to his investors, and closed my diary. "What fanciful nonsense, January. How often have I tried to cure you of it?"

He ran his thumb across the cover of my diary and then deliberately, almost mournfully, tossed it into the messy heap of lumber behind him.

"*No!* You can't—"

"I'm sorry, January. Truly." He met my eyes and made an abortive movement with his hand, as if he wanted to reach toward me. "But this is simply what must be done, for your sake. I'll expect you at dinner."

I wanted to fight him. To argue, to snatch my diary out of the dirt—but I couldn't.

I ran away instead. Back across the field, back up winding dirt roads, back into the sour-smelling hotel lobby.

And so the very beginning of my story features a skinny-legged girl on the run twice in the space of a few hours. It's not a very heroic introduction, is it? But—if you're an in-between sort of creature with no family and no money, with nothing but your own two legs and a silver coin—sometimes running away is the only thing you can do.

And anyway, if I hadn't been the kind of girl who ran away, I wouldn't have found the blue Door. And there wouldn't be much of a story to tell.

The fear of God and Mr. Locke kept me quiet that evening and the following day. I was well watched by Mr. Stirling and the nervous hotel manager, who herded me the way you might handle a valuable but dangerous zoo animal. I amused myself for a while by slamming the keys on the grand piano and watching him flinch, but eventually I was shepherded back into my room and advised to go to sleep.

I was out the low window and dodging through the alley before the sun had fully set. The road was scattered with shadows like shallow black pools, and by the time I reached the field, stars were shimmering through the hot haze of smoke and tobacco that hung over Ninley. I stumbled through the grass, squinting into the gloom for that house-of-cards shape.

The blue Door wasn't there.

Instead, I found a ragged black circle in the grass. Ash and char were all that remained of my Door. My pocket diary lay among the coals, curled and blackened. I left it there.

When I stumbled back into the sagging, not-very-grand hotel, the sky was tar-black and my knee socks were stained. Mr. Locke was sitting in an oily blue cloud of smoke in the lobby with his ledgers and papers spread before him and his favorite jade tumbler full of evening scotch.

"And where have you been this evening? Did you walk back through that door and find yourself on Mars? Or the moon, perhaps?" But his tone was gentle. The thing about Mr. Locke is that he really was kind to me. Even during the worst of it, he was always kind.

"No," I admitted. "But I bet there are more Doors just like it. I bet I could find them and write about them and they'd all open. And I don't care if you don't believe me." Why didn't I just keep my stupid mouth closed? Why didn't I shake my head and apologize with a hint of tears in my voice, and slink off to bed with the memory of the blue Door like a secret talisman in my pocket? Because I was seven and stubborn, and didn't yet understand the cost of true stories.

"Is that so," was all Mr. Locke said, and I marched to my room under the impression that I'd evaded more severe punishment.

It wasn't until we arrived back in Vermont a week later that I realized I was wrong.

Locke House was an immense red stone castle perched at the edge of Lake Champlain, topped with a forest of chimneys and copper-roofed towers. Its innards were wood-paneled and labyrinthine, bristling with the strange and rare and valuable; a *Boston Herald* columnist had once described it as "architecturally fanciful, more reminiscent of *Ivanhoe* than a modern man's abode." It was rumored that a mad Scotsman had commissioned it in the 1790s, spent a week living in it, and then vanished forevermore. Mr. Locke bought it at auction in the 1880s and began filling it with the world's wonders.

Father and I were stuffed into two rooms on the third story: a tidy, square office for him, with a big desk and a single window, and a gray, musty-smelling room with two narrow beds for me and my nursemaid. The newest one was a German immigrant named Miss Wilda, who wore heavy black woolen gowns and an expression that said she hadn't seen much of the twentieth century yet but heartily disapproved of it thus far. She liked hymns and freshly folded laundry, and detested fuss, mess, and cheek. We were natural enemies.

Upon our return, Wilda and Mr. Locke had a hurried conversation in the hall. Her eyes glittered at me like overshined coat buttons.

"Mr. Locke tells me you've been overstimulated lately, nearly hysterical, little dove." Miss Wilda often called me *little dove*; she was a believer in the power of suggestion.

"No, ma'am."

"Ah, poor dear. We'll have you right as the rain in no time at all."

The cure for overstimulation was a calm, structured environment without distraction; my room was therefore summarily stripped of everything colorful or whimsical or dear. The curtains were drawn and the bookshelf cleared of anything more exciting than *A Child's Illustrated Bible*. My favorite pink-and-gold bedspread—Father had sent it to me from Bangalore the previous year—was exchanged for starched white sheets. Samuel was forbidden to visit.

Miss Wilda's key slid and thunked in the keyhole, and I was alone.

At first I imagined myself a prisoner of war resisting the red-coats or rebels and practiced my expression of stoic resistance. But by the second day the silence was like two thumbs pressing against my eardrums and my legs shuddered and shook with the desire to run and keep running, back to that cedar-spiraled field, through the ashes of the blue Door to some other world.

On the third day, my room became a cell, which became a cage, which became a coffin, and I discovered the very deepest fear that swam through my heart like eels in undersea caves: to be locked away, trapped and alone.

Something in the center of me cracked. I tore at the curtains with clawed nails, I ripped the knobs from dresser drawers, I beat my small fists against the locked door, and then I sat on the floor and wept great hiccuping rivers of tears until Miss Wilda returned with a syrupy spoonful of something that took me away from myself for a while. My muscles turned to oiled, languorous rivers and my head bobbed loosely along the surface. The creep of shadows across the rugs became a terrible drama so absorbing there wasn't room for anything else in my head until I fell asleep.

When I woke, Mr. Locke was sitting at the side of my bed reading a newspaper. "Morning, my dear. And how are you feeling?"

I swallowed sour spit. "Better, sir."

"I'm glad." He folded his paper with architectural precision. "Listen to me very carefully, January. You are a girl of very great potential—immense, even!—but you've got to learn to behave yourself. From now on there will be no more fanciful nonsense, or running off, or doors that lead places they shouldn't."

His expression as he surveyed me made me think of old-timey

illustrations of God: severely paternal, bestowing the kind of love that weighs and measures before it finds you worthy. His eyes were stones, pressing down. "You are going to *mind your place* and *be a good girl.*"

I wanted desperately to be worthy of Mr. Locke's love. "Yes, sir," I whispered. And I was.

My father didn't return until November, looking as creased and tired as his luggage. His arrival followed its usual pattern: the wagon crunched its way up the drive and stopped before the stone majesty of Locke House. Mr. Locke went out to offer congratulatory backslapping and I waited in the front hall with Miss Wilda, dressed in a jumper so starched I felt like a turtle in an overlarge shell.

The door opened and he stood silhouetted, looking very dark and foreign in the pale November light. He paused on the threshold because this was generally the moment fifty pounds of excited young girl rocketed into his kneecaps.

But I didn't move. For the first time in my life, I didn't run to him. The silhouette's shoulders sagged.

It seems cruel to you, doesn't it? A sullen child punishing her father for his absence. But I assure you my intentions at the time were thoroughly muddled; there was just something about the shape of him in the doorway that made me dizzy with anger. Maybe because he smelled like jungles and steamships and adventures, like shadowed caves and unseen wonders, and my world was so ferociously mundane. Or maybe just because I'd been locked away and he hadn't been there to open the door.

He took three hesitant steps and crouched before me in the foyer. He looked older than I remembered, the stubble on his chin shining dull silver instead of black, as if every day he spent away from me were three days in his world. The sadness was the same as it always was, though, like a veil drawn over his eyes.

He rested a hand on my shoulder, black snakes of tattoos twisting around his wrists. "January, is something wrong?"

The familiar sound of my name in his mouth, his strange-but-not-strange accent, almost undid me. I wanted to tell him the truth—*I stumbled over something grand and wild, something that rips a hole in the shape of the world. I wrote something and it was true*—but I'd learned better. I was a good girl now.

"Everything is fine, sir," I answered, and watched the cool grown-up-ness of my voice hit my father like a slap.

I didn't speak to him over the dinner table that evening, and I didn't sneak into his room that night to beg stories from him (and he was a champion storyteller, let me tell you; he always said ninety-nine percent of his job was following the stories and seeing where they led).

But I was done with that fanciful nonsense. No more doors or Doors, no more dreams of silver seas and whitewashed cities. No more stories. I imagined this was just one of those lessons implicit in the process of growing up, which everyone learns eventually.

I'll tell you a secret, though: I still had that silver coin with the portrait of the strange queen on it. I kept it in a tiny pocket sewed in my underskirt, flesh-warm against my waist, and when I held it I could smell the sea.

It was my most precious possession for ten years. Until I turned seventeen, and found *The Ten Thousand Doors*.

The Leather-Bound Door

I wouldn't have found it if it weren't for the bird.

I was heading down to the kitchen to steal evening coffee from Mrs. Purtram, the cook, when I heard a twittering, thrashing sound and paused halfway down the second staircase. I waited until it happened again: the rushing silence of beating wings and a hollow thudding. Silence.

I followed the sound to the second-floor parlor, labeled the Pharaoh Room, where Mr. Locke's extensive Egyptian collection was housed: red and blue caskets, marble urns with wings for handles, tiny golden ankhs on leather strings, carved stone columns orphaned from their temples. The whole room had a yellowy-gold glow to it, even in the almost-dark of a summer evening.

The sound came from the southern corner of the room, where my blue treasure chest still stood. It rattled on its plinth.

After I'd found my pocket diary I hadn't been able to help circling back around to the chest every now and then and peering into its dusty-smelling depths. Around Christmas, a cut-paper puppet appeared with little wooden sticks affixed to each of her limbs. The following summer there was a tiny music box that played a Russian-sounding waltz, and then a little brown doll beaded in bright colors, and then an illustrated French edition of *The Jungle Book*.

I never asked him directly, but I was certain they were gifts from Mr. Locke. They tended to show up right when I needed them most, when my father had forgotten another birthday or missed another holiday. I could almost feel his awkward hand on my shoulder, offering silent comfort.

It seemed extremely unlikely, however, that he would intentionally hide a bird in the box. I lifted the lid, not quite believing it, and a gray-and-gold something exploded up at me as if fired from a small cannon and ricocheted around the parlor. It was a delicate, ruffled-looking bird with a marmalade-colored head and spindly legs. (I tried to look it up, later, but it didn't look like any of the birds in Mr. Audubon's book.)

I was turning away, letting the lid of the chest fall—when I realized there was something else still inside.

A book. A smallish, leather-bound book with scuffed corners and with dented imprints where the gold-stamped title had been partially scraped off: THE TEN THOU OORS. I riffled the pages with one thumb.

Those of you who are more than casually familiar with books—those of you who spend your free afternoons in fusty bookshops, who offer furtive, kindly strokes along the spines of familiar titles—understand that page riffling is an essential element in the process of introducing oneself to a new book.

It isn't about reading the words; it's about reading the smell, which wafts from the pages in a cloud of dust and wood pulp. It might smell expensive and well bound, or it might smell of tissue-thin paper and blurred two-color prints, or of fifty years unread in the home of a tobacco-smoking old man. Books can smell of cheap thrills or painstaking scholarship, of literary weight or unsolved mysteries.

This one smelled unlike any book I'd ever held. Cinnamon and coal smoke, catacombs and loam. Damp seaside evenings and sweat-slick noontimes beneath palm fronds. It smelled as if it had been in the mail for longer than any one parcel could be, circling the world for years and accumulating layers of smells like a tramp wearing too many clothes.

It smelled like adventure itself had been harvested in the wild, distilled to a fine wine, and splashed across each page.

But I'm stumbling ahead of myself. Stories are supposed to be told in order, with beginnings and middles and ends. I'm no scholar, but I know that much.

I spent the years after the blue Door doing what most willful, temerarious girls must do: becoming less so.

In the fall of 1903 I was nine and the world was tasting the word *modern* on its tongue. A pair of brothers in the Carolinas were experimenting enthusiastically with their flying machines; our new president had just advised us to speak softly but carry big sticks, which apparently meant we ought to invade Panama; and bright red hair was briefly popular, until women started reporting dizziness and hair loss and Miss Valentine's Hair Potion was revealed to be little more than red rat poison. My father was somewhere in northern Europe (my postcard showed snowy mountains and a pair of children dressed like Hansel and Gretel; the back said *Happy belated birthday*), and Mr. Locke finally trusted me enough to take me on another trip.

My behavior since the Kentucky incident had been impeccable: I didn't torment Mr. Stirling or disturb Mr. Locke's collections; I obeyed all Wilda's rules, even the really stupid ones about folding your collars straight after ironing; I didn't play on the grounds with "lice-ridden urchins just off the boat," but merely watched Samuel driving the grocery cart from the third-story window of my father's study. He still snuck story papers to me whenever he could finagle them past Mrs. Purtram, their corners dog-eared to his favorite pages, and I returned them rolled tight in the empty milk bottles, with all the best and most bloodthirsty lines circled.

He always looked up as he left, always stared long enough for me to know he'd seen me, and raised a hand. Sometimes, if Wilda wasn't looking and I was feeling daring, I touched my fingertips to the windowpane in return.

Mostly I spent my time conjugating Latin verbs and doing sums beneath the watery eye of my tutor. I sat through my weekly lessons with Mr. Locke, nodding politely while he lectured about stocks, regulatory boards that didn't know what was what, his youthful studies in England, and the three best varieties of scotch. I practiced deportment with the senior housekeeper and learned how to smile politely at every guest and client who came to call. "Aren't you a *darling* little thing," they simpered. "And so well-spoken!" They patted my hair as if I were a well-trained lapdog.

Sometimes I was so lonely I thought I might wither into ash and drift away on the next errant breeze.

Sometimes I felt like an item in Mr. Locke's collection labeled *January Scaller, 57 inches, bronze; purpose unknown.*

So when he invited me to accompany him to London—on the condition that I was willing to listen to every word he said as if they were God's own commandments—I said yes so enthusiastically that even Mr. Stirling jumped.

Half my stories and dime novels were set in London, so I was confident in my expectations: dim, foggy streets populated by urchins and nefarious men in bowler hats; black-stained buildings that loomed in a satisfyingly gloomy way over one's head; silent rows of gray houses. *Oliver Twist* mixed with Jack the Ripper, with perhaps a dash of Sara Crewe.

Maybe parts of London are really like that, but the city I saw in 1903 was almost exactly the opposite: loud, bright, and bustling. As soon as we stepped off the London and North Western Railway car at Euston station we were nearly stampeded by a group of schoolchildren in matching navy outfits; a man in an emerald turban bowed politely as he passed; a dark-skinned family was arguing in their own language; a red-and-gold poster on the station wall advertised *Dr. Goodfellow's Genuine Human Zoo, featuring Pygmies, Zulu Warriors, Indian Chiefs, and Slave Girls of the East!*

"We're already in a damned human zoo," Locke grouched, and dispatched Mr. Stirling to find a cab to take us directly to the head offices of the Royal Rubber Company. The porters crammed Mr. Locke's luggage into the back of the cab, and Stirling and I dragged it up the white marble steps of the company offices.

Mr. Locke and Mr. Stirling vanished into the dim hallways with a number of important-looking men in black suits, and I was instructed to sit on a narrow-backed chair in the lobby and not bother anyone or make any noise or touch anything. I contemplated the mural on the opposite wall, which showed a kneeling African handing Britannia a basket of rubber vines. The African wore a rather slavish, starry-eyed expression.

I wondered if Africans counted as colored in London, and then I wondered if I did, and felt a little shiver of longing. To be part of some larger flock, to not be stared at, to know my place precisely. Being "a perfectly unique specimen" is lonely, it turns out.

One of the secretaries was watching me with narrow-eyed eagerness. You know the type: one of those squat white ladies with thin lips who apparently live their entire lives longing for the chance to rap someone's knuckles with a ruler. I declined to give her the opportunity. I jumped up, pretending to hear Mr. Locke calling for me, and skittered down the hall after him.

The door was cracked. Oily lamplight oozed out, and men's voices made soft, hungry echoes against oak paneling. I inched close enough to see inside: there were eight or nine mustached men surrounding a long table piled high with all of Locke's luggage. The black cases were opened, and crumpled newspapers and straw were strewn everywhere. Locke himself stood at the head of the table, holding something I couldn't see.

"A very valuable find indeed, gentlemen, all the way from Siam, containing what I'm told is powdered scale of some kind—quite potent—"

The men listened with unseemly eagerness in their faces, their spines curving toward Mr. Locke as if magnetically compelled. There was something odd about them—a kind of collective not-quite-right-ness, as if they weren't men at all but other kinds of creatures stuffed into black-buttoned suits.

I realized I recognized one of them. I'd seen him at the Society party last July, slinking around the edges of the parlor with darting, yellowy eyes. He was a fidgety man, with a ferrety face and hair redder than even Miss Valentine's Hair Potion could manufacture. He was leaning toward Locke just like everyone else—but then his nostrils flared, like a dog getting a scent it doesn't much like.

I know people can't *smell* disobedient little girls spying on them, really I do. And how much trouble would I really have gotten in, just for looking? But there was something secretive about the meeting, something illicit, and the man was tilting his head upward as if trying to catch a strange scent and track it—

I flitted away from the door and crept back to my chair in the lobby. For the following hour I kept my eyes on the tile floor, ankles neatly crossed, and ignored the sighing, huffing sounds from the secretary.

Nine-year-olds don't know much, but they aren't stupid; I'd guessed before now that all my father's artifacts and treasures didn't end up displayed in Locke House. Apparently some of them were shipped across the Atlantic and auctioned off in stuffy boardrooms. I pictured some poor clay tablet or manuscript, stolen from its rightful home and sent circling the globe, forlorn and alone, only to end up labeled and displayed for people who didn't even know what it said. Then I reminded myself that that was more or less what happened in Locke House itself, anyway, and didn't Mr. Locke always say it was an act of "criminal cowardice" to leave opportunities unpursued?

I decided another part of being a good girl was probably keeping your mouth shut about certain things.

I didn't say anything at all to Mr. Locke or Mr. Stirling when they emerged, or during the cab ride to our hotel, or when Mr. Locke abruptly announced that he felt like a little shopping and directed the cab to Knightsbridge instead.

We walked into a department store roughly the size of an independent nation, all marble and glass. White-toothed attendants were posted like smiling soldiers at every counter.

One of them skittered toward us across the shining floor and trilled, "Welcome, sir! How may I help you? And what a darling little girl!" Her smile was blinding, but her eyes interrogated my skin, my hair, my eyes. If I were a coat she would have turned me inside out and checked my tag for my manufacturer. "Wherever did you find her?"

Mr. Locke caught my hand and tucked it protectively under his arm. "This is my…daughter. Adopted, of course. Between you and I, you're looking at the last living member of the Hawaiian royal family." And because of the confident boom of Mr. Locke's voice and the moneyed look of his suit coat, or maybe because she'd never met an actual Hawaiian, the woman believed him. I watched her suspicion vanish, replaced by fascinated admiration.

"Oh, how exceptional! We have some lovely turbans from Lahore—quite exotic, they would look so thrilling with that hair of hers—or perhaps she'd like to look at our parasols? To protect against the summer sun?"

Mr. Locke looked down at me, appraisingly. "A book, I think. Any one she likes. She's proven herself a very good girl." Then he smiled at me, an expression detectable only by the slight bending of his mustache.

I glowed; I had been weighed, and found worthy.

In the early summer of 1906 I was almost twelve. The RMS *Lusitania* had just launched as the largest ship in the world (Mr. Locke promised we'd get tickets soon); the newspapers were still full of grainy pictures of the wreckage in San Francisco after that awful earthquake; and I'd used my allowance to buy a subscription to *Outing* magazine just so I could read Jack London's new novel every week. Mr. Locke was away on business without me, and my father was, for once, home.

He was supposed to have left the day before to join Mr. Fawcett's expedition to Brazil, but there was some delay with documents getting stamped by the proper authorities and delicate instruments that required careful shipping—I didn't care. I only cared that he was home.

We ate breakfast together in the kitchens, seated at a big scarred table marked with grease spots and burns. He'd brought one of his field notebooks to review, and ate his eggs and toast with a tiny V creasing his eyebrows. I didn't mind; I had the latest installment of *White Fang*. We disappeared into our separate worlds, together but apart, and it was so peaceful and right-feeling that I found myself pretending that it happened every morning. That we were a regular little family, that Locke House was our house and this table was our kitchen table.

Except I guess if we were a regular family there would be a mother at the table with us. Maybe she'd be reading, too. Maybe she'd look up at me over the spine of her book and her eyes would crinkle, just so, and she would brush the toast crumbs from my father's scrubby beard.

It's stupid to think things like that. It just gives you this hollow, achy feeling between your ribs, like you're homesick even though you're already home, and you can't read your magazine anymore because the words are all warped and watery-looking.

My father gathered his plate and coffee cup and stood, notebook wedged beneath his arm. His eyes were distant behind the little gold-rimmed spectacles he wore for reading. He turned to leave.

"Wait." I gulped the word out and he blinked at me like a startled owl. "I was wondering if—could I help you? With your work?"

I watched him start to say no, saw his head begin a regretful shake, but then he looked at me. Whatever he saw in my face—the damp shine of almost-tears in my eyes, the hollow aching—made him draw a sharp breath.

"Of course, January." His accent rolled over my name like a ship at sea; I reveled in the sound of it.

We spent the day down in the endless cellars of Locke House, where all the uncategorized or unlabeled or broken items in Mr. Locke's collections were stored in straw-stuffed crates. My father sat with a stack of notebooks, muttering and scribbling and occasionally directing me to type out little labels on his shiny black typewriter. I pretended I was Ali Baba in the Cave of Wonders, or a knight stalking through a dragon's hoard, or just a girl with a father.

"Ah, the lamp, yes. Put that over with the carpet and the necklace, please. Don't rub it, whatever you do—although— what could it hurt?" I wasn't sure he was speaking to me until he waved me closer. "Bring it here."

I handed him the bronze lump I'd dug out of a crate labeled *TURKESTAN*. It didn't look much like a lamp; it looked more like a small, misshapen bird, with a long spout for a beak and strange symbols carved along its wings. Father stroked one finger along those symbols, gently, and oily white steam began to spool from the spout. The steam rose, coiling and writhing like a pale snake, making shapes almost like words in the air.

My father's hand swept the smoke away and I blinked. "How—there must be some kind of wick in there, and a spark. How does it work?"

He tucked the lamp back into its crate, a little half smile curling his mouth. He shrugged at me, and the half smile stretched wider, a glint of something like merriment behind his spectacles.

And maybe because he smiled so very rarely, or because it had been such a perfect day, I said something stupid. "Can I go with you?" He tilted his head, smile retreating. "When you go to Brazil. Or the place after that. Will you take me with you?"

It was one of those things you want so much it burns, so you keep it deep in the center of yourself like a banked coal. But—oh, to escape the hotel lobbies and department stores and neat-buttoned traveling coats—to dive like a fish into the thrumming stream of the world, swimming at my father's side—

"No." Cold, harsh. Final.

"I'm a good traveler, ask Mr. Locke! I don't interrupt, or touch things I oughtn't, or speak to anyone, or wander off—"

Father's brow crinkled into that puzzled V again. "Then why should you want to travel in the first place?" He shook his head. "The answer is *no*, January. It is far too dangerous."

Embarrassment and anger crept up my neck in hot prickles. I didn't say anything because then I would cry and everything would be even worse.

"Listen. I find valuable and unique things, yes? For Mr. Locke and his Society friends?" I didn't nod. "Well, they are not the only, ah, interested parties, it seems. There are others—I don't know who—" I heard him swallow. "You are safer here. This is a proper place for a young girl to grow up." That last part came out with such a rehearsed, echoey sound that I knew it was a direct quote from Mr. Locke.

I nodded, eyes on the straw-strewn floor. "Yes, sir."

"But—I will take you with me, one day. I promise."

I wanted to believe him, but I'd met enough empty promises in my life to know one when I heard it. I left without speaking again.

Safely cocooned in my room, wrapped in the pink-and-gold bedspread that still smelled of nutmeg and sandalwood, I removed the coin from its tiny pocket in my skirt and studied the silver-eyed queen. She had a mischievous, run-away-with-me sort of smile, and for a moment I felt my heart swoop like something taking flight, tasted cedar and salt in my mouth—

I crossed to my dresser and tucked her into a hole in the lining of my jewelry box; I was too old to carry around such fanciful trinkets, anyway.

In March 1908 I was thirteen, which is such an intensely awkward and self-absorbed age that I remember almost nothing about that year except that I grew four inches and Wilda made me start wearing a terrible wire contraption over my breasts. My father was on a steamer heading to the South Pole, and all his letters smelled of ice and bird shit; Mr. Locke was hosting a greasy group of Texas oilmen in the east wing of Locke House and had ordered me to stay out of their way; I was just about as lonely and wretched as any thirteen-year-old has ever been, which is very lonely and wretched indeed.

My only company was Wilda. She had grown infinitely more fond of me over the years, now that I was a "proper young lady," but her fondness only meant that she smiled too often—a creaking, cobwebbed expression that looked as if it had been stored in a musty trunk for decades—and sometimes suggested we read aloud from *Pilgrim's Progress* as a treat. It was almost lonelier than having no company at all.

But then something happened that meant I was never truly alone again.

I was copying a stack of ledger books for Mr. Locke, hunched over the desk in my father's study. There was a writing desk in my own room, but I mostly used his instead—it wasn't like he was home often enough to object. I liked the stillness of the room, too, and the way the smell of him lingered in the air like dust motes: sea salt and spices and strange stars.

And I especially liked that it had the best view of the drive, which meant I could watch Samuel Zappia's cart come swaying toward the house. He hardly ever left me story papers anymore—the habit had faded between us, like pen pals whose letters get shorter each month—but he always waved. Today I watched his breath rise in a white plume above the cart, saw his head tilt up to the study window. Was that a flash of white teeth?

His red cart had just disappeared toward the kitchen and I was considering and dismissing ways I could contrive to walk casually by in the next half hour, when Miss Wilda rapped her knuckles on the study door. She informed me, in tones of deepest suspicion, that young Mr. Zappia would like to speak to me.

"Oh." I made a stab at nonchalance. "Whatever for?"

Wilda stalked behind me like a black woolen shadow as I went down to meet him. Samuel was waiting beside his ponies, muttering into their velveteen ears. "Miss Scaller," he greeted me.

I noticed he'd been spared the misfortunes of most adolescent boys; instead of sprouting several extra elbows and galumphing around like a newborn giraffe, Samuel had grown lither, denser. More handsome.

"Samuel." I used my most grown-up voice, as if I had never once chased him across the lawn howling for his surrender or fed him magic potions made of pine needles and lake water.

He gave me a weighing sort of look. I tried not to think about my lumpy wool dress, which Wilda especially liked, or the irrepressible way my hair frizzed out of its pins. Wilda gave a threatening cough, like a mummy clearing its throat of grave dust.

Samuel rummaged in the cart for a covered basket. "For you." His face was perfectly neutral, but a faint crimp at the corner of his mouth might have been the beginnings of a smile. His eyes had a familiar, eager gleam; it was the same look he'd had when he was retelling the plot of a dime novel and was about to get to the really good part where the hero swoops in to save the kidnapped kid at just the right moment. "Take it."

At this point, you're thinking this story isn't really about Doors, but about those more private, altogether more miraculous doors that can open between two hearts. Perhaps it is in the end—I happen to believe every story is a love story if you catch it at the right moment, slantwise in the light of dusk—but it wasn't then.

It wasn't Samuel who became my dearest friend in the world; it was the animal snuffling and milling its stubby legs in the basket he handed me.

From my rare and Wilda-chaperoned trips into Shelburne, I knew the Zappias lived crammed in an apartment above the grocery in town, in the sort of sprawling, raucous nest that made Mr. Locke whuffle through his mustache and complain about *those* people. The store was guarded by an enormous, heavy-jawed dog named Bella.

Bella, Samuel explained, had recently produced a litter of burnished bronze puppies. The other Zappia children were busy selling most of them to tourists gullible enough to believe they were a rare African breed of lion-hunting dog, but Samuel had kept one. "The best one. I saved for you. See how he looks at you?" It was true: the puppy in my basket had stopped its squirming to stare up at me with damp, blue-sheened eyes, as if awaiting divine instruction.

I couldn't have known then what that puppy would become to me, but perhaps some part of me suspected, because my nose was prickling in that dangerous, you-are-about-to-cry way when I looked up at Samuel.

I opened my mouth, but Wilda made her rattly throat sound again. "I think *not*, boy," she declared. "You will take that animal right back where it came from."

Samuel didn't frown, but the smile-crimp at the corner of his mouth flattened out. Wilda snatched the basket from my clutching hands—the puppy toppled and rolled, legs paddling in midair—and thrust it back to Samuel. "Miss Scaller thanks you for your generosity, I'm sure." And she steered me back inside and lectured me for several eons about germs, the inappropriateness of large dogs for ladies, and the perils of accepting favors from men of low standing.

My appeal to Mr. Locke after dinner was unsuccessful. "Some flea-bitten thing you took pity on, I suppose?"

"No, sir. You know Bella, the Zappias' dog? She had a litter, and—"

"A half-breed, then. Those never turn out well, January,

and I won't have some mongrel chewing on the taxidermy."
He waggled his fork at me. "But I'll tell you what—one of my
associates raises very fine dachshunds down in Massachusetts.
Perhaps if you apply yourself in your lessons I could be persuaded to reward you with an early Christmas present." He
gave me an indulgent smile, winking beneath Wilda's pursed
lips, and I tried to smile back.

I returned to my ledger copying after dinner feeling sullen and strangely rubbed raw, as if there were invisible chains
chafing against my skin. The numbers blurred and prismed as
tears pooled in my eyes and I had a sudden, useless desire for
my long-lost pocket diary. For that day in the field when I'd
written a story and made it come true.

My pen slunk to the margins of the ledger book. I ignored
the voice in my head that said it was absurd, hopeless, several steps beyond fanciful—that reminded me words on a page
aren't magic spells—and wrote: *Once upon a time there was a
good girl who met a bad dog, and they became the very best of friends.*

There was no silent reshaping of the world this time. There
was only a faint sighing, as if the entire room had exhaled.
The south window rattled weakly in its frame. A sick sort of
exhaustion stole over my limbs, a heaviness, as if each of my
bones had been stolen and replaced with lead, and the pen
dropped from my hand. I blinked blurring eyes, my breath
half-held.

But nothing happened; no puppy materialized. I returned
to my copy work.

The following morning I woke abruptly, much earlier than
any sane young woman would voluntarily wake up. An insistent plink-plinking rang through my room. Wilda snuffled in
her sleep, brows crimping in instinctual disapproval.

I dove for my window in a fumbling mess of nightgown

and sheets. Standing on the frosted lawn below, wrapped in the pearly predawn mist, his upturned face crinkled in that almost-smile, was Samuel. One hand held the reins of his gray pony, who was making furtive passes at the lawn, and the other held the round-bottomed basket.

I was out the door and down the back stairs before I'd had time for anything so mundane as conscious thought. Sentences like *Wilda will flay you* or *My God, you're in your nightgown* arrived only after I'd flung open the side door and rushed out to meet him.

Samuel looked down at my bare feet, freezing in the frost, then at my desperate, eager face. He held out the basket for the second time. I scooped out the chilly, sleepy ball of puppy and held him to my chest, where he rooted toward the warmth beneath my arm.

"Thank you, Samuel," I whispered, which I know now was an utterly insufficient response. But Samuel seemed content. He bowed his head in a chivalrous, Old-World-ish gesture like a knight accepting his lady's favor, mounted his drooling pony, and disappeared across the misted grounds.

Now, let us clear the air: I am not a stupid girl. I realized the words I'd written in the ledger book were more than ink and cotton. They'd reached out into the world and twisted the shape of it in some invisible and unknowable way that brought Samuel to stand beneath my window. But there was a more rational explanation available to me—that Samuel had seen the longing in my face and decided to hell with that bitter old German woman—and I chose to believe that instead.

But still: when I got to my room and settled the brown ball of fur in a nest of pillows, the first thing I did was trawl through my desk drawer for a pen. I found my copy of *The Jungle Book*, flipped to the blank pages at the back, and wrote: *She and her dog were inseparable from that day forward.*

* * *

In the summer of 1909 I was almost fifteen and some of the selfish fog of adolescence was starting to dissipate. The second *Anne of Green Gables* book and the fifth *Oz* book were out that spring; a white, snub-nosed woman named Alice had just driven a motorcar across the entire country (a feat that Mr. Locke dubbed "utterly absurd"); there was some fuss about a coup or a revolution in the Ottoman Empire ("absolutely wasteful"); and my father had been in East Africa for months without so much as a postcard. He'd sent me a yellowed ivory carving of an elephant with the letters *MOMBASA* carved into its belly at Christmas, and a note saying he would be home by my birthday.

He wasn't, of course. But Jane was.

It was early summer, when the leaves are still dewy and new and the sky looks freshly painted, and Bad and I were curled together in the gardens, rereading all the other *Oz* books to prepare for the new one. I'd already had my French and Latin lessons for the day, and finished all my sums and bookkeeping for Mr. Locke, and my afternoons were wonderfully free now that Wilda was gone.

I think Bad deserves most of the credit, really. If you could have manifested Wilda's darkest nightmares into a physical being, it would have looked very much like a yellow-eyed puppy with overlarge paws, a surfeit of fine brown hairs, and no respect at all for nursemaids. She'd thrown a predictably impressive fit when she first found him in my bedroom, and dragged me up to Locke's office still in my nightgown.

"Good God, woman, do stop shrieking, I haven't had my coffee. Now, what's all this? I thought I was perfectly clear last night." Mr. Locke had fixed me with that *look*, ice-edged and moon-pale. "I won't have it in the house."

I felt my will shivering and warping, weakening under his gaze—but I thought of those words hidden in the back of

Kipling: *She and her dog were inseparable.* I tightened my arms around Bad and met Mr. Locke's eyes, my jaw set.

A second passed, and then another. Sweat prickled at the back of my neck, as if I were lifting some immensely heavy object, and then Mr. Locke laughed. "Keep it, if it matters so much to you."

After that, Miss Wilda seemed to fade from our lives like newsprint left out in the sun. She simply couldn't compete with Bad, who grew at an alarming pace. With me, he remained adoring and puppyish, sleeping flopped across my legs and cramming himself into my lap long past the time he could actually fit—but his attitude toward the rest of the human population was frankly dangerous. Within six months he'd successfully driven Wilda out of our room and exiled her to the serving staff's quarters; by eight months he and I had most of the third floor to ourselves.

I last saw Wilda scurrying across the broad lawn, peering back at the third-floor window of my room with the hunted expression of a general fleeing a losing battlefield. I hugged Bad so hard he yelped, and we spent the afternoon splashing along the lakeshore, giddy with freedom.

Now, lying with my head against his sun-warmed ribs, I heard the crunch and putter of a car coming down the drive.

The drive of Locke House is a long, winding thing lined with stately oaks. The cab was just pulling away as Bad and I circled around the front of the house. A strange woman was striding toward the great red stone steps, head high.

My first thought was that an African queen had been trying to visit President Taft in D.C. but found herself misdirected and arrived at Locke House by mistake. It wasn't that she was dressed especially grandly—a beige traveling coat with a neat row of black-shined buttons, a single leather valise, scandalously short hair—or that she looked particularly haughty. It was something in the unbending line of her shoulders, or the way she looked up at all the grandeur of Locke House without the slightest flicker of either admiration or intimidation.

She saw us and came to a halt before mounting the front steps, apparently waiting. We circled close, my hand on Bad's collar in case he got one of his unfortunate impulses.

"You must be January." Her accent was foreign and rhythmic. "Julian told me to look for a girl with wild hair and a mean dog." She extended her hand and I shook it. Calluses knotted her palm like a topographical map of a foreign country.

It was lucky that Mr. Locke stepped out the front door at that moment, heading for his newly shined Buick Model 10, because my mouth had fallen open and seemed unlikely to close itself again. Mr. Locke made it halfway down the stairs before he saw us. "January, how many times have I told you to *leash* that deranged animal—who in the name of God is this?" His thoughts on courtesy evidently did not apply to strange colored women who materialized on his doorstep.

"I am Miss Jane Irimu. Mr. Julian Scaller has commissioned me to be a companion to his daughter, paid from his own funds at a rate of five dollars a week. He indicated that you might be generous enough to supply room and board. I believe this letter explains my situation clearly." She extended a stained and ratty envelope to Mr. Locke. He ripped it open and read with an expression of deepest suspicion. A few exclamations escaped him: "His daughter's welfare, is it?" and "*He* has employed—?"

He snapped the letter shut. "You expect me to believe that Julian shipped a nursemaid halfway across the world for his daughter? Who is nearly grown, I might add?"

Miss Irimu's face lay in a series of wind-smooth planes, nearly architectural in their perfection, which seemed unlikely ever to be disturbed by the mobility of either smile or scowl. "I was in an unfortunate situation. As I believe the letter explains."

39

"A bit of charity work, is it? Julian always was too soft-hearted for his own good." Mr. Locke slapped his driving gloves against his palm and huffed at us. "Very well, Miss Whatsit. Far be it from me to step between a father and his daughter. I'll be damned if I'm filling up one of my good guest rooms, though—show her up to your room, January. She can take Wilda's old bed." And he strode off, shaking his head.

The silence that followed his departure was shy and slinking, as if it wanted to be awkward but didn't quite dare beneath Miss Irimu's steady eye.

"Uh." I swallowed. "This is Bad. Sindbad, I mean." I'd wanted to name him after a great explorer, but none of them seemed to fit. Dr. Livingstone and Mr. Stanley were obvious choices (Mr. Locke so admired them he even had Stanley's own revolver on display in his office, a narrow-nosed Enfield that he cleaned and oiled on a weekly basis), but they made me think of that shriveled African arm in its glass case. Magellan was too long, Drake too boring, Columbus too bumbling; in the end I'd named him after the only explorer who rendered the world stranger and more wondrous with each voyage.

Jane was watching him warily. "Don't worry, he doesn't bite," I assured her. Well, he didn't bite *often*, and the way I saw it the people he bit were probably secretly untrustworthy and had it coming to them. Mr. Locke did not find this argument compelling.

"Miss Irimu—" I began.

"Jane will suffice."

"Miss Jane. Could I see my father's letter?"

She considered me with clinical coolness, like a scientist evaluating a new species of fungus. "No."

"Then could you tell me, uh, why he hired you? Please."

"Julian cares very deeply for you. He does not wish you to be alone." Several nasty things leapt to my lips, including *Well, that's news to me*, but I kept them locked behind my teeth. Jane was still watching me with that fungus-identification expression. She added, "Your father also wishes you to be kept safe. I will ensure that you are."

I surveyed the gentle green lawns of Locke's estate and the placid grayness of Lake Champlain. "Uh-huh."

I was trying to think of a polite way to say *My father's gone mad, and you should probably leave*, when Bad stretched toward her, sniffing with an appraising, to-bite-or-not-to-bite expression. He considered briefly, then bucked his head against her hand in a shameless request for ear scratches.

Dogs, of course, are infinitely better judges of character than people. "Uh. Welcome to Locke House, Miss Jane. I hope you like it here."

She bowed her head. "I'm sure I shall."

But for the first several weeks Jane spent at Locke House, she gave no sign of liking it—or me—very much at all.

She spent her days in near-silence, prowling from room to room like something caged. She regarded me with stony resignation and occasionally picked up one of my discarded copies of *The Strand Mystery Magazine* or *The Cavalier: Weekly Stories of Daring Adventure!* with a dubious expression. She reminded me of one of those Greek heroes doomed to some endless task, like drinking from a disappearing river or rolling a stone up a mountain.

My early attempts at conversation were blighted, abortive things. I asked politely about her past and received clipped answers that discouraged further inquiry. I knew she was born in the central highlands of British East Africa in 1873, except that it wasn't called British East Africa then; I knew she spent six years in the Gospel Society Mission School at Nairu, where she learned the queen's English and wore the queen's cotton and prayed to the queen's God. Then she found herself in

41

"considerable difficulty" and took the employment opportunity my father offered her.

"Ah. Well," I said with pained cheeriness, "at least it's not so hot here! Compared to Africa, I mean."

Jane did not respond immediately, staring out the study window at the greenish-gold lake. "Where I was born, there was frost on the ground every morning," she answered softly, and the conversation died a merciful death.

I don't think I saw her smile a single time until Mr. Locke's annual Society party.

The Society party was identical every year, with slight updates in fashion: eighty of Mr. Locke's wealthiest collector friends and their wives would jam themselves into the downstairs parlors and gardens and laugh overloudly at each other's witticisms; hundreds of cocktails would be transmuted into ether-scented sweat, ascending on cigarette-smoke spirals to hang above us in a heady fug; eventually all the official Society members would slink off to the smoking room and stink up the entire first floor with cigars. Sometimes I pretended to myself it was a grand birthday party for me, because it was almost always within a few days, but it's hard to pretend it's your party when drunken guests keep mistaking you for a serving girl and asking for more sherry or scotch.

My dress that year was a shapeless froth of pink ribbons and frills that made me look like a rather sulky cupcake. I have proof, unfortunately—that was the year Mr. Locke hired a photographer as a special treat. In the picture I am stiff and vaguely hunted-looking, with my hair so brutally pinned I might be bald. One of my hands is wrapped around Bad's shoulders, and it is unclear whether I am clinging to him for strength or restraining him from eating the photographer. At Christmas Mr. Locke presented a small framed print to my father, perhaps in the charming belief that he'd take it with him on his travels. My father had held it in his hands, frowning, and said, "You do not look like yourself. You do not look like . . . her." Like my mother, I assumed.

I found the picture facedown in a drawer of his writing desk a few months later.

Even in that wedding cake of a dress, and even with Bad and Jane standing on either side of me like glum sentinels, it wasn't hard to disappear at the Society party. Most people regarded me as either a vague curiosity—having heard the rumors from Locke that I was the daughter of a Boer diamond miner and his Hottentot wife, or the heiress to an Indian fortune—or an overdressed servant, and neither group paid me much attention. I was glad, especially since I'd seen that slinky red-haired fellow, Mr. Bartholomew Ilvane, creeping along the edges of the crowd. I pressed my back to the wallpaper and wished, briefly and uselessly, that Samuel were there with me, whispering a story about a ball and a magic spell and a princess who would turn back into a serving girl at the stroke of midnight.

Mr. Locke was greeting each guest in a jovial, slightly accented boom; he'd gone to school somewhere in Britain as a young man, and liquor tended to burr his r's and slant his vowels. "Ah, Mr. Havemeyer! Thrilled you could make it, just thrilled. You've met my ward, January, haven't you?" Locke gestured at me, his favorite jade glass sloshing scotch over the rim.

Mr. Havemeyer was a tall, attenuated creature with skin so white I could see blue veins threading his wrists, disappearing beneath those pretentious leather gloves men wear to remind everyone they have a motorcar.

He waved a gold-tipped cane and spoke without looking at me. "Yes, of course. Wasn't sure I could get away, what with the strike, but I got a shipment of coolies in at the last second, thank God."

"Mr. Havemeyer is in the sugar business," Mr. Locke explained. "Spends half the year on some godforsaken island in the Caribbean."

"Oh, it's not so bad. It suits me." His eyes slid to Jane and me and his mouth curled into a smile-shaped sneer. "You ought to send this pair down to visit, if you ever grow bored with them. I'm always in need of more warm bodies."

My whole body went chill and stiff as porcelain. I don't know why—even growing up in Mr. Locke's wealthy shadow, it was hardly the first time somebody had sneered at me. Perhaps it was the casual hunger burning like an underground coal seam in Havemeyer's voice, or the sound of Jane's indrawn breath beside me. Or perhaps young girls are like camels, and there are only so many straws they can carry before they break.

All I knew was that I was suddenly shaking and cold and Bad was leaping to his feet like a gargoyle come to terrible life, teeth flashing, and there was perhaps a moment when I could have grabbed his collar but couldn't quite make myself move—and then Mr. Havemeyer was screaming in high-pitched fury and Locke was swearing and Bad was snarling around a mouthful of Mr. Havemeyer's leg—and then there was another sound, low and rolling, so incongruous I almost didn't believe it—

It was Jane. She was laughing.

In the end, things could have been much worse. Mr. Havemeyer received seventeen stitches and four shots of absinthe and was carted back to his hotel; Bad was confined to my room "for all of recorded time," which lasted the three weeks until Mr. Locke left on a business trip to Montreal; and I was subjected to a several-hour lecture on the nature of guests, good manners, and power.

"Power, my dear, has a language. It has a geography, a currency, and—I'm sorry—a color. This is not something you may take personally or object to; it is simply a fact of the world, and the sooner you accustom yourself to it, the better." Mr. Locke's eyes were pitying; I slunk out of his office feeling small and bruised.

The next day Jane disappeared for an hour or two and returned bearing gifts: a large ham hock for Bad and the newest issue of *The Argosy All-Story Weekly* for me. She perched at the end of Wilda's stiff, narrow bed.

I meant to say *Thank you*, but what came out was, "Why are you being so nice to me?"

She smiled, revealing a slim, mischievous gap between her front teeth. "Because I like you. And I do not like bullies."

After that, our fates were more or less sealed (a phrase that always makes me picture a weary old Fate tucking our futures into an envelope and pressing her wax seal over us): Jane Irimu and I became something like friends.

For two years we lived in the secret margins of Locke House, in its attics and forgotten storerooms and untended gardens. We scurried around the edges of high society like spies or mice, staying mostly in the shadows, noticed only sporadically by Locke or his assorted minions and guests. There was still something confined about her, something tense and waiting, but now at least it felt as if we shared the same cage.

I didn't think of the future much, and if I did it was with a child's desire for vague, far-flung adventures, and a child's certainty that everything would remain as it always had been. It did, mostly.

Until the day before my seventeenth birthday. Until I found the leather-bound book in the chest.

"Miss Scaller."

I was still standing in the Pharaoh Room, still holding the leather-bound book in my palm. Bad was growing bored, issuing periodic sighs and huffs. Mr. Stirling's toneless voice startled both of us.

"Oh—I didn't—good evening." I spun to face him with the book tucked behind my back. There wasn't any particular reason to hide a scuffed-up novel from Mr. Stirling, except that there was something vital and wondrous about it, and Mr. Stirling was more or less the human opposite of vitality and wonder. He blinked at me, eyes flicking to the open chest on its plinth, then inclined his head infinitesimally.

"Mr. Locke requests your attendance in his office." He paused, and something flitted darkly across his face. It might have been fear, if Mr. Stirling had been physically capable of any expression beyond attentive blandness. "At once."

I followed him from the Pharaoh Room with Bad's claws *click-click*ing at my heels. I tucked *The Ten Thousand Doors* in my skirts, where it rested warm and solid against my hip. *Like a shield*, I thought, and then wondered why the idea was so comforting.

Mr. Locke's office smelled as it always had, of cigar smoke and fine leather and the sorts of liquors that are kept in crystal decanters on the sideboard, and Mr. Locke looked as he always did: squarish and neat, seeming to reject the aging process as a waste of valuable time. He'd had the same respectable dusting of white hairs at his temples my entire life; the last time I'd seen him, my father's hair had turned almost entirely ashen.

Mr. Locke looked up from a stack of stained, weathered-looking envelopes as I entered. His eyes were gravestone-gray and serious, focused on me in a way they rarely were. "That will do, Stirling." I heard the valet retreat from the room, the brassy click of the door latch. Something fluttered in my chest, like bird wings against my ribs.

"Sit down, January." I sat in my usual chair, and Bad stuffed himself half-successfully beneath it.

"Sorry about Bad, sir, it's just Stirling seemed to be in a hurry and I didn't take him back to my room first—"

"That's quite all right." The fluttery, panicky feeling in my chest grew stronger. Bad had been banned from Mr. Locke's office (as well as all motorcars, trains, and dining rooms) since the Society party two years ago. Just the sight of him usually provoked Locke into a speech about poorly behaved pets and lax owners, or at least a grumbling snort through his mustache.

Mr. Locke's jaw worked backward and forward, as if his next words required chewing to soften them. "It's about your father." I found it difficult to look directly at Mr. Locke; I studied the display case on his desk instead, its brass-plate label gleaming: *Enfield revolver, Mark I, 1879.*

"He's been in the Far East these past few weeks, as I'm sure you know."

Father was beginning in the Port of Manila, then island-hopping his way northward to Japan, he'd told me. He'd promised to write often; I hadn't heard from him in weeks.

Mr. Locke chewed his next sentence even more thoroughly. "His reports on this expedition have been spotty. Spottier than usual, I mean. But lately they've . . . stopped coming altogether. His last report was in April."

Mr. Locke was looking at me now, expectant and intent, as if he'd been humming a tune and paused for me to finish it. As if I ought to know what he would say next.

I kept staring at the revolver, at the oiled darkness of it, the dull square snout. Bad's breath was hot on my feet.

"January, are you paying attention? There hasn't been word from your father in nearly three months. I got a telegram from another man on the expedition: no one has seen or heard from him. They found his camp scattered and abandoned on a mountainside."

The bird in my chest was scrabbling, beating its wings in frenzied terror. I sat perfectly still.

"January. He's gone missing. It seems—well." Mr. Locke

drew a short, sharp breath. "It seems very likely that your father is dead."

I sat on my thin mattress, watching the sun creep butter-soft across my pink-and-gold bedspread. Frayed threads and cotton stuffing made shadows and spires across it, like the architecture of some foreign city. Bad curled around my back even though it was too hot for cuddling, making soft, puppyish sounds deep in his chest. He smelled of summer and fresh-clipped grass.

I hadn't wanted to believe it. I'd howled, screamed, demanded Mr. Locke take it back or prove it. I'd dug bloody pink crescents in my palms with the effort of not lashing out, not smashing his little glass cases into a thousand shimmering shards.

Eventually I'd felt hands like paving stones on my shoulders, weighing me down. "Enough, child." And I'd looked into his eyes, pale and implacable. I'd felt myself flaking and crumbling beneath them. "Julian is dead. *Accept it.*"

And I had. I'd collapsed into Locke's arms and soaked his shirt with tears. His gruff murmur had rumbled against my ear. "S'all right, girl. You've still got me."

Now I sat in my room, face swollen and eyes dry, teetering on the edge of a pain so vast I couldn't see its edges. It would swallow me whole, if I let it.

I thought about the last postcard I'd received from my father, featuring a beach and several tough-looking women labeled *FISHERWOMEN OF SUGASHIMA.* I thought about Father himself, but could only picture him walking away from me, hunched and tired, disappearing through some terrible, final doorway.

You promised you would take me with you.

I wanted to scream again, felt the sound clawing and writhing in my throat. I wanted to vomit. I wanted to run away and keep running until I fell into some other, better world.

And then I remembered the book. Wondered if Mr. Locke had given it to me just for this moment, knowing how badly I would need it.

I pulled it from my skirts and traced my thumb over the stamped title. It opened for me like a tiny leather-bound Door with hinges made of glue and wax thread.

I ran through it.

The Ten Thousand Doors:
Being a Comparative Study of
Passages, Portals, and Entryways in
World Mythology

This text was produced by Yule Ian Scholar for the University of the City of Nin, in the years between 6908 and —, in partial satisfaction of his attainment of Mastery.

The following monograph concerns the permutations of a repeated motif in world mythologies: passages, portals, and entryways. Such a study might at first seem to suffer from those two cardinal sins of academia—frivolity and triviality—but it is the author's intention to demonstrate the significance of doorways as phenomenological realities. The potential contributions to other fields of study—grammalogie, glottologie, anthropology—are innumerable, but if the author may be so presumptive, this study intends to go far beyond the limitations of our present knowledge. Indeed, this research might reshape our collective understanding of the physical laws of the universe.

The central contention is simply this: the passages, portals, and entryways common to all mythologies are rooted in physical anomalies that permit users to travel from one world to another. Or, to put it even more simply: these doors actually exist.

The following pages will offer extensive evidence to defend this conclusion and will provide a set of theories concerning the nature, origins, and function of doors. The most significant proposals include:

i) that doors are portals between one world and another, which exist only in places of particular and indefinable resonance (what

51

physical-philosophers call "weak coupling" between two universes). While human construction—frames, arches, curtains, et cetera—may surround a door, the natural phenomenon itself preexists its decoration in every case. It also seems to be the case that these portals are, by some quirk of physics or of humanity, damnably difficult to find.

ii) that such portals generate a certain degree of leakage. Matter and energy flow freely through them, and so too do people, foreign species, music, inventions, ideas—all the sorts of things that generate mythologies, in short. If one follows the stories, one will nearly always find a doorway buried at their roots.[1]

iii) that this leakage and resultant storytelling have been and remain crucial to humanity's cultural, intellectual, political, and economic development, in every world. In biology, it is the interplay between random genetic mutation and environmental change that results in evolution. Doors introduce *change*. And from change come all things: revolution, resistance, empowerment, upheaval, invention, collapse, reformation—all the most vital components of human history, in short.

iv) that doors are, like most precious things, fragile. Once closed, they cannot be reopened by any means this author has discovered.

The evidence supporting theories i–iv has been divided into eighteen subcategories, presented below as

At least, that is the book I intended to write, when I was young and arrogant.

I dreamed of insurmountable evidence, scholarly respectability, publications, and lectures. I have boxes and boxes of neatly indexed note cards, each describing some small brick in a vast wall of research:

---

1. Previous scholars have been quite successful in collecting and documenting such stories, but they have failed to *believe* them, and so have failed to find the single artifact that unites every myth: doors.

See James Frazer, *The Golden Bough: A Study in Magic and Religion*, Second Edition (London: Macmillan and Co. Limited, 1900).

an Indonesian story about a golden tree whose boughs made a shimmering archway; a reference in a Gaelic hymn to the angels who fly through heaven's gate; the memory of a carven wood doorway in Mali, sand-weathered and blackened by centuries of secrets.

This is not the book I have written.

Instead, I've written something strange, deeply personal, highly subjective. I am a scientist studying his own soul, a snake swallowing its own tail.

But even if I could tame my own impulses and write something scholarly, I fear it would not matter, because who would take seriously my claims without solid proof? Proof that I cannot provide, because it disappears almost as soon as I discover it. There is a fog creeping along at my heels, swallowing my footsteps and erasing my evidence. *Closing the doors.*

The book you have in your hands is not, therefore, a respectable work of scholarship. It has not benefited from editorial oversight and contains little verifiable fact. It is just a story.

I have written it anyway, for two reasons:

First, because what is written is what is true. Words and their meanings have weight in the world of matter, shaping and reshaping realities through a most ancient alchemy. Even my own writings—so damnably powerless—may have just enough power to reach the right person and to tell the right truth, and change the nature of things.

Second, my long years of research have taught me that all stories, even the meanest folktales, matter. They are artifacts and palimpsests, riddles and histories. They are the red threads that we may follow out of the labyrinth.

It is my hope that this story is your thread, and at the end of it you find a door.

Chapter One

An Introduction to
Miss Adelaide Lee Larson and
Her Formative Explorations

Her lineage and early life—The opening of a door—
The closing of a door—The changes wrought on the
soul of a young girl

Miss Adelaide Lee Larson was born in 1866.

The world had just begun to whisper the word *modern* to itself, along with words like *order* and *unfettered free trade*. Railroads and telegraph lines snaked across frontiers like long lines of stitches; empires nibbled at the coasts of Africa; cotton mills churned and hummed like open mouths, swallowing bent-backed workers and exhaling fibrous steam.

But other, older words—like *chaos* and *revolution*—still lingered in the margins. The European rebellions of 1848 hung like gun smoke in the air; the sepoys of India could still taste mutiny on their tongues; women whispered and conspired, sewing banners and authoring pamphlets; freedmen stood unshackled in the bloodied light of their new nation. All the symptoms, in short, of a world still riddled with open doors.

But the Larson family was, on the whole, utterly disinterested in the goings-on of the wider world, and the wider world politely returned their sentiments. Their farm was tucked in a green wrinkle of land in the middle of the country, precisely where the nation's heart would be if it were a living body, which troops on both sides of the Civil War had overlooked as they marched past. The family grew enough corn to feed themselves and their four milk cows, harvested enough hemp to sell downriver to the southern cotton balers, and salted enough venison to keep their teeth from rattling loose in the winter. Their interests extended little farther than the borders of the seven acres, and their political views never grew more complex than Mama Larson's dictum that "them that has, gets." When in 1860 young Lee Larson suffered a fit of patriotism and scurried into town to cast his vote for John Bell, who promptly lost not only to Mr. Lincoln but also to Douglas and Breckenridge, it simply confirmed their clannish suspicion that politicking was a ruse designed to distract hardworking folk from their business.

None of this marked the Larsons apart from any of their neighbors. It seems unlikely that any biographer or chronicler or even a local newspaperman has ever written their names in print before now. The interviews conducted for this study were stilted, suspicious affairs, akin to interrogating starlings or white-tailed deer.

There was only one remarkable fact about the family: when Adelaide Lee was born, every last living Larson was female. Through poor luck, heart failure, and cowardice, their husbands and sons had left behind a collection of hard-jawed women who looked so similar to one another it was like seeing a single woman's life spread out in every possible stage.

Lee Larson had been the last to leave. With his characteristic lack of timing, he waited until the Confederacy was on its last shaking legs before marching southeast to join the militia. His new wife—a colorless young woman from the neighboring county—folded herself into the Larson house and waited for news. News did not come. Instead, seventeen weeks later, Lee Larson himself turned up in the night with a tattered uniform and a ball of lead in his left buttock. He left again four days later, walking westward with a haunted expression. He lingered just long enough to conceive a child with his wife.

Adelaide Lee was three when her mother succumbed to consumption and depression and faded away entirely, and thereafter she was raised by her grandmother and four aunts.

Thus Adelaide Lee was born of poor luck and poverty and raised by ignorance and solitude. Let this ignoble origin story stand as an invaluable lesson to you that a person's beginnings do not often herald their endings, for Adelaide Lee did not grow into another pale Larson woman.[2] She became something else entirely, something so radiant and wild and fierce that a single world could not contain her, and she was obliged to find others.

The name Adelaide—a lovely, feminine name that came from her great-great-grandmother, a French-German woman with the same washed-out barely-there-ness of Adelaide's own mother—was doomed to failure. Not because the child herself raised any objection to it, but simply because the name slid off her back like water off a tin roof. It was a name for a delicate girl who read her prayers every night and kept her jumpers clean and cast her eyes demurely away when adults spoke to her. It was not a name for the scrawny, grubby wildling who now occupied the Larsons' house the way a prisoner of war might occupy an enemy camp.

By her fifth birthday, every woman in the house except her aunt Lizzie (whose habits could not be changed by any force short of cannon fire) had admitted defeat and called her Ade. Ade was a shorter, harsher name, better suited to shouting warnings and admonishments. It stuck, although the admonishments did not.

Ade spent her childhood in exploration, crisscrossing through their seven acres as if she'd dropped something precious and hoped to find it again or, more accurately, like a dog on a short lead straining against her collar. She knew the land in the way a child knows the land, with an intimacy and fantasy few adults have ever managed.

---

2. As other scholars have noted (see Klaus Bergnon, "An Essay on Destiny and Blood-right in Medieval Works," delivered to the American Antiquarian Society, 1872), the significance of blood and parentage is an oft-repeated assumption in many fairy tales, myths, and fables.

She knew where the sycamores had been hollowed out by lightning and become secret hideouts. She knew where the mushrooms were likeliest to raise their pale heads in fairy rings, and where fool's gold shimmered below the surface of the creek.

In particular, she knew every board and beam in the falling-down house on their back acres, a skinny jut of hayfield that was once a separate homestead. When the Larsons had bought the property the house had been abandoned, and it spent the intervening years sinking into the earth like some prehistoric creature trapped in a tar pit. But to Ade it was everything: a moldering castle, a scout's fort, a pirate's mansion, a witch's lair.

As it was on their property, the Larson women did not expressly forbid her games. But they looked narrowly at her when she returned smelling of wood rot and cedar, and issued dire warnings about the house ("It's haunted, you know, everyone says so") and about the likely fates of those who went wandering off. "Your father was a wanderer, you know"—her grandmother gave a dark nod—"and look what good it brung us." Ade had often been invited to consider her father's life—an abandoned wife, an orphaned daughter, all for the sake of his restlessness—but it proved a toothless warning to Ade. Her father had abandoned them, certainly, but he'd also seen love and war and perhaps some of the intoxicating world beyond the farm, and such adventure seemed worth any price.

(It seems to me that Lee Larson's life was more defined by impulsivity and cowardice than an adventurous spirit, but a daughter must find what value she can in her father. Especially if he is absent.)

Sometimes Ade wandered with purpose, as when she hid aboard the Illinois Central line and made it all the way to Paducah before a railway man nabbed her, and sometimes she simply moved for the sake of motion, as birds do. She spent whole days walking along the tangled riverbank, watching the steamers huff past. She pretended sometimes she was a member of the crew leaning over the railing; more often she imagined she was the steamer itself, a thing made for the sole purpose of arriving and leaving.

If we were to draw her childhood wanderings on a map, represent her discoveries and destinations in topographic form and trace her winding way through them, we would see her as a girl solving a maze from the center outward, a Minotaur working her way free.

By fifteen she was half-mad with her own circling, heartsick with the sameness of her days. She might have turned inward then, bent by the weight of the unseen labyrinth around her, but she was rescued by an event so powerfully strange it left her permanently discontent with the ordinary and convinced of the existence of the extraordinary: she met a ghost in the old hayfield.

It happened in early fall, when the tall grasses of the field were burnt auburn and rose and the cawing of crows rang sharp through clear air. Ade still visited the old house on the back acres often, though she was too old for make-believe. On the day she saw the ghost she was planning to scale the rough blocks of the chimney and perch on the roof to watch the starlings in their mad patterns.

As she approached she saw a dark figure standing next to the ruined house. She stopped walking. There was no doubt that her aunts would advise her to turn around immediately and return home. The figure was either a stranger, who ought to be avoided at all costs, or a ghost from the house itself, which ought to be treated similarly.

But Ade found herself drawn on like a compass arrow. "Hello?" she called.

The figure twitched. It was long and lanky, boyish even from a distance. He shouted something back at her, but the words sounded jumbled in his jaw. "'Scuse me?" she called again, because good manners were advisable when dealing with either strangers or ghosts. He answered with another string of nonsense words.

Now Ade was close enough to see him clearly, and she wondered if she ought to have turned around after all: his skin was a lightless reddish-black that Ade had no name for.

The Larson household didn't subscribe to the paper on the grounds that they got all the news they needed in church, but Ade sometimes scrounged copies secondhand. She was therefore familiar with the dangers of strange black men—she'd seen the columns describing their offenses, the cartoons depicting their appetites for innocent white women. In the cartoons the men were monstrous and hairy-armed, with tattered clothes and buffoonish expressions. But the boy in the field didn't look much like the drawings in the papers.

He was young—her own age or perhaps a little less—and his body was smooth and long-limbed. He wore a strange arrangement of rough woolen cloth, draped and folded around him in an intricate swooping pattern, as if he'd stolen a ship's sail and wrapped it around his body. His features were narrow and delicate-looking, his eyes clear and dark.

He spoke again, a series of many-syllabled words arranged almost like questions. She supposed it might have been a dialect of hell, known by ghosts and demons alone. The words switched suddenly in his mouth and familiar vowels fell into place. "Pardon, lady? Can you hear me?" His accent was utterly strange but his voice was mild, mindfully gentle, as if he feared startling her.

Ade decided in that moment that her aunt Lizzie was right: newspapers weren't worth the paper they were printed on. The boy in front of her, with his startled eyes and bedsheet clothes and gentle voice, was hardly a menace to her person.

"I can understand you," she answered.

He stepped closer, bemused disbelief in his face. He stroked the heavy heads of the grass, seeming surprised to feel the bristles against his palm. Then his hand drifted upward and came to rest, pale-palmed, on Ade's cheekbone. Both of them flinched away, as if neither had believed the other might be solid.

Something about the gentleness of him, the innocence of his surprise, the delicacy of his long-fingered hands, made Ade suddenly less cautious. "Who are you? And where exactly do you come from?" If he was a ghost, he was a lost, hesitant member of the species.

He seemed to be searching in some disused closet of his memory for the right words. "I come from ... elsewhere. Not here. Through a door in the wall." He pointed back toward the dilapidated house, at the sagging front door, which had been stuck in its frame since before Ade was born, obliging her to climb through the window instead. Now the door was wedged open the width of a thin boy's chest.

Ade was a rational enough girl to know that strange boys who wandered onto your property dressed in sheets claiming to be from elsewhere ought to be treated with suspicion. He was either mad or lying, and neither one was worth her time. But she felt something shudder in her breast as he spoke, something dangerously like hope. That it might be true.

"Here." She stepped back and unrolled her flannel blanket in a red-and-white circus tent over the stiff grasses. She stomped it flat and sat, gesturing beside herself.

He looked at her with that charming surprise again, rubbing his bare arms in the autumn chill.

"Looks like the weather is warmer in elsewhere, huh? Take this." She took off her rough canvas coat, a garment handed down so many times it had lost all color and shape, and handed it to him.

He pulled the sleeves over his arms the way an animal might if he were asked to wear a second skin. Ade was certain he had never worn a coat in his life, and equally certain this was impossible.

"Well, c'mon, sit down and tell me all about it, ghost boy. About elsewhere." He stared.

If you will permit the indulgence, allow me to pause here and reintroduce the scene from the boy's perspective: he had stepped out of someplace very different from the old hayfield and, while still blinking beneath the foreign sun, seen a young woman unlike anything he had ever seen before. She came toward him in wide strides, dark-buttoned dress *shush*ing against the grasses, winter-wheat hair snarled beneath a wide hat. Now she sat below him, her upturned face clear-eyed and perhaps a little fey, and if she had asked him for anything in the world he would have given it to her.

So the boy sat, and told her about elsewhere.

Elsewhere was a place of sea salt and wind. It was a city, or perhaps a country, or perhaps a world (his nouns were imprecise on this point) where people lived in stone houses and wore long white robes. It was a peaceful city, made prosperous by trade up the coast and made famous by their skillful study of words.

"You got lots of authors, in your town?" He was unfamiliar with the word. "People who write books. You know—long, boring things, all about people who don't exist."

A look of deepest consternation. "No, no. *Words.*" He tried to explain further, with lots of stuttering sentences about the nature of the written word and the shape of the universe, the relative thickness of ink and blood, the significance of languages and their careful study—but between his limited verbs and her tendency to laugh they made little progress. He surrendered, and asked her questions about her own world instead.

She answered as well as she could but found herself limited by her shuttered life. She knew little about the nearby town, and only as much about the wider world as could be taught in two grades of education at the one-room schoolhouse. "It's not as exciting as yours, I bet. Tell me about the ocean. Do you know how to sail? How far have you been?"

He spoke and she listened, and dusk swept over the two of them like a great dove's wing. Ade noticed the settling quiet of the day and the rhythmic whip-poor-will-ing of the night birds and knew it was past time to be home but couldn't make herself turn away. She felt suspended, hovering weightless in some place where she could believe in ghosts and magic and other worlds, in this strange black boy and his hands flashing through the dimness.

"And no one in my home is like you. Did something happen, to take away your skin? Did it—what—" The boy's English devolved into a series of guttural exclamations Ade felt could be translated universally to *What the* hell *is that?* He whipped left and right, staring into the shadowed field.

"Those are fireflies, ghost boy. Last of the year. Don't you have those on the other side of your door?"

"Fireflies? No, we do not have these. What are they for?"

"They aren't for anything. Except telling you it's dark, and you're in twenty heaps of trouble if you don't get home soon." Ade sighed. "I have to go."

The boy was looking up now at the evening stars shining with disapproving brightness above them. Another string of words that Ade had no difficulty translating. "I must go also." His eyes found hers, dark and shining. "But you will return?"

"Shit, on a Sunday? After staying out late? I'll be lucky if they don't lock me in the hay barn till Christmas." It was clear the boy missed several important nouns in this statement, but he pressed her and they agreed: in three days, both would return.

"And I will take you back with me, and you will believe me."

"All right, ghost boy."

He smiled. It was such a giddy, starstruck expression, as if the boy could imagine nothing better than meeting her in this field in three days, that Ade saw no other recourse than to kiss him. It was a clumsy kiss, a dry brush that almost missed his mouth entirely, but afterward their hearts racketed strangely in their chests and their limbs tingled and shook, so perhaps it was not such a poor effort after all.

Ade left then in a whirl of skirt and red blanket, and it was several minutes before the boy could recall precisely where he was and where he ought to go next.

At home Mama Larson greeted her with a wailing diatribe on the fates of girls who stayed out alone late at night, the fear and anxiety she'd caused her dear aunts (Aunt Lizzie interrupted to say she'd been mad as a hare, not fearful, and Mama Larson could just speak for herself), and the inevitability of the decline of womanhood in this country. "And where is your *coat*, fool child?"

Ade considered. "Elsewhere," she answered, and wafted up the stairs.

The weekly trial of Sunday church was somewhat easier to bear, Ade found, when one harbored a delicious and impossible secret burning like a lantern in the center of oneself. The townspeople— who weren't really townspeople at all, but more a collection of feral persons who lived on farms just as isolated and distant as the Larson family's, who congregated only for auctions, funerals, and

God—shuffled into the pews with the same dulled expressions they wore every week, and Ade felt herself separate from them in a new and quite agreeable fashion. Preacher McDowell's sermon warbled around her like a river breaking around a stone.

The Larson women always sat in the third row from the back because Mama Larson insisted it was prideful to sit in the front row but impolite to sit in the very back, and because all of them enjoyed the thrill of superiority that came from watching the latecomers straggle in and slide into the last pew with their necks bowed. That Sunday the last pew was occupied by a few red-faced members of the Buhler tribe and the Hanson boy who was in his forties but still called "boy" because his time in the war had shaken the sense out of him. But at the very end of the sermon, as measured by McDowell's increasing volume and perspiration, a man Ade didn't recognize entered the church and tucked himself into the second-to-last row.

Ade didn't know much about the wider world, but she knew for certain this man lived there. Everything about him spoke of precision and order. His woolen coat was short and sharp, revealing a long length of pressed black trouser. His graying mustache was clipped with surgical precision. There was an almost imperceptible shuffling sound as every member of the congregation attempted to look at the stranger without anyone else seeing them look.

The service ended and the flow of people bottlenecked itself around the interloper. A few of the first-pew families had taken it upon themselves to make introductions and inquiries. They hoped he'd enjoyed their little service (although Ade was unconvinced that enjoyment was even a distant goal of Preacher McDowell's) and wondered at his occupation in the area. Perhaps he had relations nearby? Or business on the river?

"Thank you very kindly, sirs, but no, I've no interest in riverboats. I confess I'm a land man, looking for likely property." His voice carried over the heads of the congregation, nasally and foreign-sounding, and Mama Larson huffed beside Ade. No one ought to speak above a respectful murmur while under the church roof.

"I heard in Mayfield there might be some affordable acreage near here—apparently it's haunted, and not much used—and I took this opportunity to make myself known to you folks." There was a rippling beside the stranger, a pulling-away. Ade supposed they didn't much like the idea of a big-city northerner bulling into their church just to swindle them out of cheap land. They weren't far enough south for carpetbaggers to be much more than badly inked cartoons in the Sunday paper, but they knew the signs. From the tone of their muttered replies Ade guessed they were stonewalling him (*no, sir, no land hereabouts, you'll have to look somewheres else*).

The stream of people began to leave and Ade trailed behind Aunt Lizzie as they filed down the aisle. The stranger was still smiling with affable condescension at everyone, undeterred. Ade stopped.

"We got a house on our property that everybody knows is full of haunts—saw one myself, just yesterday—but it's not for sale," she told the stranger. She didn't know why she said it, except she wanted to shake the smugness out of him and prove they weren't poor rural folk who would sell land cheaply out of baseless superstition. And perhaps because she was curious, hungry for the man's worldly otherness.

"Did you now." The man smiled at her in what he must have thought was a charming manner, and leaned closer. "Permit me to walk you out, in that case." Ade found her arm clamped to his suit sleeve, her feet stumbling alongside his. Her aunts were already outside, likely fanning themselves and gossiping. "Now, what's the nature of these haunts? What did you see, precisely?"

But her desire to speak to the man had evaporated. She tugged her hand away, shrugging in a sullen, adolescent way, and would have left without speaking another word except that his eyes caught hers. They were the color of moons or coins, unspeakably cold but also somehow alluring, as if they possessed their own gravitational pull.

Even years later, curled beside me in the languorous warmth of the late-afternoon sun, Ade would shudder, just a little, as she described that gaze.

"Tell me all about it," the stranger breathed.

And Ade did. "Well, I just was going to the old cabin for no reason and there was a ghost boy waiting there. Or at least that's what I thought he was at first, on account of he was black and funny-dressed and speaking in tongues. But he didn't come from hell or anything. I don't know where he come from, exactly, except he ended up walking out of our cabin door. And I'm glad he did, I liked him, liked his hands—" She closed her teeth on the words, reeling and a little breathless.

The not-very-charming smile had returned to the stranger's face as she spoke, except now there was a kind of predatory stillness beneath it. "Thank you awfully much, Miss—?"

"Adelaide Lee Larson." She swallowed, blinked. "Pardon me, sir, my aunts are calling."

She skittered out the church doors without looking back at the stranger in the neat suit. She felt his eyes like a pair of dimes pressed to the back of her neck.

Because of her aunts' essential softheartedness, Ade's punishments never varied. She was confined to the upstairs room where they all slept (except Mama Larson, who did not sleep so much as nap haphazardly in a variety of semisupine positions downstairs) for the following two days. Ade bore this confinement with poor grace—the Larson women would spend those days haunted by bangings and thumpings above them, as if their house hosted a particularly foul-tempered poltergeist—but no real resistance. In her figuring, it was best to lull them into complacence before climbing out the window and scrabbling down the honeysuckle on the evening of the third day.

On Monday she was supplied with a basket of fresh laundry to fold and a few stacks of ripped underclothes to mend, because Aunt Lizzie insisted that lying in bed all day was more reward than punishment, and said she might run off tomorrow evening herself and they could lock her upstairs next for some bed rest. At lunch the loft grew greasy with the smell of frying bacon and beans. Ade dropped a Bible on the floor to remind them to bring her up something to eat.

But none of her aunts appeared. There was an authoritative thumping on the front door, followed by the astonished silence of five women so unaccustomed to visitors they weren't quite sure what action ought to follow a knock at the door. Then a timid chair-scraping and shuffling, and the door creaking inward. Ade lay flat on the floor and pressed her ear to the pine boards.

She heard nothing but the low, foreign rumblings of a strange man in their kitchen, and five women's voices rising and falling around it like a flock of startled river birds. Once a hearty laugh boomed upward, drum-hollow and well practiced. Ade thought of the big-city man at the church service and felt a strange darkening, a fear of something nameless hanging on her horizon.

The man left, the door closed, and the twittering of the aunts crescendoed into something like cackling.

It was an hour or more before Aunt Lizzie brought up a plate of cold beans. "And who was that at the door?" Ade asked. She was still lying on the floor, having found herself paralyzed by a combination of lassitude and dread.

"Never you mind, nosy. Just a bit of good news is all." Lizzie looked quite smug as she said it, like a woman hiding a grand surprise. Had it been one of her other aunts Ade might have bullied her for more information, but bullying Aunt Lizzie was like bullying a mountain, except mountains didn't switch you for impertinence. Ade rolled onto her back and watched the sunbeams stretch across the loft ceiling, pooling in the gullies between rafters. She wondered what the sun might look like elsewhere, in some other world, and if there were really any other worlds to see. Already the things the ghost boy told her were fading and fraying.

On the morning of the third day Ade woke with a foreboding heaviness in her limbs. Her aunts and grandmother still snored and snuffled around her in a sea of quilts and woman-flesh. Sunrise was reluctant and gray, too slow in coming.

Ade sat tense among her aunts as they dressed, wishing herself out the window and in the hayfield already. Her bones hummed and strained; her feet *tap-tap*ped on the floorboards. The loft was close and humid from their sleeping breath.

"We're going to town today," Mama Larson announced, and gestured for her town hat—an enormous white bonnet she'd purchased sometime in the 1850s, which looked and smelled increasingly like a stuffed rabbit. "But you're staying put, Ade, on account of the heart attack you gave us."

Ade blinked. Then she nodded meekly, because it seemed polite to maintain the fiction that she would obey.

By the time all the Larson women were truly gone—and it took an eternity of fussing with dresses and stockings, followed by another small eternity in the barn convincing the mules they ought to wear a harness and pull a cart before this was accomplished— Ade was almost shuddering with the urge to be elsewhere. She took a September apple and her aunt Lizzie's work coat and left at a scurrying almost-run.

There was no one waiting at the old cabin. There was, in fact, no old cabin at which to wait: the field was blank, featureless, empty but for a few sulky-looking crows and a line of fresh iron stakes driven into the earth.

Ade closed her eyes against a sudden disorienting dizziness, stumbling forward. Where the cabin used to stand she found a raw tumble of broken lumber, as if a giant's hand had reached casually from the sky to topple it.

There was nothing left of the door but a few lichen-splotched splinters.

The lamps were lit in the windows by the time she arrived home. The mules were back in the pasture looking ruffled and sweat-stained, and Ade could hear the self-satisfied cackling of her aunts in the kitchen. The laughter stopped when she opened the door.

The five of them stood gathered around the kitchen table admiring a stack of neat cream-striped shopping boxes. Packing paper seemed to drift around them in crinkling clouds, and each woman was pink-cheeked with some secret exhilaration. Their smiles were strange and girlish.

"Adelaide Lee, *where*—"

"Why are there survey stakes on our land?" Ade asked. Each of her relatives, she saw, was dressed more grandly than she had been that morning, with a profusion of velvet ribbons and even the foreign humps of bustles beneath rich-colored skirts. In her muddied dress and tangled braid, Ade felt suddenly distant from them all, as if she and her aunts were standing at opposite ends of a very large room.

It was Mama Larson who answered. "We got some luck, finally." Her hand swept in a queenly gesture at the kitchen table. "That big-city man come by yesterday and offered us good money for the old hayfield. *Real* good money." The aunts tittered. "And there wasn't a reason in the world we shouldn't take it. He handed over cash—all of it stashed in his pockets!—and I signed over the deed then and there. What's a overgrown hayfield to us, anyway?" The last phrase sounded like it had been said many times between them in the last day.

Aunt Lizzie stepped forward with a box. "Don't look so grim, Adelaide. Look, I meant to save it for your birthday, but—" She opened the box to show Ade a long length of periwinkle cotton. "Thought it'd match your eyes."

Ade found her voice had entirely deserted her. She patted Lizzie's hand, hoping they might think she was overcome with gratitude, and ran upstairs before her tears could make their treacherous paths down her cheeks.

She crawled animal-like into the sagging center of her rope bed. She felt rubbed raw, as if the grasses in the field had been sharp-edged, cutting away at that childish part of her that believed in adventure and magic.

She had lingered beside the ruins of the cabin all day, knowing the ghost boy would not appear but waiting anyway.

Perhaps there had never been an elsewhere, and she was simply young and lonely and foolish, and had dreamed up a story about a ghost boy and another world to keep herself company. Perhaps there was nothing at all except the rule-bound world of her aunts and grandmother, real as corn bread and dirt and just as dull.

She came very near to believing it. But she found there was something new in her, some wild seed buried in her chest, that could not accept the world as it was.

You see, doors are many things: fissures and cracks, ways between, mysteries and borders. But more than anything else, doors are change.[3] When things slip through them, no matter how small or brief, change trails them like porpoises following a ship's wake. The change had already taken hold of Adelaide Lee, and she could not turn away.

And so that night, lying half-heartbroken and lost in her bed, Ade chose to believe. She believed in something mad and elsewise, in the feel of the boy's dry lips against hers in the dying light, in the possibility that there were cracked-open places in the world through which strange and wonderful things might seep.

In believing, Ade felt the scattered uncertainties of her youth falling away. She was a hound that finally caught the scent it sought, a lost sailor suddenly handed a compass. If doors were real, then she would seek them out, ten or ten thousand of them, and fall through into ten thousand vast elsewheres.

And one of them, someday, might lead to a city by the sea.

---

3. This theory—described in the preface as conclusion iii—is based on decades of field research, but it is also indirectly supported by many works in Western scholarship.

Consider, for example, the *Ystoria Mongalorum*, a well-respected work of early European exploration detailing the journey of John of Plano Carpini to the Mongol court in the 1240s. In it, Carpini argues that a great change had come among the Tartars several decades previously, which could not be accounted for by reasonable means. He reported a popular Mongol myth that their Great Khan had disappeared for a time as a child, walking through a cursed door in a cave and not returning for seven years. Perhaps, Carpini theorized, he had spent the time in "a world not his own," and returned with the terrible wisdom necessary to conquer the Asiatic continent.

Perhaps one cannot walk through a door and back out again without changing the world.

A Door to Anywhere

You know the feeling of waking up in an unfamiliar room and not knowing how you got there? For a minute you're just drifting, suspended in the timeless unknown, like Alice falling forever down the rabbit hole.

I'd woken almost every morning of my life in that gray little room on the third floor of Locke House. The sun-faded floorboards, the inadequate bookshelf overflowing with stacks of paperbacks, Bad sprawled beside me like a hairy furnace: all of it was as familiar as my own skin. But still—for a single stretched moment, I didn't know quite where I was.

I didn't know why there were crusted salt trails down my cheeks. I didn't know why there was an aching emptiness just beneath my ribs, as if something vital had been cut away from me in the night. I didn't know why the corner of a book was jabbing into my jaw.

I remembered the book first. An overgrown hayfield. A girl and a ghost. A door that led marvelously elsewhere. And an eerie, echoing sense of familiarity, as if I'd heard the story before and couldn't recall the ending. How had such a thing ended up in my blue Egyptian chest? And who wrote it in the first place? And why did Ade Larson feel like a friend I'd had as a child and then forgotten?

(I could feel myself leaning desperately toward these pleasant mysteries. As if there were something else hovering just on the edges of my vision, waiting to pounce if I looked directly at it.)

There was a rustling from Jane's bed across the room. "January? Are you awake?"

Something about her voice, an uncharacteristic hesitance, a fearful softening, made me think: *She knows.*

And then: *Knows what?*

And then I remembered. *Father is dead.* The huge, cold thing sprang from the shadows and ate me whole, and everything went sort of grayish and dullish and faraway-seeming. My tale of adventure and mystery became nothing but a worn leather-bound book again.

I heard Jane rising, stretching, dressing for the day. I had the dim sense that she was going to say something to me, something comforting or consoling, and the thought was like a wire brush on rubbed-raw skin. I screwed my eyes shut and clutched Bad closer.

Then there was the creak of the window opening, and a warm, dew-heavy breeze ruffled my hair. Jane said, mildly, "Let's go out, eh? It's a lovely morning."

It was such a normal, Saturday-morning sort of thing for her to suggest. It was one of our favorite rituals, to go out on the grounds with a basket of biscuits, an armload of paperbacks, and a quilt that smelled permanently grassy from its long service as a picnic blanket. Thinking about it now—the peaceable quiet; the warm, sleepy sound of dragonflies—was like thinking of safe harbor in a storm.

God bless you, Miss Jane Irimu.

I found I was able to sit up, and then stand, and then make all my usual morning motions. It turns out that once you begin, habit and memory keep your body moving in the right directions, like a wound-up clock ticking dutifully through the seconds. I dressed at random: stockings with several holes in the heels, a plain brownish skirt, a peony blouse several inches too short on my wrists. I fended off Bad's excited nips and dragged a brush through my crackling hair (I had nursed a secret hope that puberty might domesticate my hair, but it had instead inspired it to new and greater heights).

By the time we left the room I'd achieved a false, fragile normalcy. And then I stumbled over the package waiting for me in the hall.

It was a box of such surpassing whiteness and squareness I knew it must have come from one of those exclusive shops in New York with a gold-cursive sign and gleaming glass windows. A note was propped neatly on top:

My dear girl—
Though you may feel indisposed, I request your attendance at tonight's party. I wish to give you your birthday present.

Several lines were scratched out here. Then:

I am sorry for your loss.
CL
P.S. Do your hair.

Locke hadn't dictated it to his secretary; that was his own architectural lettering. Seeing it was like feeling his icy eyes pressing me down again—*accept it*—and the cold black thing seemed to wrap itself more tightly around me.

Jane read the note over my shoulder and her lips went thin and hard as a penny. "Nothing can save you from the Society party, it seems."

The annual party—which I'd been dreading for a week or two—was tonight. I'd forgotten. I pictured myself weaving through drunken white crowds, pushing past men who laughed too loudly and sloshed their champagne over my shoes, wishing I could wipe the oily feeling of their eyes off my skin. Would everyone know about my father? Would they care? I felt the note tremble in my hand.

Jane snatched it from me and folded it into her skirt pocket. "Never mind. We've got hours yet." And she tucked my hand beneath her elbow and marched us down two flights of stairs, through the kitchens where the cooks were too harried and sweaty to notice us snatching jam and rolls and a kettle of coffee, and out into the pristine lawns of Locke House.

We wandered at first. Through the hedged gardens where the gardeners were busy murdering anything that looked too lively or untamed, along the ruffled lakeshore, where herons hooted their annoyance at Bad and waves *tap-tap*ped at the shore. We wound up in a grassy overlook far enough from the house that no garden shears had denuded it, with the countryside laid before us like a wrinkled green tablecloth.

Jane poured herself coffee and delved immediately into the seventh book in the Tom Swift series (Jane had transitioned from skeptic to addict on the subject of low-grade serial fiction; thus had Samuel's boyhood vice claimed another victim). I didn't read anything. I just lay on the quilt and stared at the soft eggshell of the sky and let the sunshine pool and sizzle on my skin.

I could almost hear Mr. Locke's huffing in my ear: *Not doing your complexion any favors, girl.* My father never seemed to care.

I didn't want to think about my father. I wanted to think about something, almost anything else. "Do you ever want to leave?" The question leapt out of my mouth before I had time to wonder where it came from.

Jane laid her book spread-eagle on the quilt and considered me. "Leave where?"

"I don't know, Locke House. Vermont. Everything."

There was a short silence, during which I realized two things simultaneously. First, that I was so selfish I'd never once asked Jane if she wanted to go home, and second, that there was nothing in the world holding her here now that my father and his weekly allowance were gone. Panic made my breath shallow and quick. Would I lose Jane, too? Would I be entirely alone? How soon?

Jane exhaled carefully. "I miss my home... more than I can say. I think of it every waking moment. But I will not leave you, January." An unspoken *yet* seemed to hang specter-like between us, or perhaps it was *until*. I felt like crying and clinging to her skirts, begging her to stay forever. Or begging to go away with her.

But Jane saved us both from embarrassment by asking lightly, "Do *you* want to leave?"

I swallowed, tucking my fear away for some future time when I would be strong enough to look directly at it. "Yes," I answered, and in answering realized it was true. I wanted wide-open horizons and worn shoes and strange constellations spinning above me like midnight riddles. I wanted danger and mystery and adventure. Like my father before me? "Oh, *yes.*"

It seemed to me I'd always wanted those things, since I was a little girl scribbling stories in her pocket diary, but I'd abandoned such fanciful dreams with my childhood. Except it turned out I hadn't really abandoned them but merely forgotten them, let them settle to the bottom of me like fallen leaves. And then *The Ten Thousand Doors* had come along and swirled them into the air again, a riot of impossible dreams.

Jane didn't say anything.

Well, she hardly needed to: we both knew how unlikely it was that I would ever leave Locke House. Odd-colored young orphan girls didn't fare well out in the wide world, with no money or prospects, even if they were "perfectly unique specimens." Mr. Locke was my only shelter and anchor now that my father was gone. Perhaps he would take pity and hire me as a secretary or typist for W. C. Locke & Co., and I would turn dull and mousy and wear thick-lensed spectacles on my nose and have permanent ink stains up both wrists. Perhaps he would let me stay in my little gray room until I grew so old and faded I became a half ghost haunting Locke House, alarming guests.

After a time I heard the regular *shush* of Jane turning the pages of *Tom Swift Among the Diamond Makers*. I stared at the sky and tried not to think about the adventures I'd never have or the father I'd never see again or the cold, black thing still wrapped around me, turning the summer sun watery and pale. I tried to think of nothing at all.

I wonder if there has ever been a seventeen-year-old girl who wanted to attend a fancy party less than I did that night.

I stood at the edge of the parlor door for several minutes or possibly a century, nerving myself to step around the corner into the chemical fog of pomade and perfume. Serving staff swept past with glittering trays of champagne flutes and fleshy-looking canapés. They did not pause to offer me anything but merely maneuvered around me as if I were a misplaced vase or an awkward lamp.

I drew a breath, brushed my sweaty palm against Bad's fur, and slipped into the parlor.

It would be overdramatic of me to claim that the entire room stood still, or that silence reigned the way it did when a princess entered her ballroom in my books, but there was a kind of silent *whooshing* around me, as if I were escorted by an invisible wind. A few conversations faltered as their participants turned toward me, eyebrows half-raised and lips curling.

Maybe they were staring at Bad, standing stiff and surly beside me. He was technically banned from all social events until the end of time, but I was betting Locke wouldn't make a fuss in public and that Bad wouldn't injure anyone seriously enough to require stitches. And anyway, I wasn't sure I could've physically made myself leave my room without him beside me.

Or maybe they were staring at me. They'd all seen me before, trailing in Locke's shadow at every Society party and Christmas banquet, alternately ignored or fussed over. *What a pretty dress you have, Miss January!* they trilled at me, laughing in the birdlike manner unique to the wealthy wives of bankers. *Oh, isn't she darling. Where did you say you found her again, Cornelius? Zanzibar?* But I'd been a little girl then—a harmless, in-between thing stuffed into dolls' clothes and trained to speak politely when spoken to.

I was not a little girl now, and they were no longer so charmed. Over the winter I'd suffered through all those mysterious, alchemical changes that transform children into sudden, awkward adults: I was taller, less soft, less trusting. My own face reflected in the gold-gilt mirrors was foreign to me, hollowed out.

And then there were Mr. Locke's gifts now on display: long silk gloves, several loops of pinkish pearls, and a drapey chiffon gown in ivory and rose that was so obviously expensive I saw women staring in disbelieving calculation. I'd even waged dutiful war with my hair, which could be defeated only by the application of a hot comb and Madame Walker's Wonderful Conditioning Treatment. My scalp still sizzled faintly.

The conversation lurched clumsily back to life. Shoulders and backs turned decisively away, and lacy fans snapped out like shields against some intruder. Bad and I slid around them and posted ourselves like mismatched mannequins in our usual corner. The guests obligingly ignored us, and I was free to slump and tug at the too-tight buttons of my dress and watch the shimmering crowd.

It was, as always, an impressive display. The household staff had polished every lamp and candlestick until the room radiated sourceless golden light, and the parquet floor was waxed to life-threatening slickness. Enormous enameled vases oozed peonies, and a smallish orchestra had been crammed between a pair of Assyrian statues. All of New England's faux-royalty preened and glittered for one another, reflected back on themselves a hundred times by the gleaming mirrors.

I noticed girls my own age scattered through the crowd, their cheeks flushed and their hair hanging in perfect silky curls, their eyes darting hopefully around the room (the gossip pages of the local paper always ran a column listing the most eligible bachelors and their rumored worth before the party). I pictured them all planning and scheming for weeks, shopping for just the right dress with their mothers, doing and redoing their hair in the mirror. And now here they were, glowing with promise and privilege, their futures laid out before them in an orderly gilt procession.

I hated them. Or I would have hated them, except that dark, formless thing was still wrapped tightly around me, and it was hard to feel anything but dull distaste.

A ringing *clink-clink-clink* sounded over the crowd and heads turned like well-coiffed marionettes. Mr. Locke was standing beneath the grandest chandelier, tapping his tumbler with a dessert spoon for attention. It was hardly necessary: Mr. Locke was always looked at and listened to, as if he generated his own magnetic field.

The orchestra stopped mid minuet. Locke raised his arms in benevolent greeting. "Ladies, gentlemen, honored Society members, let me first thank you all for coming and drinking all my best champagne." Laughter, buoyed on golden bubbles. "We are here, of course, to celebrate the forty-eighth anniversary of the New England Archaeological Society, a little group of amateur scholars who, if you'll forgive me my hubris, do their very best to contribute to the noble progression of human knowledge." A smattering of dutiful applause. "But we are also here to celebrate something rather grander: the progression of humanity itself. For it seems clear to me that the people gathered here tonight are both the witnesses and stewards of a new era of peace and prosperity from pole to pole. Every year we see the reduction of war and conflict, an increase in business and good faith, the spread of civilized government over the less fortunate."

I'd heard it all so many times I could probably deliver the rest of the speech myself: how the hard work and dedication of persons like themselves—wealthy, powerful, white—had improved the condition of the human race; how the nineteenth century was nothing but chaos and confusion, and how the twentieth promised to be order and stability; how the discontent elements were being rooted out, at home and abroad; how the savage was being civilized.

Once as a girl I'd told my father: *Don't let the savages get you.* He'd been about to leave, his shabby luggage in hand, his shapeless brown coat hanging from bent shoulders. He'd given me a half smile. *I will be quite safe,* he'd said, *as there are no such things as savages.* I could've told him that Mr. Locke and several metric tons of adventure novels disagreed with him, but I didn't say anything. He'd touched his knuckle to my cheek and disappeared. Again.

And now he's disappeared for the last time. I closed my eyes, felt the cold, dark thing wind itself more tightly around me—

The sound of my own name jarred me. "—consider my own Miss January, if you want proof!" It was Mr. Locke, jovial and booming.

My eyes flew open.

"She came to this household nothing but a motherless bundle. An orphan of mysterious origin, without so much as a penny to her name. And now look at her!"

They were already looking. An ivory ripple of faces had turned toward me, their eyes like fingers plucking at every seam and pearl. What exactly were they supposed to be looking at? I was still motherless, still penniless—except now I was fatherless, too.

I pressed my back to the wood paneling, willing it to be over, willing Mr. Locke's speech to end and the orchestra to start up and everyone to forget about me again.

Locke made an imperious come-here gesture. "Don't be shy, my girl." I didn't move, my eyes terror-wide, my heart stammering *oh no oh no oh no.* I imagined myself running away, shoving past guests and out onto the lawn.

But then I looked at Mr. Locke's proud, shining face. I remembered the solid warmth of his arms as he'd held me, the kind rumble of his voice, the silent gifts left in the Pharaoh Room all these years.

I swallowed and pushed away from the wall, stumbling through the crowd on legs gone stiff and heavy as carved wood. Whispers followed me. Bad's claws clicked too loudly on the polished floor.

As soon as I was in range Locke's arm descended and

crushed me against him. "There she is! The picture of civility. A testament to the power of positive influences." He gave my shoulders a bracing shake.

Did women actually faint, I wondered, or was that an invention of bad Victorian novels and Friday night picture shows? Or perhaps women simply contrived to collapse at convenient moments to delay the burden of hearing and seeing and feeling, just for a little while. I sympathized.

"—enough about all that. Thank you all for indulging an old man's optimism and enthusiasm, but we're here, I'm told, to enjoy ourselves." He raised his glass in a final toast—his beloved carved jade cup, translucent green. Had my father brought it to him? Stolen it away from some tomb or temple, packed it in sawdust, and sent it across the world to be clutched by this square, white hand?

"To peace and prosperity. To the future we shall build!" I dared to look up at the pale, sweating faces that surrounded us, their glasses twinkling in the chandelier's prisming light, their applause breaking around me like ocean waves.

Mr. Locke's arm unclamped from my shoulders and he spoke in a much lower voice. "Good girl. Meet us in the east smoking room at half past ten, won't you. I'd like to give you your birthday gift." He made a lazy circle with his finger to indicate the "us" he meant, and I realized the Society members had gathered like suit-wearing moths around him. Mr. Havemeyer was among them, watching me with his gloved hands resting on his cane and a polite, well-bred species of disgust on his face. Bad's hackles spiked beneath my palm and he growled so low it was like an undersea earthquake.

I spun and dove blindly away, Bad trailing stiff-legged at my heels. I aimed for our safe, invisible corner but couldn't seem to arrive. The crowd eddied and swirled in dizzy patterns, their faces leering, their smiles too wide. Something had changed—Locke's speech had dragged me to center stage, like a reluctant elephant prodded into the main ring at the circus. I felt gloved fingers stroke my skin as I passed, heard a trill of scintillated laughter. A tug on my pinned and burnt hair.

A male voice far too close to my ear: "Miss January, isn't it?" A bluish-white face loomed above me, his blond hair slicked against his skull and gold cuff links flashing. "What kind of a name is that, *January*?"

"Mine," I answered stiffly. I'd asked my father once what had possessed him to name me after a month, and particularly such a dead, frost-eaten month as January, and if there were any more normal-sounding names I could have instead. *It is a good name*, he'd said, rubbing his tattoos. And when I pressed him: *Your mother liked it. The meaning of it.*

(Don't bother looking up the meaning. Webster's says: *The first month of the year, containing thirty-one days. L. Januarius, fr. Janus, an antiquated Latin deity.* How enlightening.)

"Now, don't be rude! Take a turn outside with me, won't you?" The boy leered at me.

I hadn't spent much time with people my own age, but I'd read enough school stories to know gentlemen weren't supposed to take young ladies out alone into the dark heat of a summer night. But then, I wasn't really a lady, was I?

"No, thank you," I said. He blinked with the stunned expression of a man who knew the word *no* existed but had never actually met it in the flesh.

He leaned closer, one damp hand reaching toward my elbow. "Come, now—"

A silver tray of champagne materialized between us and a low, unfriendly voice said, "May I offer you a drink, sir?"

It was Samuel Zappia, dressed in the crisp black-and-white uniform of a hired server.

I'd barely seen him in the last two years, mostly because

the red Zappia grocery cart had been replaced by a neat black truck with a closed cab and I could no longer wave to him from the study window. I'd driven past the store with Mr. Locke once or twice and caught blurred glimpses of Samuel out back, unloading flour sacks from a truck bed and staring out at the lake with a distant, dreaming expression. I'd wondered if he still subscribed to *The Argosy*, or if he'd abandoned such childish fancies.

Now he looked clear and sharp, as if he'd come fully into focus in a camera lens. His skin was still that golden-dark color mysteriously known as olive; his eyes were still black and bright as polished shale.

They were fixed now on the blond gentleman in a flat, unblinking stare, beneath eyebrows raised in faux-polite inquiry. There was something unsettling about that stare, something so blatantly unservile that the man took a half step backward. He stared at Samuel with an expression of upper-class offense that generally sent servants scurrying to make amends.

But Samuel didn't move. A fey gleam lit in his eye, as if he were rather hoping the young man would attempt to chastise him. I couldn't help noticing the way Samuel's shoulders pressed against the seams of his starched suit coat, the wiry look of his wrist holding the heavy tray; beside him, the blond man looked as pale and squashy as unrisen dough.

He spun away, thin lips curled, and skittered back to the protection of his peers.

Samuel turned smoothly toward me, lifting a shimmery golden glass. "For the birthday girl, perhaps?" His expression was perfectly bland.

He remembered my birthday. My dress suddenly felt itchy and hot. "Thank you. For, uh, rescuing me."

"Oh, I wasn't rescuing *you*, Miss Scaller. I was saving that poor boy from a dangerous animal." He ducked his head at

Bad, who was still watching the retreating man with his hackles raised and his lips curling back over his teeth.

"Ah." Silence. I wished I were a thousand miles away. I wished I were a yellow-haired girl named something like Anna or Elizabeth who laughed like a clockwork bird and always knew just what to say.

The corners of Samuel's eyes crimped. He folded my fingers around the stem of the champagne flute, his hands dry and summer-warm. "It might help," he said, and vanished back into the crowd.

I downed the champagne so quickly my nose fizzed with it. I raided several more silver trays as I made my way through the parlor, and by the time I reached the smoking room I was placing my feet very precisely and trying not to notice the way colors sloshed and oozed at the edges of my vision. My dark veil, that invisible Thing that had curled around me all day, seemed to flicker and warp.

I took a breath outside the door. "Ready, Bad?" He dog-sighed at me.

My first impression was that the room had shrunk considerably since I'd last seen it, but then, I'd never seen it crammed with a dozen men wearing crowns of bluish smoke and conversing in low rumbles. I recognized this as one of those important, exclusive meetings that I'd never been permitted to attend: those boozy late-night congregations of men where the real decisions were made. I ought to have felt pleased or honored; instead, I tasted something bitter in the back of my throat.

Bad sneezed at the cigar-and-leather reek, and Mr. Locke turned toward us. "You made it, dear girl. Come, take a seat." He gestured to a high-backed armchair in the rough center of the room, around which the men of the Archaeological

Society were ranged as if posing for a portrait-painting. There was Havemeyer, and the ferrety Mr. Ilvane, and others I recognized from previous parties and visits: a red-lipped woman with a black ribbon around her throat; a youngish man with a hungry smile; a white-haired man with long, curling nails. There was something secretive about them, like predators stalking through tall grass.

I perched on the armchair, feeling hunted.

Mr. Locke's hand landed on my shoulder for the second time that evening. "We've asked you here tonight for a little announcement. After much careful thought and discussion, my colleagues and I would like to offer you something rather rare and much sought-after. It's quite unorthodox, but we feel it is warranted by your, ah, unique situation. January"—a dramatic pause—"we'd like to offer you formal membership in the Society."

I blinked at him. Was this my birthday gift? I wondered if I ought to be pleased. I wondered if Mr. Locke had known how, as a girl, I'd dreamed of joining his silly society and trotting around the world having adventures, collecting rare and valuable objects. I wondered if my father had ever wanted to join.

That bitter taste returned, and something else that burned ember-hot on my tongue. I swallowed it back. "Thank you, sir."

Mr. Locke's hand knocked me twice in hearty congratulations. He launched into another speech about the formal induction process and certain rituals and oaths that must be made before the Founder—see that capital *F* like a saluting soldier—but I wasn't listening. The burning in my mouth was growing stronger, scalding my tongue, and my invisible veil was crumbling to ash and char around me. The room around me seemed to pulse with heat.

"Thank you," I interrupted. My voice was flat, almost toneless; I listened to it with detached fascination. "But I'm afraid I must decline your invitation."

Silence.

A silver-eyed voice in my head was hissing at me—*be a good girl, mind your place*—but it was drowned out by the alcohol thudding in my blood. "I mean, why should I want to join your Society, really? A bunch of fussy old aristocrats who pay braver and better men to go out and steal things for you. And should one of them disappear you don't even pretend to mourn him. You just carry on—as if nothing—as if he didn't *matter*—" I broke off, panting.

You don't really realize how many small sounds a house makes—the tocking of the grandfather clock, the sighing of the summer breeze against the windowpanes, the moaning of floor joists beneath a hundred pairs of expensive shoes—until you've stunned a room into absolute silence. I clutched Bad's collar as if he were the one in need of restraint.

Mr. Locke's hand tightened on my shoulder and his munificent smile became something gritted and painful-looking. "Apologize," he breathed at me.

My jaw locked. A part of me—Mr. Locke's good girl, the girl who never complained, who minded her place and smiled and smiled and smiled—wanted to fling myself at his feet and beg for forgiveness. But most of me would rather have died.

Locke's eyes found mine. Chill, steel-colored, pressing into me like two cold hands against my face—

"Pardon me," I spat. One of the Society men gave a crack of derisive laughter.

I watched Mr. Locke work to unclench his teeth. "January. The Society is a very old, very powerful, and very prestigious—"

"Oh, yes, so *prestigious*." I sneered. "Far too prestigious for people like my father to join, no matter how much garbage he steals for you, no matter how much money you make auctioning it off in secret. Am I light-skinned enough to sign up, is that it? Is there a chart I can consult?" I bared my teeth at them. "Maybe one of you can add me to your skull collection when I die, as some sort of missing link."

The silence this time was absolute, as if even the grandfather clock were too insulted to make a sound.

"Looks like you've raised quite the little malcontent, Cornelius." It was Mr. Havemeyer, watching with a smile of purest malice and twirling an unlit cigar in his gloved fingers. "We did warn you, didn't we?"

I felt Mr. Locke inhale, whether to defend or chastise me I didn't know, but I no longer cared. I was finished with it, with them, with being a good girl and minding my place and being grateful for every scrap of dignity they tossed my way.

I stood up, feeling the champagne fizz sickeningly in my skull. "Thank you, gentlemen, for my birthday present." And I spun and marched out the dark-stained doors with Bad trotting at my heels.

The crowd had grown sweatier and louder and drunker. It was like being trapped in a Toulouse-Lautrec painting, green-lit faces spinning around me with ghoulish expressions. I wanted to set Bad on them, all teeth and burnished bronze fur. I wanted to scream myself hoarse.

I wanted to draw a door in the air, a door to somewhere else, and walk through it.

The silver tray materialized again at my elbow. Warm air whispered against the back of my neck. "Outside, west wing. Five minutes." The tray vanished, and I watched Samuel slide back into the chattering horde.

When Bad and I slipped out the west wing door, feeling like escapees from some hellish fairy ball, we found Samuel alone.

He leaned against the still-warm brick of Locke House, hands jammed in his pockets. His neat waiter's costume looked like it had recently suffered an escape attempt: his tie was loose and crumpled, his sleeves were unbuttoned, his dark coat had vanished.

"Ah, I did not know if you would come." His smile had finally extended past his eyes.

"Yes."

Silences are easier to bear outdoors. I listened to the snuffling sounds of Bad rooting through a hedgerow for some unlucky creature, and the scrape and hiss of a striking match as Samuel lit a roughly rolled cigarette. Twin flames glowed in his eyes.

He drew breath and exhaled a pearl cloud. "Listen, I—we heard about what happened. To Mr. Scaller. I am sorr—"

He was going to say how sorry he was, how tragic and sudden it had been, et cetera, and I knew with sudden clarity that I wouldn't be able to bear it. Whatever lunatic rage had allowed me to storm away from the Society had curdled and cooled, and left me very alone.

I interrupted before he could finish, gesturing abruptly at Bad. "Why did you give him to me? You never really said." My voice was too loud and false-sounding, like a poor actor in a town play.

Samuel's brows rose. He watched Bad crunching merrily on something field-mouse-sized, then gave me a one-shouldered shrug. "Because you were lonely." He twisted his cigarette out on the brick beside him and added, "And I do not like to see people outnumbered. Mr. Locke and that old German woman, bah. You needed someone on your side— like Robin Hood needed a Little John, eh?" His eyes sparked at me; I'd always made him play Little John in our games of Sherwood Forest, alternating at need to Alan-a-Dale or Friar Tuck. Samuel pointed to Bad, who was making a series of

88

unpleasant hacking sounds to dislodge the mouse bones in his throat. "This dog, he is on your side."

So casually, thoughtlessly kind. I found myself leaning closer, listing toward him like a lost ship toward a lighthouse.

Samuel was still watching Bad. "Do you swim much, these days?"

I blinked at him. "No." He and I had spent hours flailing and splashing in the lake as kids, but I hadn't set foot in the water for years. It was just one of those things I'd lost somehow, along the way of growing up.

I caught the tilted edge of his half smile. "Ah, then you are out of practice. Bet you a quarter I could beat you now."

He'd always lost our races, probably because he'd had to help in his family's store and lacked the endless summer afternoons I'd had to practice in. "A lady doesn't bet," I said primly. "But if I did, I'd be twenty-five cents richer."

Samuel laughed—a boyish, immoderate sound I hadn't heard since we were children—and I smiled rather foolishly back at him. And then somehow we were standing closer to one another, so that I had to tilt my head upward to see his face, and I could smell tobacco and sweat and something warm and green, like fresh-cut grass.

I thought a little wildly of *The Ten Thousand Doors*, of Adelaide kissing her ghost boy under the autumn constellations without a single heartbeat of doubt. I wished I were like her: feral and fearless, brave enough to steal a kiss.

Be a good girl.

. . . To hell with being good.

The thought was dizzying, intoxicating—I'd already broken so many rules tonight, left them smashed and glittering in my wake—what was one more?

Then I pictured Mr. Locke's face as I'd swept from the smoking room—the stiff lines of outrage around his mouth, the disappointment in his chilled gray eyes—and my stomach went cold. My father was gone, and without Mr. Locke I would have nothing at all in the world.

I cast my eyes to the ground and stepped away, shivering a little in the cooling night. I thought I heard Samuel exhale.

There was a short silence while I relearned the trick of breathing. Then Samuel asked, lightly, "If you could go somewhere else right now, where would it be?"

"Anywhere. Another world." I was thinking of the blue Door and the smell of the sea when I said it. I hadn't thought of it in years, but Adelaide's story had dragged it back to the surface of my memory.

Samuel didn't laugh at me. "My family has a cabin on the north end of Champlain. We used to go every summer for a whole week, but my father's health, and the shop . . . We have not gone in years." I pictured Samuel as I'd known him before, young and wiry-armed and so tanned he seemed to emanate secondhand light. "It is not a very large or very nice cabin— just a cedar-shake box with a rusted stovepipe sticking out— but it is very alone, at the edge of its own island. When you look out the windows there is nothing but lake water and sky and pine trees.

"When I get sick of all this"—he waved his hand so widely it seemed to include not only Locke House, but everything inside it, every expensive bottle of imported wine, every stolen treasure, every trilling banker's wife taking a glass from Samuel's tray without ever seeing him—"I think of that cabin. Far away from bow ties and suit coats, from rich men and poor men and the space between them. That's where I would go, if I could." He smiled. "Another world."

I was suddenly very certain he still read his story papers and adventure novels, still kept his eyes on the distant horizons.

It's a profoundly strange feeling, to stumble across someone whose desires are shaped so closely to your own, like reaching toward your reflection in a mirror and finding warm flesh under your fingertips. If you should ever be lucky enough to find that magical, fearful symmetry, I hope you're brave enough to grab it with both hands and not let go.

I wasn't. Then.

"It's late. I'm going in," I announced, and the harshness of it erased the miraculous circle we'd drawn around ourselves like a shoe smudging away a chalk line. Samuel stiffened. I couldn't bring myself to look at his face—would I have seen regret or recrimination? Desire or desperation to match my own?—but merely whistled to Bad and turned away.

I hesitated at the door. "Good night, Samuel," I whispered, and went in.

The room was dark. Moonlight drew pale edges around the ivory gown now crumpled on the floor, the burr of Jane's hair against her pillow, the curve of Bad's spine pressed against me.

I lay in bed, feeling the champagne tide retreating and leaving me beached, like some unfortunate sea creature. In its absence the Thing—heavy, black, suffocating—returned, as if it had been waiting all evening for the two of us to be alone. It slid oil-slick over my skin, filled my nostrils, pooled at the back of my throat. It whispered in my ear, stories about loss and loneliness and little orphan girls.

Once upon a time there was a girl named January who had no mother and no father.

The weight of Locke House, red stone and copper and all those precious, secret, stolen things, pressed down on me. After twenty or thirty years beneath that weight, what would be left of me?

I wanted to run away and keep running until I was out of this sad, ugly fairy tale. There's only one way to run away from your own story, and that's to sneak into someone else's. I unwedged the leather-bound book from beneath my mattress and breathed in the ink-and-adventure smell of it.

I walked through it into another world.

Chapter Two

On Miss Larson's Discovery of
Further Doors and Her Departure
from Documented History

A timely death—The boo hags of St. Ours—The hungry years and their conclusion

Mama Larson died in the bitter March of 1885, a week after the early-rising daffodils had been felled by a hard frost and eight days before her granddaughter turned nineteen. For the Larson aunts their mother's death was a tragedy on par with the falling of a great empire or the collapse of a mountain range, almost beyond understanding, and for a time the household degraded into scattered, aimless mourning.

Mourning is a self-absorbed business; it should not therefore surprise us that the Larson women failed to pay much attention to Adelaide Lee. Ade was grateful for their inattention—for if her aunts *had* considered her countenance, they would have found it very far from despair or sadness.

Standing beside her grandmother's deathbed, woolen dress still smelling of black logwood dye, Ade had felt the way a sapling might as it watched one of the old forest giants come crashing magnificently to rest: awed, and perhaps a little frightened. But when Mama Larson's final breath rattled from her ribs, Ade discovered the same thing the young sapling would have: in the absence of the old tree, there was a hole in the canopy above her.

Ade began to suspect that, for the first time in her life, she was free.

It wasn't true that she'd been unfree for the previous several years. Indeed, compared to other young women in those times, she led an unfettered and feckless life. She was permitted to wear canvas trousers and men's work hats, primarily because her aunts eventually despaired of keeping her skirts presentable; she was not expected to ensnare any eligible young bachelors, because her aunts shared a collectively dim view of men; she was not forced to attend school or find employment; and while her wandering habit was not encouraged, her aunts were at least resigned to it.

But Ade still felt as if an invisible collar rested around her throat, its leash leading back to the Larson farm. She might disappear for two or four or six days, riding a train north and sleeping in strangers' tobacco barns, but in the end she always circled back home. Mama Larson would wail about fallen women, her aunts would purse their lips, and Ade would go to sleep heartsick and dream of doors.

Her leash grew loose and frayed over the years, until it was just a single thread of love and familial loyalty. With Mama Larson's death, the thread snapped.

As happens with many caged creatures and half-domesticated young girls, it took some weeks for Ade to realize she could truly leave. She stayed for her grandmother's burial in the lumpy, ivy-eaten plot on the far side of the farm, and paid Mr. Tullsen to engrave a limestone marker (*HERE LIES ADA LARSON, 1813–1885, A MOTHER MOST DEAR*), and three weeks later she woke with her pulse beating a marching rhythm in her throat. It was a bright spring morning, full of promise. Most travelers are familiar with this kind of weather—when the wind blows westward and warm but the ground still chills the soles of your feet, when the tree buds have begun to unfurl and scent the air with secret springtime madness—and they know those days are made for leaving.

Ade left.

Each of her aunts received a kiss on the cheek that morning in order from oldest to youngest. If the kisses were more sincere than usual, and if their niece's eyes had a feverish glow, they did not notice. Only Aunt Lizzie looked up from her boiled egg.

"Where you going, child?"

"Into town," Ade said evenly.

Aunt Lizzie looked at her for a long moment, as if she could read her niece's intentions in the forward tilt of her shoulders, the slant of her smile. "Well," she sighed finally, "we'll be here when you come back." Ade barely heard her at the time, already flitting out the kitchen door like a loosed bird, but later she would return to those words and rub them for comfort until they were worn smooth as creek stones.

She went first to the sagging barn and unearthed a hammer, a pocketful of square-topped nails, a horsehair paintbrush, and a rusted paint can labeled *Prussian Blue*.

She took her supplies west toward the old hayfield. Time had stepped very lightly across the field. It had been briefly mowed and hayed by a wealthy neighbor, then abandoned again; a few crews of surveyors had scurried about with intentions of building a shipping house along the riverbank but found the ground too low-lying. Now there was only a rusted line of barbed wire with a tin sign indicating that it was private property and suggesting that trespassers should be wary. Ade ducked beneath it without breaking stride.

The cabin timbers had never been fully cleared away but were left to rot in a weedy tangle of honeysuckle and pokeberry. Ade knelt before the old lumber with her thoughts running deep and silent, like subterranean rivers, and scrounged through the pile for unrotted wood, brackets, old hinges. Farm life without uncles or brothers had left her with more-than-passable carpentry skills, and it took only an hour or so before she'd assembled a frame and rough door. She hammered the frame into the earth and hung her scrapped-together door in it. It creaked in the river breeze.

It was only when she was entirely finished, and the door was painted a deep, velvet-ocean blue, that she fully understood what she was doing: she was leaving, perhaps for a very long time, and she wanted to leave something behind. Some kind of monument or memorial, like Mama Larson's headstone, that marked her memory of the ghost boy and the cabin. She also couldn't help hoping, at least a little, that one day the door might open again, and lead elsewhere. This, in my considerable experience, was a misplaced hope. Doors, once closed, do not reopen.

Ade abandoned her aunts' tools and walked the scant miles into town. Then she tucked her hair up beneath a leather hat so shapeless and worn it lay like a sleeping animal against her skull and strode out on the docks to wait for a likely steamer. This, too, felt less like crafting a plan and more like swimming downriver, swept along by some force grander and madder than herself toward unknown seas. She did not fight it but let the invisible waters close over her head.

It took two days of loitering and begging before she found a steamer desperate enough to take her on as a deckhand. It wasn't her sex that barred her; her paint-striped trousers and baggy cotton shirt offered sufficient disguise, and her face had a freckled squareness that sidestepped beauty and landed somewhere nearer to handsome.

(This, at least, is what a daguerreotype would have recorded, if Ade had ever posed for one. But photographs, like mirrors, are notorious liars. The truth is: Adelaide was the most beautiful being I have seen in this world or any other, if we understand beauty to be a kind of vital, ferocious burning at a soul's center that ignites everything it touches.)

But still, something in her eyes made wise boatmen hesitate— something that spoke of abandon and fearlessness, a person dangerously unmoored from her own future. It was pure chance that the *Southern Queen* was piloted by an inexperienced captain who had hired three drunks and a thief upriver and was so eager to replace them that he hired Ade without asking anything beyond her name and destination. The *Queen's* logs record these as *Larson* and *Elsewhere*.

It is at this moment, just as Ade's feet danced their way onto the whitewashed deck boards of a Mississippi steamer, that we must pause. Miss Larson's life heretofore has been an unusual story but not a mysterious or unknowable one. It has been possible to act as a historian, sifting through interviews and evidences to create a tolerable narrative of a girl's growing up. But from this moment forward Ade's story grows grander, stranger, and wilder. She steps into fable and folktale, sideways and unseen, slipping through the fissures of recorded history the way smoke rises through dense canopy. No scholar, no matter how clever or meticulous, can map smoke and myth onto the page.

Ade herself has declined to divulge more than a handful of dates or details, and so from here, and for the next many years of her life, our story must become a series of scattered glimpses.

We are therefore ignorant about her months aboard the *Southern Queen*. We cannot know how the work suited her, whether her crewmates were charmed or spooked by her, or what she thought of the mud-colored towns scudding by on the banks. We cannot know if she stood on the deck sometimes with her face turned to the southern wind and felt freed from the smallness of her youth, although she was later seen aboard a very different ship in a very different place, looking out at the horizon as if her very soul had unfurled and stretched out to meet it.

We do not even know if she first heard the story of the boo hag while she worked up and down the river, although it seems very likely. It has been this scholar's experience that stories slide up and down rivers alongside boats, trailing like silver mermaids in their wake, and the tale of the boo hag was probably swimming among them in those days. Perhaps the story reminded Ade of the haunted cabin in her old hayfield and wakened the dusty promises of her fifteen-year-old self. Or perhaps it merely struck her fancy.

All we can say with certainty is this: in the warm winter of 1886, Adelaide Larson went into the St. Ours mansion in the Algiers district of New Orleans and did not emerge again for sixteen days.

We must rely here on the testimony of two locals who spoke to Ade before she walked through. Though many years passed before I was able to track them down and record their memories, Mr. and Mrs. Vicente LeBlanc insisted that their retelling was absolutely accurate because the circumstances themselves were so singular: they were strolling along Homer Street at ten o'clock in the evening, having retired from a dance hall in good spirits (Mrs. LeBlanc insisted they had been at evening mass; Mr. LeBlanc assumed an expression of studied neutrality). The couple was approached by a young woman.

"She was—well, I have to tell you she was a powerfully odd girl. Kind of grubby, and dressed like a dock worker in canvas trousers." Mrs. LeBlanc was too polite to provide additional detail, but we may also assume that she was very young, alone, wandering at night in a city she didn't know, and whiter than flour.

Mr. LeBlanc gave a conciliatory shrug. "Well, who knows, Mary. She seemed lost." He clarified: "I don't mean she was lost like a child. She wasn't worried. She was lost on *purpose*, I'd say."

The young woman asked them a series of questions. Was this Elmira Avenue? Was Fortuna Manor nearby? How high was the fence around it, and were they aware of any medium-to-large dogs in the vicinity? Finally: "Do either y'all know the story of John and the Boo Hag?"

Any right-thinking person might be forgiven for simply walking in a wide arc around such a madwoman, and casting nervous glances over their shoulders to make sure she wasn't trailing after them. But Mary LeBlanc possessed the sort of reckless compassion that led people to give money to strangers and invite beggars in for supper. "Elmira is a block west, miss," she told the strange woman.

"Huh. City could do with one or three street signs, if you ask me."

"Yes, miss." Both Mary and Vicente LeBlanc report lots of *misses* and *pardon-mes*, presumably because even a powerfully odd white woman was still a white woman. Perhaps they feared a fairy-tale-like test, where the beggar woman transforms into a witch and punishes you for your poor manners.

"And is that house on it? Fortuna something?"

The LeBlancs looked at one another. "No, miss, I never heard of it."

"Shit," said the white woman, and spat, with the half-conscious drama of a nineteen-year-old, on the cobbled street.

Then Mary LeBlanc asked, "Did you mean—there's the St. Ours place, up Elmira a ways." Vincente recalls clenching his elbow around her arm, trying his best to telegraph a warning. "It's a manor house. Been empty my whole life."

"Might be." The girl's eyes were cat-sharp on Mary's face.

Mary found herself half whispering. "Well, it's just you mentioned that story, and I always heard—they're just stories, mind, and no educated person ought to think much on them—but I always heard John Prester lived in St. Ours. And that's where he met the boo hag,[4] miss."

A Cheshire smile, all teeth and want, crept over the girl's face. "You don't say. My name's Ade Larson. Could I trouble you with another few questions, miss?"

She asked them to tell the whole story as they knew it, about the handsome young John who found himself tired and gray every morning, with tangled dreams of starlit skies and wild rides. She asked them if anybody ever went into St. Ours (sometimes, young boys, daring each other). She asked them if they came back out again (of course! Except—well, there were rumors. Boys who spent the night in there and didn't come out again for a year and a day. Boys who hid in closets and found themselves dreaming of faraway countries).

"Now, just one last crumb, my friends: How did this boo hag character get into the house in the first place? How'd she find poor John?"

---

4. I spent some time in the region researching these phenomena after speaking with the LeBlancs. It seems to me a variation of the usual hag story—old women who prey on younger people, sucking their blood or breath, perhaps even stealing their skin and going "riding" for the night. I've encountered them more often on the islands off the coast of Georgia, where the phrase *hag-ridden* is both dire and common.

Adelaide Larson was unaware of the universality of the story. She did not find her destinations by scholarly deduction or painstaking labor but by a wanderer's less certain compass.

The LeBlancs looked at one another, and even Mary's soft-heartedness was beginning to be troubled by the intensity of the young woman. It wasn't merely the oddness of her situation, dressed for labor and wandering around at night; it was the way her face seemed lit with a gaslamp glow of its own making, the way she seemed simultaneously to be the hunter and the hunted, running away from something and toward something else.

But few people can leave a story unfinished, with a raveled end left trailing. "Same way a hag gets into anybody's house, miss. They find a crack, or a hole, or a unlocked door."

The girl gave the couple a beatific smile, swept them a bow, and headed west.

She wasn't seen again for sixteen days, when a group of young boys rolling hoops down the street saw a white woman emerge from St. Ours. They described her appearance as "witchy": her practical clothing hung in ragged tatters around her, supplemented by a strange cloak of oiled black feathers; her eyes were wind-whipped and her smile at the night sky was sly, as if she and the stars were on familiar terms.

When the boys questioned her about her activities, the girl failed to provide any clear explanation beyond a few senseless descriptions of high mountain peaks and black pine boughs and lights in the sky like pink silk pinned to the stars.

When I asked her myself what she'd seen through the door—for there must have been a door—she only laughed. "Why, the boo hags, of course!" And when I frowned at her she shushed me: "Listen, not every story is made for telling. Sometimes just by telling a story you're stealing it, stealing a little of the mystery away from it. Let those witch women be, I say."

I did not know what she meant at the time. I had a scholar's hunger to reveal and explain, to make the unknown known—but in the case of the St. Ours door I was foiled. I traced her footsteps up Elmira Avenue and found a whitewashed mansion sinking into the sweet rot of magnolia blooms, simultaneously grand and half-forgotten. I made plans to return in the evening to conduct further explorations, but that was the night of the Great Algiers Fire of 1895. By midnight the sky was golden orange and by dawn the entire block, including the St. Ours mansion, was nothing but a sooty skeleton of itself.

Remember this fire. Remember that it raged from no clear origin and paid no heed to hoses or buckets of water until every grand, sagging inch of St. Ours was burned to ash.

But still, I record these recollections because St. Ours was the first door I found in this world, and the second door Miss Larson found. With the finding of a door comes change.

Later, Ade would refer to the period between roughly 1885 and 1892 as her "hungry years." When asked what she was hungry for, she laughed and said, "Same thing as you, I bet. Ways-between. Nowheres. Somewheres." She scoured the Earth, wandering and ravenous, looking for doors.

And she found them.[5] She found them in abandoned churches and the salt-rimed walls of caves, in graveyards and behind fluttering curtains in foreign markets. She found so many her imagining of the world grew lacy and tattered with holes, like a mouse-chewed map. I followed her in my own time and rediscovered as many as I could. But doors by their natures are openings, passings-through, missing-places—and it has proved difficult to record the precise

---

5. She is, perhaps, an unlikely character for a daring explorer—a poor, uneducated girl of no particular distinction. But the literature I've collected on the subject seems to indicate that doors do not tend to attract the kinds of explorers and trailblazers we might anticipate—those like Dr. Livingstone or Mr. Boone who have charged bravely into the frontier. More often, I find fellow travelers among the poor and wretched, the unwanted and homeless; those people, in short, who scurry along the margins of the world and look for ways out.

Consider Thomas Aikenhead, a young man both an orphan and a cripple, who published an ill-advised manifesto suggesting that heaven was an actual place located just on the other side of a small shabby door in an old Scottish church. He allowed for the possibility that the place was actually hell, or perhaps purgatory, but concluded that it was certainly a "warm, sunny place, much preferable to Scotland." He was hanged within the year for blasphemy.

Thomas Aikenhead, "A Tract on Magick and the Entrance to Heaven," 1695.

geometry of absence. My notes are full of dead ends and uncertainties, whispers and rumors, and even my most careful reports are full of unanswered questions hovering like gray angels in the margins.

Consider the Platte River door. Ade's iridescent trail led back up the Mississippi and westward and eventually to a gentleman named Frank C. True. When I spoke to Mr. True in 1900, he was a trickrider in W. J. Taylor's Great American Double Circus, Huge World's Museum, Caravan, Hippodrome, Menagerie and Congress of Wild and Living Animals.

Frank was a dark-haired, flint-eyed man whose charm and talent expanded his presence far past the bounds of his own small frame. When I mentioned Ade, his performer's smile turned wistful.

"Yes. Course I remember her. Why? You her husband or something?" After assuring him I was no jealous lover come to claim a decade-old slight, he sighed back into his camp chair and told me about their meeting in the hot summer of 1888.

He saw her first in the audience of Dr. Carver's Rocky Mountain and Prairie Exhibition, where Frank was wild-westing as a Genuine Plains Indian for a dollar a day. She was conspicuously alone on the wooden benches, tangle-haired and grimy, dressed with a scavenger's abandon in oversized boots and a man's shirt. She stayed through the bloody reenactment of Custer's Last Stand, cheered during the demonstration of mustang lassoing even though the "mustang" was a round-bellied pony no wilder than a house cat, and whistled when Frank won the Indian Race. He winked at her. She winked back.

When Dr. Carver's Rocky Mountain and Prairie Exhibition rolled out of Chicago the following evening, Ade and Frank were both crammed in his cubby in the performers' railcar. In this way Ade suffered precisely the sort of fall from grace her aunts and grandmother most feared, and in so doing made a discovery: fallen women are afforded a species of freedom.[6] There were certainly

---

6. There is, of course, no such thing as a fallen woman, unless we are speaking of a woman who recently tripped on the stairs. One of the most difficult elements of this

social costs—several of the women performers refused to speak to Ade at the lunch tents, and men made unfortunate assumptions about her availability—but in general Ade's horizons expanded rather than shrank. She found herself surrounded by a bustling underworld of men and women who had each fallen in their own ways through drink or vice or passion or the mere colors of their skin. It was almost like finding a door within her very own world.

Frank reports a few weeks of contentment, rattling up and down the eastern United States in the blue-and-white painted cars of the Rocky Mountain show, but then Ade began to grow restless. Frank told her stories to distract her.

"Red Cloud, I said, now, have I ever told you about him? I swear I never met a woman more in love with a good story." Frank told her about the valiant young Lakota chief who brought a new and terrible hell to the U.S. Army and the Powder River garrisons. He told her about the chief's uncanny ability to foresee the outcomes of battles using a handful of carved bones. "Now, he never would say where he got those bones, but there were rumors that he'd disappeared for a year as a boy, and returned carrying a bag of bones from some other place."

"Where did he disappear to?" Ade asked, and Frank recalled that her eyes had grown round and black as new moons.

"Somewhere up the North Platte River, I guess. Wherever it was, maybe he went back there, because he disappeared after they found gold in the Black Hills and broke the treaty. Heartbroke, I guess."

Ade was gone before dawn. She left a note, which Mr. True declined to share but which he still possesses, and the oversized boots that fit Frank better anyway. Mr. True never saw or heard from her again.

---

world is the way its social rules are simultaneously rigid and arbitrary. It is impermissible to engage in physical love before binding legal marriage, unless one is a young man of means. Men must be bold and assertive, but only if they are light-skinned. Any persons may fall in love regardless of station, but only if one is a woman and the other a man. I urge you not to navigate your own life by such faulty borders, my dear. There are, after all, other worlds.

If there was a door someplace on the North Platte, Nebraska, I never found it. The town when I found it was brutally poor, wind-scourged, bitter. An old man in a dingy barroom told me flatly that I ought to leave and not return, because if there was any such place it certainly didn't belong to me, and he couldn't see that the Oglala Lakota had ever come to any good showing off their secrets to strangers. I left town the following morning.

This was merely one of dozens of doors Ade discovered during her hungry years. Included below is a partial list of those that have been confirmed by this author:

In 1889 Ade was on Prince Edward Island working for an aged potato farmer in pursuit of something she called "silky stories," which were probably selkies. The farmer told her about a long-dead neighbor who found a young woman down by the sea caves. The woman's eyes were set oddly far apart, oily black, and she didn't speak a word of any human language. Ade spent the following days exploring the coastal caves herself, until one afternoon she failed to return. The poor potato farmer was convinced she'd drowned, until she reappeared eight days later smelling of cool, secret oceans.

In 1890 Ade was working on a steamer weaving its way through the Bahamas like a drunken seagull, when she apparently heard stories about Toussaint Louverture's rebellion and the way his troops simply melted into the highlands and disappeared, almost like magic. The shipping routes at that time curved around Haiti as if it had the plague, so Ade abandoned her post on the steamer and bribed a fisherman to take her from Matthew Town to the wrinkled green coast of Haiti.

She found Toussaint's door after weeks of stumbling along the mud-slicked logging trails of the highlands. It was a long tunnel, tangled in the roots of a gnarled acacia tree. She never described what she found on the other side, and we may never know now: the acreage was purchased, logged, and converted to sugar production several years later.

In the same year she followed stories of ice-eyed monsters whose gaze could turn unwary persons to stone and ended up in a tiny, forgotten church in Greece. There she found a door (black, frost-limned) and went through it. She discovered a wind-torn, brutally cold world on the other side, which she would have happily abandoned except that she was immediately set upon by a band of wild, pale folk dressed in animal skins. As she later reported, they stole everything she owned "down to her underthings," shouted at her for a while, then dragged her before their chieftainess, who did not shout but merely fixed her gaze on Ade and whispered to her.

"And I could almost understand her, my hand to God. She was telling me how I ought to join their tribe, fight their enemies, add wealth to their coffers, et cetera. I swear I almost did. Something about those eyes—light-colored, powerful cold. But in the end I declined." Ade did not elaborate on the consequences of her refusal, but Greek locals report seeing a wild-eyed American woman wandering the streets with nothing but a fur cloak, mild frostbite, and a rather vicious-looking spear. (My own experience with this particular door will be recounted at a later date.)

In 1891 Ade discovered a tiled archway in the shadows of the Grand Bazaar of Istanbul, and returned with great golden disks she claimed were dragon scales. She visited Santiago and the Falklands, contracted malaria in Léopoldville, and disappeared for several months in the northeast corner of Maine. She accumulated the dust of other worlds on her skin like ten thousand perfumes, and left constellations of wistful men and impossible tales in her wake.

But she never lingered anywhere for long. Most observers told me she was simply a wanderer, driven to move from place to place by the same unknowable pressures that make swallows fly south, but I believe she was something closer to a knight on a quest. I believe she was looking for one particular door and one particular world.

In 1893, in the high, snowcapped spring of her twenty-seventh birthday, she found it.

The story traveled in the usual way of stories, slithering from mouth to mouth along the railways and roads like a contagion moving along arteries. By February 1893, it had sifted into Taft, Texas, and permeated the walls of the cottonseed mill where Ade Larson was employed. Her fellow workers recall a particular lunch hour: They were gathered with their tin pails behind the mill, breathing the oil-sticky steam and the green rot scent of cottonseed hulls, listening to Dalton Gray's daily report of barroom gossip. He told them about a pair of trappers up north who came down from the Rockies raving mad, swearing on everything they held dear that they'd found an ocean at the top of Mount Silverheels.

The workers laughed, but Ade's voice thudded into their laughter like a hatchet into a stump. "How do you mean, they found an ocean?"

Dalton Gray shrugged. "How'm I supposed to know? Had it from Gene they were lost and found an old stone church from the silver-mining days and lived there for a week or two. They said it was a perfectly ordinary little church, except it had an ocean out the back door!" The laughter rallied again but petered away; Ade Larson was gathering up her uneaten lunch and walking northwest, across the mill yard toward the East Texas & Gulf Railway.

I found no trace of Ade from Texas to Colorado. She simply appears in the town of Alma a month later, like a diver surfacing, asking about boots and furs and the sorts of gear a woman would need to survive the bitter arctic spring of the Front Range. The local storekeeper remembers watching her leave with irritable pity, certain they'd find her thawing body on the trails come summer.

But instead, the woman returned down Mount Silverheels ten days later, chap-cheeked and grinning in a fortunate way that reminded the storekeeper of miners who have struck gold. She asked him where she could find a sawmill.

He told her, but added, "Pardon me, ma'am, but why would you need lumber?"

"Oh." Ade laughed, and the storekeeper would later recall it as a madwoman's full-moon cackle. "To build a boat."

The spectacle of a lone young woman with no particular carpentry skill building a sailboat in the thin-aired heights of the Rockies did not, of course, go unnoticed. Ade had cobbled together a sort of camp at the base of Silverheels that looked, as one reporter phrased it, "like a shantytown recently visited by a tornado." Pine planks lay scattered on the frozen ground, bent into tortured arcs. Borrowed tools were jumbled in the careless piles of a person who does not intend to use them more than once. Ade herself presided over the chaos in a smoke-heavy bearskin, swearing cheerily as she worked.

By April the boat had an identifiable shape; a slim, sap-scented rib cage lay in the middle of her camp like some unfortunate sea creature God had forgotten to grant skin or scales.

The first newspapermen appeared shortly thereafter, and the first printed report was a blurred sidebar in the *Leadville Daily*, unimaginatively titled *WOMAN BUILDS BOAT, PUZZLES LOCALS*. It generated enough gossip and hilarity that the story leapfrogged into larger papers, printed and reprinted and eventually trotted out in conjunction with the tale of the trappers who found an ocean. More than a month later, after Ade and her boat were long gone from Alma, it even migrated as far as the *New York Times*, under the much snappier title *LADY NOAH OF THE ROCKIES: COLORADO MAD-WOMAN PREPARED FOR THE FLOOD*.

I would give anything—every word in the Written, every star in every world, my own two hands—to unpublish that damned story.

Ade never read any of the articles about her, as far as I am aware. She simply worked on her sailboat, scabbing planks one over the other to make the hull and consulting with a local roofer who bemusedly gave her the tallow-and-spruce-sap recipe to caulk her joints. The canvas sail was a poorly stitched mess that would have appalled any one of her aunts, and it hung stiff from a stubby mast, but by the end of the month Ade was convinced it was the most glorious and seaworthy vessel in the world, or at least above ten thousand feet. She burned its name into the prow in shaky charcoal lines: *The Key*.

She walked into town that very evening and spent the last of her hoarded cottonseed wages acquiring cured ham and tinned beans, three large canteens, a compass, and the hired help of two young men who were made to understand in broken Spanish that she'd like a boat carried up a mountain. I found one of these gentlemen years later, a Mr. Lucio Martinez, and he confessed to me with bitter weariness that he wished he'd never agreed to the venture. He'd spent the better part of a decade under a cloud of baseless suspicion because he and his friend were the last living persons to have seen the mad white woman and her boat before she disappeared. The local sheriff even interrogated him a year or two after the event itself, insisting that Mr. Martinez draw him a very precise map of where Adelaide was last seen.

Ade could not have known then what miseries poor Mr. Martinez would endure when they parted ways at the peak of Mount Silverheels, and I am not sure by then she would have cared. She was driven by the pure selfishness of a knight nearing the end of their quest, and could no more turn away from her goal than a compass needle could point south.

She waited for Lucio and his friend to crisscross back down the slope, and for the half-moon to paint the pines in soft silver. Then she dragged her haphazard vessel along a deer trail to a low stone building that might once have served as a miners' church, or perhaps something older and holier.

The doorway was just as she'd found it weeks previously. It took up almost the entirety of its stacked-stone wall, framed in vast timbers gone age-black. A rough hole in the planking was the only handle, and already Ade could swear a soft breeze whistled through it carrying the smell of salt and cedar and long, sun-gilded days.

It was a smell that shouldn't have been familiar to her, but it was. It was the smell of the ghost boy's skin as they'd kissed in a late-summer field. It was the smell of elsewhere.

She opened the door and launched her boat into the strange seas of another world.

The Unlocked Door

My eyes, when I opened them, felt as if they'd been plucked from my head, rolled in coarse sand, and crammed clumsily back into my skull. My mouth was gummed and sour, and my skull seemed to have shrunk several sizes overnight. For a few disoriented seconds I forgot the half-dozen glasses of champagne from the party and wondered dizzily if the book had done this to me. As if a story could ferment in my veins, like wine, and leave me drunk.

If any story could have done it, it would have been that one. I'd certainly read better books with more adventure and kissing and less pontificating, but none of them had left me with this fragile, impossible suspicion that maybe, somehow, it was all true. That there were Doors hidden in every shadowed place, waiting to be opened. That a woman might shed her childhood skin, snakelike, and fling herself into the seething unknown.

It seemed unlikely that Mr. Locke would give me something so fanciful, no matter how sorry he felt for me. How, then, had it found its way into my treasure box in the Pharaoh Room?

But the mystery of it felt thin and distant beneath the weight of the Thing that still sat on my chest. I began to see how it would always be there, how it would cleave to my flesh like a second skin, secretly poisoning everything I touched.

I felt the damp poke of Bad's nose as he rooted under my arm, the way he had as a puppy. It was far too hot—the July sun was oozing across the floorboards now, baking against the copper roof—but I wrapped my arms around him and buried my face in his fur. We lay sweat-sticky while the sun rose and Locke House creaked and murmured around us.

I was drifting into a forced, heat-dazed sleep when the door opened.

I smelled coffee and heard familiar, decisive steps across the floor. Some secret tenseness in my chest unwound itself, exhaling relief: *She's still here.*

Jane was dressed and alert in a way that said she had been awake for a considerable time and refrained from disturbing me for as long as was decent. She balanced a pair of steaming cups on the bookshelf, dragged a spindly chair to my bedside, and sat with her arms neatly crossed.

"Good morning, January." There was something almost stern in her voice, businesslike. Perhaps a single day was the acceptable mourning period for a mostly absent father. Perhaps she was just irritated at me for sleeping late and monopolizing our room. "I heard from the kitchen girls the party was, ah, eventful."

I made a moany, I-don't-want-to-discuss-it sound.

"Is it true that you got drunk, shouted at Mr. Locke, and stormed out of the smoking room? And then—unless my informants are mistaken—disappeared with the Zappia boy?"

I repeated the moany sound, a bit louder. Jane merely raised her eyebrows. I threw an arm over my face, stared at the orangey afterglow of my eyelids, and grunted: "Yes."

She laughed, a rolling boom that made Bad jump. "There's hope for you yet. There are times I think you're too much of a mouse to make it out in the world, but perhaps I am wrong." She paused, sobering. "When I first met your father he told me you were a troublesome, feral child; I hope that's so. You'll need it."

I wanted to ask if he'd spoken often of me, and what he'd said, and if he'd ever mentioned that one day he would take me along with him, but the words clotted in my throat. I swallowed. "For what?"

That stern, very-nearly-irritated expression returned to her face. "Things can't just keep on forever the way they are, January. Things must change."

Ah. This was it, then. She was going to tell me that she would be leaving soon, returning home to the highlands of British East Africa and abandoning me alone in this little gray room. I tried to squash the scrabbling panic in my chest. "I know. You're going." I hoped I sounded cool and adult, hoped she didn't notice the way the sheets were balled in my fists. "Now that—now that Father is dead."

"Missing," she corrected.

"Excuse me?"

"Your father is missing, not dead."

I shook my head, rising up on one elbow. "Mr. Locke said—"

Jane's lips curled, and she made a gesture like a woman swatting a gnat. "Locke is not God, January."

He might as well be. I didn't answer but knew my face had gone mulish with denial.

Jane sighed at me, but her voice when she spoke again was softer, almost hesitant. "I have reason to believe—your father made certain assurances—well. I haven't given up on Julian, not yet. Perhaps you shouldn't, either."

The black Thing seemed to curl closer around me, an invisible nautilus shell protecting me from her words, hope-laced and cruel. I closed my eyes again and rolled away from her. "I don't feel like coffee. Thank you."

A sharp indrawn breath. Had I offended her? Good. Maybe she would just leave without pretending to miss me, without false promises about staying in touch.

But then she hissed, "What's that?" and I felt her hand fumble in the sheets at my back. A small squarish something slid out from beneath me.

I sat up and saw *The Ten Thousand Doors* clutched in her hands, her fingertips white where they pressed into the cover. "That's *mine*, if you don't—"

"Where did you get this?" Her voice was perfectly level but oddly urgent.

"It was a gift," I said defensively. "I think."

But she wasn't listening. She was riffling through the book with hands that shook slightly, eyes skittering across the words as if they were some vital message written just for her. I felt a strange, illogical jealousy.

"Does it say anything about the *irimu*? The leopard-women? Did he find—"

A harsh *rap-rap-rap* on the door. Bad stood, one white tooth bared.

"Miss Jane? Mr. Locke would like a private word with you, if you please." It was Mr. Stirling, sounding as usual like a typewriter that had somehow learned to walk and talk.

Jane and I stared at one another. Mr. Locke had never, in her two years at Locke House, spoken a private word to her, nor more than a dozen public ones. He regarded her as a regrettable necessity, like an ugly vase one is obliged to keep because it was a gift from a friend.

I watched Jane's throat move, swallowing whatever emotion made her palms leave dark, damp patches on the leather-bound book. "I'll be right there, Mr. Stirling, thank you."

A professionally tuned throat-clearing noise sounded on the other side of the door. "Now, if you please."

Jane closed her eyes, jaw rolling in frustration. "Yes, sir," she called. She stood, tucking my book in her skirt pocket and resting her palm against it as if reassuring herself of its existence. In a much quieter voice, she hissed, "We'll talk when I return."

I should've grabbed on to her skirts and demanded an explanation. I should've told Mr. Stirling to shut his mouth, and enjoyed the stunned silence thereafter.

But I didn't.

Jane swept into the hall and everything went silent and still again, except for the agitated swirl of the dust motes disturbed by her passage. Bad hopped to the floor, stretched, and shook himself. A mist of fine bronze hairs joined the dust, glinting gold in the sunbeams.

I fell back into the mattress. I could hear the neat snick of the gardener's shears outside on the grounds. The distant burr of a motorcar trundling past the wrought-iron gates. The too-fast patter of my heart, fluttering against my ribs like someone knocking frantically at a locked door.

Mr. Locke had told me my father was dead. *Accept it*, he'd told me, and I had. But what if—?

Sour exhaustion welled in my limbs. How many years of my life had I spent waiting for my father, believing he would return tomorrow or the next day? Rushing to collect the mail, searching for his neat handwriting in the pile? Hoping and trying not to hope for the day he would come home and say, *January, the time has come,* and I would go away with him into the shining unknown?

Surely I could spare myself this last and greatest disappointment.

I wished Jane had left my book behind. I wanted to run away again, back into Ade's quest for her ghost boy. So many years she'd spent searching on only the thinnest, most unlikely thread of hope. I wondered what she would have done in my place.

Go find out for myself. The answer came in a flat, southern-streaked voice that I thought must be Ade's own, if she'd been a person rather than a fictional character. It rang clear and strong in my skull, as if I'd heard it before. *Go find him.*

I lay very still, feeling a dangerous shivering spread from my chest like a sudden fever.

But a more grown-up, sober-sounding voice reminded me that *The Ten Thousand Doors* was just a novel, and that novels are untrustworthy advisers. They aren't concerned with rationality or sobriety; they peddle in tragedy and suspense, in chaos and rule breaking, in madness and heartache, and they will steer you toward such things with all the guile of a piper luring rats into a river.

It would be wiser to stay here, beg my way back into Mr. Locke's good graces after last night's debacle, and keep my childish dreams locked up where they belonged. Learn to forget the low, sincere sound of my father's voice as he said *I promise.*

You never came back for me. You never rescued me.

But perhaps—if I were brave and temerarious and very foolish—if I listened to that flat, fearless voice in my heart, so familiar and so strange—I could rescue both of us.

I didn't expect to see anyone on my way out. I should have— several Society men were staying as Locke's honored guests, occupying the gaudy guest suites on the second floor, and the house was still crawling with hired servants cleaning up after the party—but Running Away from Home involves a very particular and time-worn script: Bad and I were supposed to slip out the front door and down the drive like a pair of ghosts. Later Locke might storm up to my room and find my note (uninformative but apologetic, thanking him for years of generosity and kindness) and swear softly. He might stare out the window after me, far too late.

Except Mr. Locke was standing in the foyer. And so was Mr. Havemeyer.

"—just a child, Theodore. I'll have it all sorted out in a day or two." Locke was standing with his back to me, one arm making the confident gestures of a banker reassuring a nervous patron, the other holding Havemeyer's coat. Havemeyer was reaching for it, face narrowed in doubt, when he saw me standing on the staircase.

"Ah. Your prize malcontent, Cornelius." Havemeyer's smile was only a smile in the sense that his lips were curved and his teeth were bared. Locke turned. I watched his face move from cold disapproval to consternation, his mouth falling slightly open.

Under that frowning, what's-all-this-nonsense gaze, I felt myself falter. The swooping, heady confidence that had taken me this far—dressing myself in my sturdiest clothes, stuffing a canvas bag full of semirandom belongings, writing two notes and arranging them artistically—wavered, and I felt suddenly very much like a child announcing she was running away from home. It occurred to me that I'd packed at least nine or ten books, but not a single pair of spare socks.

Locke opened his mouth, chest swelling with the coming sermon, but I'd just realized something. If he was down here with Havemeyer, he was clearly finished meeting with Jane— but she hadn't come back.

"Where's Jane?" I interrupted. She was supposed to return to our room and find the note I'd hidden in *Tom Swift and His Airship*. Then she would join me in Boston, book passage on an eastbound steamer, and begin our adventure. If she wanted to; my clever plan evaded the necessity of asking her face-to-face and the possibility of hearing her say no.

Locke's face had whitened in irritation. "Return to your room, child. I'll deal with you later. In fact, you are hereby confined to your quarters until such time as I deem—"

"Where's Jane?"

Havemeyer, watching, drawled, "It's comforting to find you aren't only rude when drunk, Miss Scaller."

Locke ignored him. "January. Upstairs. Now." His voice had gone low and urgent. I looked away from his face but felt his pale eyes grasping and fastening on my flesh, prodding me backward. "Return to your *room*—"

But I was tired of listening to Mr. Locke, tired of the weight of his will crushing me smaller and smaller, tired of minding my place. "No." It came out a wavering whisper. I swallowed, touching my fingers to Bad's bronze heat. "No. I'm leaving."

I ducked my head and squared my shoulders, like a woman walking into a strong headwind, and heaved my bag down the steps and across the foyer. I kept my spine very straight.

We were almost past them, almost within reach of the brass handle of the front door, when Havemeyer laughed. It was a hideous, high-pitched hiss that made Bad's hackles rise beneath my palm. I looped my fingers through his collar.

"And where could a thing like you possibly be going?" he asked. He lifted his cane and gave my canvas sack a mocking prod.

"To find my father." I was tired of lying, too.

Havemeyer's not-smile turned saccharine. Something unseemly—anticipation? delight?—lit his eyes as he leaned toward me and curled one gloved finger beneath my chin, tilting my face upward. "Your *late* father, I think you mean."

I should've let go of Bad's collar right then and let him chew Havemeyer into red ribbons. I should've slapped him, or ignored him, or lunged for the door.

Anything but what I actually did.

"Maybe. Maybe not. Maybe he's just lost, out there somewhere. Maybe he found a Door and fell through it and he's in some other world, a better world, where there aren't people like you." As comebacks go, it was somewhere between *outright lunacy* and *pitiable*. I waited for Mr. Locke's sigh, for that sibilant sound that passed for laughter from Havemeyer.

But instead, both of them went very still. It was the kind of stillness that makes the hairs on your arms stand up, and makes you think of wolves and snakes waiting in the high grass. The kind of stillness that makes you realize you have just misstepped very badly, even if you don't see how.

Mr. Havemeyer straightened, letting my chin fall and flexing his hands in his driving gloves as if they'd grown restless. "Cornelius. I thought we'd agreed to keep certain information preserved for Society members. I thought, in fact, that it was an essential tenet of our organization, as laid down by the Founder himself." For the second time that morning, I had the sensation that the conversation was suddenly being conducted in an unfamiliar language.

"I didn't tell her a damn thing." Locke's voice was brusque, but there was a strangled note in it I might have called fear, except that I'd never heard Locke afraid.

Havemeyer's nostrils flared. "Is that so," he breathed. "Luke! Evans!" A pair of hulking men thumped down the stairs at his shout, half-packed luggage in their arms. "Mr. Havemeyer, sir," they panted.

"Escort this girl to her room, won't you, and lock her in. And watch out for the dog."

I've always hated it in books when a character freezes in fear. *Wake up!* I want to shout at them. *Do something!* Remembering myself standing there with my canvas bag hanging stupidly over my shoulder, my fingers gone slack on Bad's collar, I want to shout at myself: *Do something!*

But I was a good girl, and I didn't do anything. I was silent as Havemeyer tapped his cane to hurry his men along, as Locke huffed and protested, as heavy-knuckled hands closed above my elbows.

As Bad erupted, snarling and brave, and one of the men threw a heavy coat over his thrashing head and tackled him to the floor.

I was half dragged up the stairs and slung into my bedroom, and the lock rolled and snicked into place like the oiled metal hammer of Mr. Locke's revolver.

I didn't make any sound at all, until I heard furious barking and men swearing and then a series of boot-on-flesh thuds, and then hideous silence. And by then it was too late.

Let that be a lesson to you: If you are too good and too quiet for too long, it will cost you. It will always cost you, in the end.

Bad Bad BadBadBad. I scrabbled at the door, twisting the knob until my wrist bones creaked. Men's voices spiraled up the stairs and slid under my door, but I couldn't hear them over the rattling of the hinges and an awful, sourceless moaning. It was only when I caught Havemeyer's irritated voice on the landing—"Can someone shut her up?"—that I realized the sound was coming from me.

I stopped. Heard Havemeyer shout back down the steps, "Get that out of here and clean up this mess, Evans," and then there was nothing but the thunderous *shushing* of blood in my ears and the silent sound of my own unraveling.

I was seven again and Wilda's key had just turned in the black-iron lock and left me caged and alone. I remembered the walls pressing me between them like a botanical specimen, the sick-sweet taste of syrup on a silver spoon, the smell of my own terror. I thought I'd forgotten, but the memories were crisp as photographs. I wondered dispassionately if they'd always been there, lurking just out of sight and whispering their fears to me. If behind every good girl lurked a good threat.

Shuffling, swearing noises from the distant parlor. *Bad.*

My legs bent beneath me and I slid down the door, thinking: *This is what alone feels like.* I only thought I knew, before, but now Jane was gone and Bad was taken, and I might rot away to cotton and dust in this shabby gray room and no one on Earth would care.

That black Thing descended again and settled its coal-smoke wings around my shoulders. *Motherless, fatherless. Friendless.*

It was my own fault. My fault, for thinking I could just run away, just gather my nerve and walk out into the wide unknown like a hero beginning a quest. For thinking I could bend the rules, just a little, and write myself into some better, grander story.

But the rules were made by Lockes and Havemeyers, by wealthy men in private smoking rooms who pulled the world's riches to themselves like well-dressed spiders in the center of a golden web. People of significance; people who could never be locked away in small rooms and forgotten. The best I could hope for was a life spent creeping in their generous shadows—an in-between creature neither loved nor reviled, but permitted to scurry freely so long as I didn't cause trouble.

I pressed the heels of my palms into my eyes. I wanted to cast a spell and unspool the last three days, to find myself standing innocent and bemused in the Pharaoh Room, reaching for the blue chest. I wanted to disappear back into *The Ten Thousand Doors*, to lose myself in Ade's impossible adventures—but Jane had taken the book, and Jane was gone.

I wanted to find a Door and write my way through it.

But that was madness.

Except—there was the book, which echoed my own memory. And Jane's urgent, black-eyed expression when she held it. And Havemeyer and Locke, freezing at the barest mention of Doors. What if—?

I teetered on that invisible cliff's edge, holding myself back from the seething, teeming ocean below. I stood up, slowly, and crossed to the dresser. My jewelry box was an old sewing box I'd stood on end and stuffed with the accumulated treasures of seventeen years—feathers and stones, trinkets from the Pharaoh Room, letters from my father folded and refolded so many times the creases were translucent. I ran a finger along the lining until I felt the cool edge of a coin.

The silver queen smiled her foreign smile at me, just as she had when I was seven. The coin was heavy in my palm; quite real. I felt a dizzy rushing, as if some great-winged seabird had swooped through the center of me, trailing salt and cedar and the familiar-but-not-familiar sun of another world.

I took a breath, and then another. *Madness.* But my father was dead and my door was locked and Bad needed me, and there was no way out except through madness.

I dove over that unseen edge and plunged into the dark waters below, where the unreal became real, where the impossible swam by on glimmering fins, where I could believe it all.

And in believing came a sudden calm. I tucked the coin into my skirt and crossed to the writing desk beneath the window. I found a scrap of half-used paper and smoothed it against the desktop. I paused for a moment, gathering every speck of my dizzy, drunken belief, then took up the pen and wrote:

The Door opens.

It happened just as it had when I was seven and still young enough to believe in magic. The pen nib swirled around the period and the universe seemed to exhale around me, to shrug its invisible shoulders. The light streaming through my windows, gone dim and watery with afternoon clouds, seemed suddenly more golden.

Behind me, the hinges creaked open.

A heady, giggling sense of madness threatened to swallow me up, followed by aching tiredness—a gluey, dizzying darkness that pulsed behind my eyes—but I didn't have time for it. *Bad.*

I ran on shaking legs, flashing past a few startled guests, past display cases with their neat brass labels, and flung myself down the staircase.

The scene in the foyer had changed: Havemeyer was gone, the front door still standing open behind him, and Mr. Locke was speaking to one of his hulking manservants in a terse, low voice. The man was nodding, wiping his hands on a white towel and leaving behind rust-colored smears. Blood.

"Bad!" I'd meant to scream it, but my chest had gone airless and tight.

Their faces swung toward me. "What have you *done?*" Now I was almost whispering.

Neither of them answered me. Havemeyer's man was looking at me with an unnerved, blinking expression, like a man who doubted the evidence of his own eyes. "I locked her in, sir, I swear I did, just like Mr. Havemeyer said—how'd she—"

"Be quiet," Locke hissed, and the man's jaw snapped shut. "Get out, now." The man scurried out the door after his master, looking over his shoulder at me with fearful suspicion.

Locke turned back to me, his hands rising in either placation or frustration, I didn't care which. *"Where's Bad?"* There still wasn't enough air in my lungs, as if my rib cage were caught in a giant fist. "What did they do to him? How could you let them?"

"Sit down, child."

"The hell I will." I'd never spoken to anyone that way in my life, but now my limbs were shivering with something hot and towering. "Where is he? And Jane, I need Jane—let *go* of me!—"

Mr. Locke had crossed to the stairs and grabbed my chin roughly, fingers pressing into my jaw. He tilted my face upward, eyes on mine. *"Sit. Down."*

My legs shuddered and folded beneath me. He caught one arm and half carried me into the nearest side room—the Safari Room, a parlor filled with taxidermied antelope heads and masks made of dark, tropical wood—and slung me into an armchair. I clung to it, reeling and dizzied and still racked with that sick exhaustion.

Locke dragged another chair across the room, rucking up the rug beneath its feet, and sat so close in front of me his knees pressed against mine. He leaned back in a posture of false calm.

"I've tried very hard with you, you know," he said conversationally. "All these years spent caring for you, polishing you, *protecting* you...Of all the items in my collections, I've treasured you most of all." His fist closed in frustration. "And yet you insist on flinging yourself into danger."

"Mr. Locke, please, *Bad*—"

He leaned forward, arctic eyes on mine, hands resting on the arms of my chair. "Why couldn't you learn to *mind your place?*" His voice went low on the last three words, heavy with some foreign, guttural accent I didn't recognize. I flinched; he leaned away and drew in a long breath.

"Tell me: How did you get out of your room? And how in the name of every god did you find out about the aberrations?"

Does he mean—Doors?

For the first time since I'd heard those awful boot-on-flesh sounds, Bad was driven entirely out of my mind. But nothing seemed to replace it except the distant thought that Mr. Locke had certainly not given me *The Ten Thousand Doors*.

"It wasn't your father, I think we can be fairly sure. Those tepid little postcards barely had enough room for postage." Locke snorted through his mustache. "Was it that damned African?"

I blinked at him. "Jane?"

"Oh-ho, she does have something to do with it, then! I suspected as much. We'll track her down later."

"Track her—? Where is she?"

"She was dismissed this morning. Her services, whatever they might have been, are certainly no longer needed."

"But you can't! My father hired Jane. You can't just get rid of her." As if that mattered. As if I could get Jane back through some technicality or loophole.

"Your father no longer employs anyone, I'm afraid. Dead people rarely do. But that's not our chief concern right now." Somewhere in the conversation Locke had lost his wrathful edge and become clipped, cool, dispassionate; he might have been presenting at a board meeting or dictating orders to Mr. Stirling. "In fact, it hardly matters *how* you came by your information at this juncture; what matters is that you know entirely too much, entirely too independently, and had the infinitely poor judgment to reveal such knowledge to one of our more, mmm, imprudent members." He gave a little sigh and a what-can-you-do shrug. "Theodore employs rather rough-and-ready means, and I'm afraid he'll be even more excited by your little magic trick with the locked door. Well, he's young."

He's older than you. Is this how Alice felt, tumbling through the rabbit hole?

"And so I must find a way to keep you safe, keep you hidden. I've already made a few calls."

I floundered, free-falling. "Calls to whom?"

"Friends, clients, you know." He waved a square hand. "I've found you a place. I've been told it's very professional, very modern and comfortable—nothing like those Victorian dungeons they used to throw people into. Brattleboro has an excellent reputation." He nodded at me as if I should be pleased to hear it.

"Brattleboro? Wait"—my chest seized—"Brattleboro *Retreat*? The *asylum*?" I'd heard the name whispered among Locke's guests; it was where rich people put their mad maiden aunts and inconvenient daughters. "But I'm not crazy! They won't take me."

Locke's expression turned almost pitying. "Oh, my dear, haven't I taught you the value of money yet? And besides: as far as anyone knows you're a little half-breed orphan who heard about her father's death and started gabbling about magic doors. Took a little extra convincing for them to overlook your coloring, I admit, but I assure you: they'll take you."

It played in my head like a movie reel: the title cards flashing out Mr. Locke's lines to the audience, *"Your father is dead, January!"* and then jerky scenes of a young girl crying, raving. *"She's gone mad, poor dear!"* And then a black streetcar slides beneath a stone archway reading *ASYLUM*, lightning flashes in the background, and it cuts to a scene of our heroine strapped to a hospital bed, staring listlessly at the wall. *No.*

Mr. Locke was speaking again. "It'll only be for a few months, a year maybe. I need time to talk to the Society, let cooler heads prevail. Demonstrate your tractable nature." He smiled at me, and even through my reeling horror I saw the kindness in it, the apology. "I wish it could be otherwise, but it's the only way I know to keep you safe."

I was panting, muscles quivering. "You can't. You wouldn't."

"Did you think you could just dabble at the edges of things? Dip a toe into these waters? These are very serious matters,

January, I tried to tell you. We are enforcing the natural order of things, determining the fates of worlds. Perhaps one day you might still help us." He reached toward my face again and I recoiled. He drew a finger down my cheek the way he might have stroked a piece of imported china: delicate, covetous. "It seems cruel, I know—but believe me when I tell you this is for the best."

And, as his eyes met mine, I felt a weird, childish longing to trust him, to curl up inside myself and let the world flow around me, as I always had, but—

Bad.

I tried to run. I really did. But my legs were still weak and wobbly and Locke caught me around the middle before I'd made it out of the parlor.

He hauled me to the coat closet, clawing and spitting, and slung me inside it the way the cook slung beef sides into the icebox. The closet door slammed and I was trapped in the darkness with nothing but the musty, rich smell of unworn fur coats and the sound of my own breathing.

"Mr. Locke?" It came out quavery and high-pitched. "Mr. Locke, please, I'm sorry—" I babbled. I begged. I cried. The door didn't open.

A good heroine is supposed to sit stiff-lipped in her dungeon cell, formulating brave escape plans and hating her enemies with righteous heartiness; instead I begged, swollen-eyed and shivering.

It's easy to hate people in books. I'm a reader, too, and I know how characters can turn into Villains at the drop of an authorial hat (those capital Vs like dagger points or sharpened teeth). It just isn't like that in real life. Mr. Locke was still Mr. Locke—the man who had taken me under his suit-coated wing when my own father couldn't be bothered to raise me. I didn't even *want* to hate him; I just wanted to undo it all, to unmake the last few hours.

I don't know how long I waited in the closet. This is the part of the story where time becomes fickle and flickering.

Eventually there was an officious rap at the front door, and Mr. Locke's voice said, "Come in, come in, gentlemen. Thank God you're here." Shuffling, footsteps, door hinges. "She's a bit wild at the moment. You're sure you can cope with her?"

Another voice said it would be no difficulty at all; he and his staff were very experienced in such matters. Perhaps Mr. Locke would like to retire to another room, so as to avoid distress?

"No, no. I'd like to see it through."

More booted footsteps. Then the *slide-thunk* of the closet door unlocking and the silhouettes of three men framed in the afternoon light. Rough, gloved hands fastened around my upper arms and hauled me into the entryway, numb-legged.

"Mr. Locke, *please*, I don't know anything, I didn't mean to, don't let them take me—"

A cloth clamped itself over my nose and mouth, damp and honey-sweet. I screamed into it but it only grew larger and larger until my eyes and limbs were covered in muffling, sugared blackness.

My last sense was of distant relief; at least in the darkness I no longer had to see Mr. Locke's pitying eyes on mine.

The first thing you notice is the smell. Before you're even awake the smell twists into the darkness with you: starch and ammonia and lye, and something else that might have been panic, distilled and fermented in the hospital walls for decades. You smell yourself, too, a greasy, sweating scent like meat left out on the counter.

So when I opened my eyes—a process much like pulling apart two caramels that have melted in your pocket—I wasn't surprised to find myself in an unfamiliar room with gray-green walls. All the normal elements of a bedroom seemed to be missing, leaving only a smooth expanse of polished floor and two narrow, stingy-looking windows. Even the sunlight filtering through them was somehow muted.

My muscles felt unmoored, as if they'd come unhooked from my bones, and my head pounded. I was desperately thirsty. But I didn't really begin to be afraid until I tried to reach for my waistband to feel for the silver coin and couldn't: soft woolen cuffs circled my wrists.

Being afraid did nothing at all, of course, except make me sweatier.

I lay there with my fear and my thumping head and my gummed-up mouth for hours, thinking of Bad and Jane and my father and how much I missed the dusty, aged smell of Locke House. And how badly, deeply wrong everything had gone. By the time the nurses finally arrived I had wrung myself out with waiting.

The nurses were iron-spined women with lye-roughened hands and coaxing voices. "Let's sit up now and eat, be a good girl," they ordered, and I was. I ate something mushy and bland that might have once been oatmeal, drank three glasses of water, pissed on command in an open steel container, and even lay back down on the bed when they asked and let them refasten the cuffs around my wrists.

My only act of rebellion (and, God, how pathetically small) was to slip the coin from my waistband and clasp it hot and round in my palm. I survived the first night by holding it and dreaming of silver-faced queens sailing foreign seas, unbound.

The second morning I was convinced a legion of grim doctors would arrive at any moment to administer drugs or beatings, the way they did in the most sensational news stories about asylums. It took me many more hours of lying on my back, staring at the dingy sunlight inching across the floor, before I remembered the lesson I'd learned as a child: it isn't pain or suffering that unmakes a person; it's only time.

Time, sitting on your breastbone like a black-scaled dragon, minutes clicking like claws across the floor, hours gliding past on sulfurous wings.

The nurses returned twice and repeated their rituals. I was very biddable, and they cooed at me. When I stuttered that I'd like to speak to the doctor please, because there had been a terrible mistake and I wasn't crazy, really, one of them even giggled.

"He's very busy, pet. Your evaluation is scheduled for tomorrow, or at least before the end of the week." Then she patted my head, the way no adult would ever pat another adult's head, and added, "But you've been *very* good, so we can leave these off for tonight."

The way she said it—like I should be grateful simply to be uncuffed, to have the basic human liberty of moving my arms and touching something other than overstarched sheets—lit like a coal in my belly. If I'd let it burn it would have ignited a conflagration, a ravenous blaze that would have ripped apart my stiff sheets and smashed my oatmeal against the wall and turned my eyes white-hot. No one would have believed I was sane, after that. I smothered the coal.

They left and I stood at my window, pressing my forehead against the summer-warm glass until my feet began to ache. I lay back down.

The hour-dragons stalked me. They grew larger as the sun set, multiplying in the shadows.

I think I might have shattered into pieces that second night, and never quite found all of myself again, had it not been for an irregular, half-familiar pattering against the window. I stopped breathing.

I crept out of bed and struggled against the stiff window

latch, feeling the liquid weakness of my arms. It wedged open only a miserly few inches, but it was enough to let in a sweet summer-night smell. Enough for me to hear, far below, a familiar voice say, "January? It's you?"

It was Samuel. I felt for just a moment like Rapunzel must have when her prince finally showed up to rescue her from the tower, except that I couldn't have wedged myself out the window even if my hair had been long and golden rather than curled and matted. Still.

"What are you doing here?" I hissed down at him. I couldn't see much more than a man-shaped shadow several floors below, holding something in its hands.

"Jane sent me, she says to tell you she tried to see you, but could not—"

"But how did you know which window was mine?"

I saw his shadow shrug, one-shouldered. "I waited. I watched. Until I saw you."

I didn't say anything. I pictured him hiding in the hedges, staring up at my prison and waiting for hours and hours until he saw my face in the window—and a shiver ran down my breastbone. In my experience, the people you cared most about did not linger. They were always turning away, leaving you behind, never coming back—but Samuel had waited.

He was speaking again. "Listen, Jane says it is important that you have—"

He stopped. Both of us saw the yellow glow of lights flicking on through the first-floor windows, heard the muffled thumps of footsteps coming to investigate. "Catch!"

I caught. It was a stone tied to a length of twine. "Pull it up! Quick!" And he was gone, disappearing into the landscaped grounds just as the hospital doors creaked outward. I yanked the twine up through my window in panicky jerks and jammed the window closed. I slid down my room wall, panting as if it were me sprinting into the night instead of Samuel.

There was something smallish and square tied to the end of the line: a book. *The* book. Even in the dark I could see the half-worn lettering smiling at me like gold teeth through the gloom: *THE TEN THOU OORS*. It had been a long time since Samuel had smuggled a story to me; I wondered dizzily if he'd dog-eared his favorite scenes.

Several hundred questions occurred to me—how had Jane recognized the book, and why did she want me to have it? And how long would Samuel keep waiting for me, if I was trapped here forever?—but I ignored them. Books are Doors and I wanted out.

I crawled to the center of the floor, where there was a slanted yellow square of light from the hall, and began to read.

Chapter Three

Much on Doors, Worlds, and Words

Other worlds and the flexibility of natural laws—The City of Nin—A familiar door seen from the other side—A ghost at sea

It is a heartless thing, but it is at this juncture in our narrative that we must abandon Miss Adelaide Larson entirely. We leave her just as she sails *The Key* into a foreign ocean, with the salted wind blowing the pine sap out of her hair and filling her heart with glowing certainty.

We do not abandon her without good reason: the time has come when we ought to discuss more directly the nature of doors themselves. I must first assure you I did not delay this instruction out of any sly sense of theater, but simply because I hope by now that I have gained your trust. I hope, simply, that you will believe me.

Let us begin with the first conceit of this work: doors are portals between one world and another, which exist only in places of particular and indefinable resonance. By "indefinable resonance," I refer to the space between worlds—that vast blackness waiting on the threshold of every door, which is hideously dangerous to pass through. It is as though the borders of oneself grow dissolute with nothing pressing against them, and your very essence threatens to spill away into the void. Literature and myth are rife with tales of those who have entered the void and failed to emerge on the other side.[7] It seems therefore likely that doors themselves were originally constructed in places where this blackness is at its thinnest and least deadly: convergence points, natural crossroads.

And what is the nature of these other worlds? As we have discovered in previous chapters, they are infinitely varied and ever-changing, and often fail to comply with the conventions of our present world, which we are arrogant enough to call the physical laws of the universe. There are places where men and women are winged and red-skinned, and places where there is no such thing as man and woman but only persons somewhere in between. There are worlds where the continents are carried on the backs of vast turtles swimming through freshwater oceans, where snakes speak riddles, where the lines between the dead and living are blurred to insignificance. I have seen villages where fire itself had been tamed, and followed at men's heels like an obedient hound, and cities with glass spires so high they gathered clouds around their spiral points. (If you are wondering why other worlds seem so brimful of magic compared to your own dreary Earth, consider how magical this world seems from another perspective. To a world of sea people, your ability to breathe air is stunning; to a world of spear throwers, your machines are demons harnessed to work tirelessly in your service; to a world of glaciers and clouds, summer itself is a miracle.)

My second supposition is this: that doors generate a variable but significant degree of leakage between worlds. But what sorts

---

7. Consider all the stories of missing children, oubliettes, bottomless holes, ships sailing off the edges of oceans and into nothingness. They are not tales of journeys or passings-through; they are tales of sudden, irrevocable ending.

It is my belief that the traveler's character plays a role in their ultimate success or failure. Consider Edith Bland's seemingly innocent *The Door to Kyriel*: Five English schoolchildren discover a magic door that takes them to a new world. As the children return home, the youngest and most fearful of them falls into a "great darkness" and is never heard from again. Critics considered it too grim and strange for healthy children.

I consider it an advisement: when one enters a door, one must be brave enough to see the other side.

Edith Bland, *The Door to Kyriel* (London: Looking Glass Library, 1900).

of things leak through, and what is their fate? Men and women, of course, bringing with them the particular talents and arts of their home worlds. Some of them have come to unfortunate ends, I believe—locked in madhouses, burned at stakes, beheaded, banished, et cetera—but others seem to have employed their uncanny powers or arcane knowledges more profitably. They have gained power, amassed wealth, shaped the fates of peoples and worlds; they have, in short, brought change.

Objects, too, have trickled through the doors between worlds, blown by strange winds, drifting on white-frosted waves, carried and discarded by careless travelers—even stolen, sometimes. Some of them have been lost or ignored or forgotten—books written in foreign tongues, clothes in strange fashions, devices with no use beyond their home worlds—but some of them have left stories in their wakes. Stories of magic lamps and enchanted mirrors, golden fleeces and fountains of youth, dragon-scale armor and moon-streaked broomsticks.

I have spent most of my life documenting these worlds and their riches, following the ghost trails they leave behind them in novels and poems, memoirs and treatises, old wives' tales and songs sung in a hundred languages. And yet I do not feel I have come close to discovering them all, or even a meaningful fraction of them. It seems to me now very likely that such a task is impossible, although in my earlier years I harbored great ambitions in that direction.

I once confessed this to a very wise woman I met in another world—a lovely world full of trees so vast one could imagine whole planets nestling in their branches—somewhere off the coast of Finland in the winter of 1902. She was an imposing woman of fifty or so, with the kind of ferocious intelligence that burns bright even through language barriers and several flasks of wine. I told her I intended to find every door to every world that ever existed. She laughed and said: "There are ten thousand of them, fool."

I later learned that her people had no number higher than ten thousand, and claiming there were ten thousand of a thing meant there was no purpose in counting them because they were infinite.

I now believe her accounting of the number of worlds in the universe was perfectly correct, and my aspirations were the dreams of a young and desperate man.

But we need not concern ourselves with all those ten thousand worlds here. We are interested only in the world that Adelaide Larson sailed into in 1893. It is not, perhaps, the most fantastical or beautiful of all possible worlds, but it is the one I long to see above every other. It is the world I have spent nearly two decades searching for.

Authors introducing new characters often describe their features and dress first; when introducing a world, it seems polite to begin with its geography. It is a world of vast oceans and numberless tiny islands—an atlas would look strangely unbalanced to your eye, as if some ignorant artist had made a mistake and painted too much of it blue.

Adelaide Larson happened to sail into the near-center of this world. The sea beneath her boat had possessed many names over the centuries, as seas often do, but was at that time most often called the Amarico.

It is also customary to supply a name when introducing a new character, but the name of a world is a more elusive creature than you might suspect. Consider how many names your own Earth has been assigned, in how many different languages—Erde, Midgard, Tellus, Ard, Uwa—and how absurd it would be for a foreign scholar to arrive and give the entire planet a single title. Worlds are too complex, too beautifully fractured, to be named. But for the sake of convenience we may loosely translate one of this world's names: the Written.

If this seems an odd name for a world, understand that in the Written, words themselves have power.

I do not mean they have power in the sense that they might stir men's hearts or tell stories or declare truths, for those are the powers words have in every world. I mean that words in that world can sometimes rise from their ink-and-cotton cradles and reshape the nature of reality. Sentences may alter the weather, and poems might tear down walls. Stories may change the world.

Now, not every written word holds such power—what chaos that would be!—but only certain words written by certain people who combine an innate talent with many years of careful study, and even then the results are not the sort of fairy-godmother-ish magic you might be imagining. Even a very great word-worker could not casually scrawl a sentence about flying carriages and expect one to come winging across the horizon, or write the dead back to life, or otherwise subvert the very underpinnings of the world as they are. But she might labor for many weeks to craft a story that would increase the likelihood of rain on a particular Sunday, or perhaps she could compose a stanza that would hold her City's walls fractionally more firm against invasion, or guide a single reckless ship away from unseen reefs. There are half-forgotten stories, too faint and unbelievable even to be called legends, of greater magics—of writers who turned back tides and parted seas, who leveled Cities or called dragons down from the skies—but these tales are too unlikely to be taken seriously.

Word-magic comes at a cost, you see, as power always does. Words draw their vitality from their writers, and thus the strength of a word is limited by the strength of its human vessel. Acts of word-magic leave their workers ill and drained, and the more ambitious the working—the more it defies the warp and weft of the world as it is—the higher the toll. Most everyday sorts of word-workers lack the force of will to risk more than an occasional nosebleed and a day spent in bed, but more-gifted persons must spend years in careful study and training, learning restraint and balance, lest they drain away their very lives.

The people who have this talent are called different things on different islands, but most of us concur that they are born with a particular *something* that no degree of study can emulate. The precise nature of that something is a contentious subject among the scholars and priests. Some have claimed that it is related to their certainty of self or their scope of imagination, or perhaps simply the intractability of their will (for they are known to be obstreperous people).[8] There is also great disagreement on what ought to be done

----

8. Farfey even famously argued that it is sheer stubbornness and nothing else that grants them their power. As evidence he submitted Leyna Wordworker, the talented

with such people, and how best to limit the chaos they naturally cause. There are islands where certain faiths preach that writers are the conduits of their god's will and ought to be treated as blessed saints. There is a series of townships in the south that have proclaimed that their writers must live separately from unlettered folk, lest they infect them with their unruly imaginations. Such extremes are rare, however; most Cities find some functional-yet-respectable role for their writers, and simply carry on.

This was the way of things on the islands surrounding the Amarico Sea. Talented writers were most often employed by universities and expected to devote themselves to the civic good, and granted the surname Wordworker.

There are, as my old acquaintance would say, ten thousand other differences between that world and yours. Many of them are too insignificant to merit documentation. I could describe the way the smells of brine and sun have permeated every stone of every street, or the way the tide callers stand at their watchtowers and cry out the hour for their Cities. I could tell you of the many-shaped ships that crisscross the seas with careful writing stitched on their sails praying for good fortune and fair winds. I could tell you of the squid-ink tattoos that adorn the hands of every husband and wife, and of the lesser word-workers who prick words into flesh.

But such an anthropological documenting of facts and practices will tell you little, in the end, about the nature of a world. I will tell you instead about one particular island and one particular City, and one particular boy who would not have been remarkable at all were it not for the day he stumbled through a door and into the burnt-orange fields of another world.

If you were to approach the City of Nin in the early evening, as Adelaide eventually did, you might see it first as some hump-spined

---

author of "The Song of Ilgin," who had once saved her city from a deadly plague. She was also Farfey's wife, and apparently quite a difficult woman.
Farfey Scholar, *A Treatise on the Nature of Word-Workers* (City of Nin, 6609).

creature coiled around a stone outcropping. As you sailed closer the creature would divide itself into a series of buildings standing in rows like whitewashed vertebrae. Spiraling streets would fall like veins between the buildings, and eventually you might begin to pick out figures strolling along them: children chasing skittering cats down alleys; white-robed men and women walking down avenues with sober expressions; shopkeepers hauling their baskets back from the crowded coastline. Some of them might pause to stare out at the honey-tinted sea, just for a moment.

You might suppose that the City was a small, sea-soaked version of paradise. On the whole this impression was not inaccurate, although I admit I find it difficult to be objective.

The City of Nin was certainly a peaceful place, and neither the grandest nor poorest island City that circled the edges of the Amarico Sea. It had a reputation for fine word-working and fair traders and had gained a small degree of fame as a center of prestigious scholarship. The scholarship was rooted in Nin's vast tunneling archives, which were some of the oldest and most extensive collections on the Amarico. Should you ever find yourself on the island I urge you to visit them and wander through the endless vaults packed full of scrolls and books and pages written in every language that has ever been documented in that world.

Of course, the City of Nin suffered all the usual maladies of human cities. Poverty and strife, crimes and their punishments, disease and drought—I have not yet seen any world free entirely of such things. But none of these sins touched the childhood of Yule Ian, a dreamy-eyed boy who grew up on the eastern edge of the City in a crumbling stone apartment above his mother's tattoo shop.

He had devoted parents who were prevented from spoiling him only by the sheer number of their offspring. He had six brothers and sisters, who were, like siblings in every world, alternately his dearest friends and direst enemies. He had a narrow bunk decorated with tin stars dangling from the ceiling, which filled his dreams with gleaming planets and fanciful places. He also possessed a bound set of Var Storyteller's *Tales of the Amarico Sea* given to him by his favorite aunt, and a temperamental cat that liked to sleep on the sunbaked windowsill while he read.[9] It was a life well suited to day-dreaming and reverie, which were the things Yule loved best.

Yule and his siblings spent their afternoons working with their father on his small fishing boat or helping their mother in her tattoo shop: copying out blessings and prayers in different scripts, mixing inks, and scrubbing her tools. Yule preferred the shop to the ship, and especially loved the long afternoons when his mother permitted him to watch her pricking tiny, blood-dotted words into a customer's skin. His mother's word-working wasn't especially strong, but it was enough that her customers were willing to pay more to have their blessings written by Tilsa Ink, because her blessings sometimes came true.

His mother originally intended to apprentice him to her art, but it soon became clear that he lacked even the faintest spark of word-working talent. She might have trained him anyway, but he had no patience for the actual labor of tattooing. It was simply the *words* he loved, the sound and shape and marvelous fluidity of them, and so he drifted instead toward the scholars in their long white robes.

Every child in the City of Nin was subjected to several years of schooling, which amounted to weekly gatherings in the university courtyards to listen to a young scholar lecture them on their letters and numbers and the locations of all one hundred eighteen inhab-ited islands on the Amarico. Most children fled these lessons as soon as their parents permitted it. Yule did not. He often lingered to ask questions, and even wheedled a few extra books out of his teachers. One of them, a patient young man named Rilling Scholar, provided books in different languages, and these became Yule's most prized possessions. He loved the rolling way new syllables felt in his mind and the strangeness of the stories they brought with them, like treasures from sunken ships the waves left behind.

---

9. Cats, I have found, seem to exist in more or less the same form in every world; it is my belief that they have been slipping in and out of doors for several thousand years. Anyone familiar with house cats will know this is a particular hobby of theirs.

By age nine Yule had achieved proficiency in three languages, one of which existed only in the university archives, and by the time he turned eleven—the traditional age for such decisions—not even his mother could object to his clear destiny as a scholar. She purchased the long lengths of undyed cloth at the harbor market and only sighed a little as she wrapped her son's dark limbs in a scholar's fashion. He was out the door with an armful of books in a white-blurred instant.

His first years at the university were passed in a state of dreamy near-genius, which provoked both frustration and admiration from his instructors. He continued to learn new languages with the ease of a boy scooping water from a well but seemed unwilling to dedicate himself sufficiently to master any single one of them. He spent untold hours in the archives, turning manuscript pages with a thin wooden paddle, but frequently missed assigned lectures because he'd found an interesting passage on merfolk in a sailor's logbook, or a crumbling map marked in an unknown language. He consumed books as if they were as necessary to his health as bread and water, but they were rarely the books he had been assigned.

His most generous instructors insisted that it was purely an issue of time and maturity—eventually young Yule Ian would find a steady subject of study and dedicate himself to it. Then he might select a mentor and begin contributing to the grand body of research that made the University of Nin so prestigious. Other scholars, watching Yule prop a book of fables against the water pitcher at breakfast and turn the pages with a faraway expression, were less sanguine.

Indeed, as Yule's fifteenth birthday approached, even the most optimistic scholars were growing concerned. He showed no signs of narrowing his field of study or proposing a course of research, and did not seem in the least concerned by his approaching examinations. Should he pass them, he could be formally announced as Yule Ian Scholar and begin his ascent through the ranks of the university; should he fail, he would be politely asked to consider some other, less demanding apprenticeship.

In retrospect, it is easy to suspect that Yule's aimlessness was actually a quest, a search for some shapeless, unnamed thing that lurked just out of sight, and perhaps it was true. Perhaps he and Adelaide spent their childhoods in much the same manner, searching the limits of their worlds in search of another.

But restless quests are not the business of serious scholars. Yule was therefore summoned one day to the master's study to have "a serious discussion of his future." He arrived an hour late with his finger marking his place in *A Study of Myths and Legends in the North Sea Isles* and a bemused, distant expression. "You summoned me, sir?"

The master possessed a lined, somber face, as scholars do in most places, and venerable tattoos that wound up both arms indicating his marriage to Kenna Merchant, his dedication to scholarship, and his twenty years of admirable service to the City. His hair clung to his skull in a white scimitar, as if the heat of his working mind had burned it away from the top of his head. His eyes on Yule were troubled.

"Sit, young Yule, sit. I'd like to talk to you about your future here at the university." The master's eyes fell on the book still clutched in Yule's hands. "I will be blunt with you: we find your lack of focus and discipline of gravest concern. If you can't settle yourself to a course of study, we will have to consider other avenues for you."

Yule's head tipped curiously to one side, like a cat offered an unfamiliar bit of food. "Other avenues, sir?"

"Activities better suited to your mind and temperament," the master said.

Yule was silent for a moment but could think of nothing better suited to his temperament than spending sun-soaked afternoons curled beneath the olive trees reading books in long-forgotten languages. "What do you mean?"

The master, who had perhaps expected this conversation to involve more distressed pleading and less polite puzzlement, pressed his lips into a thin maroon line. "I mean you might apprentice elsewhere. Your mother, I am sure, would still train you as a tattooist, or you could act as a scribe for one of the word-workers on the east side, or even a merchant's bookkeeper. I could speak to my wife, if you'd like."

Only now did Yule's expression begin to reflect the horror the master anticipated. He softened again. "Well, my boy, we haven't reached that point just yet. Simply spend the next week in contemplation, consider your choices. And if you would like to stay here and take your scholar's exams...find a path."

Yule was dismissed. He found himself leaving the cool stone halls, striding through courtyards and spiraled streets, and then climbing the hills behind the City with the sun baking the back of his neck, without ever being fully aware of any particular destination. He was simply moving, fleeing the choice the master had given him.

To any other young boy hoping to join the ranks of the scholars, the choice would have been an easy one: either he proposed a line of research in American history or ancient languages or religious philosophy, or he abandoned all such aspirations and worked as a humble scribe. But to Yule both paths were unspeakably bleak. Both of them would necessitate a narrowing of his boundless horizons, an end to his dreaming. The thought of either made him feel tight-chested, as if two great hands pressed on either side of his ribs.

He could not have known it then, but it was much the same way Ade felt on the days she ran out to the old hayfield to be alone with the sound of the riverboats and the wideness of the sky. Except that Ade had grown up with the harsh boundaries of her life always close at hand and had long since set her will against them; poor, charmed Yule had simply never known such rules existed before that day.

He staggered away from his discovery, past the scrubby hillside farms, past the last packed-earth roads, scrambling along animal trails and over rocky bluffs. Eventually even the animal trails disappeared into gnarled gray stone, and the wind carried faraway smells of salt-soaked wood. He had never been so high above his City, and he found he liked the way it dwindled below him until it was just a collection of distant white squares surrounded by the vastness of the sea.

His skin itched with wind-dried sweat and his palms were rubbed raw against the stones. He knew he ought to turn around, but his legs continued carrying him onward, upward, until he pulled himself over a ledge and saw it: an archway.

A thin gray curtain hung from the arch, fluttering in its own breeze like a witch's skirt. A smell issued from it, like river water and mud and sunlight, nothing at all like the stony salt smell of Nin.

Once Yule saw the arch, he found his eyes reluctant to look anywhere else. It seemed almost to beckon him like a half-curled hand. He walked toward it with a mad feeling of hope flooding his limbs— an impossible, sourceless hope that there was something marvelous and strange on the other side of that curtain, waiting just for him.

He pulled aside the curtain and saw nothing but knotted grass and stone beyond it. He stepped beneath the arch and into a vast, swallowing darkness.

It pressed and sucked at him like tar, suffocating in its enormity, until he felt solid wood beneath his palms. He heaved against it in desperation and still-burning hope—felt it grind against long-undisturbed dirt—and then it was open, and Yule stepped out into burnt-orange grasses beneath an eggshell sky. He had only stood for a few moments, openmouthed in the strange air of another world, when she came striding toward him across the field. A young woman the color of milk and honeyed wheat.

I will not repeat the tale of that meeting a second time. You've already heard how the two young persons sat together in the early-fall chill and told their impossible truths of here and elsewhere. How they spoke in a long-dead language preserved only in a few ancient texts in Nin's archives, which Yule had studied for the sheer pleasure of new syllables dancing on his tongue. How it did not feel like a meeting of two people so much as a collision of two planets, as if both of them had swung out of their orbits and hurtled into one another. How they kissed, and how the fireflies pulsed around them.

How doomed and brief their meeting was.

Yule spent the next three days in a state of dazed elation. The scholars grew worried that his mind had been subtly damaged in some fall or accident; his mother and father, who were more familiar with the maladies of young boys, worried that he had fallen in love. Yule himself offered no explanations but only smiled beatifically and hummed out-of-key versions of old ballads about famous lovers and sailing ships.

He returned to the curtained arch on the third day just as, on the other side of an endless darkness, Ade returned to the cabin in the hayfield. You know what awaited him, of course: bitterest disappointment. Instead of a magical door leading to a foreign land, Yule found nothing but piled stones on a hilltop and a gray curtain hanging still and rotten as the skin of some dead creature. It did not lead anywhere at all, no matter how furiously he cursed it.

Eventually Yule simply sat and waited, hoping the girl might find her way through to him. She did not. You may picture the two of them—Ade waiting in the deepening night of the overgrown field with hope guttering like an overspent candle in her chest, Yule perched on the hilltop with his skinny arms held around his knees—almost like figures on either side of a mirror. Except instead of cool glass between them it was the vastness between worlds.

Yule watched constellations creep over the horizon, reading the familiar words pricked in starlight: Ships-Heaven-Sent, Blessings-of-Summer, Scholar's-Humility. They slid over him like pages from some great book, familiar as his own name. He thought of Ade, waiting in her separate darkness, and wondered what her stars told her.

He stood. He rubbed his thumb across the silver piece he'd brought with him—thinking he might show it to her as proof of his own world—and let it fall to earth. He didn't know if it was an offering or a casting-away, but he knew he didn't want to carry it any longer, to feel the knowing, silver-stamped eyes of the City Founder watching him.[10] He turned away then, and did not return again to the stone arch.

---

10. Most cities on the Amarico feature their Founders on their coinage; the City of Nin was founded by Nin Wordworker, many centuries previously, and it was her half-smiling visage that stared back at Yule from the moonlit earth. Coins are also stamped with words of power, which capture some small piece of the City's soul. A person

But doors, you will recall, are change.

The Yule who left the arch that night was therefore a somewhat different Yule from the one who had found it three days previously. Something new thudded in his chest alongside his heart, as if a separate organ had suddenly come pumping to life. It had an urgent, driving rhythm, which Yule could not fail to notice even through his misery. He pondered it as he lay in his narrow bed that night, listening to the disgruntled sounds of his siblings falling back to sleep after being woken by his return. It did not feel like despair, or loss, or loneliness. It reminded him most of the feeling he had sometimes in the archives when a scrap of writing written on ancient vellum pulled him onward, deeper, until he lost himself in a spiraling trail of stories, but even that was nothing compared to the thrumming urgency he now felt. He fell asleep worrying vaguely that he'd developed some sort of murmur in his heart.

The following morning he recognized it as something much more serious: the discovery of his life's purpose.

He lay in bed for several more minutes, contemplating the immensity of the task before him, then rose and dressed at such speed that his siblings caught only a glimpse of his white robes whipping out the door. He went straight to the master scholar's office and asked to take his exams immediately. The master reminded him gently that aspiring scholars were expected to present thorough and prepared proposals for their future studies, which convinced their fellows of their seriousness, dedication, and ability. He suggested that Yule take the necessary time to compile bibliographies and collect his sources, perhaps consult with more advanced scholars.

Yule made an exasperated noise. "Oh, very well. In three days, then. Will that do?" The master assented, but his expression said he anticipated nothing but disaster and mortification.

---

holding a coin from Nin will smell brine and bookdust, will perhaps find themselves thinking of sun-bleached streets and the joyful chatter of a peaceful city. It was this Yule had wanted to share with the girl in the field: a small silver piece of his home.

In this, as in few other things, the master was mistaken. The Yule who arrived for his examination appeared to be an entirely different boy from the one they had all known and fretted over for years. All the dreamy wonderment and misty-eyed curiosity had burned away like a sea fog beneath the sun, revealing a somber-faced young man who radiated a kind of fierce, unshakable *intention*. His proposal was a model of clarity and ambition that would require mastery of multiple languages, familiarity with a dozen different fields of study, and untold years spent combing through ancient tales and half-written stories. It was customary at the conclusion of such presentations for the scholars to voice objections and concerns to the proposal, but the room was quite silent.

It was the master himself who spoke first. "Well, Yule. I can find no fault with your course of study, save that it will take you half your life. All I would like to know is where this sudden...certainty has come from. What set you on this path?"

Yule Ian felt a tremor in his breastbone, as if there were a red thread tied around it and someone had just yanked the other end. He considered, briefly and foolishly, simply telling the truth: that he sought to follow the skittering ant-trails of words into other worlds, to find a burnt-orange field lit with fireflies, to find a girl the color of wheat and milk.

Instead, he said, "True scholarship needs neither an origin nor a destination, good master. To seek new knowledge is its own motivation." This was precisely the sort of lofty non-answer that pleased scholars best. They preened and cooed like doves around him, signing their names to his proposal with many extra flourishes. Only the master paused before signing, watching Yule the way a fisherman watches a darkening cloud on the horizon. But he, too, bent his head to the pages.

Yule left the hall that day with a formal blessing and a new name, both of which his mother tattooed in sinuous spirals around his left wrist. The words were still hot and stinging in his flesh the next day when Yule ascended the white-stone stairs that led to his favorite reading room. He sat at a yellow-wood desk overlooking the sea and opened the first sweet-smelling page of a new notebook. In uncharacteristically neat script, he wrote: *Notes and Researches vol. 1: A Comparative Study of Passages, Portals, and Entryways in World Mythology, compiled by Yule Ian Scholar, 6908.*

The title, as you have no doubt surmised, has since been revised.

Yule Ian Scholar spent a considerable portion of the next twelve years hunched over that same desk, alternately scribbling and reading, surrounded by so many towers of books that his study came to resemble a paper model of a city. He read collections of folktales and interviews with long-dead explorers, logbooks and holy texts from forgotten religions. He read them in all the languages of the Amarico Sea, and all the languages that happened to have fallen through the cracks between one world and the next over the previous several centuries. He read until there was little left to read, and he was obliged to take his researches "into the field," as he airily informed his fellows. They imagined, in the comfortable manner of scholars, that "the field" merely referred to exotic archives in other Cities and wished him well.

They did not presume that Yule would cram his shoulder bag full of journals and dried fish, pay for passage on a series of trade ships and mail carriers, and march out into the wilds of foreign islands with the focused air of a hound following an animal trail. But the trails he followed were the invisible, glimmering tracks left by stories and myths, and instead of animals he hunted doors.

In time, he found a precious handful of them. None of them led to a cedar-smelling world with inhabitants the color of cotton, but he was not discouraged. Yule was stuffed with the kind of unblemished confidence that belongs only to the very young, who have never truly known the bitterness of failure, or felt the years of their lives trickling away from them like water from cupped palms. It seemed to him then that his success was inevitable.

(Of course, I know better now.)

He often liked to imagine the scene: Perhaps he would find her home after weeks of hard traveling, and she would look up from her work to see him striding toward her, and that wild smile would split her face. Perhaps they would meet in that same field and they would run toward one another through springtime-green grasses. Perhaps he would find her in some distant city he could scarcely imagine, or in a howling thunderstorm, or on the shores of an unnamed island.

With the baseless arrogance that so often plagues young men, Yule never once considered the possibility that Adelaide would not be waiting for him. He never imagined she might have spent the past decade flitting in and out of worlds with the instinctive ease of a gull swooping from ship to ship in the harbor, without a single book or record to guide her. He certainly never imagined she might build herself a rickety boat in the mountains and sail it onto the indigo waves of the Amarico Sea.

It was such an outlandish notion, in fact, that Yule almost dismissed it entirely when he heard a strange rumor on the docks of the City of Plumm. It came to him as most rumors do: as a drifting set of jokes and have-you-heards that assembled themselves slowly into a single story. The most often-repeated details seemed to be these: There had been a strange ship sighted off the eastern coast of the City of Plumm, with sails of eerie white canvas. One or two fisherwomen and traders had approached it, curious to see what species of madman would sail a ship without blessings stitched into the canvas, but they had all veered quickly away. The ship, they claimed, was sailed by a woman as white as paper. A ghost, perhaps, or some pale undersea creature come to the surface.

Yule shook his head at the superstitions of seafolk and returned to his borrowed room in the Plumm libraries. He had come following local legends of fire-spewing lizards that lived in the centers of volcanoes and only emerged once every one hundred thirteen years, and spent his evening in careful review of his notes. It wasn't until he lay in his narrow cot, mind spiraling freely in and out of half dreams, that it occurred to him to wonder what color the ghost sailor's hair was.

Yule returned to the docks early the next morning and interrogated several startled merchants before he extracted an answer.

"It was as white as she was!" a sailor assured him in a spooked tone. "Or, well, I suppose it was more a kind of straw color. Yellowish."

Yule swallowed, very hard. "And was she coming this way? Will she come to Plumm?"

The man could offer no certainties here, for who could guess at the desires of sea witches or ghosts? "But she'll run straight into the eastern beaches if she keeps her course. Then we'll see who's telling tales, won't we, Edon?" Here he abandoned the conversation in order to elbow his doubtful shipmate and engage in a spirited debate about whether merfolk wore clothes.

Yule was left standing alone on the dock, feeling as if the world had suddenly tilted on its axis. As if he were a boy again, reaching toward that thin curtain with un-inked hands.

He ran. He didn't know the way down to the eastern beaches—a rocky, barren stretch of coast frequented only by odds-and-ends collectors and a certain breed of romantic poet—but a series of breathless questions and answers saw him perched on the edge of the sea well before midday. He curled his legs to his chest and stared out at the gold-topped waves, watching for the thin white line of a sail topping the horizon.

She did not arrive that day, or the next. Yule returned to the coast each morning and watched the sea until dusk. His mind, restless and driven for so many years, seemed to have settled in upon itself like a cat curled up to sleep. Waiting.

On the third day, a sail crept over the waves, full-bellied and perfectly white. Yule watched the ship lumbering closer, awkward and squarish in the water, until his eyes burned from salt and sun. There was a single figure aboard, facing the island with a challenging, prideful stance and a flaxen tangle of hair whipping around her head. Yule felt a hysterical desire to dance or scream or faint, but instead he simply stood and raised one arm into the air.

He saw her see him. A stillness fell over her, despite the lolling of the ship beneath her feet. Then she laughed—a wild, whooping laugh that rolled over the water to Yule like summertime thunder—removed several layers of dirt-colored clothing, and dove into the shallow waves beneath her ship without a trace of hesitation. Yule had half a second in which to wonder precisely what manner of half-wild madwoman he had been questing after for twelve years, and to doubt his sufficiency for the task, before he was splashing out to meet her, laughing and dragging his white scholar's robes through the waves.

And so, in the late spring of the year 1893 in your world, which was the year 6920 in that one, Yule Ian Scholar and Adelaide Lee Larson found one another in the noonday tides surrounding the City of Plumm. They were never willingly parted again.

The Locked Door

I dreamed in gold and indigo.

I was skimming over a foreign ocean, following behind a white-sailed ship. There was a blurred figure standing at the prow, hair running bright behind her. Her features were smeary and uncertain but there was something so familiar in the shape she made against the horizon, so whole and wild and true, that my dreaming heart broke.

It was the feeling of tears sliding down my cheeks that woke me up. I lay on the floor of my room, stiff and chilled, my face aching from where it pressed against the corner of *The Ten Thousand Doors*. I didn't care.

The *coin*. The silver coin I'd found as a girl, half-buried in the dust of a foreign world, the coin that now lay blood-warm in my palm—it was *real*. As real as the chill tile beneath my knees, as real as the tears cooling on my cheeks. I held it, and smelled the sea.

And if the coin was real...Then so was the rest of it. The City of Nin and its endless archives, Adelaide and her adventures in a hundred elsewheres, true love. Doors. Word-working?

I felt a shiver of reflexive doubt, heard an echo of Locke's voice scoffing *fanciful nonsense.* But I'd already chosen to believe, once, and written open a locked door. Whatever this story was—this unlikely, impossible fantasy of Doors and words and other worlds—it was true. And, somehow, I was a part of it. And so were Mr. Locke, and the Society, and Jane, and maybe even my poor lost father.

I felt like a woman reading a mystery novel with every fourth line missing.

There's really only one thing a person can do when they're hip-deep in a mystery novel: keep reading.

I snatched the book and flipped through the pages to find my place, but stopped: a thin slip of paper peeked out from the back pages. It was a note, written on the waxy back of a receipt labeled *Zappia Family Groceries, Inc.* It read:

HOLD ON JANUARY.

The letters were stiff capitals, written with the careful pressure of someone uncomfortable with a pen in their hand. I thought of Samuel talking about his family's cabin on the north end of the lake, his dusk-colored hands gesturing in the darkness, his cigarette drawing comet trails in the night.

Oh, Samuel.

If I hadn't been holding that scrap of paper and thinking of those hands, I might've heard the nurses' footsteps before the lock clunked and the door opened, and they stood on the threshold like a pair of gargoyles in starched white aprons.

152

Their eyes surveyed the room—unslept-in bed, unlatched window, patient on the floor with her nightgown rucked past her knees—and landed on the book. They moved toward me with such synchronous efficiency it had to have been some kind of Procedure. Procedure 4B, When an Inmate Is Out of Bed and in Possession of Contraband.

Their hands came down like harpy claws on my shoulders. I froze—I had to stay calm and sane-seeming, had to be good—but one of them scooped my book off the floor and I lunged for it. And then they were twisting my wrists behind my back and I was kicking and howling and spitting, fighting with the unscientific chaos of young children and madwomen.

But they were older and stronger and depressingly capable, and soon my flailing arms were pressed tight to my sides and my feet were half marching, half skidding out into the hall.

"Straight to the doctor, I think," one of them panted. The other nodded.

I caught glimpses of myself as I passed the windowed doors of other rooms: a dark ghost in white cotton, mad-eyed and tangle-haired, escorted by women so upright and starched they must be either angels or demons.

They steered me down two floors to an office door with gold lettering painted on the glass: *Dr. Stephen J. Palmer, Chief Medical Superintendent.* It struck me as darkly, terribly funny that all my good behavior and polite questions couldn't get me into this office, but a little howling and thrashing had brought me right to his door. Perhaps I ought to howl more often. Perhaps I ought to be again that obstreperous girl-child I was when I was seven.

Dr. Palmer's office was wood-paneled and leather-chaired, full of antique instruments and gold-framed certificates in Latin. Dr. Palmer himself was aging, aloof, with tiny half-glasses that perched on the end of his nose like a well-mannered wire bird. The asylum smell of ammonia and panic was entirely absent.

I hated him for that. For not having to breathe in the stink of it every day of his life.

The nurses corralled me into a chair and loomed behind me. One of them handed Dr. Palmer my book. It looked small and shabby on his desk, and not very magical at all.

"I think Miss January will behave herself now. Won't you, dear?" His voice had a hearty, unassailable confidence that made me think of senators or salesmen, or Mr. Locke.

"Yes, sir," I whispered. The gargoyle-nurses departed.

Dr. Palmer reshuffled a series of folders and papers on his desk. He took up his pen—a heavy, ugly specimen that looked like it could double as a rolling pin in an emergency—and I felt myself go very, very still. I'd written open one door, hadn't I?

"Now. This book." The doctor tapped the cover with a knuckle. "How did you sneak it into your room?"

"I didn't. It came in through the window." Most people can't tell the difference between truth-telling and madness; try it sometime, and you'll see what I mean.

Dr. Palmer gave me a small, pitying smile. "Ah, I see. Now. From what Mr. Locke tells me, your decline has much to do with your father. Would you like to tell me a bit more about him?"

"No." I wanted my book back. I wanted to be unchained and unfettered, to go find my dog and my friend and my father. I wanted that damn pen.

Dr. Palmer smiled his pity-smile again. "A foreigner of some sort, was he not, and colored? An aborigine or Negroid fellow?"

I considered, briefly but longingly, how nice it would feel to spit directly into his face, to spatter those neat spectacles with slime.

"Yes, sir." I tried to marshal my familiar good-girl face, to arrange my features in that dewy, biddable expression that served me so well in Locke's world. It sat wooden and stiff on my face, unconvincing. "My father worked—works—for Mr. Locke. As an archaeological explorer. He is often away."

"I see. And he passed away recently."

I pictured Jane telling me that Locke was not God and that she hadn't given up yet. *Oh, Father, I haven't given up either.*

"Yes, sir. Please"—I swallowed, tried to reassemble my good-girl mask—"when can I go home?"

Home. See that *H* like a house with two chimneys? I meant Locke House when I said it—with its familiar labyrinth of hallways, its hidden attics and warm red-stone walls—but I was unlikely ever to return there now.

Dr. Palmer was reshuffling his folders again, not looking at me. I wondered how long Mr. Locke had paid him to keep me here, mad or otherwise. "It's not clear at this time, but I shouldn't be in a rush if I were you. There's no reason you shouldn't rest here for a few months, is there? Recover your strength?"

I could think of at least thirty good reasons I didn't want to stay locked in an asylum for months, but all I said was, "Yes, sir. And can I—do you think I could have my book back? And perhaps a pen and paper? Writing...eases my mind." I attempted a timorous smile.

"Oh, not just yet. We'll discuss it again next week, if you've been on your best behavior. Mrs. Jacobs, Mrs. Reynolds, if you please—"

The door opened behind me. The sharp steps of the nurses clicked across the floor. *A week?*

I flung myself across his desk and seized the slick smoothness of the doctor's pen. I tore it from his grasp, spun away, barreled into the nurses—and then they had me, and it was over. A starched white arm crushed itself against my throat, quite dispassionately, and I felt my fingers being peeled inexorably away from the pen.

"No, please, you don't understand—" I scrabbled, bare feet sliding uselessly across the floor.

"Ether, I think, and a dose of bromide. Thank you, ladies."

My last sight of the office was Dr. Palmer placing the pen fastidiously in his pocket and tucking my book in his desk drawer.

I hissed and cried and screamed down the halls, shaking with hate and need. Faces peered out at me through the narrow door windows, pale and blank as moons. It's funny how quickly you descend from civilized young lady to madwoman; it was as if this beastly, boundaryless creature had been living just beneath my skin for years, lashing her tail.

But there are places built for holding beastly women. They hauled me into bed, fastened the cuffs around my ankles and wrists, and pressed something cold and stickily damp over my mouth. I held my breath until I couldn't and then I drifted into tarry blackness.

I don't want to talk much about the next few days, so I won't.

They were dull and gray and long. I woke at odd, arrhythmic times of the day with the sick tang of drugs on my breath; at night I dreamed I was suffocating but couldn't move. I spoke to other people, I think—nurses, other inmates—but the only real company I had was the silver queen on her coin. And the hateful, stalking hours.

I tried to hide from the hours by sleeping. I lay very still and closed my eyes against the dull sameness of the room and made my muscles go slack and soft. Sometimes it worked, or at least I achieved a stretch of time that was even grayer and duller than the rest, but mostly it didn't. Mostly I just lay there, staring at the pink veins of my eyelids and listening to the *shush-shush* of my blood.

Nurses and orderlies appeared every few hours, slate schedules clutched in their hands, to unfasten me from bed and prod me into motion. There were meals to be eaten under close supervision, starched white gowns to be worn, baths to be taken in rows of tin tubs. I shivered beside the fish-pale nakedness of two dozen other women, all of us made ugly and unsecret, like snails pulled from their shells. I watched them furtively— twitching or weeping or silent as tombstones—and wanted to scream: *I'm not like them, I'm not mad, I don't belong here.* And then I thought: *Maybe they didn't belong here, either, at first.*

Time went strange. The hour-dragons stalked and circled. I heard their belly scales susurrating against the tile in my sleep. Sometimes they crept into bed and stretched out beside me the way Bad used to, and I woke wet-cheeked and terribly alone.

At other times I would be engulfed instead by righteous rage—How could Locke betray me into this hell? How could I let them hurt Bad? How could my father leave me here, alone?—but eventually rage burns out and leaves nothing but ash, a muted landscape drawn in charcoal gray.

And then on the fifth or sixth (or seventh?) day of my imprisonment, a voice said, "You have a visitor, Miss Scaller. Your uncle came to see you."

I had my eyes screwed shut, hoping that if I feigned sleep long enough my body would give up and play along. I heard the click of the door, the scrape of a chair. And then a voice drawled, "Good lord, it's half past ten in the morning. I would make a Sleeping Beauty joke, but it's only half-true, isn't it?"

My eyes snapped open and there he was: alabaster-white, cruel-eyed, hands like white-gloved spiders resting on his cane. Havemeyer.

The last time I'd heard his voice, he'd been ordering his men to get rid of the mess that was my dearest friend.

I lunged for him. I'd forgotten that I was despairing, weak, cuffed to my bed; I only knew I wanted to hurt him, bite him, rake my nails down his face—"Now, now, let's not get excited. I'll have to call the nurses in, and you're no good to me drugged and drooling."

I snarled and twisted against my restraints. He chuckled. "You were always so biddable, so civilized at Locke House. I told Cornelius not to believe it."

I spat at him. I hadn't intentionally spit on anyone since Samuel and I were kids holding contests on the lakeshore; it was comforting to see I hadn't entirely lost my aim.

Havemeyer wiped his cheek with one gloved finger, his amusement turning brittle. "I have some questions for you, Miss Scaller. Cornelius would have us believe this is all blown out of proportion, that you simply eavesdropped on your betters, that you're distraught over your father, that you're no threat, really, et cetera, et cetera. I think otherwise." He leaned forward. "How did you find out about the fractures? Who have you been talking to?"

I bared my teeth at him.

"I see. And how did you get out of your room? Evans was sure he locked you in, and he's not foolish enough to lie to me."

My lips curved into a not-smile. It was the kind of expression that makes you think *That person is unhinged* and *Someone should lock them up*; I found I didn't care. "Maybe I cast a magic spell, Mr. Havemeyer. Maybe I'm a ghost." The smile turned into a lopsided snarl. "I'm mad now, didn't you hear?"

He tilted his head at me, considering. "That vile dog of yours is dead, in case you were wondering. Evans tossed it in the lake. I would apologize, but someone ought to have done it years ago, if you ask me."

My body recoiled like a kicked animal. My ribs were shattered shards, pressing into the soft meat of my insides. *Bad, Bad, oh Bad*—

"It seems I have your full attention. Good. Now, tell me,

158

have you ever heard of *upyr*? *Vampir*? *Shrtriga*?" The words rolled and hissed in his mouth. They reminded me, for no clear reason, of the trip I'd taken with Mr. Locke to Vienna when I was twelve. It'd been February and the city was shadowed, wind-scoured, old. "Well, the name hardly matters. I'm sure you've heard of them in general outline: things that creep out of the black forests of the north and feast on the lifeblood of the living."

He was removing the glove from his left hand as he spoke, tugging on each white fingertip. "Lies spread by superstitious peasants, in the main, repeated in story papers and sold to Victorian urchins." Now his hand was entirely free, fingers so pale I could see blue veins threading them. "Stoker should've been summarily executed, if you ask me."

And he reached toward me. There was perhaps half a second before his fingertip touched me when all the fine hairs on my arm stood straight and my heart seized and I knew, in a scrabbling, animalish way, that I shouldn't let him touch me, that I should scream for help—but it was too late.

His finger was cold against my skin. Beyond cold. An aching, burning, tooth-hurting absence of heat. My body warmth drained desperately toward it, but the cold was ravenous. My lips tried to form words but they felt numbed and clumsy, as if I'd been out walking in freezing wind.

Havemeyer made a soft sighing sound of deepest contentment, like a man warming his hands by the fireplace or taking his first sip of hot coffee. He pulled his finger reluctantly away from my skin.

"Stories always have a grain of truth, don't you find? I believe that was the principle that kept your father trotting around the globe, digging up scraps for his master." His cheeks were flushed an unhealthy consumptionish crimson. His black eyes danced. "So tell me, my dear: How did you find out about the fractures?"

159

My lips were still numb, my blood sluggish and congealed-feeling in my veins. "I don't understand what—why—"

"Why we're so concerned? Cornelius would give you a speech about order, prosperity, peace, et cetera—but I confess my own purposes are not so lofty. I merely wish to preserve this world as it is: so accommodating, so obligingly full of undefended, unmissed people. My interest is therefore personal and passionate. It would be wise to tell me everything you know."

I looked at him—still confidently smiling, running his bare thumb across his fingernails—and was more afraid than I'd ever been in my life. Afraid I would drown in a sea of madness and magic, afraid I would betray someone or something without really knowing how, but mostly afraid he would touch me again with those cold, cold hands.

A sharp rap at the door. Neither of us made a sound.

Mrs. Reynolds entered anyway, her shoes tapping officiously across the tile. "It's time for her bath, I'm afraid, sir. Family are asked to return later."

Barely contained rage curled Havemeyer's lips away from his teeth. "We're busy," he hissed. In Locke House, it would've been enough to send nearby staff scurrying for cover.

But this was not Locke House. Mrs. Reynolds's eyes narrowed, lips pursed. "I'm sorry, sir, but regular schedules are very important for our patients here at Brattleboro. They're easily agitated and require a sober, predictable life to keep them calm—"

"*Fine.*" Havemeyer breathed deeply through his nose. He shook out his glove and pulled it over his bare hand. Something about the showy slowness of the gesture made it obscene.

He leaned toward me, hands crossed atop his cane. "We'll talk more soon, my dear. Are you free tomorrow night? I'd hate to be interrupted again."

I licked my slowly warming lips, tried to sound braver than I felt. "Don't—don't you have to be invited in?"

He laughed. "Oh, my dear, don't believe everything you read in the story papers. You people are always trying to invent *reasons* for things. Monsters only come for bad children, for loose women, for impious men. The truth is that the powerful come for the weak, whenever and wherever they like. Always have, always will."

"Sir." The nurse stepped toward us.

"Yes, yes." Havemeyer flapped a hand at her, smiled a hungry smile at me, and left.

I listened to the merry tapping of his cane down the halls.

Halfway through my bath I started to shake and couldn't stop. The nurses fussed and rubbed warm towels down my arms and legs, but the shaking only intensified and then I was crouched naked on the tile floor, holding my own shoulders to keep them from shattering. They took me back to my room.

Mrs. Reynolds lingered to fasten the cuffs around my goose-fleshed arms. I seized her hand with both of mine before she could finish.

"Could I—do you think I could have my book back? Just for tonight? I'll be good. P-please." I wished I'd had to feign that stutter, wished it were all some clever ruse designed to lull them into trusting me before I made my daring escape— but I was precisely as terrified and hopeless as I seemed, and I just wanted to hide from the howling thoughts in my head. Thoughts like: *Havemeyer is a monster* and *The Society is full of monsters* and *What does that make Mr. Locke?* And: *Bad is dead.*

I didn't really think she would say yes. The nurses had treated us so far like bulky, poorly behaved furniture that needed regular feeding and grooming. They spoke to us, but in the light, chattering way a farmer's wife might speak to her chickens. They fed and bathed us, but their hands were rough stones against our flesh.

But Mrs. Reynolds paused and looked down at me. It almost seemed accidental, that looking, as if she'd forgotten for a half second that I was an inmate and saw instead a young girl asking for a book.

Her eyes skittered away from mine like startled mice. She tightened the cuffs until I could feel my pulse thumping in my fingertips and left without looking at me again.

I wept then, unable even to wipe the glistening snot-trail away from my lip, unable to press my face into the pillow or curl my head into my knees. I kept crying anyway, listening to the shuffling sounds of women in the halls until the pillowcase was damp beneath my head and the hallways went silent. The electric lights buzzed and crackled as they clicked off.

It was harder, in the darkness, not to think about Mr. Havemeyer. His white fingers spidering toward me out of the gloom, his blue-tinged flesh glowing in the moonlight.

And then a key scraped and thunked and my door eased open. I spasmed against my restraints, heart seizing, already seeing his black-suited form edge into the room, his cane *tap-tapping* nearer—

But it wasn't Havemeyer; it was Mrs. Reynolds. With *The Ten Thousand Doors* tucked beneath her arm.

She scurried to my bedside, a furtive white smear in the darkness. She tucked the book beneath my sheets and unfastened my cuffs with fumbling fingers. I opened my mouth but she shook her head without looking at me, and left. The lock snicked behind her.

I just held it, at first; rubbed my thumb against the worn lettering, inhaled the faraway, free scent of it.

And then I edged into the slanting moonlight, opened the book, and ran away.

Chapter Four

On Love

Love takes root—Love takes to the sea—The
simultaneously predictable and miraculous
results of love

It is fashionable among intellectuals and sophisticates to scoff at
true love—to pretend it is nothing but a sweet fairy tale sold to children and young women, to be taken as seriously as magic wands
or glass slippers.[11] I feel nothing but pity for these learned persons,
because they would not say such foolish things if they had ever
experienced love for themselves.

I wish they could have been present at the meeting of Yule Ian
and Adelaide Lee in 1893. No one watching their bodies crash
together in the waist-deep surf, watching their eyes glow like light-
houses leading stray ships home at last, could have denied the presence of love. It hung between them like a tiny sun, radiating heat,
remaking their faces in red and gold.

But even I must admit that love is not always graceful. After
Ade and Yule peeled themselves apart they were left standing in
the waves, staring at the perfect stranger before them. What do
you say to a woman you had met only once in a hayfield in another
world? What do you say to a ghost boy whose boot-leather eyes have

---

11. I hope you are sufficiently familiar with the nature of doors by this juncture to
assume that both magic wands and glass slippers exist in plentitude, in some world or
other.

haunted you for twelve years? Both of them spoke at once; both of them stuttered to silence.

Then Ade said, passionately, "Shit," and after a pause, *"Shit."* She ran her fingers through her hair and smeared seawater on too-warm cheeks. "Is it really you, ghost boy? What's your name?"

The question was a perfectly natural one, but it dimmed the sun between them. Both of them became abruptly aware of how unlikely it was that two people who did not even know one another's names should be in love.

"Yule Ian." It came out in a rushing whisper.

"Nice to meet you, Julian. Could you give me a hand?" She gestured back toward her boat, now bobbing amiably southward. It took long minutes of wrangling and thrashing before the two of them had the little ship hauled into the bay and anchored to a standing stone in the surf. They worked in silence, studying the movements of each other's bodies, the miraculous geometry of bone and muscle, as if it were a secret code they'd been assigned to translate. Then they stood on the shore in the red bloom of sunset, and it became difficult to look directly at one another again.

"Would you like—I have a place to stay, in the City." Yule thought of his cramped room on a washerwoman's second floor, and wished very much that he were inviting Ade to a castle or palace or at least one of the costly balconied bedrooms rented by traveling merchants. Ade nodded, and they wound back up through the City of Plumm side by side. The backs of their hands brushed timidly together sometimes on the narrow streets but never lingered. Yule felt the heat of those passages like matches struck against his skin.

In his room he perched her on the end of the unmade cot and skittered briefly in circles, consolidating piles of books and raking empty ink bottles into corners. Ade didn't say anything at all. If Yule had known her for longer than a few hours in her youth, he would've realized how very unusual this was. Adelaide Lee was a woman who wore her desires openly, without shame or artifice, and generally expected the world to accommodate them. But now she sat in a cluttered room that smelled of ocean and ink, and could not find the right words.

Yule sat hesitantly beside her. "How have you come here?" he asked.

"Sailed through a door on a mountaintop back in my world. Sorry it took me so long to get here, it's just there are an awful lot of doors out there." A little of her usual swagger slunk back into her voice.

"You were looking for this world? For me?"

Ade tilted her head at him. "Of course."

Yule smiled, hugely, and it seemed to Ade it was a smile stolen from a much younger boy. It was the same smile he'd given her in the field when she promised to meet him in three days, giddy at his own good luck, and it was suddenly clear to Ade what she ought to do next.

She kissed him. She felt the grinning curves of his lips reshape themselves against hers, his delicate scholar's hands settle lightly on her shoulders. Ade pulled back very briefly to look at him—the red-edged dark of his skin, the very different smile now gleaming at her like a scimitar moon, the seriousness of his eyes on her face—then laughed, once, and pushed him downward.

Outside Yule's room, the City of Plumm sank into a sweet evening stupor, its citizens caught in that quiet hour after dinner but before nightfall. Beyond Plumm the Amarico Sea *shush-shush*ed itself against a thousand tarry hulls and rocky islands, and blew salt-heavy breezes through doors into other skies, and all the ten thousand worlds reeled in ten thousand twilit dances. But for the first time in their lives, neither Ade nor Yule cared about these other worlds, for their own universe was now contained in a narrow cot on a washerwoman's second floor in the City of Plumm. It was some days before they emerged.

Once we have agreed that true love exists, we may consider its nature. It is not, as many misguided poets would have you believe, an event in and of itself; it is not something that *happens*, but something that simply *is* and always has been. One does not fall in love; one discovers it.

It was this archaeological process that so occupied Ade and Yule during their days in the washerwoman's room. They discovered their love first through the strange and miraculous language of the body: through skin and cinnamon-sweat, the pink-edged creases left by rumpled sheets, the deltas of veins charting the backs of their hands. To Yule it was an entirely new language; to Ade it was like relearning a language she thought she already knew.

But soon spoken words filtered into the spaces between them. Through the underwater heat of the humid afternoons and into the relief of the cool nights, they told one another twelve years of stories. Ade told her story first, and it was a thrilling confabulation of starlit train rides and foot-worn journeys, of leaving and coming, of doors standing slantwise in the dusk, half-open. Yule found he couldn't listen to her without a pen in his hand, as if she were an archival scroll sprung to life, which he had to document before she vanished.

She finished with the story of Mount Silverheels and the door to the sea, and only laughed when Yule pressed her for details and dates and specifics. "That's exactly the kind of nonsense that ruins a good yarn. No, sir. About time you told me *your* story, don't you think?"

He lay on his stomach on the cool stone floor, legs tangled in sheets and forearms smeary with ink. "My story is your story, I think." He shrugged.

"How do you mean?"

"I mean...That day in the field changed me just as it changed you. Both of us have spent our lives seeking out the secrets of doors, haven't we, following stories and myths." Yule laid his head on his arm and looked up at the golden sprawl of her in his cot. "Except my quest involved much more time in libraries."

He told her about his dreamy childhood and dedicated youth, his respected scholarly publications (which never directly asserted the existence of doors but merely presented them as mythological constructions offering valuable social insights), his unending quest to discover the truest nature of the doors between worlds.

"And what have you found out, Julian?" He reveled in the foreign, rolled-together way she said his name.

"Some," he said, gesturing at the many volumes of *A Comparative Study of Passages, Portals, and Entryways in World Mythology* that lay stacked on the desk. "And not enough."

She stood and leaned over his desk, perusing the angles of foreign words on the page. Her body looked strangely calicoed to Yule, her skin shifting dramatically from palest milk to burnt freckles. "All I know is there are these places—sort of thinned-out places, hard to see unless you're doing a certain kind of looking—where you can go to somewhere else. All kinds of somewhere elses, some of them packed full of magic. And they always *leak*, so all you have to do is follow the stories. What else you got?"

Yule wondered if all scholars dedicated their lives to questions that other people had already casually answered, and if they found it vexing or pleasing. He suspected Ade would often be both. "Not very much," he told her dryly. "There are, as you say, thinned-out places, where worlds bleed into one another. But I have this idea that this leakage is somehow...important. Vital, even."

Doors, he told her, are change, and change is a dangerous necessity. Doors are revolutions and upheavals, uncertainties and mysteries, axis points around which entire worlds can be turned. They are the beginnings and endings of every true story, the passages between that lead to adventures and madness and—here he smiled—even love. Without doors the worlds would grow stagnant, calcified, storyless.

He ended with a scholar's solemnity. "But I don't know where the doors come from in the first place. Have they always been there, or were they created? By who, and *how*? It might cost a word-worker her life to split the world open like that! Although—perhaps not, if the worlds are already hovering so close together. Perhaps it is more like drawing aside a veil, or opening a window. But they would first need to be persuaded that it was even possible, and I doubt—"

"Why's it matter so much where they came from?" Ade had lain down beside him while he spoke, watching him with a mix of admiration and levity.

"Because they seem so *fragile*. So easily closed. And if they can be destroyed but not created, won't there be fewer and fewer doors over the years? The thought... haunted me. I thought I might never find you." The weight of twelve years of fruitless searching pressed down on the two of them.

Ade flung an arm and leg over Yule's back. "That doesn't matter anymore. I found you anyhow, and there won't be any more closed doors for us." She said it so fiercely and fearlessly, a tigress growl rumbling in her ribs, that Yule believed her.

It took another generous handful of days before Ade and Yule could simply lie still and quiet beside one another in the cot, without the frenzied need to know one another. They had unearthed the rough shape of the love between them and were content to let the rest of it proceed more sedately, unfurling like an endless sea before their prow.

To Ade, it was a kind of homecoming: after years of rootless wandering, years of drifting down the subtle trails of stories with a restless ache in her heart, she found herself at last content to be still. To Yule, it was a departure. He had lived his life within the comforting confines of research and scholarship, driven to pursue his studies with single-minded fervor, rarely looking up toward the horizon. But now he found himself adrift, unmoored— what did his studies matter now? What were the mysteries of doors compared to the far grander mystery of Ade's long white heat stretched beside him?

"What do we do now?" he asked her one morning.

Ade had been half drowsing in the pink-pearl light of dawn. The worry in his voice made her laugh. "Anything we like, Julian. You could show me your world, for starters."

"All right." Yule was quiet for several long breaths. "There's something I would like to do, first." He rose and scrabbled through his desk for a pen and a thick, jellied bottle of ink. He crouched beside the cot and stretched her left arm straight against the sheets. "When something happens, something important, we write it down.

If it is something important that everyone ought to know, we write it down here." He tapped the softness of her inner wrist.

"And what are you going to write?"

His eyes, when they met hers, went solemn and dark as underground pools. Ade felt a slight tremor in her belly. "I would like to write: *On this day in the summer of 6920, Adelaide Lee Larson and Yule Ian Scholar found love, and did swear to keep it eternally.*" He swallowed. "If you do not object, I mean. Written this way, in this ink, the words will last some weeks but they can still be washed away. It is only a kind of promise."

Ade's heart thrummed. "What happens if I decide I don't want to wash it off?"

Silently, Yule held up his left arm. Tattoos wound around it in tight, dark lines, naming him Scholar and listing his most prestigious publications. Ade looked at the markings very seriously for a moment, like a woman seeing her future and giving herself one last chance to turn away, then met Yule's gaze. "Why bother with the pen, then. Where can we get ourselves tattooed?"

A great bubble of giddy relief burst in Yule's chest. He laughed, and she kissed him, and when they left the washerwoman's home that afternoon there was fresh black ink circling their entwined hands, spelling out their futures for the world to see.

They spent the following hours shopping in Plumm's bright-awninged marketplace. Yule negotiated for dried fruits and oats in short, practical phrases of American-common while Ade gathered a trail of fascinated onlookers like a ship's wake behind them. There were giggles and shrieks from skinny-armed children, pitying mutters from market women, rumbling gossip from the fishers who'd heard rumors of the ghost woman.

Yule hired a wobbly cart to pull their supplies down to the eastern beach, where Ade's fat little ship still bobbed in the bay. They spent the night tucked beneath a spare scrap of canvas in the boat bottom, listening to the sluicing of waves against the pine-tarred hull and watching the night wheel over them like a dancer's star-studded skirt. Ade nestled into the softness of his arm and thought about happily-ever-afters and sweet-tasting endings. Yule thought about once-upon-a-times and bold beginnings.

At dawn they departed. When asked what she wanted to see, Ade replied, *"Everything,"* so Yule obediently charted a course toward everything. They docked first at the City of Sissly, where Ade could admire the pink domes of the local chapels and taste the pepper-bite of fresh gwanna fruit. Then they stayed three nights on the abandoned Island of Tho, where the ruins of a failed City loomed like broken gray teeth against the sun, before skipping along a string of low, sand-scoured islands too small to be named. They walked the streets of the City of Yef and slept in the cool grottoes of the City of Jungil, and walked across the famed bridge connecting the twin Cities of Iyo and Ivo. They sailed north and west, following the summer currents out of the sweating heat of the equator, and saw Cities so distant even Yule had only read their names on his charts.

Yule's scholar's stipend, meant for the renting of small rooms and the eating of plain meals, was not so generous that they could supply themselves endlessly from City markets. Instead Yule fumbled to recall his father's long-ago lessons in knot tying and hook setting, and fished for their dinner. Ade cut and bent thin saplings and built them a kind of arched bower in the stern of the ship where they could shelter from the sun and rain. In the crowded City of Cain, Yule bought a spool of waxed thread and an iron needle as long as his palm. They spent a day floating in Cain's harbor while Yule stitched blessings into their scandalously bare sailcloth. He wrote all the usual prayers for good weather and safe passage, but where most ships added some specific dedication—to fruitful fishing or profitable trading or comfortable travel—he wrote only *to love*. Ade saw the word twined around her wrist mirrored on the sail, and kissed his cheek, laughing.

It was difficult to imagine an ending to those golden months they spent on *The Key*. The summer heat faded and was replaced with the cool, high winds of the trading season, when the Amarico was so trafficked with ships the sea itself was scented with spice and oil and fine flaxen paper. Yule and Ade traced love-drunk spirals through the currents, winding back southward on white-edged waves, planning no further than the next island, the next City, the next night spent curled together on some empty beach. Yule thought they might go on forever like that.

Yule was, of course, mistaken. True love is not stagnant; it is in fact a door, through which all kinds of miraculous and dangerous things may enter.

"Julian, love, wake up." They had spent the night on a small, pine-covered island, occupied only by woodsmen and goatherds. Yule was nestled deep in their bed of canvas and cloth, sweating out the juniper-berry wine of the previous evening, but he peeled his eyes open at Ade's call.

"Nng?" he asked articulately.

She was sitting with her back to the sea, crosshatched by the dawn light slinking through pine branches. Her straw-colored hair hung around her shoulders in a jagged line where she'd made Yule cut it with his fishing knife, and her skin had turned a rawish, unlikely shade of burnt brown. She wore the practical wrapping of a sailor woman but hadn't yet mastered the folds and tucks it required, so that her clothes hung around her body like loose netting. Yule thought she was the most beautiful thing in his or any other world.

"There's something I need to tell you." Ade was rubbing the black words still staining her left wrist. "Something pretty big, I guess."

Yule looked more closely at her, but her expression was unfamiliar to him. In their months together he'd seen her exhausted and elated, furious and fanged, bored and brave; he'd never seen her fearful. The emotion sat like a foreign tourist on Ade's features.

She blew out a breath and closed her eyes. "Julian. I think— well, I *know*, actually, I've been pretty sure for a while now—I'm going to have a baby."

The world hung suspended. The waves ceased their slapping, the pine boughs no longer brushed together, even the small creatures in the earth stopped their burrowing. Yule wasn't certain his heart was still beating, except that he didn't seem to be dead.

"Well, you don't have to look so damned surprised. I mean, two people doing what we've been doing for half a year, you'd have to be downright stupid not to think we might—that I might—" Ade sucked her breath through tight-clenched teeth.

But it was difficult for Yule to hear her clearly, because the momentary silence had given way to something raucous and celebratory, as if his own stuttering heart had been replaced with a City parade. He strove to respond gently, cautiously. "What will you do?"

Ade's eyes widened and her fingers splayed helplessly over her own stomach, as if warding him away. "Doesn't seem like I have much choice, does it."[12] But there was no bitterness or regret in her voice, only that chill fear. "But men do, don't they. Lord knows my father wasn't—he didn't—what will *you* do?"

And Yule realized then what should have been obvious: it wasn't the baby Ade was frightened of, but *him*. It was such an enormous relief that Yule laughed, a great shout of joy that scattered the birds perched above them and made Ade bite her cheek with sudden hope.

Yule tossed his blankets aside and crawled to her. He took her hands—scarred and burnt, blunt-nailed and beautiful—in his. "Here's what I will do, if you will let me: I will take you back to Nin and marry you, and find someplace to make a home for us. And the three of us—or four of us? Or six?—wait till you meet my brothers and sisters—will spend our winters in Nin and our summers sailing, and I will love you and our child more than any man has loved anything. I will never leave either of you as long as I live."

He watched the fear in her face vanish. It was replaced by some burning, luminous thing that made Yule think of sea divers

---

12. In fact, she did have a choice. Ade had perhaps forgotten that she was in Yule's world, rather than her own, and Yule's world had word-workers. Pregnancy is a fragile, uncertain thing, especially at the beginning, and any sufficiently skilled and well-compensated word-worker may usually write away an unwanted child while it is still only a faint glimmer of potential in its mother's body.

standing at the edges of cliffs or word-workers staring at the blank page. "Yes," she said, and their whole lives lay in that single word.

If only Yule had been a better man, he might have kept his promise—to his daughter, if not to his wife.

Yule's own mother tattooed their wedding vows on their arms. She worked with her white-knotted hair pulled back beneath a kerchief and her needles up-and-downing in the same rhythm Yule knew from childhood. It still seemed to him a kind of magic to see words emerging in the blood-and-ink trail of the needle like dawn following some old god's chariot. For Ade the ritual lacked the weight of tradition, but she still caught her breath at the strange beauty of dark lines twisting up her forearm, and when she pressed her arm against Yule's so their red-black wounds touched, and spoke the inked words out loud, she still felt something tectonic shifting beneath her feet.

The traditional Signing of the Blessings followed their vows. Yule's parents—wearing bemused, affable expressions that indicated they didn't quite understand how their son came to be married to a milk-pale foreigner with nothing to her name but the world's ugliest boat, but were happy for him anyway—hosted the gathering, and all Yule's cousins and stoop-backed aunties and university fellows came crowding in to have their prayers for the newlyweds recorded in the family book. They lingered to eat and drink themselves into a traditional stupor, and Ade spent her third night in the City of Nin crammed into Yule's childhood bed, watching his cut-tin stars twirl overhead.

It took another week for Yule to wrangle a new arrangement between himself and the university. He announced that he had finished with his researches in the field and needed time and quiet to compile his thoughts, and would also like a stipend large enough to support a wife and child. They balked; he insisted. In the end, and after much muttering about his expected future contributions to the university's reputation, the master required him to teach three times a week in the City square and provided him enough pay to afford a small stone house on the high northern hillside of the island.

The house was a tired, settling sort of structure, half-buried in the hill behind it, which emitted a strong smell of goats on warm afternoons. It had only two rooms, a blackened oven occupied by several generations of mice, and a bed of straw-stuffed canvas. The mason who chiseled their names into the stone mantel thought privately it was a grim, lean home for a young family, but to Yule and Ade it was the most beautiful building ever to claim four walls and a rooftop. This is the mad Midas touch of true love, which transforms everything it touches to gold.

Winter crept over Nin stealthily, like a great white cat made of chill mists and sharp-edged winds. Ade was entirely unimpressed by it, and laughed at Yule as he wrapped woolen cloths around his chest and shivered by the bread oven. She went on long walks through the hills, dressed only in her summer things, and returned with wind-scoured cheeks.

"Won't you take something warmer?" Yule pleaded one morning. "For his sake?" He snaked an arm around the gentle slope of her belly.

She laughed at him, pulling away. "*Her* sake, I think you mean."

"Mm. Well, perhaps you'd wear—this?" he said, and pulled from behind his back a brownish, rough-looking canvas coat, as foreign to his world as it was familiar in hers.

She fell still. "You kept it? All these years?"

"Of course." He whispered it into the salt-smelling tangle of hair at the back of her neck, and her walk that morning was somewhat delayed.

Spring in Nin was a season of saturation. Warm rains turned every trail to mud and every stone to moss. Their neat-folded clothes molded in their stacks and bread grew stale almost before it cooled. Ade spent more time down in the City with Yule, swaying up and down rain-slicked streets and practicing her abysmal Amarican on every passing citizen, or working with Yule's father to scrub small, shelled creatures off the keels of his fishing boats. She took care of *The Key*, too, adjusting and rebuilding under Yule's father's direction until it sat a little more jauntily at the dock, its mast thinner and taller and its hull well sealed. She liked to watch it rocking in the waves and feel her baby rolling beneath her ribs. *One day she'll be yours*, Ade told her, *one day you and* The Key *will sail off into the sunset.*

In midsummer, in the sun-bleached month Ade called July, Yule returned to their home to find Ade swearing and bent over, pearled sweat slicking her skin.

"Is it—he's coming?"

"...She," Ade panted, and she looked at Yule with the expression of a young soldier charging into her first battle. Yule gripped her hands, their tattoos twining like paired snakes up their wrists, and made the same desperate, silent prayers that every father makes in that moment: that his wife would live, that his child would be whole and healthy, that he would hold them both in his arms before dawn.

And, in the world's most often-repeated and transcendent miracle, his prayers were granted.

Their daughter was born just before sunrise. She had skin the color of cedarwood and eyes like wheat.

They named her for an old, half-forgotten god from Ade's own world, whom Yule had studied once in an ancient text preserved in Nin's archives. He was a strange god, depicted in the faded manuscript with two faces staring both backward and forward. He presided not over one particular domain but over the places between—past and present, here and there, endings and beginnings—over doorways, in short.

But Ade thought Janus sounded too much like Jane, and she'd be damned if any daughter of hers would be named Jane. They named her after the god's own month instead: January.

Oh my sweet daughter, my perfect January, I would beg for your forgiveness, but I lack the courage.

All I can ask for is your belief. Believe in doors and worlds and the Written. Believe most of all in our love for you—even if the only evidence we've left you is contained in the book you now hold.

The Door of Blood
and Silver

When I was a child, breakfast was twenty minutes of absolute silence seated across from Miss Wilda, who believed that conversation interfered with digestion and that jam and butter were only for holidays. After her departure I joined Mr. Locke for breakfast at his enormous polished dining table, where I did my best to impress him with my good posture and ladylike silence. Then Jane arrived and breakfasts became stolen coffee in a forgotten sitting room or jumbled attic room, where everything smelled of dust and sunlight and Bad could disperse fine bronze hairs on the armchairs without rebuke.

At Brattleboro, breakfast was the splat of porridge ladled

into tin bowls, the pale filtering of light from high windows, the click of the attendants' heels down the aisles.

Good behavior had granted me the right to join the murmuring flock of women who ate in the dining hall. I was seated that morning beside a mismatched pair of white women: one of them was old, narrow, and pursed-looking, with her hair drawn into a bun so severe it tugged her eyebrows into little arches; the other was young and wide, with moist gray eyes and chapped lips.

Both of them stared as I sat down. It was a familiar stare: a mistrustful, what-exactly-are-you stare that felt like a knife blade pressed to my flesh.

But not that morning. That morning my skin was shining plated armor, it was silver snakeskin, it was invulnerable; that morning I was the daughter of Yule Ian Scholar and Adelaide Lee Larson, and those eyes could not touch me.

"You going to eat that?" The gray-eyed girl had apparently determined I wasn't so odd she couldn't ask for my biscuit. It sat half-sunk in my porridge, a flattish lump the color of fish scales.

"No."

She took the biscuit, sucking the dampness out of it. "I'm Abby," she offered. "That's Miss Margaret." The older woman didn't look at me, but her face pinched further inward.

"January Scaller," I said politely, but I thought: *January Scholar*. Like my father before me. The thought was a lantern glow in my chest, a brightness so real I thought it must be leaking from me like light around a closed door.

Miss Margaret gave a faint, high-bred snort, perfectly calibrated to be mistaken for a sniff. I wondered what she'd been before she was a madwoman—an heiress? A banker's wife? "And what kind of a name is that, exactly?" She still wasn't looking at me but addressed her question to the air.

The lantern in my chest glowed brighter. "Mine." All

mine. Given to me by my own true parents, who loved one another, who loved me—who had abandoned me, somehow. The lantern glow dimmed a little, flickering in a sudden draft.

What happened to that little stone house on the hillside, to *The Key*, to my mother and father?

I almost didn't want to know. I wanted to linger as long as I could in the fragile, fleeting past, in that brief happily-ever-after when I'd had a home and a family. Last night I'd stuffed *The Ten Thousand Doors* beneath my mattress rather than read another page and risk losing it all.

Abby was blinking her damp eyes into the sudden silence. "I got a telegram from my brother this morning. I'm going home on Tuesday, or maybe Wednesday, he said." Margaret snorted again. Abby ignored her. "Do you think you'll stay long?" she asked me.

No. There was too much to do—finish my damn book, find Jane, find my father, write it all *right* again—to stay locked up here like some tragic orphan girl in a Gothic novel. Plus, if I stayed past dark I was three quarters certain a vampire would climb through my window and eat me.

I had to find a way out. And wasn't I the daughter of Yule and Ade, born beneath the sun of another world? Wasn't I named after the god of in-betweens and passageways, the god of Doors? How could I be locked away, really? My very blood seemed a sort of key, an ink with which I could write myself a new story.

Ah. Blood.

A slow smile peeled my lips back over my teeth. "No, I don't think so," I answered breezily. "I've just got so much to do." Abby nodded contentedly and launched into a long and unlikely story about the picnic she would have when she arrived back home, and how her brother really missed her very much, and it wasn't his fault she was such a trying sister.

We left the hall in the same gray lines. I tried to make my

shoulders curve inward and my back stoop, like everyone else's, and when Mrs. Reynolds and another nurse escorted me into my room I said "Thank you" in a soft, docile voice. Mrs. Reynolds's eyes flicked up to mine, then away. They did not cuff me to the bed when they left.

I waited until their steps had clicked down the hall to the next locked door, then dove for my mattress. I ran my fingertips along the spine of my father's book, lightly, but left it where it lay. Instead, I found the cool silver of the coin from the City of Nin.

It sat heavy in my palm, wider than a half-dollar and twice as thick. The queen smiled up at me.

Slowly, I scrubbed the edge of the coin against the rough cement stucco of the wall beside my bed. I held it back up to the light and saw that the smooth curve of the coin had been worn away, ever so slightly.

I smiled—the desperate smile of a prisoner as she digs her escape tunnel—and pressed the coin back against the wall.

By dinner, my arm muscles were wrung-out rags and my finger joints ached where they curled around the coin. Except that it wasn't a coin anymore. There were two angled sides leading to a single point, with nothing left of the queen's face except one wise eye in the center. I kept scraping after dinner, because I wanted to be sure it was sharp enough and also because I was scared.

But night was coming—I watched the light on my bare walls turn from rose to palest yellow to dim ash—and Havemeyer would return soon. Creeping like a penny-dreadful monster along the halls, reaching his cold fingers out for me, drinking the warmth from my flesh...

I rolled back my blankets, pressed bare feet to the floor, and crept to the locked door.

The coin lay gleaming and thin in my palm, transformed

into a tiny blade or a sharp silver pen nib. I touched it lightly to my fingertip, thought of Havemeyer's hungry eyes, and pressed down.

By moonlight, blood looks like ink. I knelt and drew my finger across the floor in a shaky line, but the blood beaded and pearled on the slick-polished tile. I squeezed my hand, forced the reluctant drops into a puddled, smeary *T*, but I already knew it wouldn't work: it would take too much blood, and too much time.

I swallowed. I laid my left arm across my knees and tried to think of it as paper or clay or slate, something not-alive. I touched the silver knife to my skin, right where the stringy muscle of my forearm joined up to my elbow.

I thought *Hold On January*, and began to write.

It hurt less than I'd thought it would. No, that's a lie—it hurt precisely as much as you'd think to carve letters into your own flesh, deep enough for blood to boil up like red oil wells; it's just that sometimes pain is too unavoidable, too necessary to feel.

THE DOOR

I was careful to cut my lines away from the ropy veins in the middle of my forearm, out of a dim sense that I might exsanguinate myself on the hospital floor and cut my whole escape attempt tragically short. But I was equally afraid of cutting too lightly, as if it might signal some secret hesitancy or unbelief. It's believing that matters, remember.

THE DOOR OPENS FOR HER.

The coin edge bit and twisted around the period, and I believed it with all my shaken heart.

The room did that same almost-familiar reshuffling of itself, a subtle wrenching, as if an invisible housewife were tugging at the corners of reality to shake out the wrinkles. I screwed my eyes shut and waited, hope thudding through my veins and dripping out onto the floor—God help me if it didn't work—in the morning they'd find me lying in the curdling muck of my own blood—at least Havemeyer wouldn't have any life-heat left to steal—

The lock clicked. I opened my eyes, blinking through sudden exhaustion. The door swung inward just slightly, as if pulled by a faint breeze.

I slouched forward and rested my forehead against the tile, letting waves of fatigue roll and crash over me. My eyes wanted to close; my ribs ached as if I'd swum to the bottom of the lake and back.

But he was coming, and I couldn't stay.

I limped back to the bed in a three-limbed crawl, smearing red behind me, and fumbled for my book. I hugged it close to me, just for a moment, breathing in that spice-and-ocean smell. It smelled exactly like my father's ancient, shapeless coat, which he left draped over the back of his chair at dinner whenever he was home. How had I never realized that before?

I tucked the book beneath my arm, gripped the coin-knife tight in my palm, and left.

There was no Threshold here, of course, but stepping from my room into the hall was still crossing from one world into another. I swept down the hall with my stiff gown rustling against my legs and blood *drip-drip*ping behind me in a long line of spatters. I thought absurdly of bread-crumb trails leading through dark fairy-tale forests, and quashed a slightly hysterical urge to laugh.

I crept down two flights of stairs and into the pristine white of the front lobby. I passed doors with neat gold lettering on the glass, blinking blurring eyes at the titles. *Dr. Stephen J. Palmer.* I had an irrational urge to slip into his office and upend all his neat files and folders, shred all his careful notes—perhaps steal that hideous pen of his—but I kept padding forward.

The entranceway was cool marble beneath my bare feet. I was reaching for the stately double-paned doors, already smelling summer grass and freedom, when I realized two things simultaneously: first, that I could hear raised voices echoing on the floor above, a rising clamor of alarm, and that I'd left a spattered red trail through the halls leading directly to the front doors. And second, that there was a blurred figure standing on the other side of the door, drawn in shadow and moonlight. The tall, attenuated silhouette of a man.

No.

My legs went weak and slow, as if I were wading through knee-deep sand. The silhouette sharpened as it came closer. The doorknob turned, the door opened, and Havemeyer stood framed on the threshold. He had abandoned his cane and gloves, and his white-spider hands hung naked by his sides. His skin was lambent and alien in the darkness, and I suddenly thought how strange it was that he seemed so human by daylight.

His eyes widened as he saw me. He smiled—a predatory, life-hungry smile, and God help you if you've ever seen a smile like that on a human face—and I ran.

The voices had grown louder, and electric lights snapped and buzzed ahead of me. White-frocked nurses and staff were scurrying toward me, shouting and scolding. But I could feel Havemeyer behind me like a malevolent wind and I kept running until I was nearly face-to-face with them. They slowed, hands raised in placating gestures, voices soothing. They seemed reluctant to touch me, and I had a brief disorienting vision of myself through their eyes: a feral, in-between-girl with blood staining her nightgown and words carved like prayers into her flesh. Teeth bared, eyes fear-black. Mr. Locke's good girl had been replaced by someone else entirely.

Someone who wasn't prepared to surrender.

I dove sideways through an unlabeled wooden door. Brooms

and buckets crashed around me in the dark, an ammonia-and-lye smell: a janitor's closet. A dangling pull-cord turned on the light and I jammed a stepladder inexpertly beneath the doorknob. Heroes were always doing that in my stories, but it looked much more tenuous in real life.

Running footsteps pounded outside the door and the knob gave a violent rattle, followed by swearing and shouting. An ominous thump shook the ladder. My pulse rocketed and I fought the panicky whine in my throat. There was nowhere left to run, no doors left to open.

Hold On January. The stepladder made a worrying splintery sound.

I needed to run, far and fast. I thought of the blue door to the sea; of my father's world; of Samuel's world, his cabin by the lake. I looked down at my left arm, thrumming now with pain like a marching band in the distance, and thought: *Why the hell not?*

I hesitated for a half second. *It comes at a cost,* my father had said; *power always does.* How much would it cost to split the world open like this? Could I afford to pay it, shivering and bleeding in a broom closet?

"Come, now, Miss Scaller," a voice hissed through the door. "How childish." It was a very patient voice, like a wolf circling a treed animal, waiting.

I swallowed cold terror, and began.

I started high on my shoulder, where I could barely reach, and kept my letters tight and small. *SHE WRITES A DOOR*

The thundering sounds on the closet door paused, and that cold voice said, "Out of my *way.*" Then came harassed-sounding bickering, shuffling footsteps, and much stronger, frame-rattling thuds.

OF BLOOD

Where? My eyes felt distant in my skull, as if they longed to soar upward and leave my bleeding, hurting body on its own.

I didn't have an address, couldn't even point to the place on a map, but it didn't matter. Believing is what matters. Willing.

AND SILVER. I curled the blade around the final letter and thought of Samuel.

The new letters quashed up next to the first sentence I'd written, so that it all ran together in a single story I desperately, madly believed: *She writes a Door of blood and silver. The Door opens for her.*

The stepladder gave a final, fatal crunch. The door pressed inward against the tumble of cleaning supplies and broken wood. But I didn't care, because at the same moment I felt the swirling, shifting madness of the world reshaping itself, followed by the most unlikely thing in the world: a fresh breeze against my back. It smelled of pine needles and cool earth and warm July lake water.

I turned and saw a strange, gaping wound in the wall behind me, a hole that glinted with rust and silver. It was an ugly, crudely drawn thing, like a child's chalk sketch made real, but I recognized it for what it was: a Door.

The closet door was wedged halfway open and a white-fingered hand was reaching around its edges. I scuttled backward, sliding through my own blood and realizing from the queer ache in my jaw that I was grinning a fierce, flesh-rending grin, like Bad when he was a few seconds away from biting somebody. I felt the Door at my back—a blessed absence, a pine-scented promise—and crammed myself through it, shoulders scraping raw against the rough-hewn edges.

I fell backward into the swallowing darkness and watched as faces and hands swarmed into the closet, a many-armed monster reaching after me. Then the nothingness of the Threshold ate me.

I'd forgotten how empty it was. *Empty* isn't even the right word, because something that's empty might once have been full, and it was impossible that anything had ever existed in the Threshold. I wasn't entirely sure I existed, and for a terrible moment I felt the edges of myself dissipating, unraveling.

That moment scares me even now, with solid wood beneath me and warm sun on my face.

But I felt the worn leather of *The Ten Thousand Doors* beneath my blood-sticky fingers and thought of my mother and father diving from world to world like rocks skipping across some vast black lake, unafraid of falling. Then I thought of Jane and Samuel and Bad, and then, as if their faces were a map unfurling in the void, I remembered where I was going.

Rough edges pressed against me again, and a darkness formed that was infinitely less dark than the Threshold. Musty wooden floorboards appeared beneath me. I fell forward and curled my fingernails against the floor as if I were clinging to a cliff face, the edges of my book pressing painfully, wonderfully against my ribs. My heart, which seemed to have disappeared in the Threshold, thundered into existence again.

"Who's there?" A shape moved across the floor, casting moon-edged shadows over me. Then, *"January?"* The voice was low and female, rolling through the vowels of my name in a fashion both foreign and familiar. The word *impossible* sprang to mind, but the past few days had fatally weakened my entire concept of what was and wasn't possible, and it slunk furtively away again.

Oily golden light flared. And there she was: short hair limned with lamplight, dress disheveled, mouth slightly open as she knelt beside me.

"Jane." My head felt far too heavy. I laid it down and spoke to the floor. "Thank God you're here. Wherever here is. I know where I was aiming, but you never know, with Doors, do you." My words were soupy and slurred-sounding in my

ears, as if I were shouting underwater. The lamplight seemed to be dimming. "But how did you get here?"

"I think the more interesting question is how *you* got here. 'Here' being the Zappia family cabin, by the way." The dryness of her tone felt brittle, forced. "And what happened to you—there's blood everywhere—"

But I was no longer listening. I'd heard a sound from the shadowy edges of the room—a lurching, dragging sound, followed by the click of claws on wood—and ceased to breathe. The footsteps padded closer, moving with an uneven hesitancy. *Impossible.* I raised my head.

Bad limped into the light. One eye was swollen, his back leg was hovering and shaking above the ground, and his head hung low and haggard. For a stretched half second he blinked at me, as if unsure it was really me, and then we dove toward one another. We collided, a desperate mess of dark limbs and yellow fur. He rooted around my neck and armpits as if trying to find a place he could crawl into, making a hoarse, puppyish whine I'd never heard from him before. I wrapped my arms around him, resting my forehead against his shivering shoulder and saying all the stupid, inane things you say when your dog is hurt (*I know, love, it's all right, I'm here, I'm sorry, I'm sorry*). Some jagged, broken thing in my chest began to mend.

Jane cleared her throat. "I hate to interrupt, but should there be anything...else, coming out of this hole?"

I went still. Bad's tail ceased its thumping against the floor. Scuffling, creeping sounds echoed behind me, like something crawling closer. I looked back over my shoulder at my Door— a ragged black tear, as if reality had been careless and caught itself on a loose nail—and saw, or thought I saw, a malevolent gleaming in its depths, like a pair of hungry eyes.

"He's coming for me." My voice was calm, almost detached,

while my thoughts ran in terrified circles. Havemeyer would emerge, white and wicked, and take whatever it was he wanted from me. Others would follow once they gathered their courage. They'd lock me up forever, if there was anything left of me to lock up, and probably Jane too. Certainly nothing good would happen to an African woman found in the company of a clinically insane fugitive at midnight. And who would take care of poor, battered Bad?

"I think I have to—I have to close it." Anything open can be closed. Hadn't my father discovered that when the Door closed between the City of Nin and my mother's field? He'd never known why or how it happened, but then, my father was a scholar: his tools were careful study and rational evidence and years and years of documentation.

My tools were words and will, and I was out of time. I found my coin-knife, so blood-crusted it no longer gleamed silver. I pulled my knees under my belly and laid my poor, aching arm before me. I pressed the coin to my skin a final time, blinking a little against the weird blurring and unblurring of the room.

"*No!* January, what are you—" Jane tugged my hand away.

"Please." I swallowed, swaying a little. "Please trust me. Believe me." There was no reason in the world she should. Anyone else would have happily dragged me back to the doctors with a note pinned to my chest suggesting they lock me in a small room without any sharp objects for the next century or so.

(This was the true violence Mr. Locke had done to me. You don't really know how fragile and fleeting your own voice is until you watch a rich man take it away as easily as signing a bank loan.)

The scuffling sounds grew louder.

Her eyes flicked to the hole in the wall behind me, and to the congealed lettering on my arm. A strange expression moved across her face—shrewdness, perhaps? A wary under-standing?—and she let go of my hand.

I chose a bare, unbloodied patch of skin, and began to carve a single word: *JU*

Movement in the blackness, the harsh sound of breathing, a white-spider hand reaching out of the darkness toward me—
JUST.

The Door opens just for her.

I felt the world pull itself back together, like skin pulling tight around a scar. The blackness receded, the white hand spasmed—there was a terrible, inhuman screech—and then I was staring at nothing but a patch of unremarkable cabin wall.

The Door was closed.

Then my cheek was pressed to the floor and Jane's cool hand was on my forehead. Bad limped closer and lay down with his spine pressed against me.

My last, wavering sight was of three odd, pale objects lying in a row on the floorboards. They looked like the white ends of some unusual mushroom, or maybe candle stubs. I'd already closed my eyes and begun to drift into a pain-hazed sleep when I recognized them for what they were: three white fingertips.

I was somewhere else for a while. I don't know where, exactly, but it felt like another kind of Threshold: lightless and endless, a silent galaxy without stars or planets or moons. Except I wasn't passing through; I was just—suspended. Waiting. I remember a vague sense that it was a nice place, free of monsters and blood and pain, and I'd quite like to stay.

But something kept intruding. A warm, breathing some-thing that nestled against my side and rooted in my hair, making small, whimpering sounds.

Bad. Bad was alive, and he needed me.

So I rose up out of the black and opened my eyes.

"Hello, you." My tongue was cottony and thick, but Bad's ears pricked. He made that whining sound in his chest again, somehow inching closer to me despite the absence of spare inches, and I laid my cheek on the warm slab of his shoulder. I made a motion to throw my arms around him but desisted with a small yelp.

It hurt. Everything hurt: my bones felt bruised and aching, as if they'd been forced to bear some impossible load; my left arm was too hot and throbbing, wrapped tightly in strips of sheet; even my blood beat sluggishly in my ears. In all, it seemed a fair price to pay for rewriting the very nature of space and time and crafting a Door of my own making. I blinked away an urge to laugh or possibly cry, and looked around.

It was a small cabin, like Samuel had said, and a little forlorn: the stacks of blankets were musty, the cookstove was rusting in orange flakes, the windows were cobweb-clogged. But the smell—oh, the smell. Sunshine and pine, lake water and wind— it was as if all the smells of summertime had soaked into the walls. It was the perfect, scientific opposite to Brattleboro.

It was only then that I noticed Jane, sitting at the foot of my bed with a steaming tin mug in her hands, watching Bad and me with a quirk at the corner of her mouth. Something about her had changed in the week we'd been apart. Maybe it was her clothes—her usual stodgy gray dress had been replaced by a calf-length skirt and loose cotton blouse—or maybe it was the sharp glitter of her eyes, as if she'd dispensed with a mask I hadn't known she was wearing.

I found myself suddenly uncertain. I looked at Bad's back as I spoke. "Where did you find him?"

"On the beach, in that little cove past the house. He was..." She hesitated, and I glanced up to see that the quirk in her mouth had flattened out. "Not in very good shape. Half-drowned, beaten bloody...It looked to me like someone dropped him over the bluff and hoped he'd drown." She lifted one shoulder. "I did the best I could for him. I don't know if that leg will ever be right." My fingers found clipped patches of fur and stubbly lines of stitches. His back leg had been splinted and wrapped.

I opened my mouth, but no words emerged. There are times when *thank you* is so inadequate, so dwarfed by the magnitude of the debt, that the words wilt in your throat.

Jane, in case you ever read this: *Thank you.*

I swallowed. "And how did...how are you here?"

"As you might have surmised, Mr. Locke called me down to his office to inform me that my services would no longer be needed. I became...agitated, and was escorted from the grounds by that damned eerie valet of his, without even packing my things. I came back that night, of course, but you were already gone. A failure for which I am"—her nostrils flared— "deeply sorry."

She gave her shoulders a shake. "Well. Brattleboro is a white institution, I'm told. I was not permitted to visit you. So I went to the Zappia boy, figuring Italian is close enough to white, but his visitation was also denied. Apparently he delivered my package by more, ah, efficient means." Her smile reappeared and widened enough to show the slim gap between her teeth. "Quite a devoted friend, isn't he?"

I didn't find it necessary to respond to that. She continued, primly. "And a very nice young man. He gave me this address, a place to think and plan, a place to sleep, since I was no longer welcome at Locke House."

"I'm sorry." My voice was small, feeble-sounding in my ears.

Jane snorted. "I'm not. I have despised that house and its owner since the moment I arrived. I tolerated it solely on the basis of a bargain your father and I struck. He asked me to protect you, in exchange for...something I wanted very badly."

Her expression turned inward, burning with a kind of bottomless, bleak rage that made my breath catch. She swallowed it away. "Which he is no longer in a position to provide."

I wrapped my arm tighter around Bad and made my voice as even and neutral as I could. "So you'll be leaving now. Going home."

I saw her eyes widen. "Now? And leave you sick and injured, hunted by gods-only-know-what? Julian might've broken the terms of our deal, but you and I have an entirely separate arrangement." I blinked at her, stupidly. Jane's expression softened as much as I'd ever seen it. "I am your friend, January. I will not abandon you."

"Oh." Neither of us spoke for a time. I let myself fall back into a sweaty half doze; Jane prodded the cookstove to life and reheated her coffee. She returned to the edge of the bed, scooting Bad's hind end aside and perching beside me. She held *The Ten Thousand Doors*—ruffled-looking, smeared with rust-red stains—on her knees, one thumb stroking the cover.

"You should sleep."

But I found I couldn't, quite. Questions buzzed and hummed in my ears, gnatlike: What had my father promised Jane? How had they met, really, and what was the book to her? And why had my father come to this gray, dull world at all?

I fidgeted beneath the quilt until Bad sighed at me. "Would—do you think you could read to me? I just finished the fourth chapter."

Jane's gap-toothed grin flashed at me. "Of course."

She opened the book and began to read.

Chapter Five

On Loss

Heaven—Hell

No one really remembers their own origins. Most of us possess a kind of hazy mythology about our early childhood, a set of stories told and retold by our parents, interwoven with our blurred baby memories. They tell us about the time we nearly died crawling down the stairs after the family cat; the way we used to smile in our sleep during thunderstorms; our first words and steps and birthday cakes. They tell us a hundred different stories, which are all the same story: *We love you, and have always loved you.*

But Yule Ian never told his daughter those stories. (You will permit me the continued cowardice of third-person narration, I hope; it is foolish, but I find it lessens the pain.) What, then, does she remember?

Not those first few nights when her parents watched the rise and fall of her rib cage with a kind of terrified elation. Nor the hot, raised feeling of fresh tattoos spiraling beneath their skin, spelling out new words (*mother, father, family*). Nor the way they sometimes looked at one another in the predawn glow, after hours of pacing and rocking and singing nonsense songs in half a dozen languages, with all their emotions written raw on their faces—a kind of stunned exhaustion, a slight hysteria, an unspeakable longing to simply *lie down*—and knew themselves to be the most profoundly lucky souls in ten thousand worlds.

She is unlikely to recall the evening her father climbed back up to the little stone house and found her sleeping beside her mother on the hillside. She was openmouthed, naked except for the cotton cloth tied around her waist, a faint breeze brushing through her curls. Ade was curled around her, a golden-white curve like a lioness or a nautilus, nestled into her milk-sweet breath. It was nearly the end of summer and the evening shadows were creeping toward the two of them on chill tiptoes—but hadn't reached them yet. The two of them were still shining, untouched, whole.

Yule stood on the hillside watching them, feeling an exultant, vaulting joy edged with melancholy, as if he were already mourning its loss. As if he knew he could not live in heaven forever.

It hurts me to speak of such things now. Even now as I write this—cowering in my tent in the foothills outside Ulaanbaatar, alone but for the scratching of my pen and the ice-rimed howling of wolves—I am grinding my teeth against waves of pain, an ache that settles in my limbs and poisons my marrow.

Do you recall the time you asked me about your name, and I said your mother liked it? You left annoyed, dissatisfied, the line of your jaw so precisely like hers I could hardly breathe. I tried to return to my work but couldn't. I crawled into bed, racked and shuddering, thinking of the shape of your mother's mouth when she said your name: January.

I missed dinner that night and left the next morning before dawn. You were rousted from bed to see me off, and your face through the carriage window—sleep-tousled, vaguely accusing—haunted me for months afterward. In the pain of my loss, I gave you the pain of absence.

I cannot fill that empty place now; I cannot dive backward in time and force myself to fling open the carriage door and run back to you, gather you close to me, and whisper in your ear: "We love you, we have always loved you." I have left it too late, and you are nearly grown. But I can give you at least an accounting of the facts, long overdue.

This is why you were raised in the pine-pocked snows of Vermont rather than the stone islands of the Amarico Sea in the world of the Written. This is why your father's eyes touch your face only rarely and lightly, as if you were a tiny sun that might blind him. This is why I am nearly six thousand miles away from you, hand cramping from the cold, alone but for the twin harpies of despair and hope hovering always by my side.

This is what happened to Yule Ian Scholar and Adelaide Lee Larson after the birth of their daughter, in the raw spring of the Written Year 6922.

It was earliest spring when Yule first noticed an expression on his wife's face he had not seen before. It was a kind of wistfulness, a tendency to gaze out at the horizon and sigh and forget, for a moment, what she was doing. At night she twisted and chafed, as if the quilt were a burdensome weight on her body, and woke before dawn to make tea and stare again out their kitchen window toward the sea.

One night as they lay breathing together in the dark, wrapped in the green smell of spring, Yule asked, "Is there something wrong, Adelaide?"

He asked in the language of the City of Nin, and she responded in the same manner. "No. Yes. I do not be knowing." She reverted to English. "It's just I'm not sure I like staying all tied up to one place. I love her, I love you, I love this house and this world, but . . . I feel like a mad dog on a short leash, some days." She rolled away from him. "Maybe everybody feels this way at first. Maybe it's just the season getting to me. I always did say springtime was made for leaving." Yule did not answer but lay awake listening to the distant sighing of the sea, thinking.

The following day he left the house early, while Ade and January were still sprawled in bed and the sky was not truly light but merely dreaming pale dreams. He was gone several hours, during which time he spoke to four people, spent the entirety of their modest savings, and signed three separate statements of debt and ownership. He returned to the stone cottage out of breath and beaming.

"How was teaching?" Ade asked. ("Ba!" January added imperiously.)

Yule plucked the baby from Ade's arms, winked, and said, "Come with me."

They spiraled down into the City, past the square and the university, past his mother's tattoo shop and the shoreline fish market, out onto the sun-warmed pier. Yule led her to the very end and stopped before a shapely little boat, larger and sleeker than *The Key*, with hastily stitched blessings in the sail for speed and adventure and freedom. There were supplies packed in canvas bags—nets and tarps, water barrels and smoked fish, dried apples, juniper wine, rope, a bright copper compass—and a tidy covered cabin at one end with a straw mattress inside.

Ade was quiet for so long that Yule's heart began to jitter and flutter with doubt. It is never advisable to make decisions before dawn or without consulting one's spouse, and he had done both.

"Is this ours?" Ade asked, finally.

Yule swallowed. "Yes."

"How did you—why?"

Yule lowered his voice and slipped his hand into hers so that their tattoos merged into a single black-inked page. "I will not be your leash, my love." Ade looked at him then, with a soaring expression so full of love that Yule knew he had done something not merely kind but utterly vital.

(Do I regret it? Would I take it back, if I could? Tell her to resign herself to home and hearth, to give up her wandering ways? It depends which weighs more: a life, or a soul.)

January, who had been clapping her hands at a huddle of harassed gulls, grew bored. The ship caught her attention instead, and she made the squawking sound they normally interpreted as "Give me that immediately."

Ade pressed her forehead to her daughter's. "I couldn't agree more, darlin'."

Two mornings later the City of Nin was shrinking behind them and the eastern horizon was clean and bright ahead of them, and Ade was kneeling in the prow, wearing her own shapeless farmer's coat and cradling her child close against her chest. Yule couldn't be sure, but he thought she might be whispering to January, telling her how it felt to have waves rolling beneath your feet, see strange cities silhouetted at twilight and hear unknown languages singing through the air.

They spent the following months like a small flock of birds on some circuitous migration of their own design, wheeling from City to City but never perching anywhere for long. Ade's skin, which had grown milk-soft over winter, turned freckled and burnt again, and her hair became a bleached, knotted mess reminiscent of a horse's mane. January turned a hot red-brown, like coals or cinnamon. Ade called her a "natural-born wanderer," on the theory that any baby who learned to crawl on the gentle swaying of the deck boards, who bathed in salt water and used a compass as a teething toy, ought to be destined for a journeying sort of life.

As spring deepened and the islands greened, Yule began to suspect their wandering was not entirely rudderless. They seemed to be heading east, however erratically and indirectly, and so he was not entirely surprised when Ade announced, one evening, that she missed her aunt Lizzie.

"I just think she ought to know I'm not molding in a ditch somewheres, and I think she'd like to see a new Larson girl. And a man who stuck around." What she did not say, but what Yule strongly suspected, was that she was homesick for the first time in her life. She spoke in the evenings about the smell of the Mississippi on a summer afternoon, the china-blue color of the sky above the hayfield. Something about having a child bends you back to your beginnings, as if you have been drawing a circle all your life and now are compelled to close it.

They restocked at the City of Plumm, where Ade and Yule had first found one another the year before. A few marketgoers remembered them, and word spread that the merwoman had married the scholar and produced a (disappointingly normal) girl-child, and by the time they departed there was a small crowd on the beach. January alternated between screeching at them in delight and burying

197

her face in her mother's shoulder, while Ade supplied satisfyingly nonsensical answers to their questions ("Where are we headed? To a mountaintop in Colorado, if you want to know the truth"). By sunset it had become a sort of picnic, and they shoved off with the warm glow of bonfires against their backs. The crowd watched them go with expressions ranging from curiosity to hilarity to alarm, calling out warnings and well-wishes as the sky turned from pink silk to blue velvet above them.

(I have thought often of these people in the years since, watching us sail away into the empty eastern sea. Did any of them come looking for us, when we failed to return? A curious trader or worried fisherman? What a slim hope to rest my heart upon.)

Yule wasn't accustomed to making such a fuss, but Ade laughed at him. "I've left a trail of faces just like that behind me in three dozen worlds. It's good for 'em. Trying to explain things that can't be explained is how you get stories and fairy tales, I figure." She looked down at January, curled in her lap and chewing pensively on her own knuckle. "Our girl will be a fairy tale before she can walk, Jule. Isn't that something? A natural-born wanderer if there ever was one."

Ade charted their course into the night, navigating by starlight and memory, with January sleeping against her chest. Yule watched from the cabin and drifted into dreams of his daughter as a grown woman: how she would speak six languages and outsail her father, how she would have her mother's brave and feral heart, how she would never be root-bound to a single home but would instead dance between the worlds on a path of her own making. She would be strong and shining and powerfully, beautifully strange, raised in the light of ten thousand suns.

Yule woke before dawn, when Ade crawled into the cabin and settled January between them. He fell back to sleep with his arm over both of them.

The wind grew wilder and colder away from the City islands. They spent the following days cutting across some unseen current, waves slapping against their hull like warnings and their sail

198

alternately stretched taut and luffing. Ade grinned into the salt spray like a hunting hawk with her quarry in sight. January crawled from stern to prow with a rope tied round her middle, rolling sometimes with the waves. Yule watched the horizon for Ade's door.

It appeared at dawn on the third day: two black crags emerging from the sea like dragon teeth, tilted toward one another with their stone tips nearly touching, so that a narrow passage of open sea lay between them. Morning fog curled and steamed around the doorway, obscuring and then revealing it. *Appears to avoid easy discovery,* Yule wrote in his journal, *which substantiates my initial premise.*

He tucked his notes away and stood in the prow with January bundled in his arms, her sleep-soft face peering out from the folds of Ade's worn coat. The sea had gone still and silent; their prow slid across it like a pen across the page. The shadow of the stones fell over the boat. Just before they slid into the passageway, across the threshold and into the black maw of the space between worlds, Yule Ian turned back to look at his wife.

Ade was crouched at the rudder, wide shoulders braced against the current, jaw set, eyes alive with fierce joy: in the thrill of diving through another doorway, perhaps, or in the glory of a life without borders or barriers, or in the simple pleasure of going home. Her hair was gathered in a loose honey-colored snarl over one shoulder, tangling with the winding lines of her tattoo. She'd changed since that first day Yule saw her in the cedar-strewn field more than a decade before—she was taller, broader, with merry lines gathering at the corners of her eyes and the first wisps of white hair curling at her temples—but no less luminous.

Oh, January, she was so lovely.

She looked up just as we crossed into the blackness and grinned her crooked, wild grin at the two of us.

That smile, a white-gold smear against the mist, still hangs like a painted portrait before my eyes. It marks the last moment the world was whole, the last moment of our brief, fragile family. The last moment I saw Adelaide Larson.

The blackness took us. The suffocating absence of the in-between. I closed my eyes against it, my coward's heart trusting that Ade would see us through.

And then a rending, splintering sound that wasn't a sound, because there could be no sound in that airless place. My feet heaved beneath me and I thought wildly of sea monsters and leviathans, of vast tentacles encircling our ship—and then an enormous, sourceless pressure descended on us. It was as if the in-between itself were being bitten in half.

I was breathless, blind, panicked. But there was a fraction of a second—suspended now in my memory like an axis point around which all else turns—when I might have chosen differently. I might have dived back toward the stern, toward Ade. I might have died, or been damned to unravel in the endless in-between, but at least I would have done so with Adelaide at my side.

Instead, I planted my feet and curled myself around you.

I think of this moment often. I do not regret it, January, not even at my darkest and most despairing.

The moment passed. The crushing intensified, until you and I were flattened against the groaning hull, our lungs empty and our skulls aching. My arms were a vise around you and I was no longer sure whether I was protecting you or crushing you—my eyes pressed inward—my teeth ground against one another—

Air. Thin, frost-sharp, smelling of pine and snow. We burst through some unseen barrier and our ship scudded against the ground. We were pitched forward, smashed against the cold earth of another world.

Here my memories grow reeling and confused, blinking in and out like a bad bulb in a projector; I believe my head knocked against some stone or flying timber. I remember you, tensed and screaming in my arms and therefore impossibly, wonderfully alive. I remember staggering upright, spinning back toward the scattered remains of our ship and looking desperately for some flash of white or gold, except my eyes weren't focusing right and then I was back on my knees. I remember looking for the great timber-frame door Ade told me about and finding nothing but rubble and ash.

I remember shouting her name and receiving no answer.

I remember a figure looming out of the shadows, silhouetted by the dawn.

Something connected with the back of my head and the world fragmented. My nose crashed against pine needles and stone and the ocean-taste of blood filled my mouth.

I remember thinking: *I am dying.* And I remember feeling a distant, selfish relief, because by then I knew: Ade had not come through the door with us.

The Ivory Door

As a general rule I'm not a person who cries much. When I was younger I cried over everything from sneers to sad endings, and even once over a puddle of tadpoles that dried up in the sun, but at some point I learned the trick of stoicism: you hide. You pull yourself inside your castle walls and crank up the drawbridge and watch everything from the tallest tower.

But I cried then: lying bloody and exhausted in the Zappia family cabin, with Bad beside me and Jane's voice rolling over us, telling my father's story.

I cried until my eyes were prickly-feeling and the pillow was soggy with snot. I cried as if I'd been assigned to cry the unshed tears of three people instead of one: my mother, lost in the abyss; my father, lost without her; and me, lost without either of them.

Jane finished reading and didn't say anything, because what do you say to a grown woman crying herself to sleep? She closed the book gently, as if the pages were flesh that might be bruised, and tucked the pink quilt around me. Then she drew the curtains against the midday sun and sat in a rocking chair with her cold coffee. Her face was so still and smooth-planed I suspected fierce emotions lurking beneath it; she'd learned the trick of stoicism, too.

I fell asleep watching her through hot, puffy eyes, my arm around the rise and fall of Bad's ribs.

I have dreaming memories of Jane moving around the cabin, leaving once and returning with an armload of firewood for the cooling evening, working at the table on something dark and metal, her face inscrutable. Once I half roused to see the door propped open and Jane and Bad both sitting on the stoop, framed in summer moonlight like a pair of silver statues or guardian spirits. I slept better after that.

I woke fully the following morning, when the sun was drawing the first faint line against the western wall, a bluish-pale light that told me it was far too early for civilized people to be awake. I watched the line turn taffy-pink and listened to the birds begin their hesitant scales and felt, for perhaps the first time in my life, truly safe.

Oh, I know: I grew up in a sprawling country estate, I traveled around the world with first-class tickets, I wore satin and pearls—hardly a perilous childhood. But it was borrowed privilege and I knew it. I'd been Cinderella at the ball, knowing all my finery was illusory, conditional, dependent on how successfully I followed a set of unwritten rules. At the stroke of midnight it would all vanish and leave me exposed for what I truly was: a penniless brown girl with no one to protect her.

But here in this cabin—musty, forgotten, perched on a pine-covered rock a dozen miles away from the nearest town—I felt truly, finally safe.

Jane had evicted Bad from the bed at some point in the night and taken his place beside me, and only the black burr of her hair was now visible. I tried not to disturb her as I climbed over the headboard. I stood for a moment, swaying and sick with tiredness that had nothing to do with how much I'd slept, and then stole a lightly mildewed blanket from the corner. I whispered Bad's name and we limped together to the front step and sat, watching the morning steam coil off the lake in puffy white curls.

My thoughts drew circles in my skull, returning again and again to the same fragments and trying to fit them together like shards of some broken, precious thing: the Society, the closing Doors, Mr. Locke. My father.

There was still a chapter or so left to read, but it wasn't hard to fill in the missing years. My father had been stranded in this miserable world with his baby daughter, had found himself employment that permitted travel, and spent seventeen years looking for a way back home—back to her. My mother.

But I'd *found* their Door, hadn't I? The blue Door in the field, with the silver coin waiting on the other side, which had so briefly opened. And my father had never known, had perhaps died searching for the Door that his own daughter had opened. It was so... *stupid*. Like one of those tragic plays where everyone dies at the end from a series of preventable poisonings and misunderstandings.

Although perhaps it hadn't all been preventable or accidental. Someone had been waiting outside that mountaintop Door; someone had closed it. My father's book was riddled with references to other Doors closing, to some nameless force stalking his footsteps.

I thought of Havemeyer telling me he wished to preserve the world as it was, thought of Locke inviting me into the Society with a grand speech about order and stability. *Doors are change*, my father had written. But... did I really believe the New England Archaeological Society was a secret organization of malevolent Door-closers? And if they were—had Mr. Locke known? Was he the capital-*V* Villain of this story?

No. I wouldn't, couldn't believe it. This was the man who had sheltered my father and me, opened his own house to us. The man who had given me nursemaids and tutors and fancy dresses, the man who had left me seventeen years of gifts in that blue treasure box. And such unusual, thoughtful gifts— dolls from faraway countries, spice-scented scarves, books in languages I couldn't read—perfectly suited to a lonely girl who dreamed of adventure.

Mr. Locke loved me. I knew he did.

The ammonia-stink of Brattleboro seemed to waft from my skin, a dull reeking. He'd done that. He'd sent me to that place, locked me away where no one could hear me or see me. To protect me, he'd said, but I wasn't sure I cared about the why.

By the time Jane emerged—eyes narrowed at the sun, hair slightly flattened-looking on one side—my legs were numb and the lake steam had sizzled away. She sat beside me without saying anything.

"Did you know?" I asked, after a silence.

"Did I know what?"

I didn't bother to answer. She gave a short, resigned sigh. "I knew some of it. Never the whole story. Julian was a private man." That past tense, slinking through sentences like a snake in the grass, waiting to bite me.

I swallowed. "How did you meet my father, really? Why did he send you here?"

A longer sigh. I imagined I could hear a kind of release in it, like the unlocking of a door. "I met your father in August 1909 in a world of wereleopards and ogres. I very nearly killed him, but the light was fading and my shot went wide."

Until that moment, I didn't think people's jaws actually dropped in real life. Jane looked rather pleased with herself, watching me sidelong. She stood up. "Come inside. Eat. I'll tell it to you."

"I found the door the fourth time I ran away from the mission school. It wasn't easily found: the northern side of Mount Suswa is riddled with caves and the door was hidden down a twisting, narrow tunnel that only a child would think worth exploring. It shone at me through the shadows, tall and yellow-white. Ivory."

I'd traded my starched and bloodied smock for a spare blouse and skirt from Jane and raked my fingers through my hair (to no discernible effect) and now we sat across from one another at the dusty kitchen table. It felt almost normal, as if we were hidden in one of the attics of Locke House, drinking coffee and discussing the latest issue of *The Sweetheart Series: Romantic Adventures for Young Girls of Merit*.

Except that it was Jane's story we were discussing, and she hadn't started at the beginning. "Why did you run away?"

Her lips pursed slightly. "The same reason everyone does."

"But didn't you worry about—I mean, what about your parents?"

"I had no parents." She hissed a little on the *s*. I watched her throat move as she swallowed away her anger. "I only had my little sister left, by then. We were born in the highlands on my mother's farm. I don't remember much of it: the tilled earth, black as skin; the smell of fermenting millet; the scrape of the shaving blade against my skull. *Mucii*. Home." Jane shrugged.

"I was eight when the drought came, and the railroad. Our mother took us to the mission school and said she would return with the rain in April. I never saw her again. I like to think she died of some fever in the work camps, because then it is possible to forgive her." Her voice oozed with the bitterness of abandonment, of waiting and waiting for a parent who never returned; I shivered in recognition.

"My sister forgot her entirely. She was too young. She forgot our language, our land, our names. The teachers called her Baby Charlotte, and she introduced herself as Baby." Another shrug. "She was happy." Jane paused, the muscles of her jaw hard as marbles, and I heard the unsaid *I was not.*

"So you ran. Where did you go?"

Her jaws unclenched. "Away. I had no place to go. I returned to the mission twice on my own, because I got sick or hungry or tired, and once tied behind an officer's horse because I'd been caught stealing buns from the barracks. The fourth time I was older, nearly fourteen. I made it much farther." I saw myself briefly at fourteen—uncertain, lonely, wearing pressed linen skirts and practicing my penmanship—and found I could not imagine running alone through the African bush at that age. Or any age. "I made it all the way home, except it wasn't home anymore. There was just a big ugly house with shingles and chimneys, and little blond children playing out front. A black woman in a white apron was watching them." She shrugged again; I began to see them as practical gestures, designed to shed the weight of resentment threatening to settle on her shoulders. "So I kept running. South, where the highlands fold up into valleys and mountains. Where the trees are dry and wind-burnt and food is scarce. I grew thin. The cattle herders watched me pass and said nothing."

I made a sound, a sort of disbelieving *tsk*, and Jane spared me a pitying look. "The empire had arrived by then, with its borderlines and deeds and railroads and Maxim guns. I was not the only motherless, feral child running through the bush."

I was silent. I thought of Mr. Locke's lectures on Progress and Prosperity. There were never any orphan girls or stolen farms or Maxim guns in them. Bad, lying beneath my chair with his splinted leg sticking stiffly out from his body, shifted so that his head was more completely covering my foot.

Jane continued. "I found the ivory door and went through. I thought at first I had died and passed into the world of spirits and gods." Her lips parted in an almost-smile, and her eyes crimped with some new emotion—longing? Homesickness? "I was in a forest so green it was almost blue. The door I'd come through was behind me, set among the exposed roots of a vast tree. I wandered away from it, deeper into the woods.

"I know now how foolish that was. The forests in that world are full of cruel, creeping things, many-mouthed monsters with a bottomless hunger. It was mere luck—or God's will, as the mission workers would have it—that I found Liik and her Hunters before anything else found me. It didn't feel all that lucky at the time: I stepped around a tree trunk and found an arrowhead inches from my face."

I covered my gasp with a cough, hoping to sound less like a small child listening to a campfire story. "What did you do?"

"Not a damn thing. Surviving is often a matter of knowing when you're beat. I heard rustling behind me and knew others were emerging, that I was surrounded. The woman holding the bow was hissing at me in a language I didn't know. Apparently I didn't look like much of a threat—a hungry girl-child, wearing a white cotton shift with the collar torn off—because Liik lowered her weapon. Only then could I get a proper look at them all."

The hard lines of Jane's face softened, just a little, warmed by fond reminiscence. "They were women. Muscled, golden-eyed, impossibly tall, with a kind of rolling grace that made me think of lionesses. Their skin was mottled and spotted and their teeth when they smiled were sharp. I thought they were the most beautiful things I'd ever seen.

"They took me in. We couldn't understand one another but their instructions were simple ones: follow, eat, stay, skin this creature for dinner. I patrolled with them for weeks, maybe months, and learned many things. I learned to creep through the woods in silence, and to oil bowstrings with fat. I learned to eat meat raw and blood-warm. I learned that all the ogre-stories I'd ever heard were true, and that monsters lurked in the shadows."

Her voice had gone rhythmic, nearly hypnotic.

"I learned to love Liik and her Hunters. And when I saw them change—their skins sloughing and shifting, their jaws lengthening, their bows clattering forgotten to the forest floor—I was envious, rather than afraid. I'd been powerless my whole life, and the shape of the leopard-women as they leapt into battle was the shape of *power* written on the world." I didn't think I'd ever heard such emotion in Jane's voice; not when a book ended poorly or the coffee was burned or a party guest said something scathing behind their gloved hand. Hearing it now felt almost intrusive.

"The patrol ended, eventually, and the women took me home: a village surrounded by fruit trees and farmlands, hidden in the cauldron of a dead volcano. Their menfolk greeted them in the streets with fat babies on their hips and fresh beer in clay pots. Liik spoke to her husbands and they looked at me with pity in their eyes. They led me to Liik's home and fed me, and I spent that night and the next and the ones after that sleeping in a pile of soft furs surrounded by the gentle snoring of Liik's children. It felt"—Jane swallowed, and her voice sounded briefly constricted—"like home."

There was a small silence. "So you stayed there? In the village?"

Jane smiled, crooked and bitter. "I did. But Liik and her Hunters did not. I woke one morning to find that all of them had gone back to the forests, to the patrol, and left me behind." She'd gone very brusque; how much had that second abandonment hurt? "I knew enough of the language by then to understand what the husbands were telling me: the forest was no place for a creature like me. I was too small, too weak. I should stay in the village and raise babies and grind tisi-nuts into flour and be safe." Another crooked smile. "But by then I was very good at running away. I stole a bow and three skins of water and made my way back to the ivory door."

"But—"

"Why?" Jane rubbed her finger along the wood grain of the table. "Because I didn't want to be safe, I suppose. I wanted to be dangerous, to find my own power and write it on the world."

I looked away, down to Bad now growling phantom-growls in his sleep. "So you left the leopard-women's world. Where did you go?" People never got to stay in their Wonderlands, did they? Alice and Dorothy and the Darlings, all dragged back to the mundane world and tucked into bed by their handlers. My father, stranded in this dull reality.

Jane gave a great, scornful *ha*. "I went straight to the nearest British outpost, stole a Lee-Metford rifle and as much ammunition as I could carry, and went back through my ivory door. Two weeks later I walked back into the village, my rifle over my shoulder and a stinking, blood-crusted skull under my arm. I was hungry and thin again, my cotton shift was a tattered wrap around my waist, I'd broken two ribs in the battle—but I could feel my eyes burning with pride." They were doing so now, gleaming dangerously through the cabin shadows.

"I found Liik in the village street and rolled the ogre skull at her feet." The gap between her front teeth winked as her smile widened. "And so I patrolled with the leopard-women for the next twenty-two years. I had twelve kills to my name, two husbands and a hunt-wife, and three names in three languages. I had an entire world, full of blood and glory." She leaned toward me, eyes fixing on mine like a black hunting cat, invisible tail lashing. Her voice when she spoke again was lower, rougher. "I would have all of that still, if your father had not arrived in 1909 and closed my door forever."

I found myself wholly, profoundly speechless. Not out of shyness or uncertainty, but because all the words had apparently been shaken out of my skull and left nothing behind them but a dull, staticky buzzing sound. Maybe if we'd had longer I would've recovered, said something like *My father, closing Doors?* or maybe *How do you know?* or, perhaps most honest and necessary of all: *I'm sorry.*

But I didn't say any of that, because there was a sudden pounding at the cabin door. A chill, drawling voice called: "Miss Scaller, my dear creature, are you in there? We never finished our conversation."

There was a single, crystalline moment of stillness.

Then the latch lifted and the cabin door swung toward us. Jane's chair clattered backward as she stood, hands plunging into her skirts. Bad clawed to his feet, hackles high and lips peeled back. My own body felt as if I'd been submerged in cold honey.

Havemeyer stood on the threshold. But he was hardly the same man who'd attended Society meetings and snubbed us at Christmas parties: his linen suit was wrinkled and faintly gray with too many days' wear; his skin was flushed; something about his smile had gone sickeningly wrong. His left hand was a wad of wrapped gauze, soggy brown with blood. His right hand was bare.

But it wasn't Havemeyer who brought me stumbling to my feet, my hands reaching uselessly toward the door. It was the young man he half dragged beside him, battered and dazed.

Samuel Zappia.

Samuel's hands were bound behind his back and his mouth had been jammed with cotton gauze. His skin, normally the color of browned butter, had gone a sick yellow, and his eyes reeled in his skull. The prey-animal panic in them was familiar to me; if I'd looked into a mirror after Havemeyer touched me, I'd have seen the identical expression on my own face.

Samuel blinked into the gloom of the cabin. His eyes focused on me and he made a hoarse sound through the gauze, as if the sight of me had been an invisible blow.

Jane was in motion. Everything about her promised violence—the angle of her shoulders, the length of her stride, her hand emerging from her skirt with something dully gleaming—but Havemeyer raised his bare right hand and placed it around Samuel's neck, hovering just above the warmth of his skin.

"Now, now, ladies, settle down. I shouldn't like to do anything regrettable."

Jane wavered, hearing the threat but not understanding it, and I found my voice. "Jane, *no!*" I stood shakily, bandaged arms outstretched as if I could restrain either Jane or Bad if they lunged for Havemeyer. "He's some kind of, of vampire. Don't let him touch you." Jane went still, radiating red tension.

Havemeyer gave a short laugh, and the laugh was just as wrong-seeming as his smile. "You know, I feel similarly about that appalling animal beside you. How *did* he survive? I know Evans isn't bright, but I thought he could at least drown a dog properly."

Rage curled my nails into my palms and hardened my jaw. Havemeyer's not-smile widened. "Anyway. I've come to continue our conversation, Miss Scaller, as you missed our previous appointment. Although I confess my original purposes have been somewhat amended since your little magic trick." He waved his bandaged, bloody left hand at me, eyes flashing with malice. I watched the muscles of Samuel's neck move as he swallowed.

"It appears you're quite a remarkable creature—we're all unusually talented people, each in our separate ways, but none of us can open a hole in the world where there was none. Does Cornelius know? It would be just like him, collecting all the best things and locking them away in that mausoleum he calls a house." Havemeyer shook his head fondly. "But we've agreed he can't keep you to himself any longer. We'd very much like to speak with you further." My eyes flicked around the room—from Jane to Bad to Havemeyer's white fingers held like a knife blade to Samuel's throat—as if I were solving a math equation again and again, hoping for a different answer.

"Come with me—immediately and without fuss—and I won't suck the life out of your poor little grocery boy."

And Havemeyer let his fingertips rest, with obscene tenderness, against Samuel's skin. It was like watching a flame flicker in the wind: Samuel's entire body seized and shuddered, his breath drawing harshly against the cotton gauze. His legs sagged.

"No!" I was moving forward, reaching for Samuel and half catching him as he pitched forward. Then both of us were on the floor, Samuel's shivering weight slumped over my knees, my left arm burning as the barely scabbed wounds split and bled. I tugged the sodden cotton from his mouth and he breathed easier, but his eyes remained vague and distant.

I think I must have been whispering words (*no, no, Samuel, please*) because Havemeyer *tsk*ed. "There's no need for hysterics. He's perfectly fine. Well, not *perfectly*—he was quite uncooperative with me when I tracked him down last night. But I was insistent." The not-smile returned. "All I had to go on when you vanished—taking some of me with you, of course— was his little love note. Which you so heartlessly left behind at Brattleboro, and which he so foolishly composed on the back of a Zappia Family Groceries receipt."

Hold On January. Such a small, brave act of kindness, repaid with suffering. I'd thought only sins were punished.

"He'll recover, if nothing else unfortunate befalls him. I'll even leave the dog alone, and your maid." Havemeyer's voice was confident, almost casual; I pictured a butcher calling a reluctant cow onto the slaughterhouse floor. "Simply come with me now."

I looked at Samuel's pale face below me, at Bad with his splinted leg, at Jane, jobless and homeless on my behalf, and it occurred to me that, for a supposedly lonely orphan girl, there were a surprising number of people willing to suffer on my behalf.

Enough.

I slid Samuel off my lap as gently as I could. I hesitated, then let myself brush a dark curl of hair away from his clammy forehead, because I was probably never going to get another chance and a girl should live a little.

I stood. "All right." My voice was a near-whisper. I swallowed. "All right. I'll go with you. Just don't hurt them."

Havemeyer was watching me. There was a kind of cruel confidence in his expression, the swagger of a cat stalking something weak and small. He reached his bare hand toward me, white and somehow hungry-looking, and I stepped toward him.

There was a scrabbling behind me, a snarl, and Bad leapt past me in a streak of bronze muscle.

I had a sudden movie-reel memory of Mr. Locke's Society party the year I was fifteen, when it had required the intervention of several party guests and a butler to dislodge Bad's teeth from Havemeyer's leg.

There was no one to intervene this time.

Havemeyer made a shrill not-very-human sound and staggered backward. Bad growled through his mouthful of flesh and planted his feet as if they were playing tug-of-war for possession of Havemeyer's right hand. If Bad hadn't been already injured, if his splinted back leg hadn't folded beneath him, maybe he would've won.

But Bad stumbled, whimpering, and Havemeyer ripped his hand away in a spatter of blackish blood. He clutched both hands to his chest—the left one bound in gauze, missing three waxen fingertips, the right one now punctured and torn—and looked at Bad with an expression of such wrath that I knew, with perfect clarity, that he would kill him. He would bury his ruined hands in Bad's fur and hold on until there was no warmth left in him, until the amber light of his eyes went cold and dull—

But he was unable to do so, because there was a metallic click, like flint-stones striking—and then a sudden thunderclap.

A small hole appeared in Havemeyer's linen suit, directly above his heart. He blinked down at it in confusion, then looked up with an expression of absolute incredulity.

Darkness bloomed around the hole in his chest and he fell. It wasn't a theatrical or graceful collapse, but more of a sideways, melting-candle slump against the doorway.

He took a hideous, wet-sounding breath, as if he were sucking tar through a straw, and met my eyes. He smiled. "They'll never stop looking for you, girl. And I promise"—the tar-sucking sound again, as his head slumped forward—"they'll find you."

I waited for the next gargled breath—but it didn't come. His body looked somehow smaller as he lay there, like one of those desiccated spider-corpses that collect in windowsills.

I turned slowly around.

Jane stood with her legs planted wide, arms raised and perfectly steady, both hands wrapped tight around—

You know how it feels when you see a familiar object out of its usual context? As if your eyes can't quite make sense of the shapes they're seeing?

I'd only ever seen that Enfield revolver in its glass case on Mr. Locke's desk.

A single coil of oily smoke rose from the barrel as Jane lowered it. She inspected the revolver with a cool, detached expression. "I'm a little surprised it fired, to be honest. It's an antique. But then"—she smiled, a vicious, gleeful smile, and I suddenly saw her as she must have once been: a young Amazon reveling in the thrill of the hunt, a hunting cat prowling through the jungles of another world—"Mr. Locke always kept his collections in very good shape."

Of the four of us—five of us? Did Havemeyer count?—only Jane seemed fully in possession of her own body. Bad hopped in agitated, three-legged circles around Havemeyer and made whimpering, muttering sounds, apparently complaining that he'd been cheated of a good fight. I sank back to my knees beside Samuel, who was stirring weakly, grimacing and twitching as if he were locked in some unpleasant dream battle. I felt my pulse *thud-thud*ding through my bleeding, bandaged arm and thought, inanely: *It's not like our story papers at all, Samuel.* Shouldn't there be more blood? More fuss?

Jane didn't seem concerned. She laid a cool hand against my face and met my eyes with a weighing expression, like a person checking a recently dropped china doll for fractures.

She nodded once—a questionable diagnosis, because I felt pretty fractured—and began moving purposefully around the cabin. She unfolded a moth-chewed sheet beside Havemeyer, rolled his body neatly onto it, and hauled him out the door. There was a series of unpleasant, meaty thunks as he cleared the threshold—*Thresholds are awfully dangerous places*, I thought, with a semihysterical hiccup of laughter—and then nothing but the *shush* of something heavy dragging through pine needles.

Jane returned with two rusting buckets of lake water, her sleeves rolled up to the elbow, looking for all the world like an industrious housewife rather than a murderess. She saw me and stopped, sighing a little. "See to Samuel, January," she said softly.

It seemed to me she was also saying: *Pull it together, kid*, and maybe *Everything will be all right*. I nodded, a little shakily.

It took half an hour to get Samuel settled, even with his dazed cooperation. First I had to wrangle him to the bed and coax him sufficiently awake to crawl into it. Then I had to convince him to relax his feverish grip on my wrist—"It's all right, you're safe, Havemeyer's—well, he's gone, anyway— that *hurts*, Sam, Jesus"—and then build up the fire and pile extra blankets over his still-shivery legs.

There was a wood-on-wood scrape as Jane dragged a chair beside mine. She used a handful of skirt to scrub her still-damp hands. The blotches they left behind were stained pale pink.

"When he hired me to look after you," Jane said softly, "your father told me there were people following him, chasing him. He said one day they might catch him. And then they might come for his daughter, whom he kept as safe as he could." She paused, and her eyes flicked toward me. "I told him, by the way, that daughters do not want to be kept safe, that they would prefer to be with their parents—but he did not answer."

I swallowed, quelling the child in me that wanted either

to stamp her foot and say *How come?* or to throw herself into Jane's arms and wail inconsolably. *Too late for either.*

Instead, I said, "But what was my father even *doing*? And if there *were* mysterious villains following him around the world—and I guess I shouldn't roll my eyes, because you did just shoot an actual vampire—who are they?"

Jane didn't answer immediately. She leaned forward and picked my father's leather-bound book from the floor beside the bed. "I don't know, January. But I think they may have caught up with your father, and come for you. And I think you ought to finish this book."

How fitting, that the most terrifying time in my life should require me to do what I do best: escape into a book.

I took *The Ten Thousand Doors* from her hand, tucked my feet beneath me, and opened the book to the final chapter.

Chapter Six

The Birth of Julian Scaller

A man shipwrecked and saved—A man hunting and hunted—A man hoping

Yule Ian drifted in roiling darkness, unanchored from his body. This was, he felt, for the best, and he determined to remain adrift as long as he could.

It wasn't easy. The darkness was marred sometimes by strange voices and lantern light, by the inconvenient demands of his body, by dreams that left him gasping and awake in a room he didn't know. Once or twice he heard the piercing, familiar crying of a baby and felt a stabbing in his chest, like broken pottery shards grinding against one another, before diving back into oblivion.

But—fitfully, reluctantly, slowly—he felt himself healing. There were hours at a time now when he lay fully awake but motionless and silent, as if reality were a tigress who might overlook him if he was sufficiently quiet. He could no longer escape the brusque, morose-looking man with a black leather bag who came to check his temperature and change the bandaging wrapping his skull. He could ignore his questions, though, and lock his jaw against the steaming bowls of broth set on the bedside table. He could also ignore the squat little woman who trundled in sometimes to badger him about his daughter—was he the father? Why had he taken her up that mountain, alone? Where was her mother?—by the crude

221

but effective means of pressing his injured skull into the mattress until the pain and darkness swallowed him up again.

(Among the many things that haunt me about my own cowardice, perhaps the worst is the knowledge of what your mother would've said if she'd seen me then. I took a bitter satisfaction in the thought that she was gone, and I could not therefore disappoint her.)

Yule woke some days or weeks later to find a stranger sitting at his bedside—a wealthy-looking man in a black suit, blurred slightly in his squinting vision.

"Good morning, sir," the man said pleasantly. "Tea? Coffee? Some of this rather vicious bourbon these mountain savages drink?"

He closed his eyes.

"No? Wise choice, my friend, there's a whiff of rat poison about it." Yule heard a tinkle and splash as the stranger poured himself a measure. "The proprietor here tells me you were addled in the accident, that you haven't said two words together since they dragged you in here. He adds that you're stinking up his best room, though I find the word 'best' to be highly flexible in this case."

Yule did not answer.

"He went through your things, of course, or at least such things as could be fished from the strange wreckage on the mountaintop. Rope, canvas, salted fish, rather odd clothing. And bundles and bundles of pages written in some kind of gibberish, apparently, or code. The town is neatly divided into those who believe you're a foreign spy sending missives back to the French—except who ever heard of a colored spy?—and those who think you were perfectly mad prior to your head injury. Personally, I suspect neither."

Yule began pressing his head against the straw-stuffed mattress. Small, fizzing constellations burst against his eyelids.

"Enough, boy." The man's voice changed, shedding its unctuous skin as if dropping a fur coat to the floor. "Has it occurred to you to wonder why you are sleeping in a nice warm room, benefiting from the dubious skills of the local doctor, rather than dying slowly in the street? Did you think it was the goodwill of the natives?" He laughed, short and sneering. "Goodwill doesn't extend to penniless, tattooed

Negroes—or whatever you are. I'm afraid it's entirely my will—and my money—that keeps you so comfortable. So I think"—and Yule felt an ungentle grip turn his chin toward the stranger—"you owe me your fullest attention."

But Yule found himself far past any of the usual bounds of social convention and reciprocation, and his primary thought was that his path toward the perfect darkness of death would be much faster without this man's intervention. He kept his eyes closed.

There was a pause. "I am also making weekly payments to a certain Mrs. Cutley. Should I cease to do so, your daughter would be tossed on a train to Denver and stuck in a state orphanage. She'd either grow up lice-ridden and mean, or die young of consumption and loneliness, and no one in this world would care which."

That pottery-shard feeling stabbed his chest again, accompanied by a kind of silent shout in his skull that sounded very much like Adelaide's voice saying *Over my dead body.*

Yule's eyes opened. The dim setting-sun light felt like several hundred needles inserted into his skull, and at first all he could do was blink and gasp. The room came slowly into focus: small, grubby, furnished in rough-cut pinewood. His bed was a knot of stained sheets. His own limbs, emerging from the tangle at careless, random angles like debris from a flood, looked thin and wasted.

The stranger was watching him, eyes pale as dawn, jade-glass tumbler in one hand. Yule licked his cracked lips. "Why?" he asked. His voice was lower and rougher than it had been before, as if he'd replaced his lungs with rusting iron bellows.

"Why have I acted so magnanimously on your behalf? Because I happened to be in the area considering some mineral investments— the market is saturated, incidentally, and I'd advise against it just now—and heard rumors about a tattooed madman shipwrecked on a mountaintop, raving about doors and different planets and a woman named, unless my informants are mistaken, *Adelaide.*" The man leaned forward, the fine fabric of his suit *shush*ing a little. "Because I am a collector of the unique and valuable, and I suspect that you are both.

223

"Now." He produced a second glass—a muddy cup quite unlike his own carved-green cup—and filled it with more of the greasy liquor. "You are going to sit up and drink this, and I will pour you another and you'll drink that as well. Then you are going to tell me the truth. All of it." On those last words the man caught Yule's eyes and held them.

Yule sat up. He drank the liquor—a process very much like swallowing lit matches—and told his story.

"I first came to this world in 1881, by your calendar, and met a girl named Adelaide Lee Larson." His voice absented itself briefly, and returned as a whisper: "I loved her from that day forward."

Yule spoke slowly at first, in short, bare sentences, but quickly found himself stumbling into paragraphs and pages, until he was speaking in an endless, gasping stream. It didn't feel particularly good or bad, but merely necessary, as if those pale eyes were twin stones sitting on his chest, forcing the words out of him.

He told the stranger about the closing of the door and his subsequent dedication to the scholarly study of doors. About Adelaide's own explorations and their reunion on the shores of the City of Plumm. About their daughter, and their journey back to the mountaintop door, and the breaking of the world.

"And now I don't know—I don't know what to do, or where to go. I have to find another door home, I have to know if she survived—I'm sure she did, she was always so tough—but my baby girl, my January—"

"Stop blubbering, boy." Yule hiccuped to a stop, his hands twisting in his lap, rubbing the words on his arm (*scholar, husband, father*) and wondering if any of them were still true. "I am, as I said before, a collector. As such I employ a handful of field agents to gallivant about the world collecting things—sculptures, vases, exotic birds, et cetera. Now it seems to me these—doors, you call them?—could lead one to objects of particular rarity. Bordering on the mythological, even." The man leaned forward, radiating hunger. "Is that not so?"

Yule blinked at him, dimly. "I suppose—yes, it is so. In my researches I noted that things that are commonplace in one world may be perceived as miraculous in another, due to the transition in contextual cultural understa—"

"Precisely. Yes." The man smiled, sat back, and removed a fat stub of cigar from his coat pocket. Then came the sulfur smell of a struck match and the bluish stink of tobacco. "Now, it seems to me we might strike a mutually profitable arrangement, my boy." He shook the match out and flicked the remains to the floor. "You are in need of shelter, food, employment, and—unless I am much mistaken—funding and opportunity to search for a way back to your dear likely departed wife."

"She isn't—"

The man ignored him. "Consider it done. All of it. Room and board, and an unlimited stipend for research and travel. You can look for your door as long as you like anywhere you like, but in exchange—" He smiled, teeth shining ivory through the cigar smoke. "You'll help me create a collection that makes the Smithsonian look like a pauper's attic. Find the rare, the strange, the impossible, the otherworldly—the powerful, even. And bring it back to me."

Yule's eyes focused on the man more clearly than they previously had, his pulse rocketing with a sudden surge of hope. He swore, softly, in his own language. "And perhaps—a wet nurse, to travel with me? Just for a little while, for my little girl—"

The man whuffled through his substantial mustache. "Well, as to that…This world isn't a particularly safe place for young girls, you'll soon find out. I rather thought she could stay with me. My house is quite large and"—he coughed, looking away from Yule for the first time and fixing his gaze instead on the far wall—"I have no children of my own. It would be no trouble."

He looked back at Yule. "What do you say, sir?"

Yule could not speak for a moment. It was everything he could have hoped for—sufficient time and money to search for a door back to the Written, a safe place for January, a way forward out of the darkness—but he found himself hesitating. Despair, once established, can be quite difficult to uproot.

225

Yule took a breath and extended his hand in the manner Adelaide had once shown him. The stranger took it, with a smile that revealed a higher-than-necessary number of teeth.

"And what's your name, dear boy?"

"...Julian. Julian Scaller."

"Cornelius Locke. Thrilled to have you on board, Mr. Scaller."

As a young man in the Written, Julian searched for doors with the boundless confidence of a young person in love who assumes the world will contort itself to accommodate his desires. There were times—after fruitless weeks of trawling through the archives of some distant City, eyes aching from twisting themselves around half a dozen languages, or after miles of hiking across jungly hillsides without the slightest sign of a door—when he felt doubt creep in. Treacherous thoughts slunk through his skull as he lay in the unguarded place between sleeping and waking, thoughts like *What if I grow old searching for her, and never find her?*

But by morning such thoughts had burned away like mist at dawn and left nothing behind them at all. He simply rose, and kept searching.

Now, trapped in Adelaide's world, I search with the desperation of an old man who understands that time is a precious and finite thing, beating away like a second hand in my chest.

Some of that time I've spent simply learning how to navigate this world—a place I find baffling, sometimes cruel, and profoundly unwelcoming. There are rules about wealth and status, borders and passports, guns and public restrooms and the shade of my skin, all of which change according to my precise location and timing. In one place it might be perfectly permissible to visit the university library and borrow a few books; yet the same action in another place might inspire a call to the local police, who dislike my attitude, arrest me, and refuse to release me until Mr. Locke wires an apology and an upsetting amount of money to the Orleans County station. Under certain conditions I might meet with other scholars in my field and hold forth on the archaeological value of mythmaking;

at other times I am treated like a rather clever dog that has learned to speak English. I have been feted by Persian princes for my discoveries; I have been spat on in the street for failing to cast my eyes aside. I am invited to dine at Cornelius's table, but never to join his Archaeological Society.

In fairness, I have also seen the beautiful and admirable in this world: a group of girls flying kites in Gujarat, moving in a pink and turquoise blur; a blue heron fixing me with its golden stare on the banks of the Mississippi; two young soldiers kissing in a dim alley in Sebastopol. It is not a wholly evil world, but it will never be mine.

I've wasted more time fulfilling my end of Cornelius's bargain. And what a devil's bargain it's turned out to be: my papers at the border identify my occupation as an *exploratory archaeological researcher*, but they might more accurately say *well-dressed grave robber*. I once overheard the Uyghurs of China refer to me by a long and complicated name filled with fricatives and unpronounceable combinations of consonants—it means *the story-eater*.

This is what I am, what I have become: a scavenger scouring the earth, burrowing into its most secret and beautiful places and harvesting its treasures and myths. Eating its stories. I have chiseled out sections of sacred art from temple walls; I've stolen urns and masks and scepters and magic lamps; I've unearthed tombs and stolen jewels from the arms of the dead—in this world and a hundred others. All for the sake of a rich man's collection on the other side of the world.

What a shameful thing, that a Scholar of the City of Nin should become a story-eater. What would your mother say?

I would do worse things to find my way back to her.

But I'm running out of time. Your face is my hourglass: each time I return to Locke House it's as if I've been gone for decades rather than weeks. Entire lifetimes have bloomed and faded for you, months of secret trials and triumphs that have subtly molded your features into someone I hardly recognize. You've grown tall and silent, with the mistrustful stillness of a doe just before she bolts.

Sometimes—when I'm either too tired or too drunk to steer my thoughts away from dangerous places—I wonder what your mother would think if she could see you. Your features so plainly and painfully her own, but your spirit tightly laced beneath good manners and the invisible burden of unbelonging. She had dreamed for you a different life, one profoundly and perilously free, unbounded, every door standing open before you.

Instead, I've given you Locke House and Cornelius and that awful German woman who looks at me as if I am unwashed laundry. I've left you alone, orphaned, ignorant of the wondrous and terrible things seething just beneath the surface of reality. Cornelius says it's for the best; he says it isn't healthy for young girls to grow up with their heads full of doors and other worlds, that the time isn't right. And after all he's done—rescuing us, employing me, raising you as he might his own daughter—who am I to object?

And yet: If I ever find your mother again, will she forgive me?

This is something I do not let myself think. I will begin again on a fresh sheet of paper so I do not see the words glaring up at me from the page.

Men like myself cannot see anything beyond our own pain; our eyes are inward-facing, mesmerized by the sight of our own broken hearts.

This is why I didn't notice for so long: the doors are closing. Or, perhaps more accurately, the doors are being closed.

I should have seen it sooner, but I was even more obsessed in the earliest years, convinced that the very next door would open onto the cerulean seas of my homeland. I followed myths and stories and rumors, I looked for upheavals and revolutions, and at their twisted roots I often found doorways. None of them led me back to her, and so I abandoned them all as quickly as I could, taking time only to scavenge and plunder. Then I packed their stolen treasures in sawdust, scrawled *1611 CHAMPLAIN DRIVE, SHELBURNE, VERMONT* on the crate, and departed for the next steamer, the next story, the next door.

I did not linger long enough to see what came next: unexplained forest fires, unscheduled demolitions of historic buildings, floods, property development, cave-ins, gas leaks, and explosions. Sourceless, blameless disasters that turned the doors to rubble and ash and broke the secret links between the worlds.

When I finally recognized the pattern—sitting on a hotel balcony reading an article in the *Vancouver Sun* about a mine-shaft collapse where I'd found a door only the week before—I did not at first blame human agency. I blamed time. I blamed the twentieth century, which seemed hell-bent on Ouroboran self-destruction. I thought doors might not belong in the modern world, that all doors were destined to close eventually.

I should have known: destiny is a pretty story we tell ourselves. Lurking beneath it there are only people, and the terrible choices we make.

Perhaps I knew the truth, even before I had proof. I felt myself growing suspicious, worrying that strangers were watching me in Bangalore restaurants, hearing footsteps behind me in the alleys of Rio. Around that time I began writing my missives back to Cornelius in a code of my own invention, convinced that some unknown entity was intercepting my reports. It made no difference; the doors kept closing.

I reasoned with myself: What did it matter that these particular doors were destroyed? They were all the wrong doors. None of them would take me back to Ade, to our stone house above the City of Nin, to that moment when I climbed the hillside and saw the two of you curled on the quilt: golden, whole, perfect.

But even in the depths of my self-pity, another thought occurred to me: *What happens to a world without doors?* Hadn't I concluded that doors introduce change, back when I was a Scholar rather than a grave robber? I'd hypothesized that doors were vital avenues, allowing the mysterious and miraculous to flow freely between worlds.

Already I imagine I see the effects of their absence in this world: a subtle stagnation, a staleness, like a house that has been left shut up all summer. There are empires upon which the sun will never set, railways that cross continents, rivers of wealth that will never run dry, machines that never grow tired. It's a system too vast and ravenous to ever be dismantled, like a deity or an engine, which swallows men and women whole and belches black smoke into the sky. Its name is Modernity, I am told, and it carries Progress and Prosperity in its coal-fired belly—but I see only rigidity, repression, a chilling resistance to change.

I believe I already know what happens to a world without doors.

But to stop looking for doors would be to stop looking for your mother, and I *cannot*. I cannot.

I began retracing Ade's decade-old footsteps, on the theory that the door to the Written might be hidden in some other world. It was not always easy, piecing together the stories she told me with stories overheard in busy streets or dingy bars, gin-soaked and garbled, but I was persistent. I found the St. Ours door, the Haitian door, the selkie door, a dozen others—all of them are gone now. Burnt, collapsed, destroyed, forgotten.

It wasn't until 1907 that I caught a glimpse of my pursuers. I'd finally found the Greek door—a cold stone slab in an abandoned church—which led to a world Ade had once described as a "black pit of hell." I had no interest in repeating her experiences (she was, by her testimony, nearly shanghaied by an ice-eyed chieftainess), and so did not linger long inside it. I wandered for less than a day, creeping fearfully through the snow, but found nothing alive and nothing worth stealing. There were only endless rows of black pines and a distant horizon the color of gunmetal, and the wracked remains of some sort of fort or village. If there were any other doors in that place, I did not linger to find them.

I crawled back through the stone door into the mold-splotched interior of St. Peter's Church. It was only after I'd emerged—shivering in heaving spasms, inhaling the salt and lime smell of a Mediterranean evening—that I noticed something standing on the tile floor that hadn't previously been there: a pair of black-booted feet.

They belonged to a tall, heavy-browed man wearing the brass-buttoned uniform and round cap of a Greek police officer. He did not look particularly surprised to see a snow-dusted foreigner crawling out of the wall, but merely a little inconvenienced.

I scrambled to my feet. "Who—what are you doing here?"

He shrugged and spread his hands. "Exactly as I please." He spoke guttural, accented English. "Although I am I think a little early." He sighed and made a show of brushing off a pew and sitting down to wait.

I swallowed. "I know what you're here for. Don't try to pretend. And I won't let you, not this time—"

His mocking laughter punctured my daring little speech. "Oh, don't be foolish, Mr. Scaller. Return to that nasty little hut on the shore, buy yourself a steamer ticket in the morning, and forget about this place, eh? You have finished here."

It was all my most paranoid fantasies come true: he knew my name, knew about the shack I'd rented from a fisherwoman, perhaps knew the true nature of my researches.

"No. I won't let it happen again—"

The man waved a dismissive hand at me, as if I were a child resisting bedtime. "Yes, you will. You will leave without any fuss. You will not tell another soul. And then you will sniff out the next door for us like a good dog."

"And why's that?" My voice had gone high and taut and I wished, piercingly, for Adelaide. She was always the brave one.

He watched me almost pityingly. "Children," he sighed. "They grow up so fast, yes? Little January will be thirteen in just a few months."

We stood in silence while I listened to the sound of my own heart beating and thought of you, waiting for me an ocean away.

I left.

I purchased my steamer ticket the following morning and bought a paper from the Foreign Affairs stand in Valencia three days later. On the sixth page, printed in blurred Greek type, was a small column about a sudden and inexplicable rock slide on the coast of Crete. No one had been hurt, but a road had been buried and an old, mostly forgotten church had been reduced to rubble. The local police chief was quoted describing the event as "unfortunate, but inevitable."

You will find below a partial reproduction of a list recorded in my notes in July 1907. It is such a scholar's impulse, to cope with a dangerous and murky situation by sitting at his desk and writing a list. What would your mother have done, I wonder. One imagines a great deal more noise and disruption, and perhaps a body count.

I titled the page *Various Responses to the Continuing Situation Regarding the Nefarious Closing of Doors and Potential Risks to Immediate Family Members* and underlined it several times.

A. Expose the plot. Publish findings thus far (write to the *Times*? Take out an ad?) and denounce the activities of shadowy organization. Points in favor: could be done quickly; minimal disruption to January's life. Points against: likelihood of total failure (would papers publish findings without evidence?); loss of Cornelius's trust and protection; danger of (violent) retribution from unknown parties.

B. Go to Cornelius. Explain my fears more fully and request additional security for January. In favor: Locke's considerable resources could command a high degree of safety. Against: He hasn't been sympathetic to my concerns thus far; the terms *delusional paranoias* and *ridiculous flimflammery* have been used.

C. Remove January to safe, secondary location. If she were hidden in some other stronghold, very quietly, pursuers might not find her. In favor: J kept safe. Against: difficulty of finding safe location; difficulty of managing Cornelius's attachment to J; uncertainty of success/risk to J's safety; maximum disruption of daily life.

I believe she loves Locke House, despite everything. When she was young I would often arrive to find a flustered nursemaid and an absent daughter, and she would be discovered hours later building sand castles on the lakeshore, or playing endless games with the grocer's son. Now I find her walking the halls with one hand on the dark wood paneling, as if she is stroking the spine of some great sprawling beast, or curled with her dog in a forgotten armchair in the attic. Would it be right to steal the only home she's ever known, when I have stolen so much else from her already?

D. Run away, take refuge in another world. I could find a door and go through it, taking January with me, and build a new life for the two of us in some safer, brighter world. In favor: ultimate safety from pursuers. Against: see above. And I am far from certain that all worlds connect to one another—were we to flee to another world, could I ever find the Written again? And if Ade should claw her way back home, would she ever find us?

There was no *E. Continue on precisely as before*, but this is the course I ultimately chose. Life has a kind of momentum to it, I've found, an accumulated weight of decisions which becomes impossible to shift. I continued my thieving, chiseling away stories and boxing them up so that a rich man might brag to his rich friends; I continued my desperate search, following stories and unearthing doors; I continued to let them close behind me. I stopped looking over my shoulder.

I made only three changes. The first involved an ivory door in the mountains of British East Africa and an uncomfortably close encounter with a Lee-Metford rifle, and ended in forging a passport and purchasing train tickets for a Miss Jane Irimu. It is not necessary to recount the full story of our meeting here, but only to note that she is one of the most fearless and casually violent persons I have ever met, and that I caused her inadvertent but terrible heartache. She also has a very particular empathy to your situation and it is my belief that she will protect you far more capably than I have. You ought to ask her for the full story one day.

The second change was to find an escape route for the two of you, a bolt-hole which I hope you will never make use of. I will not describe it with any detail here—lest some prying, unfriendly eye come across this book—except to say there is one door I found which has not yet been closed. I traveled under an assumed name to discover it and burned my notes and papers once I had. I blamed my delayed return on stormy seas, and I suppose by then I had been so often absent from Locke House that neither Cornelius nor you asked anything further. I spoke of my true purpose to only one living soul; should you ever need a place to run, a place to hide from whatever it is that pursues me—follow Jane.

The third change is this book you now hold in your hands. (Assuming I've had it bound. Otherwise I refer to a messy pile of typewritten papers tied together with packing twine and the shed skin of a flying snake, which I found in a viciously unpleasant world through a door in Australia.)

I spend my evenings now gathering the disparate and wandering pieces of my own story—our story, I should call it—shepherding them into a straight line, and recording them as neatly as I can on the page. It is taxing work. Sometimes I am too exhausted from a day's fruitless tramping through the Amazon or the Ozarks to write more than a sentence before bed. Sometimes I spend the entire day trapped in my camp by poor weather with nothing but a pen and paper for company, but still fail to write a single word because I've become trapped in the mirrored halls of my own memory and cannot escape (the nautilus-curve of your mother's body around yours; the white-gold smear of her smile in the misted dawn of the Amarico).

But I persist in writing, even when it feels like pressing forward through an endless briar patch, even when the ink looks smeary-red in the lamplight.

Perhaps I keep writing because I was raised in a world where words have power, where curves and spirals of ink adorn sails and skin, where a sufficiently talented word-worker might reach out and remake her world. Perhaps I cannot believe words are entirely powerless, even here.

Perhaps I simply need to leave some record, however wandering and unsubstantiated, so that another living soul can learn the truths I have worked so hard to unearth. So that someone else might read it and believe: there are ten thousand doors between ten thousand worlds, and someone is closing them. And I am helping them do it.

Perhaps I write out of an altogether more desperate and naive hope: that someone braver and better than myself might atone for my sins and succeed where I failed. That someone might fight back against the shadowy machinations of those who wish to sever this world from all its cousins and render it barren, rational, profoundly alone.

That someone, somehow, might forge themselves into a living key, and open the doors.

END

Post Script

(Apologies for my penmanship—what would my mother say?—but I am in a great hurry, and don't have time to get this typed and bound like the rest.)

My dearest January,

I found it. *I found it.*

I am camped on one of the cold, wind-scoured islands north of Japan. Near the shore there's an association of bamboo-grass huts and corrugated-tin shanties that might generously be called a village, but up on this mountainside there's nothing but knotted grass and a few des-iccated pines clinging gamely to the ashy soil. Before me stands an interesting formation: some of the tree boughs have twisted themselves into a sort of arch, looking out over the sea.

If seen from the proper angle, it looks almost like a doorway.

I found it by following the stories: Once there was a fisherman who folded the pages of books and turned them into sailing ships. The ships were fleet and light, and their sails were stained with ink. Once there was a little boy who disappeared in midwinter and returned sunburnt and warm. Once there was a priest with prayers written on his skin.

I knew where it led before I stepped through it. Worlds, like houses, have very particular smells, so subtle and complex and varied you barely notice them, and the smell of the Written filtered through the pine boughs like a delicate fog. Sun, sea, the dust of crumbling book spines, the salt and spice of a thousand trade ships. Home.

I am going through it as soon as I can. This very evening. I was careful on my journey here, but I fear I wasn't careful enough. I fear they will find me—the door-closers, the world-killers. I hesitate even to look away from the doorway and down at this page, lest some spectral figure leap from the shadows and close it forever.

But I will delay long enough to finish this. To tell you where I have gone and why, and send you this book through the Azure Chests of Tuya and Yuha—a rather useful pair of objects I found through a door in Alexandria, and one of the few treasures I declined to surrender entirely to Cornelius. I gave him one, but kept the other for myself.

I've sent you trinkets and toys before—did you recognize them for what they were? The insufficient offerings of an absent father? A coward's attempt to say: _I think of you_ *always, I love you, forgive me?* I feared your disappointment, your rejection of my paltry, pitiful gifts.

This book is my last such gift. My final insufficiency. It is a profoundly imperfect work, as you know very well by now, but it is the truth—a thing you deserved long before now, but which I could not give you. (I tried, once or twice. I came into your room, opened my mouth to tell you everything—and found myself voiceless. I fled from you and lay gasping in my own bed, almost choking on the weight of unsaid words in my throat. I suppose I am truly that much of a coward.)

Well, no more silences. No more lies. I don't know how often you visit the Azure Chest, so I've found a way to ensure that you find the book in a timely fashion—the birds here are trusting creatures, unfamiliar with the dangers of humankind.

It contains only one falsehood of which I am aware: the claim that I wrote it for the sake of Scholarship or Knowledge or Moral Necessity. That I was trying to "leave a record behind me" or "document my findings" for some murky future reader, who might bravely take up my mantle.

The truth is that I wrote it for you. I was always writing for you, every moment.

Do you remember when you were six or seven and I returned from the Burmese expedition? It was the first time you didn't run into my arms when I arrived (and how I longed for and dreaded those arrivals, when your dear hourglass face would tell me how much time I'd wasted). Instead you simply stood in your starched little dress, looking up at me as if I were a stranger on a crowded train car.

Too many times, your eyes said. _You left me too many times, and now something precious and fragile has broken between us._

I wrote this book in the desperate, pitiable hope that I could repair it. As if I could atone for each missed holiday and absent hour, for all the years I spent wrapped in the selfishness of grief. But here, at the end, I know I cannot.

I am leaving you again, more profoundly than I have ever done before.

I can give you nothing but this book, and a prayer that this door will not be closed. That you will find a way to follow me one day. That your mother is alive and waiting, and one day she will hold you again and what is shattered will be made whole.

Trust Jane. Tell her—tell her I am sorry.

The door calls me in your mother's voice. I must go.

Forgive me. Follow me.

YS

I can't do it.

I tried, January. I tried to leave you. But I merely stood on the threshold of my door, frozen, smelling the sweetness of my home world and willing myself to take that last, final step forward.

I cannot. I cannot leave you. Not again. I am packing my things, returning to Locke House. I will bring you back here with me, and we will go through together or not at all. I am so sorry, gods, so sorry—I am coming.

Wait for me.

RUN JANUARY
ARCADIA
DO NOT TRUST

The Driftwood Door

I found Jane by following the rhythmic grind and thunk of a shovel in rocky earth. She worked steadily, digging in a low-lying spot in the center of the island, alone except for a fetid, marshy smell and the whining drone of several million mosquitoes.

And, of course, Mr. Theodore Havemeyer.

He was nothing but a stained bundle of sheets, muddy-white and vaguely larval. His hand—a colorless claw, dotted with oozing punctures roughly the size of Bad's teeth—protruded from the wrapping. It cast a too-large shadow in the late-afternoon light.

"Couldn't we just, I don't know, toss him in the lake? Or leave him?"

The crunch of the shovel biting into the ground; the *shush*

241

of dirt sliding off it. Jane did not look up at me, but a humorless smile appeared on her face. "You think the Havemeyers of the world just disappear? You think no one comes looking?" She shook her head and added comfortingly, "It's good and wet here; he won't last long."

This, I found, made me feel slightly ill, so I perched on a moss-eaten boulder and watched the crows gather along the pine boughs above us like poorly behaved funeral attendees, cawing and gossiping.

The splintery handle of the shovel appeared in my vision. I took it, and made several subsequent discoveries: first, that digging is very hard and I was still weak and sick-feeling from escaping Brattleboro. Second, that human bodies are fairly large and require substantial holes. And third, that digging leaves plenty of room in your skull for thinking, even when sweat pricks your eyes and the skin of your palms stings in a raw, you-already-have-blisters kind of way.

My father didn't abandon me. He turned back for me. The thought was a small sun burning behind my eyes, too bright to look at safely. How long had I longed for some small proof of his love for me? But his love for my mother, his selfish sadness, had always been stronger—until the last. Until it hadn't, and he'd turned away from the Door he'd wanted for seventeen years.

So where is he? I wavered a little on that thought, pictured the mad scrawl of those final words—*RUN JANUARY, ARCADIA, DO NOT TRUST*—and retreated.

What did this final chapter tell me, really, that I hadn't already suspected? Well, first: that Mr. Locke had known full well that my father was Door-hunting, and had even hired him specifically to do so. I pictured the basement rooms of Locke House with their endless aisles of crates and cases, the rooms bristling with glass cases and neat labels—how many of those treasures were stolen from other worlds? How many of them were imbued with strange powers or uncanny magics?

And how many had he sold or bartered away? I remembered the meeting I'd seen in London as a girl, the secret auction of valuable objects. There'd been Society members present, I was sure—that ferrety red-haired man, at least—so I supposed the Society, too, knew about my father and the Doors and the things he stole. And it must be the Society who stalked after him, haunting him, closing his Doors. But why, if they wanted the treasures he stole for them? Or perhaps they wanted to hoard the treasures for themselves, then seal the Doors against any further leakage. They'd like that; I'd spent enough time around rich and powerful men to know their affection for phrases like *maintaining exclusivity* and *manufacturing demand through rarity.*

It made sense, almost. But who had closed my mother's Door, that first Door in the field, all those years ago? And the mountaintop Door? My father hadn't even been employed by Mr. Locke then. Had it been random misfortune, or had the Society been closing Doors for far longer than my father's personal quest? They'd mentioned a Founder, once or twice, in reverent tones—perhaps the Society was far older than it seemed.

It didn't make sense, either, that they would harm their prize Door-hunter, but something had certainly prevented my father from coming back. Something had driven him to scrawl those last three lines. And now the Society wanted me. *They'll never stop looking for you, girl.*

There was a horrible, meaty crunch behind me.

I turned to find Jane crouched over Havemeyer's body with a mallet and a clinical expression. A peeled wooden stake now protruded from the white bundle, roughly where his heart would be.

Jane shrugged at me. "Just in case."

I teetered for a moment between horror and humor, but I couldn't help it: I laughed. It was an oversized, tiptoeing-toward-hysteria kind of laugh. Jane's eyebrows rose, but then her head tilted back and she laughed alongside me. I heard a little of the same relief in her voice, too, and it occurred to me that her attitude of cool nerve and confidence might not, in fact, be wholly true.

"You have read *entirely* too many penny dreadfuls," I admonished her. She shrugged again, unrepentant, and I went back to my digging. It felt easier, somehow, as if something heavy had been perched on my shoulders and had flapped away at the sound of our laughter.

I worked in silence for another minute or so, and then Jane began to speak. "In my world, it's wisest to shoot anything strange or unusual you might meet in the forests, and this is why I almost killed your father the first time I saw him. My first shot went wide, though. Give me that, if you aren't going to dig."

My shovelfuls had grown scant and random; I scrabbled out of the hole and Jane took my place. Her voice matched the jab-and-toss rhythm of her digging. "He began shouting and waving his arms, switching between a dozen or so languages. One of them was English; it had been a very long time since I'd heard English spoken aloud, and never by a dark-skinned, tattooed man who looked like a professor. So I did not shoot him."

The hole was now well past Jane's waist, and every shovelful made a soupy, sucking sound. Gnats hovered like overeager dinner guests at its edges. "I took him back to my camp, fed him, and we traded stories. He asked if I'd ever found another door in this world, or heard any stories about written words coming true. No, I answered, and his shoulders slumped. I felt I should apologize, but did not know for what.

"Then he gave me a warning: *The doors are closing behind me,* he said. *Someone is following me.* He begged me to return to my native world with him. He told me he knew what it was like to be trapped in a world not your own, urged me to go back with him. I refused."

"Why?" I perched at the edge of the hole, arms wrapped around my own knees. My borrowed skirt was already hopelessly muddied and stained, and for a disorienting moment I felt as if I'd been zipped backward to a time when I was young and obstreperous and gleefully unkempt.

Jane climbed out of the hole and perched beside me. "Because the place you are born isn't necessarily the place you belong. I was born into a world that abandoned me, stole from me, rejected me, is it so surprising I found a better one?" She sighed, long and regretful. "But I wanted to make one last trip through the door, just in case this madman was correct and it was my only chance. Julian stayed camped at the foot of Mount Suswa while I went searching for more ammunition and for—for news of my sister." Jane's eyes flickered like lanterns in a gust of winter air, and the question *what happened to her?* died in my throat. There was a little silence, and when she spoke again her tone was brusque. "I returned to Julian's camp. He asked me to stay again, and I laughed in his face—I'd seen what my home had become. White women watching me from train windows, poachers wearing foolish hats and posing for pictures beside animal carcasses, potbellied children begging in English, *please-sah, please-sah.* No. So Julian escorted me back to my ivory door to say good-bye. Except there was something strange waiting in the cave."

Jane was staring into the grave, face taut. "Piles of gray sticks bundled together, and wires running out, and a faint fizzing sound. Your father yelled and shoved me away, and then everything came apart. An explosion that scorched the backs of my arms and tossed both of us forward like matchsticks.

I don't know if I lost consciousness, but it felt like I blinked and suddenly there was a man standing above me, wearing a tan British uniform. And behind him, where the cave should have been, was nothing but rubble and dust.

"His lips were moving, but something was wrong with my ears. Then he drew his pistol and pointed it at Julian. He should have pointed it at me—I was the one with a weapon— but he didn't." Jane's lip curled. "When I die, I hope at least I don't look so damn surprised."

I did not look at Havemeyer's body, did not think about the neatness of the hole that had appeared in his chest.

"I didn't even wait for his body to hit the ground: I threw myself at the mountainside, tearing away stones and earth. By the time Julian stopped me my hands looked like bushmeat. He held me back and said, 'I'm sorry, I'm sorry' until I understood: I was trapped here, in this world, forever."

I'd never seen Jane cry, but I could feel a kind of rhythmic shuddering moving through her, like thunderclouds scudding across the bay. Neither of us spoke for a time but simply sat in the cooling evening and listened to the hollow, mournful hooting of a loon across the lake.

"Well. In this world you cannot be black-skinned and found near a dead white man in uniform. I used a stone to smash the body up and dragged him near the rubble, so there would be no bullet wound to scandalize a search party, and then we ran.

"We were on the train to Khartoum when your father asked where I would go next. I told him I wanted to find another way in, a back door, and he smiled sadly at me. 'I've been looking my whole life for another door to my home world,' he told me. 'But I'll look for yours, too, if you do something for me.' And he asked me to come to a rich man's house in Vermont and protect his daughter."

Another silent wave shook her. Her voice remained perfectly even. "I kept my end of the bargain. But Julian...didn't."

I cleared my throat. "He's not dead." I felt her go very still beside me, tense with hope. "I finished his book. He found a Door in Japan that led back to his own world but he didn't go through it—he tried to come back for me"—that small sun blazed again, briefly, then faltered—"but he never made it, I guess. He says to tell you"—I swallowed, tasting the shame of it on my tongue—"he's sorry."

Air hissed through the gap in Jane's teeth. "He promised me. He *promised*." Her voice was strangled, almost swallowed by emotion: bitterest betrayal, jealousy, and the sort of rage that leaves bodies in its wake.

I flinched and her eyes flicked toward me, then widened. "Wait. January, you made a passage between the asylum and this cabin. Could you do it for me? Could you write me home?" Her face shone with desperate hope, as if she expected me to produce a pen from my pocket and draw her Door in the air between us, as if she were about to see her husbands and wife again. She looked younger than I'd ever seen her.

I found I couldn't look at her as I answered. "No. I—my father's book says there are places where worlds rub against one another, like the branches of two trees, and that's where Doors are. I don't think a Door here, in Vermont, could ever reach all the way to your world."

She made an impatient, dismissive sound. "Fine, but if you went with me to Kenya, to my ivory door—"

Mutely, I lifted my bandaged left arm and held it level with her eyes. It shook and shivered after only a few seconds, and after a few more I dropped it back to my side. "Opening the way from the asylum to here almost killed me, I think," I told her softly. "And that was a Door within the same world. I don't

247

know what it might take to reopen a Door between two worlds, but I doubt I have it."

Jane exhaled very slowly, staring at my hand where it lay against the earth. She didn't say anything.

She stood abruptly, dusting her skirt and reaching for the shovel again. "I'll finish here. Go see to Samuel."

I fled, rather than see Jane cry.

Both Bad and Samuel looked like they'd died and been reanimated by a sorcerer of questionable skill. Bad—dotted with dried blood, patchworked with bandages and stitches—had crammed himself in bed between Samuel and the wall, and now slept with his chin propped adoringly on Samuel's shoulder. Samuel's skin was an unhealthy mushroomy color between white and yellow, and his breathing beneath the quilt stuttered and shivered.

His eyes opened to gummy slits when I perched on the bedside. Improbably, he smiled. "Hello, January."

"Hello, Samuel." My return smile was a timid, tremulous thing.

He extricated an arm and patted Bad's side. "What did I tell you, eh? Bad is on your side."

My smile sturdied. "Yes."

"And," he said more softly, "so am I."

His eyes were steady, glowing with some sourceless warmth; looking into them was like holding my hands above a banked fireplace in February. I looked away before I said or did something stupid. "I'm sorry. For what happened. For what Havemeyer did to you." Was my voice always that high-pitched?

Samuel shrugged, as if being tortured and kidnapped were a tiresome inconvenience. "But you will explain exactly what he was, of course, and what these doors are that so upset him, and how you got here without my daring rescue." He

248

was sliding out from beneath the quilt as he spoke, arranging himself against the pillows as though every inch of him were bruised.

"Daring rescue?"

"It was going to be spectacular," he sighed mournfully. "A midnight raid—a rope through the window—a getaway on white horses—well, gray ponies—it would've been just like one of our story papers. All wasted."

I laughed for the second time that evening. And then— haltingly, messily, fearing that Samuel would either laugh at me or pity me—I told him everything. I told him about the blue Door in the overgrown field; about my father and mother and how neither of them was dead or perhaps both of them were; about the New England Archaeological Society and the closing Doors and the dying world. Mr. Locke, keeping my father like a leashed hound and me like a caged bird. The Written, and the way certain willful persons are able to rewrite existence. And then I told him about the silver coin that became a knife, and showed him the words I'd written in my own flesh.

The skin beneath my bandages was pale and puckered with fresh scabs, like some injured lake creature that had washed ashore. Samuel touched the jagged curve of the *J* carved into my skin.

"You did not need rescuing, then, it seems," he said, a wry twist in his smile. "Stregas rescue themselves in all the stories."

"Stregas?"

"Witches," he clarified.

"Oh." Sure, I'd been hoping for something a little more complimentary but—*he believed me*, without even a flicker of doubt. Maybe all those years of sneaking pulpy monster stories when he was supposed to be manning the shop counter had rotted his brain just like his mother said they would. Maybe he just trusted me.

Samuel continued, speculatively. "They always end up alone in the stories—witches, I mean—living in the woods or mountains or locked in towers. I suppose it would take a brave man to love a witch, and men are mostly cowards." He looked directly at me as he finished, with a kind of raised-chin boldness that said: *I am not a coward.*

I found I couldn't say anything at all. Or even think, much.

After a moment he smiled again, gently, and said, "So these Society people. They will keep looking for you, won't they? For the things you know, and the things you can do."

"Yes, they will." Jane's voice came from behind me. She stood in the doorway, framed by the last red rays of sunlight, her mouth set in a grim line. Something about her reminded me of my father, and the way grief stooped his shoulders and carved lines on his face.

Jane moved stiffly to the water bucket to rinse her dirt-grimed arms, saying, "We need a plan, and a place to hide." She patted herself dry. "I suggest Arcadia, the name your father gave me for a world hidden on the southern coast of Maine. It is inhospitable and inaccessible, or so I am given to understand, which makes it an excellent place to disappear. I know the way." Jane's voice was perfectly even, as if a hostile and alien world was a perfectly ordinary destination, like the bank or the post office.

"But surely we don't need to—"

"January," she interrupted, "we have no money, no place to live, no family. I am black in a nation that abhors blackness, foreign in a nation that abhors foreigners. And worst of all we are memorable—an African woman and an in-between girl with wild hair and a scarred arm." She turned her hands palm up. "If the Society wants to find you, they will. And I doubt Mr. Havemeyer was the worst of them."

Samuel shifted against his pillows. "But you are forgetting— Miss January is not defenseless. She could write you anything you pleased, it seems to me. A fortress. A door to Timbuktu, or Mars. An unfortunate accident for Mr. Locke." He sounded rather hopeful about that last possibility; he had growled in a very Bad-like manner when I told him about Brattleboro.

A sour smile twisted Jane's face. "Her powers are not unlimited, I am told."

I felt a prickle of defensiveness, doused in shame. "No." It came out slightly choked-sounding. "My father says word-working comes at a cost. I can't just rip things up and stick them back together however I like." I snuck a sidelong look at Samuel, my voice lowering. "I'm not much of a witch, I'm afraid."

He twitched his hand so that it lay very near to mine on the blankets, our fingertips almost touching. "Good," he whispered. "I'm not that brave."

Jane cleared her throat rather markedly. "Now, getting there will be challenging. We have two hundred miles to cross without being recognized or followed, and not much money to do it with. I am afraid"—she smiled a tight, chill smile—"Miss Scaller will have to become accustomed to a rather different standard of living."

That stung. "I *have* traveled a bit, you know." I had luggage with my name stamped on little brass plates; my passport looked like a well-thumbed paperback novel.

Jane laughed. It wasn't a very cheerful sound. "And in all your travels, have you spent a single night in a bed you made yourself? Cooked a single meal? Have you ever even seen a second-class ticket?" I didn't say anything, damningly, but merely glared. "We'll be sleeping in the woods and begging rides, so adjust your expectations accordingly."

I couldn't think of an especially clever reply, so I switched subjects. "I'm not convinced we should even go to this Arcadia place. My father disappeared in *Japan*, if you recall, and we ought to go look for him, at least—"

But Jane was shaking her head tiredly. "They'll be expecting that above all. Maybe someday, after some time has passed, when it's safer."

To hell with safer. "Maybe—maybe we could go to Mr. Locke for help." Samuel and Jane both emitted sounds somewhere between disbelief and outrage. I forged on, shoulders squared. "I know, I know—but look: I don't think he wanted me or my father hurt or dead. He just wanted to get a little richer and have a few more rare objects to stick in display cases. He might not even know about the Society closing the Doors, or maybe he doesn't care—and he loved me, I think. At least a little. He could help us hide, lend us some money, get us to Japan…" I trailed off.

Jane's eyes filled with something tarry and oozing: pity. It's surprising how much pity can hurt. "You'd like to go off adventuring and save your father, like a fairy-tale hero. I understand. But you are young and penniless and homeless, and you've never really seen the ugly side of the world. It would swallow you whole, January."

Beside me, Samuel said, "And if Mr. Locke was trying to protect you before, he has done a very bad job so far. I think you should run."

I went mute, feeling my whole future twist and warp dizzyingly beneath my feet. I'd been waiting for my life to snap back to normal, as if everything that'd happened since my father's disappearance were a movie and soon the card would say *THE END* and the lights would buzz back to life and I'd find myself safely back at Locke House, rereading *The Rover Boys on Land and Sea.*

But all that was permanently in the past, like a dragonfly preserved in amber.

Follow Jane. "All right," I whispered, and tried not to feel like I was seven again, eternally running away. "We'll go to

Arcadia. And will you—will you stay there with me? Or go home?"

She flinched. "I have no home." I met her eyes and found that the pity in them had curdled into something ragged and despairing. It made me think of ancient ruins or decaying tapestries, of things that have lost the thread of themselves.

She teetered for a moment on the edge of saying something further—recriminations or rebukes or regrets—then turned and left the cabin with her back very straight.

Samuel and I were quiet in her absence. My thoughts were a flock of drunk birds, ricocheting between despair (*Would we both be homeless forever? Would I spend my life running?*) and a childish, bubbling excitement (*Arcadia! Adventure! Escape!*) and the distracting warmth of Samuel's hand still lying beside mine on the quilt.

He cleared his throat and said, not very casually, "I intend to go with you. If you allow it."

"*What*—you can't! Leave your family, your home, your, your profession—it's far too dangerous—"

"I was never going to be a good grocer," he interrupted mildly. "Even my mother admits it. I have always wanted something else, something bigger. Another world would do."

I gave an exasperated half laugh. "I don't even know where we're going, or for how long! My future is all tangled and messy, and you can't sign up for all that out of, of *goodness* or *pity* or—"

"January." His voice had gone lower and more urgent, which made my heart do a funny *duh-dump* against my ribs. "I do not offer out of pity. I think you know this."

I looked away, out the cabin window at the blueing evening, but it didn't matter: I could still feel the heat of his gaze against my cheek. The banked coals had sparked and caught flame.

253

"Maybe," he said slowly, "maybe I did not make myself clear before, when I said I was on your side. I meant also that I would like to be *at* your side, to go with you into every door and danger, to run with you into your tangled-up future. For"—and a distant part of me was gratified to note that his voice had gone wobbly and strained—"for always. If you like."

Time—an unreliable, fractious creature since the asylum—now absented itself entirely from the proceedings. It left the two of us floating, weightless, like a pair of dust motes suspended in afternoon sunlight.

I found myself thinking, for no particular reason, of my father. Of the way he'd looked as he walked away from me all those times, shoulders bent and head bowed, dusty coat hanging loose on his frame. Then I thought of Mr. Locke: the warmth of his hand on my shoulder, the jovial boom of his laugh. The pity in his eyes as he'd watched me drugged and dragged from his house.

In my life I'd learned that the people you love will leave you. They will abandon you, disappoint you, betray you, lock you away, and in the end you will be alone, again and always.

But Samuel hadn't, had he? When I was a child trapped in Locke House with no one but Wilda for company, he'd slipped me story papers and brought me my dearest friend. When I was a madwoman locked in an asylum without hope or help, he'd brought me a key. And now, when I was a runaway pursued by monsters and mysteries, he was offering me himself. *For always.*

I felt the lure of that offer like a hook behind my heart. To be not-alone, to be loved, to have that warm presence always at my shoulder...I stared hungrily into Samuel's face, wondering if it was a particularly handsome one and realizing I could no longer tell. It was only his eyes I saw, ember-bright, unwavering.

It would be so easy to say yes.

But I hesitated. My father had written about True Love like it was gravity—something that simply existed, invisible and inescapable. Was it True Love that made my breath catch and my heart seize? Or was I merely scared and lonely, reeling from exhaustion, clinging to Samuel like a drowning woman offered a buoy?

Samuel was watching my face, and whatever he saw made him swallow. "I've offended you. Forgive me." His smile curdled with embarrassment. "It is only an offer. To consider."

"No, it's not—I just—" I started the sentence without knowing where it was going, half-terrified of where it might end, but then—with a sense of timing that bordered on the divine—Jane returned.

She had an armload of mossy firewood and a closed expression, like a sutured wound. She saw us and paused, her eyebrows lifting in a my-my-what-have-I-interrupted sort of expression, but proceeded to the stove without comment. Bless her.

After a minute or two (during which Samuel and I both exhaled and shifted our hands farther apart), Jane said mildly, "We should sleep early tonight. We leave in the morning."

"Of course." Samuel's voice was perfectly even. He levered himself off the bed, face paling with the effort, and ducked his head graciously toward me.

"Oh no, you don't have to—I can sleep on the floor—"

He feigned deafness, spreading a few mousy-smelling blankets in the corner and crawling into them. He rolled his face to the cabin wall, shoulders curving inward.

"Good night, Jane. January." He said my name carefully, as if it were barbed.

I climbed into bed beside Bad and lay stiff and aching, too tired to sleep. My eyelids felt hinged and hot; my arm throbbed. Jane propped herself in the rocking chair in front of the stove with Mr. Locke's revolver in her lap. Faint coal light glowed from the grate, drawing the planes of her face in soft orange.

She wore her grief more openly now that she was unobserved. It was the same expression I'd seen so many times on my father's face, when he paused in his writing and stared out the gray windows as if wishing he could sprout wings and dive through them.

Was theirs the only future I could look forward to? Was I doomed to grim survival in a world that wasn't my own? Grieving, unmoored, terribly alone?

Bad gave one of those soft dog yawns and stretched beside me.

Well, not entirely alone, at least. I fell asleep with my face pressed into the sunshine smell of his fur.

Traveling with Jane across New England was nothing at all like traveling with Mr. Locke, except that both of them had similarly clear ideas about who was in charge. Jane issued orders and instructions with the calm confidence of someone used to seeing them followed, and I wondered if she'd led her own bands of hunters back in her adopted world, and how hard it had been for her to impersonate a maid in this one.

She woke Samuel and me in the predawn gloom, and we were halfway across the lake before the first honeyed line of sunlight crept above the horizon. The four of us crammed into the Zappias' rowboat rather than risk the ferry and its curious eyes, and took turns rowing toward the dull gaslight glow of the shore.

Rowing, I discovered, is quite as difficult as shoveling dirt. By the time the hull scuffed against coarse sand, my palms had progressed past blistered and were approaching bloodied, and Samuel was moving like someone several decades older than his actual age. Jane looked perfectly fine, except for the grave dirt and blood still staining her skirt.

I should've predicted the way people would scurry away from us as we straggled into town, clutching their hats and muttering. We made an unsettling gang: an armed black woman, a sickly young man, a glaring dog, and an odd-colored girl with ill-fitting clothes and no shoes. I tried to ask one of the scurrying women for directions to the nearest train station, but Jane stamped on my bare foot.

"Well, excuse *me*, but I thought you said we'd take the train?"

Jane sighed at me. "Yes, but as we will not be purchasing tickets, it's best not to draw attention to ourselves." She jerked her head at the railway snaking east out of town. "Follow me." She walked on without waiting for assent.

Samuel and I looked at one another for almost the first time since our conversation the night before. He raised his brows, eyes sparking with humor, and made a grand after-you bow.

Jane led us to a small, mostly empty train yard, where we slunk aboard a flat railcar labeled *MONTPELIER LUMBER CO.* and waited. Within the hour we were hurtling east, deafened by the roar and rattle of the rails, coated in coal smoke and dust, grinning like children or madmen. Bad's tongue lolled in the wind.

The next two days are blurred in my memory, lost in a haze of heat and aching feet and the ever-present fear that there were eyes on the back of my neck, hunting me. I remember Jane's voice, cool and certain; a night spent curled in an overgrown field with the sky hanging like a spangled quilt above me; greasy fish sandwiches bought from a roadside store; a ride from a farmer hauling blueberries to Concord in a mule-drawn cart, and another from a chatty postal carrier at the end of his route.

And I remember Jane lifting her face to the breeze as we limped down an unnamed road just over the Maine state line. "Smell that?" she asked.

I did: brine and cold stone and fish bones. The ocean.

We followed the road until it turned to smooth pebbles and salt-stunted pines, our footsteps muted in the moonlight. Jane seemed to be navigating from my father's instructions rather than any map or memory of her own. She muttered to herself, occasionally reaching out to touch an odd-shaped rock or squinting up at the stars. The rhythmic rushing of the sea drew closer.

We rounded a dense wall of pines, scrabbled down a short bluff—and there it was.

I'd been to the seaside dozens of times: I'd strolled along the beaches of southern France and sipped lemonade on the coast of Antigua; I'd taken steamers across the Atlantic and watched the neat parting of the sea before us. Even storms felt small and distant from inside a hotel or a steel hull. I'd thought of the ocean as something pleasant and pretty, a slightly bigger version of my own familiar lake. But standing there on the rock ledge with waves crashing beneath me and the vastness of the Atlantic roiling like the black contents of a witch's cauldron—it seemed to be something else entirely. Something wild, something secretive, something that might swallow you whole.

Jane was picking her way down a lichen-slick path, hugging the cliff side. Samuel and I followed, Bad scrabbling ahead of us. My lungs felt strangely constricted, my pulse shuddering in anticipation: *A Door.* A real, actual Door, the first I'd seen since I was a half-feral child running through the fields.

A Door my father had left hidden and open just for me. Even now, when he was trapped or caged or dead on the other side of the planet, he had not abandoned me. Not entirely. The thought warmed me, like a candle flame held safe against the whipping sea wind.

Jane had disappeared into a low, damp crevice. I leaned

forward eagerly, but Jane reemerged tugging a jangled pile of planks and rotten twine behind her. She sighed heavily. "Well, it was too much to hope it would last in this weather, I suppose. We might be able to float the supplies alongside us with whatever's left." And then she began—methodically and quite unself-consciously—to undress.

"Jane, what are you—where's the Door?"

She did not answer but merely pointed out to sea.

I followed her finger and saw a lumpy gray smudge on the horizon, with patches of bare rock gleaming silver in the starlight. "An island? But surely we can't—you're not *swimming* to it?"

"Inaccessible. Inhospitable. Just as advertised, I believe." Her tone was dry. She was already splashing into the sea, her underthings shining white, her limbs vanishing into the dark. Bad dove joyfully after her.

I turned to Samuel in search of an ally and found him unbuttoning his shirt. "Bet you the last loaf of bread I can beat you," he murmured, as if we were children playing in the lake rather than weary, desperate adults standing on the coast of a cold sea, running away from God-knew-what. I laughed, helplessly.

I caught the bright curve of his answering smile, glimpsed the paleness of his chest, and then he was wading after Jane and Bad. There was nothing to do but follow him.

I shouldn't have been surprised at the cold—it was summer, but summer in Maine is a fleeting, cautious creature that disappears as soon as the sun sets—but I don't think it's possible to step into water that cold without being surprised. Swimming through it was like swimming through a cloud of stinging insects. We clung to the rotten raft-planks with frozen fingers, tugging our belongings alongside us, our breath coming in thin gasps. Even Bad was lifting his head high out of the water as if trying to levitate rather than swim. The salt seeped through my bandages, burrowing into the words carved on my arm. If I could have turned back, if I could have given up and crawled back home to the rosy fireplaces of Locke House, I would have. But I couldn't. So I kept reaching my stinging arms out into the chill black sea, kept inching closer to the gray blur of the island.

And then somehow my knees were scraping stone and Jane was heaving the raft up the shore and Samuel's breath was a harsh wheeze beside me. He crawled a few feet farther and collapsed in a goose-fleshed heap, face pressed into the pebbled shore. "I do not," he gasped, "like the cold. Anymore."

I remembered the piercing chill of Havemeyer's touch, Samuel's sickly face as he fell, and fear sent me scrabbling to his side. I touched his back, numb-fingered. "Are you all right?"

He propped himself on one elbow and craned his head wearily upward. He blinked at me, clearing the salt water from his eyes, and his face went curiously blank. I became aware that the ocean had transformed my underthings from shapeless cotton sacks into something more like a second skin, clinging and nearly translucent. Neither of us moved. I felt frozen, snared by his oil-and-ember eyes—until Bad positioned himself several inches away and shook, spraying us in freezing salt water.

Samuel closed his eyes very deliberately and returned his forehead to the pebbles. "Yes. I am," he sighed. Then he staggered upright and limped to the raft. He returned with his own mostly dry shirt and draped it over my shoulders without letting his fingers brush my skin. It smelled of flour and sweat.

"Almost there. We'll go through, I think, before we make camp." Even Jane sounded weary now.

We stumbled after her, winding up the shore and climbing a low bluff on shaking legs. The wind whipped us dry, leaving a white rime of salt on my skin.

On the far side of the island, perched like the skeleton of some long-dead guardian, stood the abandoned bones of a lighthouse. Its tower sagged and leaned and its paint, which might once have been cheery white-and-red, had weathered to the same grayish-brown as the rock beneath it. Where there should have been a doorway there was only a gaping mouth. Jane ducked through it first, picking her way over tumbled rafters and missing floorboards, and Bad and I followed.

Standing inside was like standing in the rotted rib cage of a sea creature, dark and strewn with seaweed. A single bright moonbeam shone through the broken window and illuminated a door on the western wall, where there had been no door on the outside. My heart shivered in my chest.

The Door was old-looking, even older than the lighthouse decomposing around it, built of lashed-together driftwood and strips of curving ivory. A faint breeze whistled through the gaps, carrying a hot, dry smell like hayfields in the August sun.

Jane tugged the whalebone handle and it flowed smoothly toward her, oiled and silent. She looked back at us, flashed her gap-toothed grin, and stepped into the black.

I rested one hand on Bad's skull and reached the other toward Samuel, impulsively. "Don't be afraid, and don't let go."

He met my eyes. "I won't," he said, and his fingers wrapped tight around mine.

We stepped across the Threshold together. The nothingness was just as terrifying, just as empty, just as suffocating as it had been before—but somehow it felt less vast with Samuel and Bad beside me. We sailed through the dark like a trio of comets, like a many-legged constellation spinning through the night, and then our feet crunched on dry grass.

We stood in the orange, alien dusk of another world. I had a single reeling second to see the endless golden plain, the sky so wide open it felt like an ocean suspended above me—before a rough voice spoke.

"Jesus, it's a goddamned parade. All right, folks, you're going to stop where you are and turn around real slow. And then you're going to tell me what your business is, and how in the name of sweet Christ you found our door."

The Burning Door

When you've stepped into a foreign world and you're cold and weak-limbed and only half-dressed, you tend to do as you are told. The three of us turned slowly around.

Facing us was a rangy, raggedy old man, very much like a scarecrow if scarecrows grew patchy white beards and wielded spears. He wore a vaguely martial-looking gray coat, a pair of rough sandals made of rope and rubber, and a bright feather tucked into the white tangle of his hair. He grunted, jabbing the spear point toward my belly.

I raised shaking hands. "Please, sir, we're just trying to—" I began, and it was no effort at all to sound pitiful and terrified. But the effect was undercut somewhat by Bad, who was making a sound like an idling engine, hackles spiked, and Jane, who had drawn Mr. Locke's revolver and pointed it directly at the old man's chest.

His eyes flicked to the gun and back to me, hardening. "Go ahead, miss. But I bet I could gut this girl before I bled out. You want to make the same bet?" There was a brief stillness, during which I imagined how unpleasant it would be to be disemboweled by a rusty homemade spear and silently swore at my father for his poor judgment—and then Samuel stepped between us.

He leaned gently forward until the spear point dimpled his shirt. "Sir. There is no need for this. We don't mean any harm, I swear to you." He made a sharp *put down your weapon, woman* gesture at Jane, who ignored him entirely. "We're just looking for a, ah, place to hide for a little time. We didn't mean to intrude." The old man's eyes remained narrowed and suspicious, a pair of damp blue marbles set in deep folds of flesh.

Samuel licked his lips and tried again. "Let us try again, yes? I am Samuel Zappia, of Zappia Family Groceries in Vermont. This is Mr. Sindbad, more often called Bad; Miss Jane Irimu, who will lower her gun *very soon*, I am sure; and Miss January Scaller. We were told this was a good place to—"

"Scholar?" The man spat the word, tilting his chin at me.

I nodded over Samuel's shoulder.

"You Julian's girl, then?"

My skin prickled at the sound of my father's name. I nodded again.

"Well, shit." The spear point dropped abruptly earthward. The man leaned comfortably against it, picking at his snaggled teeth with one fingernail and squinting amiably at us. "Sorry to scare you, hon, that's my mistake. But the whole point of guard duty is to guard, ain't it, and you can't be too careful. Why don't y'all follow me and we'll get you some hot food and a place to set down. Unless"—and here he gestured toward the gnarled, age-wracked tree just behind us, at the narrow Door nestled in its roots—"there's anybody likely to come running through after you?"

Samuel and I stared at him in slightly stunned silence, but Jane made a considering sound. "Not immediately, I shouldn't think." The revolver had vanished again into her tight-knotted bundle and Bad's growls had turned to intermittent grumbles. His tail gave the smallest of wags, not indicating friendliness so much as a cessation of open hostilities.

"Well, c'mon, then. Might make it back for dinner if we hustle." The man turned toward the setting sun, bent to pluck a rusted red bicycle from the tall grass, and began wheeling it down a narrow track. He whistled tunelessly as he walked.

We exchanged a series of looks, ranging from *what the hell* to *at least he's not trying to kill us anymore*, and followed him. We waded across the plain with the last red sunbeams warming our cheeks, driving the frigid Atlantic from our bones. The old man alternated between whistling and chatting, entirely undeterred by our weary, edgy silence.

His name, we learned, was John Solomon Ayers, called Sol by his friends, and he'd been born in Polk County, Tennessee, in the year 1847. He'd joined the 3rd Regiment of the Tennessee Infantry when he was sixteen, deserted at seventeen when he realized he was likely to die miserable and hungry on behalf of some rich cotton grower who wouldn't give a bent penny for him, and was promptly taken prisoner by the Yanks. He'd spent a few years in a Massachusetts prison before busting out and running for the coast. He'd stumbled into this world and been here ever since.

"And have you been, uh, all alone? Until my father came through?" It would, I felt, explain a few of Solomon's more eccentric qualities. I pictured him squatting alone in a dirt hovel, whistling to himself, perhaps shunned by the natives...

And where *were* the natives of this world? Were they likely to swoop down on us in a thundering horde? I glanced up at the bare horizon but saw nothing more alarming than a low line of hills and a jumble of sand-colored stones ahead.

Solomon cackled. "Lord, no. Arcadia—that's what we call it, who knows what it used to be called—is about halfway toward being a proper city these days. Not that I've seen many of those. We're nearly there, now." No one answered him, but Jane's face expressed deepest skepticism.

The tumbled stones loomed larger as we walked, growing into massive boulders that leaned against one another at precarious angles. A few birds—eagles, maybe, or hawks, the same shimmering golden color as the feather in Sol's hair—watched us mistrustfully from their craggy perches. They took flight as we approached, seeming by some trick of the fading light to vanish into the sky.

Solomon led us to a gap between the two largest stones, which formed a shadowed tunnel with a strange, shining curtain strung across it. It was only when we stood before it that I realized it wasn't fabric at all, but dozens of golden feathers tied and dangling like soft wind chimes. I could see through them to the other side of the standing stones: a few empty hills, endless swaying grasses, the last rose glimmer of the sun as it set. No secret cities.

Solomon leaned his bicycle against the stone and crossed his arms, staring at the feathers as if waiting for something to happen. Bad gave an impatient whine.

"Excuse me, Mr. Ayers," I began.

"Sol's fine," he said absently.

"Right. Um, excuse me, Sol, what are you—" But before I could find a polite way to ask if he was an honest-to-God madman who spent his spare time knitting feathers into curtains, or if he had an actual destination in mind, I heard padding footsteps. They came from the darkness behind the curtain, but there was nothing there except stone and dusty earth—

Until a wide hand swept the feathers aside and a squat woman in a black stovepipe hat stepped out of the empty air and stood before us, arms crossed and eyes narrowed. Jane said a series of words I didn't recognize, but which I was sure were impolite.

The woman was roundish and brownish, with silver-streaked hair. She wore a collection of clothes just as motley as Solomon's—including a silver-buttoned tailcoat, pants sewn from burlap, and some sort of bright beaded collar—but somehow contrived to look imposing rather than comical. She glared at each of us in turn with heavy-lidded eyes.

"Guests, Sol?" She said the word *guests* the way you might say *fleas* or *influenza*.

Solomon gave an exaggerated bow. "May I introduce our most esteemed chieftainess—don't growl at me, darlin', you know you are—Miss Molly Neptune. Molly, you remember that black fella with the tattoos, name of Julian Scholar? Came through a few years back and mentioned a daughter?" He turned both palms toward me like a fisherman displaying a particularly large catch. "She's finally come to call."

Molly Neptune looked only slightly appeased. "I see. And these others?"

Jane lifted her chin. "Are her companions. Charged with keeping her alive and safe." *Companions.* See the curve of that *C* like a pair of outstretched arms? It implied the sort of friends who might slay dragons or go on hopeless quests or swear blood oaths at midnight. I swallowed the urge to fling myself at Jane in gratitude.

Molly ran her tongue over her teeth. "Doesn't look like you've done too good a job, so far," she observed. "She's three quarters drowned, half-naked, and banged up all over." Jane's jaw tightened, and I tried to pull Samuel's shirt cuffs lower over the grayish bandaging around my wrist.

The woman sighed. "Well, never let them say Molly Neptune doesn't keep her word." And, with a slightly mocking flourish, she drew back the feathered curtain.

The view between the stones—that dull triangular patch of sky and grass—disappeared and was replaced by a confused jumble of shapes. I ducked under Molly's arm and into the short tunnel, trying to squint the images into focus. Steep stairs rising up hillsides; thatched roofs and clay bricks; a rising murmur of voices.

A city.

I stepped out into a sandstone plaza with my mouth hanging slightly open. The empty hills had been suddenly populated by a messy sprawl of buildings and streets, as if some enormous child had tossed his blocks into the valley and wandered away. Everything—the narrow roads, the walls, the low houses and domed temples—was built of yellow clay and dried grass. It glowed gold in the cooling dusk: a secret El Dorado hidden on the coast of Maine.

Except there was something weirdly dead-looking about it, as if I were standing in the leftover bones of a city rather than the thing itself. Tumbled-down bricks and slumping buildings dotted the hillsides, surrounded by broken statues of winged men and eagle-headed women. In some places gnarled trees had rooted themselves in rotted-thatch roofs, and tufts of grass sprouted in the cracked streets. The fountains were all dry.

A ruin. But not an empty one: children laughed and screeched as they rolled a rubber tire down an alley; laundry zigzagged from window to window on what looked like telegraph wires; greasy cook smoke hung low over the square.

"Welcome to Arcadia, Miss Scholar." Molly was watching me with a slightly smug expression.

"I—what *is* this place? Did you build all this?" I gestured a little wildly at the eagle-headed statues, the rows of clay houses. Samuel and Jane had emerged behind us with similar expressions of startled awe.

Molly gave a small shake of her head. "Found it." A bell clanged twice from somewhere in the city, and she added, "Dinner's ready. C'mon."

I trailed after her, feeling like a cross between Alice and Gulliver and a stray cat. Questions buzzed in my skull—if these people didn't build the city, then who did? And where were they now? And why was everyone dressed like some weird cross between a circus performer and a tramp?—but a heavy, mute exhaustion had fallen over me. It was the weight of a new world pressing against my senses, perhaps, or maybe the half mile of freezing ocean I'd swum across.

We joined a stream of other people who gawked at us curiously. I gawked back; I'd never seen such a wildly disparate group of humans in my life. It reminded me of the London train station when I was a girl—*a human zoo*, Locke had called it.

There was a freckled, redheaded woman wearing a canary-colored dress and carrying a toddler on one hip; a group of giggling girls with their hair braided in intricate swirls around their heads; an ancient-looking black woman speaking some language that involved periodic clicks and tocks; a pair of older men walking with their fingers interlaced.

Solomon saw me staring and grinned. "Runaways, like I said. Every type of person that ever needed a place to run has ended up in Arcadia at one time or another. We got a few Indians, some Irish girls who didn't care for the cotton mills, some colored folks whose ancestors jumped overboard on the way to the auction block, even a couple of Chinamen. After a few generations we get all mixed together. Take Miss Molly— her granddaddy was a Indian witch doctor, but her mama was a Georgia slave that run up north." He sounded rather proud, as if he'd personally invented her.

"So none of you are actually *from* here. From this world." Jane was listening from Solomon's other side with her eyebrows drawn together.

Molly answered. "When my grandfather first found this place it was empty except for eagles and bones. Not a single living soul, and not much food or water—but no white men, either. It suited him just fine."

"Although a few of us white fellas have slipped in sideways, since then," Solomon stage-whispered. Molly swatted at him without looking backward and he dodged, and something in the ease of their motions made me think they'd been friends for a very long time.

We ate outdoors, seated at a series of long tables made of weathered wood that looked suspiciously like it had once belonged to the lighthouse floor. We were too stunned and exhausted to do much more than chew, and the Arcadians seemed content to leave us be. They chattered and argued like a great, untidy family, laughing as they exchanged heaping bowls of food: dark bread the approximate texture of unleavened bricks, baked yams, unidentifiable meat on skewers that Bad heartily approved of, and something alcoholic served in tin soup cans that only Jane dared to drink.

My shoulder leaned against Samuel's as the sky blackened and the wind chilled, and I found myself entirely unable to pull away. It was so warm, so familiar in this foreign world. Samuel did not look at me, but I saw the corners of his eyes crimp.

We slept that night in one of the unclaimed houses, lying on the clay floor in a nest of borrowed blankets and quilts. I lay staring at the stars glimmering through the missing hunks of thatch, at all the constellations I couldn't name.

"Jane?" I whispered.

She made an annoyed, half-asleep sound.

"How long do you think we'll have to stay here before the Society gives up on us? When will it be safe to go look for my father?"

There was a brief silence. "I think you should go to sleep, January. And learn to live with what you have."

What did I have? My father's book and my silver coin-knife, both wrapped tight in a stolen pillowcase. Bad, snoring lightly beside me. Jane. Samuel. My own unwritten words waiting to change the shape of the world.

Surely all that outweighed what I didn't have: a mother, a father, a home. Surely it would be enough.

I woke abruptly, feeling like something that had washed up on the shore and been left to cure in the sun: salty, sweaty, sour-smelling. I might've forced myself back to sleep through sheer force of will, except that Bad yipped in greeting.

"Morning to you, too, dog." It was Molly Neptune's slow, graveled voice.

I sat up. So did Samuel. Jane made a pathetic flopping motion, like a beached fish, then pressed her face deeper into the blankets.

"That was Sol's brew she was drinking last night. She'll survive." Molly stepped across the threshold and settled herself cross-legged on the floor. "Probably." She produced two jars of plums and a half loaf of dense bread. "Eat. And we'll talk."

"About what?"

Molly removed her stovepipe hat and considered me gravely. "This is not an easy world to survive in, January. I don't know how much your father told you"—*far too little, as usual*—"but it's dry, harsh land. We can't say for sure what happened to the original inhabitants, but my grandfather had a theory that this was the original Dawn Land our stories talk about, and that our ancestors communed closely with these people. Perhaps, then, they suffered the same sicknesses and evils that came to us. Except they didn't make it."

She shrugged. "It doesn't matter, really. But it means that everyone here must do their fair share to keep us from going the same way. We need to determine what your fair share might be."

I felt a queasy pang of doubt—what could I contribute to these tough, practical people? Accounting? Latin lessons?— but Samuel was nodding comfortably. "What work is there to help with?"

"Oh, all kinds. We haul water from a spring to the north, we farm what we can, we hunt prairie rats and deer... We make everything we need. Almost." Molly's eyes on us were sharp, watchful, as if testing our cleverness.

I didn't feel clever. "So... what do you do? If it isn't enough?"

But it was Samuel who answered. He held the jarred plums up to the light and ran his thumb over the embossed glass. *BALL MASON JAR CO.*, it read. "They steal." He did not sound particularly perturbed by this.

The folds around Molly's eyes deepened with grim humor. "We scavenge, boy. We find, we borrow, we buy. And sometimes we steal. We figure your world stole enough from each of us, it won't hurt it to give us some back."

I tried and failed to picture the Arcadians strolling casually into the small towns of Maine without being immediately noticed, apprehended, and possibly imprisoned. "But how—?"

"Very carefully," Molly answered dryly. "And if it does not go as planned, we have these." She reached two fingers beneath her beaded collar and extracted a shimmering golden feather. "You saw the eagles as you walked in, yes? Each of them sheds just a single feather in their lifetimes. The children search the plains for them every morning and every evening, and when they find one we call a citywide meeting to decide who carries it. They're our most precious possessions." She brushed the edge of the feather, delicately. "If I were frightened or cornered, and if I were to blow my breath against this feather, you would no longer see me sitting before you. It tricks the eye in some way we don't understand and frankly don't care to—all we know is that, to the casual observer, you become almost invisible." She smiled. "A thief's dream. No one has ever followed us back to the lighthouse."

Jane, who had struggled up to one elbow and was listening now with puffy-eyed effort, made a grunt of enlightenment. "But then how did Julian find you?" she asked. Her voice sounded as if her throat had been lined with sand in the night.

"Well, there are still rumors. Stories about mischievous spirits that haunt the coast, stealing pies from windowsills and milk from cows. Julian knew how to follow a story. We are fortunate that there are few men like him. Well"—Molly heaved herself back to her feet, dusting her tailcoat—"we can hardly send the three of you out scavenging if you're wanted criminals."

"We're not—" Samuel began.

Molly flapped an annoyed hand at him. "Are there powerful people after you? People with money and influence and patience?" We exchanged uneasy looks. "Then you'll be criminals soon, if you aren't already, and we sure as hell don't have feathers to spare on you. We'll have to find other work for you."

This threat proved to be both earnest and immediate; the three of us spent the next week laboring alongside the Arcadians.

I—as the member of our party with the fewest practical skills—was sent to work with the children. The children were unnecessarily amused by this. They taught me how to skin prairie rats and haul water with almost offensive enthusiasm, and delighted in the discovery that I was slower and clumsier than the average Arcadian nine-year-old.

"Don't worry," advised a gray-eyed, dark-skinned girl on my second morning. She wore a grimy lace frock and a pair of men's work boots. "It took me years to get really good at balancing the water buckets." Demonstrating both maturity and nobility, I resisted the urge to knock the bucket off her head.

Even Bad was more useful than me; once his leg had healed enough to remove the splint, he was recruited to join Jane and the hunters. They trotted out onto the plains before dawn each morning, armed with a truly random assortment of weapons and traps, and returned with limp rows of furred bodies slung over their shoulders. Jane was unsmiling, but she moved with a predatory ease I'd never seen in the narrow halls of Locke House. I wondered if this was how she'd looked as she'd prowled through the forests of her lost world, hunting with the leopard-women; I wondered if her Door was closed forever. Or if I could open it, if I were brave enough to try.

Samuel seemed to be working everywhere with everyone simultaneously. I saw him repairing a thatched rooftop; bent over a steaming copper cauldron in the kitchens; stuffing mattresses with fresh-dried grasses; tilling the gardens and sending clouds of yellow dust into the air. He was always smiling, always laughing, his eyes glowing as if he were on some grand adventure. It occurred to me that perhaps he'd been right: he wouldn't have made a very good grocer.

"Could you be happy here? Truly?" I asked him on the fourth or fifth evening. It was the slow-moving, after-dinner time of the day when everyone lounged, full-bellied, and Bad crunched contentedly on the small bones of prairie rats.

Samuel shrugged. "Perhaps. It would depend."

"On what?"

He didn't answer immediately but looked at me in a steady-eyed, serious way that made my ribs tighten. "Could you be happy here?" I shrugged back, eyes sliding away. After a short silence I moved to sit with Yaa Murray, the gray-eyed girl, and cajoled her into braiding my hair. I fell quiet beneath the hypnotic twist and tug of her fingers.

Could I truly be happy never knowing my father's fate? Never seeing the seas of the Written or the archives of the City of Nin? Leaving the Society to their obscure machinations, their malevolent Door-closing?

But then—what else *could* I do, really? I was a misfit and a runaway, like everyone else here. I was young and soft and untried. Girls like me do not fling themselves against the crushing weight of fate; they don't hunt villains or have adventures; they hunker down and survive and find happiness where they can.

The sound of running steps thudded down the street and Yaa's fingers froze in my hair. The comfortable babble of the Arcadians ceased.

A boy came hurtling into the square, chest heaving and eyes wild. Molly Neptune stood up. "Something wrong, Aaron?" Her voice was a mild rumble, but her shoulders were squared with tension.

The boy bent in half, panting, his eyes white-ringed. "It's—there's a old lady down by the tree, real upset, saying a man chased her through the door. No sign of him now." Fear clotted my throat like cold cotton. *They found us.*

But the boy was still trying to speak, looking up into Molly's eyes and moving his lips soundlessly.

"What else, boy?"

He swallowed. "It's Sol, miss. His throat's been cut clean open. He's dead."

★   ★   ★

If Mr. Locke had successfully taught me anything, it was how to be quiet when I wanted to howl or shriek or claw the wallpaper to ribbons. My limbs stiffened like stuffed appendages tacked onto some poorly taxidermied subject, and a ringing silence filled my skull. I tried hard not to think anything at all.

While Molly shouted orders and Jane and Samuel sprang to their feet to help—I didn't think: *Oh God, Solomon.* I didn't think about his jaunty golden feather, his scarecrow clothing, his genial winks.

When a crowd of people departed and left the courtyard mostly empty except for children and their mothers, I didn't feel the fear slinking snakelike through my belly, didn't think: *Will I be next? Are they already here?*

And when they returned, when Molly Neptune herself lay the scrawny, white-draped form on the table, her eyes like open graves, I didn't think: *My fault. All my fault.* Bad leaned his warm weight against my leg and I felt a tremor run through me, a shiver of grief.

Samuel entered the courtyard in a hunched shuffle, guiding a frail-looking woman in long gray skirts. She clutched pathetically at his arm, blinking watery eyes over the twisted root of her nose. He seated her carefully, adjusting her shawl with such tenderness that I wondered if he was thinking of his own grandmother—a cackling crow of a woman I'd seen perched on the Zappias' porch, muttering Italian curses at Mr. Locke's Buick as it rolled by. I wondered if Samuel would ever see her again. *My fault.*

The old woman's eyes flicked from face to face until they landed on me. Her mouth gaped, moist and unpleasant, and I flinched. It was a familiar sensation—I'd been stared at by rude old white women for seventeen years as they speculated whether I was from Siam or Singapore—but it jarred me. I'd

276

already gotten used to the luxury of invisibility among the Arcadians.

Jane was speaking in low, urgent tones with Molly and the other hunters, discussing rotating patrols and all-night watches. A flock of women had encircled the old lady, cooing with pity. She answered their questions in a tremulous, timid voice—yes, she'd been rowing along the coast, but she'd gotten lost; yes, a man in a dark coat had chased her; no, she didn't know where he'd gone. Her eyes skittered over mine too often as she spoke. I looked away but could still feel the clingy, cobwebbed sensation of her eyes on my skin.

I found myself resenting her. How had she even found the lighthouse? Why had she invaded this tiny, fragile paradise, bringing death on her heels?

Samuel came to collect me eventually, like a shepherd gathering a wayward sheep. "There is nothing else we can do tonight, except sleep." I trailed after him through the dark, cracked streets.

Several times I thought I heard footsteps shuffling behind us, or long skirts trailing on stone, or breath rattling from an aged chest. I chastised myself—*don't be stupid, she's a harmless old woman*—until I noticed Bad standing stiff as a copper statue, staring behind us with his lips peeled back and a growl radiating in his chest.

A silent coldness slipped over me, like when you dive too deep in the lake and stir up the winter-chilled waters at the bottom. I nudged Bad with my knee, dry-mouthed. "C'mon, boy."

I lay beside Samuel in the moon-streaked dark of our adopted house, thinking things like *surely not* and *it's impossible* and then reflecting on the word *impossible* and its many abrupt fluctuations in recent days and continuing to stare sleeplessly at the ceiling.

Jane came in sometime after midnight and crawled into her blanket pile. I waited for her breathing to deepen, for the soft whistle of her not-quite-snore, and then crept to her side. I slid Mr. Locke's revolver carefully from her skirts and stuffed it beneath my waistband. It rested cold and heavy against my thigh as I ducked out of the house and into the bright black night.

I followed our street upward, Bad padding at my side, until it petered into tufted grass and tumbled brick. The plains rose around me, painted silver by the half-moon. I waded through the grasses, trying to ignore the sweat prickling my palms, the quivering in my belly that said this was a very, very stupid idea.

Then I stopped. I waited.

And waited. Minutes thudded by, measured in too-fast heartbeats. *Be patient. Be brave. Be like Jane.* I tried to stand the way she would, tense and ready as a long-legged hunting cat, rather than shivering and uncertain.

A whispering shuffle sounded behind me, so soft it might have been some small creature runneling through the grass. Bad growled, low and deep, and I believed him.

I drew the revolver from my skirt, turned, and pointed it at the hunched figure behind me. I saw the long twist of her nose, the saggy folds of flesh at her throat, the tremor of her hands as she raised them.

I strode closer. "Who are you?" I hissed.

How terribly, painfully cliché. Even with blood pulsing in my skull and my throat terror-tight, I felt conscious that I was doing a fairly poor impression of one of the Rover Boys, if the Rover Boys had ever threatened any innocent old ladies.

The woman was breathless and stammering with fear. "My—my name is Mrs. Emily Brown and I just got a little turned around, I swear, please don't hurt me, miss, please—"

I almost believed her. I felt myself shrinking, retreating, except—there was something wrong with her voice. It didn't actually *sound* like an old woman's voice, now that I was standing close to her; it sounded like a younger person doing a slightly rude impression of an old woman, high and shaky.

Her hand began to creep toward her skirts, voice still babbling with terror. Something silver glinted up at me from the black folds of cloth. I froze, had a half second's vision of how disappointed Jane would be if I let a little old lady slit my throat—then knocked her hand away and scrabbled the knife out of her dress pocket. Something black and flaky crusted the blade.

I threw it into the darkness and leveled the gun back at her chest. She'd stopped babbling.

"Who. Are. You." It sounded much better this time, almost menacing. I wished the gun would stop shaking.

The woman's mouth closed in an ugly seam. She glared for a moment, narrow-eyed, then clucked her tongue in disgust. She fished a cigarette from her pocket and struck a match, puffing until her cigarette glowed and crackled. White smoke streamed from her nostrils in a sigh.

"I said—"

"I see now why Cornelius and Havemeyer had such difficulty with you." Her voice was much lower and sleeker-sounding now, slightly oily. "You're a troublesome thing, aren't you?"

It's an odd feeling, having one's wildest suspicions proved true. It's satisfying to find you aren't insane, of course, but somewhat disheartening to realize you are indeed being hunted by a shadowy organization of apparently infinite reach.

"Who—you're from the Society, aren't you? Did you kill Solomon?"

The woman raised her eyebrows and flicked ash from her cigarette in a casual, masculine gesture. "Yes."

I swallowed. "And are you some kind of, of shapeshifter, or something?"

"Goodness, what an imagination." She reached behind her head and made a strange twisting gesture in the air, as if she were untying an invisible knot, and—

Her face sagged and fell. She caught it in her hand, except it wasn't a wrinkled, age-spotted hand anymore, and the mouth now smiling nastily at me wasn't a damp gash. Only the watery eyes were unchanged.

It was the red-haired man from Mr. Locke's Society gatherings: ferrety, thin-faced, wearing a dark traveling suit now rather than gray skirts.

He swept me an insincere bow, absurd in the empty darkness of a dead world, and held the mask up in the silvered moonlight. Horsehair straggled from it in tangled ropes. "Some Indian thing—a false-face, I think they call it? Your own dear father acquired it for us ages ago from a fracture south of Lake Ontario, and we've found it *quite* useful. Ugly old women are such unremarkable creatures." He tucked the mask into his breast pocket.

I swallowed shock, tried to make my voice sound menacing rather than stunned. "And how did you find me?"

"I'm generally agreed to be the best hunter, when things require hunting." He sniffed dramatically, inhaling smoke, and laughed. Bad growled, the sound rolling across the plain, and Mr. Ilvane's confident smile dimmed a little.

He reached into his breast pocket again and removed something tarnished and coppery-green. "And I had this, of course."

I darted forward, snatched it, stepped back again. It was a sort of compass, except that there were no letters or numbers or even little tick marks indicating degrees. The arrow settled abruptly, pointing in a direction that I was fairly certain wasn't north. I tossed it into the grass, heard it clatter against his knife.

"But *why*?" I waved the gun a little wildly, watched his

eyes track it nervously. "I'm not doing you any harm. Why not just leave me alone? What do you *want*?"

He gave a coy shrug, smiling at my frustration, my fear.

I was abruptly, entirely sick of it—of secrets and lies and almost-truths, things I half knew and half suspected, patched-together stories that were never told in order from beginning to end. It seemed to be an unspoken agreement in the world that young girls without money or means were simply too insignificant to be told everything. Even my own father had waited until the very last moment to tell me his whole truth.

Enough. I felt the weight of the gun in my palm, an iron authority that meant—just for a moment—I could change the rules. I cleared my throat. "Mr. Ilvane. Please sit down."

"Pardon me?"

"You can stand if you like, but you're going to tell me a very long story, and I'd hate for your legs to tire." He lowered himself to the earth, legs crossed and face sullen.

"Now." I steadied the barrel directly over his chest. "Tell me everything, from the beginning. And if you make any sudden movements, I swear I'll let Bad eat you." Bad's teeth were bared and shining blue-white; Ilvane's throat bobbed in a swallow.

"Our Founder came through his fracture in the seventeen-somethings, in England or Scotland, I don't recall. He possessed an uncanny ability to sway people to his cause—it didn't take him long to rise up in the world, and to see the world for what it was: a mess. Revolutions, upheavals, chaos, and bloodshed. *Waste.* And at the root of it all there were the aberrations—unnatural holes letting in all sorts of mischief. He began to repair them wherever he found them.

"At first the Founder worked alone. But soon he began recruiting others: some like himself who were immigrants to this

world, others who simply shared his interest in cultivating order."
I pictured Mr. Locke, young and ambitious and greedy—an ideal
recruit. It must have been easy. "Together we made it our business to cleanse the world and keep it safe and prosperous."

"And to steal things, of course," I added.

He made a come-now sort of pout. "We found that certain
objects and powers, when used sparingly by wise hands, could
aid us in our mission. As do more material forms of wealth—
all of us worked to gain positions of prestige and power. We
pool our money and fund expeditions into every corner of the
world, looking for fractures.

"By the sixties we adopted a name and a respectable function: the New England Archaeological Society." Ilvane made a
little ta-da gesture with his hands and continued with earnest
urgency. "And it's been working. Empires are growing. Profits
are rising. Revolutionaries and rabble-rousers are thin on the
ground. And we cannot, will not, let a spoiled little interloper
like *you* ruin all our efforts. So tell me, girl—what objects or
powers do you have?" His eyes on me were damp and bright.

I took a step backward. "It—that doesn't matter. Now, stand
up—" I wasn't sure what I was going to do—march him back
into the city and deliver him to Jane like a cat depositing something unpleasant for her owner?—but Ilvane smiled suddenly.

"You know, your father thought to thwart us. Look what
happened to him." He clucked his tongue.

I stopped moving. I may even have stopped breathing.

"You killed him, didn't you." All that grown-up-sounding
authority had leaked out of my voice.

Mr. Ilvane's smile grew wider and sharper, foxlike. "He'd
found us a fracture in Japan, as I'm sure you've realized. It was
generally his custom to wander around inside for a day or two
and return with a few interesting trinkets for Locke, and then
depart. But this time he lingered. And I grew bored of waiting,

bored of wearing this hideous thing—" He tapped his breast pocket above the old-woman mask.

"One day he caught sight of me on the mountainside. He recognized me." Ilvane shrugged, falsely apologetic. "The look on his face! I'd say he went white as a sheet, but with that complexion of his...'You!' he cried. 'The Society!' Well, really, imagine being surprised after seventeen years of being kept on a leash. Then he said some rather intemperate, tiresome things. Threatened to expose us—who would believe him, I ask you?—raved about saving his little girl, told me he'd keep this door open if it was the last thing he did...All very dramatic."

My pulse whispered *no-no-no*. The gun was trembling again.

"Then he rushed back to his camp like an absolute madman. I followed."

"And you killed him." Now my voice was less than a whisper, a strangled breath. After all this hoping and waiting and not knowing, after all this—I pictured his body frozen and forgotten, picked over by seabirds.

Ilvane was still smiling, smiling. "He had a rifle, you know. I found it in his things, after. But he didn't even try to reach it—he was *writing* when I dragged him out of his tent, writing as if his life depended on it. Fought me tooth and nail just to put his journal back in its box. Honestly, you should be thanking me for relieving you of such an unstable fellow."

I could almost see his hand, dark and ink-twined, scratching out those last desperate words: *RUN JANUARY, ARCADIA, DO NOT TRUST*. Trying to warn me.

Now Ilvane's smile prismed and blurred in my sight.

"I set the fracture ablaze. It was dry pine, went up like a torch. Your father wept, January, he *begged*, before I shoved him through. I caught sight of his hands, briefly, flailing back through the flames, then nothing. He never emerged."

Ilvane watched me as he finished, his eyes hunger-bright. He wanted tears, I knew. He wanted heartbreak and despair, because my father was trapped forever in some other world and I was permanently, terribly alone. But—

Alive, alive, alive. Father is alive. Not wracked and rotting on some foreign hillside, but *alive*, and finally gone home to his own true world. Even if I would never see him again.

I closed my eyes and let the twin waves of loss and joy crash over me, let my legs go limp and my knees crunch to earth. Bad's nose snuffled worriedly at my neck, checking for injuries.

Too late, I heard the scuffling sounds of Ilvane moving. My eyes snapped open to find him scrabbling sideways for his knife and the copper compass.

"No!" I shouted, but he was already running back toward the city, a black-and-red shadow darting through the grass. I fired the gun high into the night, saw him duck, and heard the echoing pound of his feet on the empty street. He disappeared into the tangle of abandoned houses.

Bad and I tore after him. I hardly knew what I'd do if I caught him—the revolver hung heavy in my hand, and the image of Solomon's white-draped body flashed sickeningly before me—but I couldn't let him leave, couldn't let him tell the Society where I was, where Arcadia was—

Two tall figures reeled into the street ahead. Jane reached an arm out to catch me. "We heard a shot—what—"

"Ilvane. From the Society. Went that way—think he's trying to get back to the Door—" My words sputtered between gasps of air. Jane did not wait for clarification but simply ran, flowing down the hill in a long-striding lope several times faster than mine. Samuel fell in with Bad and me, stumbling over humped bricks and cracks.

We skidded into the courtyard to find Jane crouching before the feather-curtained tunnel, lips peeled back in a hunter's triumphant grin. Ilvane stood several paces away, eyes wild and nostrils flared in animal desperation.

"That, I think, is enough," Jane said coolly, and reached into her skirt pocket for Mr. Locke's revolver. But then her face went slack. Her leopardess smile vanished.

Because it wasn't there. Because I'd stolen it from her.

There was a single stretched second in which I fumbled with the gun, sweaty thumb slipping on the hammer, and Ilvane watched Jane's empty hand emerge from her skirts. He smiled. And then he struck.

There was a slash of silver, the gleam of something wet and wine-colored in the moonlight—and then he was gone, the golden curtain fluttering in his wake.

Jane fell to her knees with a soft, surprised sigh.

No. I don't remember if I screamed it, if the word shattered against the clay ruins and echoed up the alleys, if there were answering shouts of alarm and running footsteps.

I remember kneeling beside her, clutching at the long, gaping edges of the cut, seeing my own hands blacken with blood. I remember Jane's expression of distant surprise.

I remember Samuel crouching on her other side, his guttural hiss—*"Bastard"*—and the sight of his back disappearing through the curtain after Ilvane.

And then there were other hands pressing beside mine—competent, probing hands—and a clean, crushed-mint smell. "S'all right, child, just give me some room." I drew back to let the gray-haired woman bend closer over Jane, an old-fashioned lantern sputtering beside her. I held my blood-gummed hands awkwardly away from my body, as if hoping someone would tell them what to do.

The woman called for clean cotton and boiled water and someone skittered to obey. Her voice was so calm, so unhurried, that the tiniest curl of hope unwound in my stomach.

"Is she—will she—" My voice raw-sounding, like something recently peeled.

The woman cast a harassed eye over her shoulder. "All this is just mess and show, girl. He didn't get anything she can't do without." I blinked at her and she softened. "She'll be fine, long as we can keep infection out."

I went slack with relief, muscles unspooling like cut wires. I pushed sticky palms into my eyes, pressing back the hysterical tears that sizzled just below the surface, and thought: *She's alive. I didn't kill her.*

I stayed that way, half-slumped over my knees and weak with relief, until the feathered curtain rustled again. It was Samuel, and I knew from the grim line of his mouth that Mr. Ilvane had escaped back through the Door.

Samuel did not look at the people now filling the square with fearful whispers, or at the ruby gleam of blood in the lantern light. He strode straight to me, feet bare and shirt half-buttoned, eyes roiling with some dark emotion. It was only when he stood directly above me that I knew what it was: fear.

"I followed him to the tree," he said softly. "I tried to follow him farther, tried to go through after him. But"—and I knew what he would say, knew it as surely as if I'd stood beside him on that empty plain—"there was nothing, no way through."

Samuel swallowed. "The door is closed."

The Lonely Door

Samuel had spoken softly, his voice a tired rasp, but trag-edy has its own terrible volume. It rolls and cracks, shakes the ground beneath your feet, lingers in the air like summer thunder.

The Arcadians gathered in the courtyard fell silent, their eyes turned toward us in a dozen shades of disbelief and terror. The quiet stretched, taut as piano wire, until one man issued a strangled curse. Then came a rising clamor of panicked voices.

"What will we do?"

"My babies, my babies need—"

"We'll starve, every last one of us."

An infant woke and wailed in his mother's arms, and she gazed down at his crumpled face in listless despair. Then a wide form shouldered past her and moved to the front of the crowd. Molly Neptune's stovepipe hat was missing and the upward glow of the lantern painted shadowed hollows over her face.

She held up two hands. "Enough. If the way is closed, we'll find another way through. We'll find another way to survive. Aren't all of us here survivors, one way or the other?" She surveyed them with a kind of fierce love, willing strength into their shaking limbs. "But not tonight. Tonight we'll rest. Tomorrow, we'll plan."

I found myself leaning into the rumble of her voice, letting it beat back the tide of guilt and horror that threatened to swallow me—until her eyes met mine, and I watched all the warmth flow out of her face like dye running in the rain. It left nothing behind but bitter regret. Regret that she'd ever seen my father, perhaps, or ever offered Arcadia as a refuge; regret that she'd let me set foot in her fragile kingdom with monsters on my heels.

She turned away and addressed the woman still bent over Jane. "Will she live, Iris?"

Iris ducked her head. "Likely, ma'am. Except it's deep in some places, and messy, and..." I saw the pink dart of her tongue as she moistened her lips, the fearful flick of her eyes toward the feathered curtain. "And we're out of iodine. Even salt water might do the job, but we, we can't..." Her voice trailed to a racked whisper.

Molly Neptune rested a hand gently on her shoulder and shook her head. "No use worrying now. You'll do the best you can for her, and that's it." She called for two young men to help roll Jane onto a sheet and carry her into a nearby house. Iris trailed behind them, hands hanging bloody and empty at her sides.

Molly's eyes raked over us once more and her lips rippled as if she wanted to say something, but she turned away and followed the last trailing group of Arcadians back up the dark streets. Only now, when her people couldn't see her, did she allow her shoulders to bow in defeat.

I watched her until she disappeared into the depths of her doomed, beautiful city. I wondered how long they could last without supplies from their home world, and if a second city would die here among the bones of the first.

I closed my eyes against the weight of guilt settling on my shoulders, heard the click of claws and the scuff of worn shoes as Samuel and Bad approached. They settled on either side of me, warm and constant as a pair of suns. What would happen to them, trapped in this starved world? I pictured Bad with sharp ribs and dull fur; Samuel with the ember-glow gone dull in his eyes. Jane might be swallowed by fever before she could even feel the desperate bite of hunger in her belly.

No. I wouldn't let it happen. Not when there was a chance— even the slimmest, wildest chance—that I could prevent it.

"Samuel." I was hoping to sound brave and resolute, but I just sounded tired. "Will you please go back to the house and get my father's book for me? And an ink pen?"

He went very still beside me, and I knew he understood what I intended to do. A small, treacherous part of me hoped he would grab my hands and beg me not to do it, like an actor in a moving-picture romance, but he didn't. I supposed he didn't much want to die in Arcadia either.

He stood, slowly, and left the square. I sat beneath the half-moon, arm tight around Bad, and waited.

He returned with the leather-bound book and a pen clutched in his hands. I flipped to the last rustle of blank pages in the back and tore them gently away from their binding, not looking at Samuel's worry-dark eyes, his solemn mouth. "Would you—will you come with me?"

He reached for my hand in answer and I hesitated—I'd never

accepted his offer, never told him yes—but then I reflected that we were both trapped in a dying world for the rest of our short lives, and laced my fingers through his.

We walked together out of the city and into the deep blue night, with Bad slipping like an amber-eyed ghost through the grass ahead of us. It was so late the moon was skulking near the horizon and the stars seemed to hang low and close around us.

The tree emerged from the darkness like a gnarled, many-fingered hand reaching toward the sky. Neat planks of wood nestled among its bulbous roots, looking strangely forlorn—a Door, now reduced to a mere door. A heavy stink of smoke and char filtered through it, and I knew the lighthouse was burning on the other side. I imagined that my father's final Door had the same funeral-pyre reek.

I walked until I was so close I could have stroked my fingers along the dark wood of the door, and stopped. I stood unmoving, palms sweating against the crumpled pages, the pen heavy in my hand.

Samuel let the silence stretch, then asked, "What's wrong?"

I laughed—a despairing, humorless huff. "I'm afraid," I told him. "Afraid that I'll fail, that it won't work, that I'll—" I broke off, the iron tang of fear filling my mouth. I remembered the bone-deep bite of exhaustion in my limbs, the sick reeling of the room around me after I'd written my way out of the asylum. How much more would it take to open a way between two worlds?

My father had said Doors existed in places of "particular and indefinable resonance," thinned-out places where two worlds brushed delicately against one another. *Perhaps it is more like drawing aside a veil, or opening a window.* A thin supposition on which to bet my life.

Samuel was squinting up at the stars, his expression casual. "Do not do it, then."

"But Jane—Arcadia—"

"We will find a way to survive, January, trust us that far. Do not risk yourself if it will not work." His voice was even and calm, as if we were discussing the likelihood of rain or the unreliability of train schedules.

I looked down, uncertain and ashamed by my uncertainty.

But then I felt a hesitant touch beneath my chin, a gentle push as Samuel tipped my face upward with two fingers. His eyes were earnest, his mouth half-curled with a sideways smile. "But if you are willing to try, I believe in you. Strega."

A heady warmth sizzled over me, as if I were standing in the center of a blazing bonfire. I didn't recognize it, didn't know what to call it—but then, no one had ever believed in me before. Or they'd believed in some other, less able version of me. Locke and my father and Jane had each believed in the timid January who had haunted Locke House, who so desperately needed their protection. But Samuel was looking at me now as if he expected me to eat fire or dance on rain clouds. As if he expected me to do something miraculous and brave and impossible.

It felt like donning a suit of armor or sprouting wings, extending past the boundaries of myself; it felt an awful lot like love.

I looked into his face for another greedy second, letting his faith soak into my skin, then turned to the door. I breathed the smoke-and-ocean air into my lungs, felt Samuel's trust at my back like a warm wind filling a ship's sail, and touched the pen to the page.

The Door opens, I wrote, and I believed every letter of it.

I believed in the black gleam of the ink in the night, in the strength of my own fingers wrapped around the pen, in the reality of that other world waiting just on the other side of some invisible curtain. I believed in second chances and righted wrongs and rewritten stories. I believed in Samuel's belief.

A wind blew noiselessly across the plain as I lifted the pen away from the door. The stars pulsed above me and the moon-shadows drew mad patterns in the dirt. I felt myself smiling, distantly, and then everything slid sideways and Samuel's arms were warm around me.

"Is it—did you—"

I nodded. There was no need to check; I could already hear the rhythmic crash of the Atlantic, could already feel the infinite emptiness of the Threshold stretching beyond the Door. A triumphant laugh rolled in Samuel's chest, rumbling against my cheek, and then I was laughing with him because it had *worked*. It had worked, and I wasn't dead—it had been almost easy, compared to the words I'd carved into my own arm at Brattleboro. Like drawing aside a veil.

We staggered back toward the city, dizzy with relief, leaning drunkenly into one another. I could almost pretend we were two ordinary young people stealing an unchaperoned stroll past their curfew, sure they'd catch hell in the morning but too giddy to care.

Until Samuel said, quietly, "This means we are safe, you know. They think this world is gone forever, don't they, so they will not come looking. We could stay, at least for a while."

There was a question in his voice, but I didn't answer it. I pictured Ilvane's spinning copper compass and the way he'd sniffed the air like a hound on a trail. He would find me again.

And when he did, would I be cowering in some other world? Hiding behind the protection of better and braver people? A movie reel spun and clicked in my skull: Samuel falling pale and lifeless to the cabin floor; Solomon wrapped in that white sheet; Jane lying in her own blood, eyes on the stars.

No.

I might be young and untried and penniless and everything else, but—I clutched the pen in my hand until my knuckles were white crests—I was not powerless. And now I knew no Door was ever truly closed.

I looked sideways at Samuel's silhouette in the graying almost-dawn. "Yes," I answered him. "Of course we'll stay."

I've always been a good liar.

I wrote three letters before leaving.

Dear Mr. Locke,

I want you to know I'm not dead. I almost didn't write this letter at all, but then I pictured you worried and irritable, pacing your office or yelling at Mr. Stirling or smoking too many cigars, and figured I owed you this much.

I want you to know, too, that I don't hate you. I think perhaps I should: you knew my father's true history but kept it from me; you're part of an archaeological society that's actually some kind of malevolent cult, you fired Jane, let them hurt Sindbad, shipped me off to Brattleboro—but I don't. Quite.

I don't hate you, but I don't particularly trust you, either—were you really trying to protect me? From creatures like Havemeyer and Ilvane? If so, you should know your protection was woefully inadequate—so forgive me for not telling you precisely where I'm going next.

I wish I could come back to Locke House, to that little gray room on the third floor, but I can't. Instead, I'm following my father. I'm going home.

I'm sorry I couldn't be your good girl any longer. But not very.

Love,
J

Jane,

Just in case: I'm officially willing you my entire book collection. Consider this letter a binding legal contract. Maybe one day you can show up at an estate sale and show it to the auctioneer and walk away with the first edition of <u>The Jungle Book</u> or the entire run of <u>Pluck and Luck.</u>

It's funny—all that time I spent longing for a chance to escape, to fling myself into the endless horizon without worrying about keeping my skirts pressed or using the right fork or making Mr. Locke proud—and now…Now I think I might trade it for another rainy afternoon rereading romance novels with you, curled in the towers of Locke House like stowaways in some vast, land-bound ship.

But looking back, I realize both of us were secretly waiting. Holding ourselves in careful, painful suspension, like women stand-ing at the station with our luggage neatly packed, looking expectantly down the tracks.

But my father never came back for me, or for you, and now it's time to stop waiting. Leave the luggage at the station and run.

Jane: you are released from the promises you made to him. I am my own keeper now.

I might wish you'd move to Chicago and find a comfortable job as a bank security guard, or go back to Kenya and meet a nice young lady who helps you forget about the leopard-women and their wild hunts—but I know you won't. I know you'll keep looking for your ivory Door. Your home.

And—though the word of a Scholar might not be worth much to you anymore—I want you to know:

So will I.

Love,
J

S—

~~I wish we had more~~
~~I have always to~~

It's so typical of me to leave the most difficult letter for last, as if it would magically become easier. I don't have much space so I'll be brief:

My answer is yes. For always.

Except that there are monsters pursuing me, haunting my footsteps, breathing down my collar. And I will not, cannot place you in their path. I'm strong enough to face my monsters alone—you showed me that, just a few hours ago. (It turns out that only in loving you am I brave enough to leave you. There's some terrible irony there, don't you think?)

So go home, Samuel. Go home and be whole and safe and alive, and forget all this dangerous madness about Doors and vampires and secret societies. Pretend it's all just the plot of a particularly outlandish paperback, something we can laugh about on the lakeshore.

And look after Bad, won't you? I don't seem to have taken very good care of him so far, and I think he'd be safer with you.

J

P.S. Actually Bad is coming with me. I don't deserve him, but that's just how it is with dogs, isn't it?

I slunk into the kitchens and stole a sack of oats, four apples, and a few salted hunks of prairie rat for Bad. I stuffed it all into a pillowcase with my silver coin-knife and my father's book and slipped back into the streets of Arcadia, now glowing pink in the rising dawn. I had nearly reached the feather curtain when a graveled voice stopped me.

"Headed out so soon?"

Bad and I froze like a pair of deer caught in the headlights of Mr. Locke's Model 10. "Ah. Morning, Miss Neptune."

Molly looked like she hadn't slept either—the lines in her face were deep-carved cobwebs and her hair was a black-and-silver tangle—but she'd recovered her stovepipe hat and beaded collar. She squinted at me with flint-chip eyes. "You won't last three days out on the plains, girl. I'd stay, if I were you."

She thought I was slinking away into the hills, running away from my guilt. I felt my shoulders straightening and a smile curving my lips. "Thank you, but there are things I need to attend to back home. Back through the Door."

Watching the realization settle over her face was like watching a woman age in reverse. Her spine unbent and her eyes went round with hope. "No," she breathed.

"We opened it last night," I told her softly. "We didn't want to wake everyone, so we—well, Samuel—was going to tell you in the morning."

Molly closed her eyes, then buried her face in her hands, shoulders heaving. I turned to leave. "Wait." Her voice was tear-thick and shaky, unlike her usual growl. "I don't know who or what is chasing you, and I don't know how it followed you here, but be careful. Sol"—I heard her swallow, choking back grief—"Solomon's feather, the one he wore in his hair—it's gone."

A chill prickled my spine as I imagined the golden feather clutched in Ilvane's hand, the horror of being hunted by something you couldn't see. I made myself nod calmly. "I'm sorry for the loss of the feather. Thank you for warning me." I adjusted the pillowcase on my shoulder, not looking at her. "Don't tell Samuel, please. I wouldn't want him to . . . worry."

Molly Neptune ducked her head. "Good luck, January Scholar."

I left her sitting in the warming sunlight, looking up at her city like a mother surveying her sleeping children.

The Door seemed somehow smaller by day, dark and narrow and terribly lonely. It brushed softly against the grass as I pulled it shut behind me and stepped into the void between the worlds.

When you travel with money, you follow a smooth, well-worn path through the world. Wood-paneled train cars lead to shiny black cabs, which lead to hotel rooms with velvet curtains, each step effortlessly following the last. When I'd traveled with Jane and Samuel the path had grown narrow and twisting, frequently terrifying.

Now I was alone, and the only path was the one I left behind me.

Bad and I stood for a moment in the charred skeleton of the lighthouse, looking through the mist to the pocked and rugged coast. I felt like an explorer at the precipice of some new, wild world, armed only with ink and hope; I felt like my mother.

Except that she hadn't been pursued by invisible monsters with fox-toothed smiles. The giddy grin faded from my face.

I floated my pillowcase on an unburnt plank from the light-house and waded back into the icy sea with Bad at my side. Clouds settled like eiderdown around us, a feathered fog that swallowed everything: the sound of my splashing, the sight of the shore, the sun itself. It was only by the rough scrape of stone beneath my fingers that I knew we'd reached the other side.

We climbed the cliffside on jellied legs, found the road, and began to walk. At least I had boots this time, although I'd had difficulty in identifying them as such when Molly presented them to me—they'd looked more like the remains of small, unfortunate creatures. I thought briefly of the shined, patent-leather shoes Mr. Locke had bought me as a girl, with their narrow toes and stiff heels; I didn't miss them.

By midmorning I'd realized fewer trucks or cars were will-ing to stop for an in-between girl and her vicious-looking dog, without Samuel's respectable whiteness nearby. People swerved around me without slowing; it was as if I'd fallen through the cracks, slipped down into some invisible underworld that decent people preferred to ignore.

It was a horse and buggy that eventually stopped beside me, with a jangle of harnesses and a querulous "Dammit, Rosie, I said *whoa*." The driver was a raggedy, nearly toothless white woman wearing yellow boots and a strange sort of home-sewn poncho. She let Bad ride in the cart among her potatoes and string beans, and even gifted me a sack of them when she let me off near Brattleboro.

"Don't know where you're headed, but it seems far." She sniffed, then offered: "Keep your dog close, don't take rides from men in nice cars, and steer clear of the law." I suspected she'd fallen through the cracks, too.

I made it across the New York State line just as the day

purpled into dusk. I'd only taken one more ride, perched in the back of an empty logging truck with a dozen or so stolid, sawdusted men who did their best to ignore me. One of them fed Bad the leftover rinds from his bacon sandwich. He raised one hand in a sort of salute when they left me standing at a crossroads.

I slept that night in a three-sided sheep shed. The sheep *baa*ed suspiciously at us, watching Bad with their queer, sideways eyes, and I fell asleep missing the soft sounds of Jane and Samuel beside me.

I dreamed of white fingers reaching toward me, and a fox-toothed smile, and Mr. Havemeyer's voice: *They'll never stop looking for you.*

It took me five days, three hundred miles, a road map stolen from the Albany train station, and at least four near-misses with local law enforcement to reach the western edge of New York State. I might've traveled faster, except for the wanted poster.

I'd stopped at a post office on the second morning to mail Mr. Locke's letter, after some sweaty-palmed hesitation outside. But he deserved to know I wasn't trapped forever in a desolate, foreign world, didn't he? And if he tried to come after me, my letter would lead him on a rather inconvenient detour to Japan. Locke didn't know there was another way home, a back Door just waiting to be unlocked.

I pushed the letter across the counter, and then I saw it: a fresh white poster tacked to the wall. My own face looked down from it, printed in smeary black and white.

MISSING CHILD. Miss January Scaller, seventeen, has gone missing from her home in Shelburne, Vermont. Her guardian urgently seeks information

relating to her whereabouts. **She has a history of hysteria and confusion and should be approached with
caution. She may be in the company of a colored
woman and an ill-behaved dog. SUBSTANTIAL
REWARD OFFERED. Please contact Mr. Cornelius Locke. 1611 Champlain Drive, Shelburne, Vt.**

It was the picture from Mr. Locke's party, the one my father
had never liked. My face looked round and young, and my
hair was so ferociously pinned that my eyebrows were slightly
raised. My neck stuck out from its starched collar like a turtle
tentatively looking out of its shell. I checked my own reflection
in the post office window—dust-grimed and sun-darkened,
my hair suspended in an unruly knot of braids and twists—and
thought it unlikely that anyone would recognize me.

But still: a chill, creeping fear slunk up my spine at the
thought that every stranger on the street might know my
name, that every police officer might be looking for the timid
girl in the picture. It seemed to me the Society hardly needed
their masks and feathers and stolen magics when they had all
the mundane mechanisms of civil society at their fingertips.

I stuck to the winding back roads after that, and took fewer
rides.

By the time I reached Buffalo, though, I was hungry and
worn enough to take a risk. I staggered into the front office of
the Buffalo Laundry Co. and begged for paying work, half-
expecting to be tossed out into the street.

But apparently there were three girls out sick and a big load
of uniforms recently arrived from the reform school, so the
proprietress handed me a starched white apron, informed me
that I would earn thirty-three and one-half cents every hour,
and placed me under the jurisdiction of a muscly, humorless
white woman named Big Linda. Big Linda looked me over

with an expression of deepest misgiving and set me to shaking out wet clothes and feeding them into the mangle.

"And keep your damn hands away from the rollers, if you like your fingers," she added.

It was hard. (If you don't think laundry is hard, you've never lifted several hundred soaked wool uniforms in the steamy heat of a washroom in July.) The air felt like something you drank rather than breathed, a cottony steam that seemed to pool and slosh in my lungs. My arms were wobbly-feeling and shaky after an hour, aching after two, and numb after three. A few of my not-quite-healed scabs split and wept.

I kept going, because the week's travel had taught me that much: how to keep going even when your hips ache and your dog's limp has become a three-legged hop; even when all you found for dinner were three unripe apples; even when every stranger and every gust of wind might be your enemy, finally catching up with you.

And yet—here I was. Sweating and aching in the bowels of the Buffalo Laundry Co., but alive, unbound, entirely myself for the first time in my life. And entirely alone. I had a brief vision of olive hands flashing in the night, dark eyes lit with a cigarette glow—and felt a sudden hollowness in my chest, a rawness like the space left behind by a pulled tooth.

No one spoke to me that entire shift except a dark-skinned woman with a half-moon smile and a southern drawl. The smile vanished when she saw me. She raised her chin at me.

"And just what exactly happened to you?" I shrugged. She looked down at my dust-caked skirt, my scarecrow frame. "Been walking a while on an empty stomach, I'd say."

I nodded.

"Got more walking to do?" I nodded again. She sucked her teeth pensively, dumped another load of clothes into my cart, and left shaking her head.

Big Linda told me I could sleep in the rag pile—"But only for tonight, mind, this isn't a damn hotel"—and Bad and I slept curled around one another like a pair of birds in a lye-scented nest. We woke to the first-shift bell ringing in the pre-dawn black, and I discovered two things waiting beside our nest: a greasy ham hock with all the fat and gristle still hanging off it for Bad, and an entire pan of corn bread for me.

I worked another half shift, doing rough multiplication in my head, then marched to the front office and told the proprietress that I was very sorry but I had to leave now, and could I please have my payment in the form of a check. She pursed her lips and offered her thoughts on vagrants, layabouts, and girls who didn't know a good thing when it came to them—but she wrote the check.

In the alley outside I dug the ink pen out of my pillowcase and pressed the check against the brick wall. I added a wobbly zero and a few extra letters, biting my lip. The check fluttered in a sudden wind that wasn't there, the lettering blurring and curling, and I rested my head against the steam-warmed brick, dizzied. It shouldn't have worked—the ink was a different color and crammed rather obviously into the blank space, and whoever heard of a laundress with a $40 check rather than a $4 one—but I'd *believed* it as I wrote it, and so did the bank teller.

By midafternoon I was boarding the New York Central Line, a precious train ticket clutched in my hand with the letters *LOUISVILLE, KY.* printed in neat red ink.

My pillowcase looked especially stained and grubby beside the gleaming leather suitcases in the luggage rack, like an underdressed party guest hoping to go unnoticed. I felt sort of stained and grubby myself; every other passenger was wearing pressed linen and high-necked gowns, their hats perched at fashionable angles and their shoes gleaming with fresh polish.

A rumbling shudder rolled through the carriage, like a dragon shaking itself from sleep, and the train pulled out of the shade of Buffalo Central and into the lazy sunlight of a summer afternoon. I pressed my forehead against the warming glass and slept.

I dreamed, or maybe just remembered: a different train heading in the same direction, ten years previously. A scrubby town on the Mississippi; a blue Door standing alone in a field; a city that smelled of salt and cedar.

My father's city. My mother's city, if she was somehow alive. Could it ever be my city? Assuming I could open the Door again, even though it was nothing now but a pile of ash. Assuming the Society didn't get me first.

I dozed and woke, interrupted by the roll-and-stop of the train at every station, the porter's shouted announcements and periodic demands to see my ticket, the thud and shuffle of passengers departing and arriving. None of them sat next to me, but I felt their eyes on me. Or thought I did; several times I flicked my head sideways, trying to catch them staring, but their faces were all politely averted. Bad lay tense over my feet, ears pricked.

I slipped a hand into my pillowcase and held the silver coin-knife tight in my fist.

The train sat unmoving for a full half hour in Cincinnati while the carriage grew stuffy and crowded with new passengers. Eventually a porter came shoving through the aisle. He strung a chain across the back of the car and hung a neat white placard on it: *COLORED SEATING*.

There was no Mr. Locke to protect me now. No private compartment with meals delivered by smiling porters, no comfortable veil of money between me and the rest of the world.

The porter strode back down the aisle prodding people with a stubby baton: a brown-skinned woman and her three children, an old man with a poof of white hair, a pair of young men with broad shoulders and mutinous expressions. The porter rapped his baton against the luggage rack. "This train abides by state law, boys, and the next stop's in Kentucky. You can either move back or get off and walk, doesn't bother me which." They slunk to the back.

The porter hesitated at my seat, squinting at my red-glazed skin as if consulting a mental color chart. But then he looked at my grimy hem and scarred arm and entirely disreputable dog and jerked his head to the back.

Apparently, without money I wasn't perfectly unique or in-between or odd-colored; I was simply colored. I felt something cold settle over me at the thought, a weight of rules and laws and dangers that hung on my limbs, pressed on my lungs.

I shuffled to the back without protest. I didn't plan to be stuck in this stupid world with these stupid rules for much longer, anyhow.

I clung to the end of an overcrowded bench in the very back, the coin damp in my fist. It was only once the train was moving again that I noticed Bad staring fixedly into the aisle beside me, the faintest burr of a growl in his throat. There was no one there, but I thought I could hear a soft, steady rustling, almost like breathing.

I thought of Solomon's missing golden feather and clutched my pillowcase tighter, feeling the corner of my father's book press into my stomach. I kept my eyes carefully on the blue-green roll of the countryside.

Forty minutes later the porter shouted, "Turners Station, last stop till Louisville," from the front of the carriage. The train slowed. The door rolled open. I hesitated, barely breathing, and then dove for the exit with Bad scrabbling behind me.

I felt my shoulder slam into something solid in midair, heard a muttered curse—

And then there was something sharp and cold pressed against my throat. I stood very still.

"Not this time," hissed a voice in my ear. "Let's get out of this crowd, shall we?" Something prodded me forward and I stumbled onto the wood-planked platform. I was marched into the station, his breath hot against my ear and the knife tip biting into my neck. Bad watched me with worried, glaring eyes. *Not yet*, I thought to him.

The bodiless voice turned me through a peeling white door labeled *LADIES* and into a dim, green-tiled room. "Now, turn around slowly, there's a good girl—"

Except I wasn't a good girl anymore.

I drove my fist up and back over my shoulder, the coin-knife wedged between my knuckles. There was a terrible, wet *pop* beneath my hand and a shattering scream. The blade dragged away from my throat in a hot line and went skittering across the tile. "*Damn* you—"

Bad, seeming to decide that even invisible creatures could be bitten with sufficient effort, snarled and snapped at the air. His teeth closed around a mouthful of something and he growled in satisfaction. I dove for the knife, held it tight in blood-slick hands, and called Bad. He trotted to my side, licking red from his lips and glaring at his invisible prey.

Except he wasn't quite invisible anymore. If I squinted I could almost see a racked shimmer in the air, a heaving chest and a thin face oozing with dark wetness. A single, hateful eye was fixed on me.

"Your compass, Mr. Ilvane. Give it to me."

He hissed, low and vicious, but I raised the knife toward him and he dug something copper-colored out of his pocket. He slid it resentfully across the floor.

I grabbed for it without taking my eyes away from him. "I'm leaving now. I'd advise you not to follow me again." My voice hardly shook at all.

He gave a dark crack of laughter. "And where will you run to, little girl? You've no money, no friends left to protect you, no father—"

"The trouble with you people," I observed, "is that you believe in *permanence*. An orderly world will remain so; a closed door will stay closed." I shook my head, reaching for the door. "It's very...limiting."

I left.

Out in the genteel bustle of the station I pressed my shoulder faux-casually against the bathroom door and fished Samuel's pen out of my pillowcase-sack. I held it tight for a moment, feeling an echo of remembered warmth, then dug the tip into the peeling paint of the door.

The door locks, and there is no key.

The words were scratched deeply into the paint, jittering along the wood grain. The dull scrape of metal on metal sounded through the door, a permanent sort of clunk, and I gave a little gasp at the sudden weight of exhaustion pulling at my limbs. I leaned my forehead against the wood, eyes closed, and raised the pen again.

The door is forgotten, I wrote.

And then I was blinking up from the floor, knees aching where I'd fallen. I lay there for a while, unmoving, wondering if the stationmaster would come investigate the poor vagrant girl collapsed on his floor, or if I might just sleep for an hour or so. My eyes ached; my throat was stiff with dried blood.

But—it had worked. The bathroom door had become vague and blurred, something too mundane for my eyes to linger on. No one else in the little station seemed to see the door at all.

I vented a small, tired *ha*, and wondered how long it would last. Long enough to run, I supposed. Providing I could stand up.

I dragged myself to a bench on the platform and waited with my red-inked ticket clutched in one hand. I boarded the next train south.

I sat, watching the country turn rich and wet, the hills rising and diving like great emerald whales, and thought: *I'm coming, Father.*

My Mother's Door

The last three hundred miles reeled past as if I were wearing a pair of those magical boots that take you seven leagues forward with every step. I remember them only as a series of jarring *thuds*.

Thud. I am stepping off the train into the sweating sprawl of Union Train Station in Louisville. Even the sky is busy, a criss-crossed mess of electric lines and church spires and shimmery waves of heat. Bad presses close to my knees, hating it.

Thud. I'm standing in a dusty lot outside the station begging for a ride from a truck with *BLUE GRASS BREWING* printed on the side in black block letters. The driver tells me to go back where I came from; his friend makes obscene kissing sounds.

Thud. Bad and I are swaying westward in a creaking wagon

piled head-high with earthy, green-smelling hemp stalks. A solemn black man and his solemn young daughter sit on the bench up front. Their clothes have that calicoed, mismatched look that only happens when fabric has been patched and repatched until almost nothing original remains, and they look at me with worried, warning eyes.

Thud. Ninley, finally.

It had both changed and not changed in the last decade. So had the world, I supposed.

It was still scrubby and reluctant-looking, and the towns-folk still glared in aggrieved half squints, but the streets had been paved. Automobiles putted up and down them, alongside newly rich men in three-piece suits with embarrassingly large pocket watches. The river was crowded with chugging steamers and flatboats. Some sort of mill—a hulking, ugly thing—now brooded on the shore. Steam and smoke hung above us, transformed into oily pink clouds by the setting sun. Progress and Prosperity, as Mr. Locke would say.

I'd been driven and hunted on the journey here, but now that I'd arrived I found myself strangely reluctant to take the last few steps. I bought myself a sack of peanuts at Junior's River Supply with the last of my laundry money and found a tobacco-slimed bench to sit on. Bad perched like a bronze sentinel at my feet.

A shift bell rang, and I watched thin-faced women scurrying in and out of the mill, their fingers curled into callused claws at their sides. I watched the bent black backs of men loading coal onto docked steamers, and the rainbow sheen of oil on the river's surface.

Eventually a sweaty little man in a stained apron emerged from the cookhouse to tell me the bench was for paying customers, and to imply heavily that I should leave Ninley before nightfall if I knew what was good for me. It would never have happened if Mr. Locke had been with me.

But then, if Mr. Locke had been with me, I probably wouldn't have lingered insolently on the bench, staring at the man with my hand on the back of Bad's buzzing skull. I wouldn't have stood and stepped slightly too close to him, and savored the way he shriveled like something left on the windowsill too long. I certainly wouldn't have curled my lip and said, "I was leaving anyway. *Sir.*"

The little man scurried back to his kitchen and I sauntered back toward the center of town. I caught a wavery glimpse of myself in a plate-glass window—mud-caked, oversized boots, sweat drawing damp lines through road dust at my temples, pinkish-white scars scrolling haphazardly from wrist to shoulder—and it occurred to me that my seven-year-old self— that dear temerarious girl—would've been rather taken with my seventeen-year-old self.

Perhaps the manager at the Grand Riverfront Hotel recognized me, too, because he didn't immediately order my vagabondish self thrown out of his establishment. Or maybe Bad made people hesitate to throw me anywhere.

"Good evening. I'm trying to find the, uh, Larson family farm. South of here, I think?"

His eyes widened at the name, but he hesitated, as if debating the morality of directing a creature like me toward an innocent family. "What's your business?" he compromised.

"They're...family. On my mother's side."

He gave me a you're-not-a-very-good-liar look, but apparently the Larson women hadn't inspired sufficient loyalty in the townsfolk to keep him from directing me south, past the mill, two miles down. He shrugged. "Doesn't look like much, these days. But she's still in there, last we heard."

Those final two miles were longer than regular miles. They felt stretched and fragile beneath my feet, as if a too-heavy footfall might shatter them and leave me stranded in the nowheresville of the Threshold. Maybe I was just tired of walking. Maybe I was afraid. It's one thing to read a storybook version of your mother's life and choose to believe it; it's quite another to knock on a stranger's door and say, *Hello, I have it on good authority that you're my great (great?) aunts.*

I let my fingers graze Bad's spine as we walked. Dusk settled over our shoulders like a damp purple blanket. The river—the churn and clank of boat traffic, the *shush* of water, and the tangy smell of catfish and mud—was slowly beaten back by honeysuckle and cicadas and some bird that cooed the same three syllables in a lilting circle.

It was all so familiar and so foreign. I pictured a young girl in a blue cotton dress running down this same road on cinnamon-stick legs. Then I pictured another girl, white and square-jawed, running before her. Adelaide. *Mother.*

I would've missed it if I hadn't been looking: a narrow dirt drive crowded on either side by briars and untrimmed boughs. Even once I'd followed the track to its end I was uncertain—who would live in such a huddled, bent-backed cabin, half-eaten by ivy and some sort of feral climbing rose? The wooden-shake shingles were green with moss; the barn had collapsed entirely.

But a single ancient mule still stood in the yard in a three-legged doze, and a few chickens roosted in the remains of the barn, clucking sleepily to themselves. A light—dim, mostly obscured by dingy white curtains—still flickered in the kitchen window.

I climbed the sagging front steps and stood unmoving before the front door. Bad sat beside me and leaned against my leg.

It was an old door, nothing but a series of gray planks so time-worn the grain of the wood had weathered into ridges like the whorls of fingerprints. The handle was a strip of oil-dark leather; candlelight peered through the cracks and knot-holes like an inquisitive housewife.

It was my mother's door, and her mother's door.

I exhaled, raised my hand to knock, and hesitated at the last moment because what if it was all a beautiful lie, a fairy-tale spell that would be broken the moment my hand touched the unyielding reality of that door—what if an old man answered and said "Adelaide who?" Or what if Adelaide herself opened the door and it turned out she'd found her way back into this world after all but never come looking for me?

The door opened before I brought myself to touch it.

A very old, very querulous-looking woman stood on the threshold, glaring up at me with an expression that was (impossibly, dizzyingly) familiar. It was a grandmotherly, young-people-these-days sort of look, as seamed and wrinkled as walnut meat. I had a disorienting sense of having seen it from a much lower vantage point, perhaps as a child—

And then I remembered: the old woman I'd bumped into when I was seven. The woman who'd stared at me with an expression like a lightning-struck tree and asked me just who the hell I was.

I'd run from her then. I did not run now.

Her eyes—red-rimmed, weepy, blurred with blue-white clouds—found mine and widened. Her mouth untwisted. "Adelaide, child, what'd you do to your *hair*?"

She blinked up at the half-braided mass piled behind my head, circled by a fuzzy reddish halo of escaped hairs. Then she frowned again and refocused on my face, her gaze circling like a compass needle unable to find true north. "No—no, you're not my Ade…"

"No, ma'am." My voice came out far too loud, ringing like a struck bell in the soft evening. "No. I'm January Scholar. I think you might be my aunt. Adelaide Larson is—was—my mother."

The old woman made a single sound—a soft exhalation, as

if a blow she'd braced for had finally arrived—and then collapsed and lay on the threshold as motionless and crumpled as a
pile of tossed laundry.

The insides of the Larson house matched its outsides: scraggly
and poorly tended, with very little evidence of human habi-
tation. Vines crept in around rotten windowsills and jars of
preserves gleamed murky gold in the last evening light. Something had nested in the rafters and left white spatters on the
floorboards.

The old woman (my aunt?) was birdlike in my arms,
hollow-boned and fragile. I propped her in the only piece of
furniture that wasn't covered in fabric scraps or dirty dishes—a
rocking chair so ancient there were shiny grooves worn in the
floorboards beneath it—and briefly considered doing something drastic and dime-novelish to wake her, like tossing cold
water in her face. I let her be.

I rummaged through the kitchen instead, which prompted
a lot of skittering and squeaking from its occupants, followed
by the unpleasant snap-crunch of Bad's jaws. I unearthed three
eggs, a mold-spotted onion, and four potatoes so wizened
and curled they could have been in one of Mr. Locke's glass
cases (*Amputated ears, 4 ct., unlikely to be edible*). A voice very
like Jane's hissed in my head: *Have you ever cooked a single meal
yourself?*

How hard could it be?

The answer—as you may or may not know depending on
your experience with rusted iron skillets, wavering candlelight, and finicky cookstoves that are either lukewarm or the
temperature of the sun itself—is: very hard indeed. I chopped
and clanged and opened the stove door several hundred times
to prod the fire. I experimented with covering and uncovering
the pan, which seemed to have no effect whatsoever. I fished

out a potato chunk and found it somehow both burnt and undercooked; even Bad hesitated to eat it.

It was all a very effective distraction. I hardly had room for thoughts like: *My mother must've stood right here*; or, *I wonder if she's still alive, somehow, and if my father found her*; or, *I wish one of them had taught me how to cook.* I barely even thought about the blue Door, now so near I imagined I could hear its ashes whispering and lamenting to themselves.

"Can't decide if you're trying to burn the house down or make dinner."

I dropped the poker I'd been holding, lunged for the swinging stove door, burned myself, and spun to face the old woman. She was still slumped in the rocking chair, but her eyes were candlelit slits. She wheezed at me.

I swallowed. "Uh. Making dinner, ma'am—"

"That's Great-Aunt Lizzie, to you."

"Yes. Great-Aunt Lizzie. Would you like some potatoes and eggs? That's what those crispy brown flakes are, between the potatoes. I think maybe salt would help." I scraped the food onto two tin plates and scooped water out of a barrel on the counter. It tasted green and cedary.

We ate in silence, except for the crackling of burnt food between our teeth. I couldn't think of anything to say, or I could think of a hundred things to say and couldn't choose between them.

"I always thought she'd come home, someday." Aunt Lizzie spoke long after Bad had finished licking our plates, and the windows had faded from indigo to black velvet. "I waited."

I thought of all the various truths I could tell her about the fate of her niece—shipwrecked, sundered, stranded in an alien world—and settled on the kindest and simplest one. "She died when I was very young, in a terrible accident. I don't know much about her, really." Lizzie didn't answer. I added, "But I know she wanted to come home. She was trying to get here, she just . . . never quite made it."

There was another of those huffs of air, as if she'd been struck in the chest, and Lizzie said, "Oh."

Then she began to cry, very suddenly and very loudly. I didn't say anything, but ooched my chair closer to hers and placed a hand on her heaving back.

When the sobs had receded to stuttering, snot-thick breaths, I said, "I was wondering if you—if you could tell me about her. My mother."

She was quiet again for so long I thought I'd offended her in some inscrutable way, but then she creaked to her feet, fished a brown glass jug out from the pantry, and poured me a greasy glass of something that smelled and tasted like lantern oil. She shuffled back to her rocking chair with the bottle and resettled herself.

Then she began to speak.

I won't tell you everything she told me, for two reasons: first, because there's a good chance you'd die of boredom. She told me stories about my mother's first steps and the time she climbed into the barn loft and jumped out because she thought she could fly; about her hatred of sweet potatoes and her love of fresh honeycomb; about the perfect June evenings the Larson women spent watching her cartwheel and careen through the yard.

Second, because they are each precious and painful to me in some secret way I can't explain, and I'm not ready to show them to anyone else yet. I want to hold them for a while in the quiet undercurrents of myself, until their edges are worn smooth as river stones.

Maybe I'll tell you about them, someday.

"She used to love the back acres, and that rotten old cabin, before we sold 'em. I'll tell you: that's something I regret."

"What, selling the hayfield?"

Lizzie nodded and took a contemplative sip of the lantern-oil liquor. (Mine remained untouched; the fumes alone were enough to singe my eyebrows.) "The money was nice, I won't lie, but that big-city man was no good. Never did a thing with the property, either, just plowed over the cabin and let the place rot. Ade stopped going out thataways, afterward. Always seemed like we'd done her wrong somehow."

I considered telling her that she'd sold her property to some shadowy Society member and closed the doorway between two lovestruck children, consigning them both to lives of endless wandering. "At least you don't have any neighbors," I offered, lamely.

She scoffed. "Well, he never did nothing with it, but he still comes around every ten-year or so. Says he's checking up on his investment, bah. You know back in—what, '02, '01?—he had the nerve to come knocking on my door and ask if I'd seen any suspicious characters around. Said there'd been some kind of *activity* on his property. I told him *no, sir* and added that a man who could afford fancy gold watches and hair dyes—because let me tell you he hadn't aged a *day* since we signed the contract—could afford to build a damned fence, if he was so worried, and not go hassling old women." She took another gulp from the brown glass bottle and muttered herself into silence, complaining about rich folk, young folk, nosy folk, Yankees, and foreigners.

I'd stopped listening. Something in her story was bothering me, prickling in the tired depths of my brain like a burr caught in cotton. A question was forming, rising to the surface—

"To hell with all of 'em, I say," Lizzie concluded. She screwed the cap back onto her vile brown bottle. "Time we got to bed, child. You can have the upstairs; I do my sleeping right here." A pause, while the bitter lines framing Lizzie's mouth softened. "Take the bed under the window, on the north side, won't you. We always meant to get rid of the damn thing, once we understood she wasn't coming back, but somehow we never did."

"Thank you, Aunt Lizzie."

I was two steps up the stairs when Lizzie said, "Tomorrow maybe you can tell me how a colored girl-child with a mess of scars and a mean-lookin' dog ended up on my doorstep. And what took you so damned long."

"Yes, ma'am."

I fell asleep in my mother's bed, with Bad pressed against my side and the smell of dust in my nose and that shadowy question still looming, unspoken, in my skull.

I had that nightmare about the blue Door and the hands reaching for me, except this time the hands weren't white and spidery, but thick-fingered and familiar: Mr. Locke's hands, reaching toward my throat.

I woke with Bad's nose snuffling beneath my chin and greenish sunlight filtering through the vine-eaten window. I lay for a while, stroking Bad's ears and letting my heart thud itself quiet. The room around me was like an exhibit in a grubby museum. A stiff-bristled brush lay on the dresser with a few wiry white hairs still snarled around it; a framed daguerreotype of a chinless Rebel soldier sat propped on a dresser; a series of children's treasures (a chunk of fool's gold, a broken compass, a rock studded with dull white fossils, a moldy satin ribbon) perched in a neat line on the windowsill.

My mother's whole world, until she ran away to find others. This was what she'd been sailing toward before she died, this shabby house that smelled of old woman and bacon fat. Her home.

Did I have a home to sail back to? I thought of Locke

House—not the stupid, sumptuous parlors crowded with stolen treasures, but my favorite lumpy armchair. The little round window where I could watch storms coming across the lake. The way the stairwell always smelled of beeswax and orange oil.

I did have a home. I just couldn't go back to it. *Like mother, like daughter.*

Lizzie's breakfast appeared to be nothing but ferociously bitter coffee, boiled and strained through a black-stained scrap of cloth. I'd never tried drinking cyanide, but I imagined the sensation of hot liquid burning through your stomach lining is similar.

"Let's hear it, then," Lizzie said, and made a harassed, get-on-with-it gesture.

So I told her how an in-between girl ended up on her doorstep twenty-something years after her niece vanished.

I didn't tell the truth—because then my only remaining relative would think I was insane, and I'd developed something of an allergy to people thinking I was insane—but I tried to make sure all the important bits were true. My father was a foreigner ("Bah," muttered Lizzie) who met my mother by pure chance when he was passing through Ninley. They found one another again after years of searching, got legally married ("Well, thank God for that") and lived on my father's wages as a professor of history (skeptical silence). They were journeying back to Kentucky when there was a terrible accident and my mother was killed (that hit-in-the-chest sound again), and my father and I were more or less adopted by a wealthy patron (more skeptical silence). My father spent the last decade and a half conducting research all over the world; he never remarried (a noise of grudging approval).

"And I grew up in Locke House, in Vermont. I had everything any girl could want." *Except family or freedom, but who's counting?* "I traveled everywhere with my, uh, foster father. I even came here once, I don't know if you remember."

Lizzie squinted at me, then gave a little *huh* of recognition. "Ah! Didn't think you were real. Used to be I'd see Adelaide all over the place, but it always turned out to be some girl with a yellow braid, or a man in an old coat. She used to wear my coat around, ugliest thing you ever saw...Well. When was that? How'd you end up here?"

"It was 1901. I'd come with my foster father to..."

The number *1901* echoed weirdly as I said it.

Lizzie had said last night that her mysterious property buyer reappeared in 1901, and wasn't it rather strange that we were both in Ninley in the same year? Perhaps we were even here at the same time. Perhaps our paths had crossed at the Grand Riverfront Hotel—could it have been that governor with the skull collection? I tried to remember how my father's book had described him: clipped mustache, expensive suit, cold eyes. Eyes the color of moons or coins...

My thoughts slowed, as if they were slogging through hip-deep syrup.

The question—that formless black ghost that had been haunting me all night—came suddenly into focus. And I knew as it did so that it was something I desperately didn't want to ask.

"Sorry, but—you know the man who bought your back acres? What was his name, did you say?"

Lizzie blinked at me. "What? Well, we never got his first name, and isn't that an odd thing, to sell your land without knowing a fellow's Christian name. But he had a queer way about him, and those eyes..." She shivered, just a little, and I pictured a pair of glacial eyes pressing against her skin.

"But it says his company name right on the contract: W. C. Locke & Co."

★ ★ ★

It's hard to remember precisely how I reacted.

Maybe I screamed. Maybe I gasped and covered my mouth with my hands. Maybe I fell backward in my chair into deep, cold water and kept falling down and down, a final glittering stream of bubbles escaping back toward the surface—

Maybe I cleared my throat and asked my aunt Lizzie to repeat herself, please.

Mr. Locke. It had been Mr. Locke who had met my fifteen-year-old mother after Sunday church, who had interrogated her about ghost boys and cabin doors, who had purchased the Larson women's back acres and closed their Door.

Are you really surprised? The voice in my head was tart and grown-up sounding. It made, I supposed, a fair point: I'd already known Mr. Locke was a liar and a thief and a villain. I knew he was a Society member and therefore dedicated to the destruction of Doors; I knew he had recruited my father with all the callous self-interest of a rich man purchasing a race-horse, and had profited from his torment for seventeen years; I knew his love for me was conditional and fragile, abandoned as easily as selling an artifact at auction.

But I hadn't known, or permitted myself to know, that he was so cruel. Cruel enough to knowingly close my father's Door not once but twice—

Or maybe he didn't know the blue Door was anything special. Perhaps he never connected it to the strange, tattooed fellow he found years later. (This, I recognize now, was a desperate, absurd hope, as if I could somehow discover a clue that would redeem Mr. Locke and make him again the distant-but-beloved almost-father-figure of my childhood.)

I dumped out the contents of my reeking, stained pillow-case, ignoring Lizzie's squawked "Not on my kitchen table, child!" I seized the leather-bound book, my father's book, the book that had sent me on this mad, wandering trail back to my own beginnings. It shook slightly in my hands.

I turned to the final chapter, the part where Mr. Locke miraculously shows up to rescue my grieving father. And there it was: *1881. A girl named Adelaide Lee Larson.* Surely Locke had recognized the name and date. A trapped, panicky feeling rose in my throat, like a small child who has run out of excuses.

He knew. Locke *knew.*

When he met my father in 1895 he already knew all about the Larsons and their back acres and the Door in the field. He'd been the one to close it, after all. But he hadn't said a word to my poor, foolish father. Not even—and this time I felt myself actually gasp, and heard Lizzie's tongue cluck in irritation— not even when he found the Door open again in 1901.

If Mr. Locke had loved my father and me at all, he would have left my blue Door standing and sent him a telegram within the hour: *Come home Julian STOP Found your damn door.* My father would've skimmed across the Atlantic like a skipped stone. He would've burst into Locke House and I would've run into his arms and he would've whispered into my hair, *January, my love, we're going home.*

But Mr. Locke hadn't done any of those things. Instead, he'd burned the blue Door to ash, locked me in my room, and left my father stranded for ten more years.

Oh, Father. You thought of yourself as a knight under the generous patronage of some wealthy baron or prince, didn't you? When really you were a bridled horse running beneath the whip.

The book was still in my hands. My thumbs were pressed bloodless-white against the pages. A suffocating heat gathered in my throat—a final, terrible betrayal, a swelling rage—and some distant part of me was almost frightened by the sheer immensity of it.

But I didn't have time for rage, because I'd just remembered the letter I mailed to Mr. Locke. *I'm going home*, I'd told him. I had imagined, when I wrote it, that Mr. Locke would assume I was headed for the Door Ilvane had destroyed in Japan, or even the Door the Society had closed in Colorado. I'd thought he didn't know about this first Door, except as a passing reference in my father's story, closed decades before.

Oh, hell.

"I have to go. Right now." I was already standing, already reeling toward the door with Bad scrabbling to catch up. "Which way to that old hayfield? Never mind, I'll find it—it was on the river, wasn't it?" I rummaged freely through Lizzie's things as I spoke, tugging out drawers wedged tight in the summer heat, looking for—*yes*. A few faded pages of newsprint. I jammed them back into my pillowcase with everything else: Ilvane's greenish compass, my silver coin-knife, my father's book, Samuel's pen. It would have to be enough.

"Hold up, girl, you're half-dressed—" I was three quarters dressed, at least—I just wasn't wearing shoes and my blouse was buttoned sideways. "What do you want with that place, anyhow?"

I turned back to face her. She looked so shrunken and fragile in her rocking chair, like something plucked from its shell and slowly fossilizing. Her eyes on me were red-rimmed and anxious.

"I'm sorry," I told her. I knew what it felt like to be always alone, always waiting for someone to come home. "But I have to go. I might already be too late. I'll come back to visit, though, I swear."

The lines around her mouth twisted into a bitter, hurting sort of smile. It was the smile of someone who has heard promises before, and knows better than to believe them. I knew what that was like, too.

Without thinking I crossed back to the rocking chair and kissed my aunt Lizzie on the forehead. It was like kissing a page in an ancient book, musty-smelling and dry.

She huffed a half laugh. "Lord, but you are just like your mother." Then she sniffed. "I'll be here when you come back."

And I left my mother's house with the pillowcase clutched tight in my hand and Bad flying like a sleek bronze spear at my side.

The Ash Door

He was already waiting for me, of course.

You know that feeling when you're in a maze and you think you've almost made it out, but then you turn the corner and *bam*, you're back at the entrance? That warped, eerie feeling of having fallen backward in time?

That was how it felt to see the overgrown field and the black-suited shape waiting for me in the center of it. Like I'd made a mistake somewhere and circled back to the day when I was seven and found the Door.

Except the scene had changed, subtly. When I was seven the grasses had been orange and autumn-dry, and now they were several hundred shades of green and studded with yellow bursts of goldenrod. I'd been neatly dressed in blue cotton, terribly alone except for my pretty little pocket diary, and now I was barefoot and dirt-grimed, with Bad padding beside me.

And I'd been running away from Mr. Locke then, rather than toward him.

"Hello, January. Sindbad, always a pleasure." Mr. Locke looked a little travel-rumpled but otherwise precisely the same: square, pale-eyed, supremely confident. I remember being surprised, as if I expected him to be wearing a black cape lined with red silk or twirling a long mustache with a sinister smile, but he was just comfortable, familiar Mr. Locke.

"Hello, sir," I whispered. The will to be polite, to maintain civility and normalcy, is fearfully strong. I wonder sometimes how much evil is permitted to run unchecked simply because it would be rude to interrupt it.

He smiled in what he must have believed was a charming, friendly manner. "I was just starting to suspect I'd missed you, and you were already gallivanting off God-knows-where."

"No, sir." The jagged tip of the pen pressed into my palm.

"How lucky. And—good Lord, child, what have you done to your arm?" He squinted. "Tried to copy Daddy's tattoos using a butcher knife, did you?"

The next *No, sir* caught in my throat and refused to come out. My eyes had fallen on the weedy, mostly vanished circle of ash that had once been my blue Door, and standing before me was the man who had burned it down, betrayed my father, locked me away—and I didn't owe him good manners. I didn't owe him anything at all.

I unbent my shoulders and raised my head. "I trusted you, you know. So did my father."

The joviality slid from Locke's face like clown paint washing away in the rain. His gaze on me turned watchful and narrow-eyed. He didn't answer.

"I thought you were helping us. I thought you *cared* about us." *About me.*

Now he raised a placating hand. "Of course I do—"

"But you betrayed us both, in the end. You used my father, lied to him, had him locked forever in another world. And then you lied to me, told me he was *dead*—" My voice was rising, boiling up from my chest. "You told me you were *protecting* me—"

"January, I have protected you since the moment you came into this world!" Locke moved closer to me, hands outstretched as if he intended to place them on my shoulders. I stepped backward and Bad came to his feet, hackles rough, lips peeled back. If Mr. Locke hadn't been firmly on his Please Do Not Ever Bite list, I think his teeth would've found flesh.

Locke retreated. "I thought Theodore had that animal dumped in the lake. Drowning doesn't seem to have improved his temper much, does it?" Bad and I glared.

Locke sighed. "January, listen to me: when you and your father crashed through that door in Colorado just as we were closing it, my associates were all for smashing your skulls and leaving you for dead on the mountainside."

"From my father's account, you gave it a good try," I said coldly.

Locke made a dismissive, gnat-swatting gesture. "A misunderstanding, I assure you. We were there because your mother had raised quite a fuss in the papers. Everybody made fun of the madwoman and her ship in the mountains, but we suspected there was more to it—and we were right, were we not?" He cleared his throat. "I'll admit my man was a bit, ah, overexcited about your father, but the poor fellow had been tearing down a doorway when half a damned ship sailed through it! And anyway there was no lasting harm done. I had the two of you well taken care of while I consulted with the others."

"The Society, you mean." Locke inclined his head in a genteel bow. "And they all advised you to commit double homicide, did they? And I'm supposed to be—to be *grateful*, that you didn't do it?" I wanted to spit at him, scream at him until he understood how it felt to be small and lost and worthless. "Do they hand out medals for not murdering babies? Perhaps just a nice certificate?"

I expected him to shout at me, perhaps even hoped he would. I wanted him to abandon this pretense of goodwill and good intentions, to cackle with glee. That was what villains were supposed to do; that was what gave the heroes permission to hate them.

But Locke merely looked at me with one side of his mouth twisted up. "You're upset with me. I understand." I sincerely, deeply doubted it. "But you were exactly what we'd been striving so hard to prevent, you see, exactly what we'd sworn ourselves against: a random, foreign element, with the potential to instigate all sorts of trouble and disruption, which ought to be stamped out."

"My father was a grieving scholar. I was a half-orphaned baby. What sort of trouble could we cause?"

Locke bowed again, his smile gone a little tight. "So I argued. I brought them all around, eventually—I am *very* persuasive when I wish to be." A small, black laugh. "I explained about your father's notes and papers, and his particular and personal motivation to seek out additional fractures. I suggested I might foster you myself, watch you carefully for any useful, unusual talents, and turn them to our purposes. I *saved* you, January."

How many times had he told me that, growing up? How many times had he retold the story of finding my poor father and taking him under his wing, of giving us fine clothes and spacious rooms, and how dare I talk to him like that? And every time I would wilt with guilt and gratitude, like a pet whose leash has been tugged.

But now I was free. Free to hate him, free to run from him, free to write my own story. I turned the pen in my hand.

"Listen, January, it's getting hot." Locke mopped the pearled sweat from his forehead theatrically. "Let's you and I head back into town and discuss everything in a more civilized setting, hm? This has all been nothing but a series of misund—"

"No." I had a suspicion he wanted to get me away from here, away from the susurrating green field and the black remains of the Door. Or maybe he just wanted to get me back to town where he could call the police or the Society. "No. I think we're through talking, actually. You should leave."

My voice had been so emotionless it could have been a conductor's announcement on a train, but Mr. Locke threw up his hands in defense. "You don't understand—you've suffered some personal misfortunes, I admit, but try not to be so self-ish. Think about the good of the *world*, January! Think about what these 'doors'—fractures, we call them, or aberrations—promote: disruption, madness, magic…they overturn *order*. I've seen a world without order, defined by constant competition for power and wealth, by the cruelties of change."

Now he did reach for me, resting his hand clumsily on my shoulder and ignoring Bad's snarl. His eyes—colorless, glacial—stared into mine. "I wasted my youth in a world like that."

What? My fingers around the pen went slack.

He spoke slowly, almost gently. "I was born into a cold, vicious world, but I escaped and found a better one. A softer world, full of potential. I have dedicated my life, and the better part of two centuries, to its betterment."

"But—you—two *centuries*?"

Now there was pity in his voice, syrup-sweet and rancid. "I traveled in my youth, you see. Happened to find a fracture in the middle of Old China, and a very special jade cup—you've seen it, I'm sure. It has the property of extending one's life span. Perhaps indefinitely. We shall see." I thought of Lizzie saying he hadn't aged a day; thought of my father's silvering hair, the lines framing his mouth.

Locke sighed, and said softly, "I first came into this world in 1764, in the northern mountains of Scotland."

In England or Scotland, I don't recall.

I thought I'd circled back to the beginning of my own labyrinth. I thought I knew where I was. But now everything warped strangely in my vision and I realized I was still wandering in the heart of the maze, entirely lost.

"You're the Founder," I whispered.

And Mr. Locke smiled.

I stumbled backward, clutching at Bad's fur. "But how could— no. It doesn't matter, I don't care. I'm leaving."

I fumbled for the newsprint pages, held the pen tight in shaking fingers. *Run away, run away.* I was through with this world and its cruelties, its monsters and betrayals and stupid colored sections on its stupid trains—

"Is that how you do it? Some sort of magic ink? Written words? I should have suspected as much." Locke's voice was genial, quite calm. "I don't think so, my dear." I glanced up at him, the split nib already touching the page—

—and his eyes caught me like two silver fishhooks. "*Drop that*, January, and *be still*." The pen and paper fell from my hands.

Locke retrieved them, tucked the pen in his coat pocket, shredded the newsprint, and tossed the remains behind him. They fluttered like yellow-white moths into the grass.

"You are going to listen to me now." My pulse beat turgid and reluctant in my skull. I felt suspended, like some unlucky prehistoric girl preserved forever in a glacier. "When you're done listening, you're going to understand the work to which I've dedicated my life. And, I hope, how you might help me."

And so I listened, because I had to listen, because his eyes were hooks or knives or claws fastened tight in my flesh.

"How is it your stories always start? *Once upon a time* there was a very unlucky little boy. He was born into a nasty, brutal, bitter world, a world too absorbed in killing and being killed even to name itself. The locals in your world called it Ifrinn, I later learned, and that's what it was: hell. If hell were dark and frigid."

He wavered oddly between accents, his tone swerving between dry narration and bitter anger. It was as if the Mr. Locke I'd grown up with—his voice, his mannerisms, his posture—was just a sort of party mask, behind which lurked someone much older and stranger.

"This unlucky boy fought in four battles before he was fourteen. Can you imagine? Boys and girls dressed in mangy animal skins, half-feral, running among the soldiers like hungry scavengers... Of course you can't.

"We fought for such meager rewards. A few snow-covered acres of good hunting ground, the rumor of treasure, pride. Sometimes we didn't even know why we fought, except that our chieftainess willed it. How we loved her. How we hated her." My expression must've changed, because Locke laughed. It was a perfectly normal-sounding laugh, the same jovial boom I'd heard how many hundreds of times, but it made the fine hairs on my arms stand upright.

"Yes, *both*. Always both. I imagine it's much the same way you feel about me, really, and don't think the irony is lost on me. But I was never cruel to you, the way our rulers were." Now his tone turned almost anxious, as if he were afraid one or both of us might not quite believe him. "I never made you do anything against your own interest. But in Ifrinn they *used* us, like soldiers use bullets. It was too damned cold to live clanless and hungry, but we might have tried anyway if it weren't for the Birthright."

I heard the capital *B* pressing up through Locke's sentence, casting a bulbous shadow behind it, but didn't understand it.

"I should've started with the Birthright. I've gotten it all jumbled up." Locke dabbed sweat from his lip. "This storytelling rubbish is harder than it looks, eh? The Birthright. Around sixteen or seventeen, a very few children in Ifrinn manifest a, ah, particular ability. It's easy, at first, to mistake the children as bullies or charmers. But they possess something much rarer: the power to rule. To sway men's minds, to bend their wills like smiths bend hot iron...And then there are the eyes, of course. The final sign."

Locke leaned toward me and widened his own ice-pale eyes for my inspection. Softly, he asked, "What color would you call them? We had a word for it that English doesn't supply, which referred to a very particular kind of snow that has fallen and refrozen, so that there's a gray translucency to it..."

No, I thought, but the word felt weak and distant in my head, like someone calling for help a long way away. A broken grass-stem poked into the bare arch of my foot; I pressed down against it, felt it peel away a semicircle of skin, felt the prickle of raw skin in the open air.

Locke's face was still close to mine. "You already know all about the Birthright, of course. Such a willful little girl you were."

Like smiths bend hot iron. I saw myself briefly as a piece of worked metal glowing dull orange, hammered and hammered—

Locke straightened again. "The Birthright was an invitation to rule. We were expected either to challenge our present chieftainess in a battle of wills, or skulk off and form our own miserable clan. I challenged her as soon as I could, the old bitch, left her weeping and broken, and claimed my Birthright at sixteen." His voice was savage with satisfaction.

"But nothing lasted in that world. There were always new clans, new leaders, new wars. Challengers to my rule. Dissidence. There was a night raid, a battle of wills, which I lost, and I ran away and... You know what I found, of course."

My mouth moved, soundless. *A Door.*

He smiled indulgently. "Quite right. A crevice in a glacier that led to another world. And oh, what a world it is! Rich, green, warm, populated by weak-eyed people who cave to my slightest suggestion—everything Ifrinn was not. It took only a few hours before I returned to the fracture and smashed it to rubble with my bare hands."

I gasped, eyes wide, and Locke scoffed. "What? You think I should've left it wide open, so some Ifrinn bastard could sneak out after me? Could ruin my lovely, soft world? *No.*" He was strident and principled, like a priest trying hard to save his sinful flock. Except there was something else panting beneath the preaching, something that made me think of cornered dogs and drowning men, a kind of clawing terror. "This is what I'm trying to tell you, January—you call them 'doors,' as if they were necessary, everyday sorts of things, but they're quite the opposite. They let in all manner of dangerous things."

Like you. Like me?

"I found a town big enough to grant a little anonymity. Clothes and food were easy for a Birthrighted man to acquire. So was a rather nice home, and an obliging young woman to teach me the language." A smug smile. "She told me stories about great winged snakes that lived in the mountains with hoards of gold, and how you must never look them in the eyes lest they steal your soul." A fond chuckle. "I confess, I've always liked nice things—what is Locke House if not a dragon's hoard?"

Locke began to pace in irregular circles, fishing a half-chewed cigar from his coat pocket and gesticulating against the noon-blue sky. He told me about his early years spent studying language, geography, history, economics; his travels abroad and his discovery of additional aberrations, which he plundered and destroyed at once; his conclusion that his new world was still plagued by all manner of mess and malcontent ("First the Americans, then the damned French, even the Haitians! One after the other!") but was steadily improving under the guidance of orderly new empires.

I listened, with the sun pulsing against my skin like a hot yellow heartbeat and the words *be still* circling inside my head like harpies. I felt twelve again, being lectured at in his office and staring at his Enfield revolver in its glass case.

He joined the Honorable East India Company in 1781. He rose through the ranks quickly, of course—"And it wasn't all my Birthright, either, don't look at me like that"—made himself a largish fortune, pursued business ventures of his own, retired and rejoined the company several times to allay suspicion about his age, built himself homes in London, Stockholm, Chicago, even a green little estate in Vermont in the 1790s. He alternated between his homes, of course, selling and repurchasing them half a dozen times.

For a long time, he'd thought it would be enough.

But then in 1857 a certain group of mutinous colonial subjects rose up, set a few British forts aflame, and ran victorious through the countryside for almost a year before being brutally subjugated once more.

"I was there, January. In Delhi. I went around to every mutineer I could find—which wasn't many, as the captain had been firing them from cannons—and all of them told me the same story: an old Bengali woman in Meerut had slipped through a strange archway and returned twelve days later. She

334

had spoken with some sort of oracular creature that told her she and all her people would one day be free from foreign rule. And so they'd taken up arms against us."

Locke's hands rose into the air in remembered outrage. "A fracture! A damned door, lurking beneath my very nose!" He exhaled forcefully and tucked his thumbs behind his belt, as if willing himself calm. "I came to realize the urgency of my mission, the importance of closing the fractures. I took it upon myself to recruit others to my cause."

And thus was the Society formed, a secretive association of the powerful: an old man in Volgograd who kept his heart in a little velvet box; a wealthy heiress in Sweden; a fellow in the Philippines who transformed into a great black boar; a handful of princes and a dozen members of Congress; a white-skinned creature in Rumania who fed on human warmth.

Now Locke spiraled back to face me in his pacing, snagged my eyes with his own. "We have done our work well. For half a century we've labored in the shadows to keep this world safe and prosperous—we've closed dozens of fractures, maybe hundreds— we've helped build a stable, bright future. But, January"—his gaze intensified—"it isn't enough. There are still murmurs of discontent, threats to stability, dangerous fluctuations. We need all the help we can find, frankly, especially now that your father is gone."

His voice fell to a rumbling whisper. "Help us, dear child. *Join* us."

It was well past noon now, and our shadows had begun to creep cautiously out from under us, shattering into dark spindles in the tall grass. The river and the cicadas made a kind of rushing thrum beneath the soles of my feet, as if the earth were humming to itself.

Mr. Locke breathed, waiting.

Words pressed at the roof of my mouth, words like *Thank you* or *Yes, of course, sir* or maybe *Give me some time.* They were pleased, flattered words, oozing with girlish gratitude that he loved me and trusted me and wanted me by his side.

I wondered if they were my words or Mr. Locke's, delivered to me through his white-eyed gaze. The thought was sick-making, dizzying—infuriating. "*No.* Thank you." I hissed it between locked teeth.

Locke clucked his tongue. "Don't be imprudent, girl. Do you think you'd be permitted to wander freely, with your habit of opening things that ought to be left closed? The Society would not suffer such a creature to live."

"Mr. Ilvane already indicated as much. As did Mr. Havemeyer."

Locke huffed in exasperation. "Yes, I'm terribly sorry about Theodore and Bartholomew. They were both given to extremes, and to violent solutions. No one will miss Theodore much, I assure you. I'll admit there were some concerns about Miss Whatsit and your little grocer boy, but I've dealt with them now."

Dealt with—but they were supposed to be safe, supposed to be hidden in Arcadia—a soft wailing sound rang in my ears, as if I were hearing someone crying from a long ways away. I stepped forward, half stumbling on something buried in the ash pile.

"Jane—S-Samuel—" I could barely speak their names.

"Are both perfectly fine!" I went weak with relief and found myself kneeling in the ash with Bad propping me up on one side. "We found them creeping down the coast of Maine after you. We hardly caught a glimpse of Miss Whatsit—awfully quick on her feet, the thieving bitch—but we'll find her eventually, I'm sure. The boy, though, was quite cooperative."

A ringing silence. The cicadas hummed and thrilled. "What did you do to him?" It was a whisper.

"My, my, is this a crush, after a decade of Little Miss Leave Me Alone I'm Reading?" *If you've killed him, I will write a knife into my hand, I swear I will—* "Calm yourself, January. My methods of interrogation are far less, hm, primitive than Havemeyer's. I simply asked him a few questions about you, realized you'd unwisely told him all about Society business, and told him to forget the entire affair. Which he obligingly did. We sent him trotting off home without a care in the world."

Mr. Locke's smile—comforting, assured—told me he didn't understand what he'd done.

He didn't understand the horror of it, the violation. He didn't understand that reaching into someone's mind and sculpting it like living clay is a species of violence far worse than Havemeyer's.

Was this what he'd done to me, my whole life? Forced me to become someone else? Someone biddable and demure and good, who didn't run off into hayfields or play on the lakeshore with the grocer's son or beg on a weekly basis to go adventuring with her father?

Be a good girl, and mind your place. Oh, how I'd tried. How I'd worked to fit myself inside the narrow confines of the girl Mr. Locke told me to be, how I'd mourned my failures.

He didn't understand how much I hated him then, as I knelt in the ashes and tall grasses, my tears turning to muddy paste on my cheeks.

"So you see, everything is taken care of. Join the Society and all this nonsense will be forgotten. The invitation is still open, just as I promised." I could barely hear him over my roaring, keening fury. "Don't you see you're *meant* to do this? I've raised you at my side, let you see the world, taught you everything I could. I never felt it would be entirely wise to—ah"—Locke coughed in brief embarrassment—"to have a child of my own—what if he was Birthrighted? What if he came to challenge my rule? But just look at you! My adopted child has turned out to be nearly as willful, nearly as powerful as any true-born son of mine could be." His eyes on me were lit with pride, like an owner admiring his best horse. "I don't know precisely what you're capable of, I admit, but let us find out together! Join us. Help us protect this world."

I knew when Mr. Locke protected something he locked it away, stifled it, kept it preserved like an amputated limb in a glass case. He'd been protecting me my entire life, and it'd nearly killed me, or at least my soul.

I wouldn't let him continue to do that to the world. I *wouldn't*. But how could I not, when he could remake my will with a mere look? I buried my hands in the weedy ashes around me, an unvoiced wail caught in my throat.

It is at that moment I made two interesting discoveries: The first was a hunk of charcoal lurking beneath the surface layer of rain-leached ash and mud. The second was the burnt, rotting remains of my pocket diary. The diary my father had placed in the blue chest a decade ago, just for me.

The cover, once softest calfskin, was now stiff and cracked, burnt black around the edges. Only the first three letters of my name were still visible (see the unfurled curve of that *J*, like a rope dangling out a prison window?). Pieces of it crumbled and flaked away as I opened it; the pages inside were fire-chewed and dirty.

"What's that? What—put that down, January. I mean it." Locke's feet stumped toward me. I brought the charcoal to the page, made a single sinuous line. *God, I hope this works.*

"I'm not joking—" A sweaty hand circled my chin and

forced my face upward. I met those pale, cutting eyes. "*Stop, January.*"

It was like being submerged in a winter river. An incalculable weight crushed me downward, pressed me, tugged at my clothes and limbs and urged them in a single direction—and wouldn't it be so much easier if I just let the river take me, instead of gritting my jaw and refusing—I could go back *home* again, could curl back into my former good-girl place like a loyal hound at her master's feet—

It became a question, as I stared into Mr. Locke's bone-pale eyes, of how thoroughly he'd succeeded in making me be a good girl who knew her place. Had his will entirely eclipsed my own? Had he scrubbed away my natural self and left nothing but a china-doll version behind? Or had he merely stuffed me into a costume and forced me to play a part?

I thought abruptly of Mr. Stirling—the eerie emptiness of him, as if there were nothing at all lurking beneath his good-valet mask. Was that my future? Was there anything left of that obstinate, temerarious girl-child who found a Door in the field, all those years ago?

I thought of my desperate escape from Brattleboro; the midnight swim to the abandoned lighthouse, and my wandering, dangerous route southward. I thought of every time I'd disobeyed Wilda or snuck a story paper into Locke's office rather than read *The History of the Decline and Fall of the Roman Empire*; of the hours I'd spent dreaming of adventure and mystery and magic. I thought of myself here, now, kneeling in the dirt of my mother's home in defiance of Havemeyer and the Society and Mr. Locke himself—and rather suspected there was.

Could I choose, now, who I wanted to be?

The river surged and rushed against me, willing me down, down, down—but it was as if I'd turned into something impossibly heavy, a lead statue of a girl and her dog standing together, unbothered by the crushing river.

I pulled against Locke's hand on my chin, broke away from his eyes. The charcoal moved on the page. *SHE—*

Locke stumbled backward and I heard him scrabbling at his waist. I ignored him. *SHE WRITES—*

Then came the soft *shush* of metal on leather and a syncopated *click-click*. I knew that click; I'd heard it in the Zappia family cabin just before the thunderclap of sound had killed Havemeyer; I'd heard it in the fields of Arcadia, when I'd fired wildly after Ilvane.

"January, I don't quite know what you're doing, but I can't allow it." I noted, distantly, that I'd never heard Mr. Locke's voice shake before, but I couldn't seem to care; I was distracted by the thing in his hands.

A revolver. Not the old, beloved Enfield that Jane had stolen, but a much sleeker, newer-looking gun. I stared dumbly down the black-tunnel barrel of it.

"Just put it down, dear." He sounded so calm and authoritative that he might have been chairing a board meeting, except for the subtle tremor of his voice. He was afraid of something—me? Or Doors, and the ever-present threat that something more powerful than himself was lurking on the other side? Maybe all powerful men are cowards at heart, because in their hearts they know power is temporary.

He smiled, or attempted to smile; his mouth stretched in a bare-toothed grimace. "These doors of yours are meant to stay closed, I'm afraid."

No, they aren't. Worlds were never meant to be prisons, locked and suffocating and safe. Worlds were supposed to be great rambling houses with all the windows thrown open and the wind and summer rain rushing through them, with magic passages in their closets and secret treasure chests in their attics.

Locke and his Society had spent a century rushing madly around that house, boarding up windows and locking doors.

I was so very tired of locked doors.

SHE WRITES A DOOR OF—

I suppose, looking back, that I hadn't ever been properly afraid of Mr. Locke. My childish heart refused to believe that the man who had sat beside me on a hundred different trains and steamers and ferries, who smelled of cigars and leather and money, who was always there when my own parents weren't— could ever really hurt me.

I might even have been right, because Mr. Locke didn't shoot me. Instead, I saw the black glint of the barrel swing to the right. It paused, pointed at Bad, at the spot where his hairs met in a ridged seam down his chest.

I moved. My scream was eaten by a booming crack.

And then Mr. Locke was yelling, swearing at me, and I was running my fingers over Bad's chest whispering *oh God no* and Bad was whimpering but there was no wound, no hole, his skin was as smooth and whole as it had been before—

Then where was all this smeary red coming from?

Oh.

"Can't you ever, just once, mind your damned *place*—"

I sat back on my heels, watching blood slide down the dirt-dark skin of my arm in neat runnels, like a street map to a foreign city. Bad's whiskers trailed through it as he investigated the dark hole in my shoulder, his ears pulled flat in concern. I tried to reach my left hand up to comfort him, but it was like tugging a broken puppet string.

It didn't hurt, or maybe it did hurt but the pain didn't want to be pushy about it. It waited politely at the edges of my vision, like a well-bred houseguest.

I'd dropped my charcoal. My sentence lay unfinished beside a smallish pool of redness forming at the end of my fingertips.

Well. It would have to do, because I certainly wasn't lingering in this vicious, white-toothed world where the people you loved could do such terrible things to you.

I've always been good at running away.

I extended my finger, almost lazily, and drew it through the muddy puddle of blood. I wrote in the earth itself, in red-mud letters that glistened in the summer afternoon. The cicadas made the bones of my hand buzz.

SHE WRITES A DOOR OF ASH. IT OPENS.

I believed in it the way people believe in God or gravity: with such unswerving intensity they hardly notice they're doing it. I believed I was a word-worker, and that my will could reshape the very warp and weft of reality itself. I believed that Doors existed in rare places of resonance between worlds, where the skies of two planets whispered against one another. I believed I would see my father again.

An eastward wind blew suddenly up from the riverbank, but it didn't smell catfishy and damp like it should have. Instead it smelled dry and cool and spice-laden, like cinnamon and cedar.

The wind scudded over the ash pile. It swirled, like one of those strange dust devils you see sometimes teasing leaves into the air, and ashes and rain-rotted charcoal and dirt flung themselves upward. They hung for a moment between Mr. Locke and me, an arch framed in blue summer sky. I saw Locke's face slacken, his gun wavering.

Then the ash began to . . . spread? Melt? It was as if each speck of dirt or char were actually a drop of ink in water, and now delicate tendrils were spiraling toward one another, connecting, melding, darkening, forming a curved line in the air until—

An archway stood before me. It looked strangely fragile, as if it might crumble back to ash at the slightest touch, but it was a Door. I could already smell the sea.

I reached for my discarded pillowcase and climbed unsteadily to my feet, exhaustion blurring my eyes, bits of dirt and grass embedded in my kneecaps. I saw Mr. Locke's grip seize around the revolver again. "Now, just, just stop. We can still make this right. You can still come back with me, come home—everything can still be fine—"

That was a lie; I was dangerous and he was a coward, and cowards don't let dangerous things live in their spare bedrooms. Sometimes they don't let them live at all.

I stepped toward the ash door and met Mr. Locke's eyes for the last time. They were white and barren as a pair of moons. I had a sudden childish urge to ask him a question—*Did you ever really love me?*—but then the barrel of the gun drifted upward again and I thought, *I suppose not.*

I dove through the ash archway with Bad leaping at my heels and my heart *thud-thud*ding in my chest and the crack of a second shot ringing in my ears, following me into the black.

The Open Doors

I had entered the Threshold four times before. *Perhaps*, I thought as I fell into the echoing black, *the fifth time won't be so bad*.

I was, of course, wrong. Just as the sky doesn't turn less blue the more times you see it, so the atomless, airless nothing of the space between worlds does not grow less terrifying.

The darkness swallowed me like a living thing. I tilted forward, falling but not falling because in order to fall there has to be an up and a down and in the Threshold there's only the endless black nothing. I felt Bad brush past me, legs paddling ineffectually against the emptiness, and scooped my arm around him. He kept his eyes fixed on me. It occurred to me that dogs are probably never lost in the in-between, because they always know precisely where they are going.

And so, this time, did I. I felt my father's book wedged tight against my ribs, and followed the cedar-and-salt smell of his home world, *my* home world, toward that white-stone city.

I could still feel the hungry tugging of the darkness, but it was as if something bright and shining in me had finally unfurled and filled me to my edges. I was weak, riddled with hurts—betrayal, abandonment, the tiny black hole in my shoulder, a new something-very-wrong in my left hip that I didn't want to think about—but I was entirely myself, and I was not afraid.

Until I felt a hand close around my ankle.

I didn't think he would follow me. I want you to understand that—I didn't mean for it to happen, any of it. I thought he would stay behind in his safe little world and crush my Door back to ash and char. I thought he would sigh regretfully, cross out my entry in his mental ledger book (*In-between girl, magic powers suspected, value unknown*) and then go back to his twin passions of amassing wealth and closing Doors. But he didn't.

Maybe he loved me, after all.

I think I even caught a glimpse of love when I turned back to look at his face—or at least a possessive, conditional, desire-to-own—but it was quickly subsumed beneath his towering fury. There is nothing quite like the anger of someone very powerful who has been thwarted by someone who was supposed to be weak.

His fingers burrowed into my flesh. His other hand still held the shining revolver, and I saw his thumb move. There was no sound in the Threshold, but I imagined I could hear that ominous *click-click* again. *No no no*—I could feel myself slowing, floundering in the black, fear blurring my goal—

But I had forgotten Bad. My first friend, my dearest companion, my terrible dog who had always seen the Please Do Not Ever Bite list as a fundamentally negotiable document.

He arched backward, yellow eyes gleaming in the fierce joy of an animal doing what he loves best, and buried his teeth in Locke's wrist.

Locke's mouth opened in a soundless scream. He let go of me. And then he was floating, falling alone in the empty vastness of the Threshold and his eyes had gone white and wide as china plates.

For all the Doors he'd closed, I wondered how long it had been since he'd stepped through one, since he'd seen the Threshold. He seemed to have forgotten his rage, his direction, the gun in his hand—now there was nothing in his face but wild terror.

He could still have followed me.

But he was too afraid. He was afraid of change and uncertainty, of the Threshold itself. Of things outside his power, and things in between.

I watched the darkness nibble, delicately, at the edges of him. His right hand and his revolver vanished. His entire arm. His eyes—his powerful, pale eyes, which had brought him such wealth and such status, which had subjugated enemies and persuaded allies and even reshaped stubborn young girls, temporarily—could do nothing against the darkness.

I turned away. It was not an easy turning-away; a part of me still wanted to reach my hand back to him, to save him; another part of me wanted to watch him vanish, piece by piece, to pay for every betrayal and every lie. But I felt my home world still waiting for me, certain and steady as the North Star, and I could not go toward it if I were still looking back.

My bare foot found solid, warm stone.

I knew nothing but sunlight, and the smell of the sea.

It was sunset when I opened my eyes. I could see the sun sinking like a squat red coal into the western ocean. Everything was soft around the edges, lit by a pinkish-gold glow that reminded me for a sleepy moment of the quilt my father had given me when I was a girl. *Oh, Father, I miss you.*

I must have sighed aloud, because there was a smallish explosion beside me that was Bad springing to his feet as if fired from a dog-sized cannon. He landed awkwardly on his bad leg, yipped, and contented himself with wriggling all over and burying his face in my neck.

I threw my arms around him, or tried to—only my right arm obeyed with any real enthusiasm. The left one just sort of flopped over, fishlike, and lay still. It was at that moment, as I stared in mild dismay at my disobedient arm, that the politely waiting pain cleared its throat, stepped forward, and introduced itself.

Damn, I thought, cogently. Then, after another few heartbeats, during which I could feel every fiber of torn muscle in my shoulder and every shuddering bone in my left hip, I revised it: *"Shit."*

It actually helped a little; Mr. Locke had forbidden me to swear when I was thirteen and he'd caught me telling the new kitchen boy to keep his goddamned hands to himself. I wondered how long it would take before I stopped discovering these petty little laws that'd governed my life, and whether I would only reveal them by breaking them. It was a rather cheerful thought.

And then I wondered how long it would take before I stopped seeing Mr. Locke devoured by incarnate darkness, and sobered a little.

I pulled myself to my feet—slowly and painfully and with lots more swearing—and tucked *The Ten Thousand Doors* beneath my arm. The city lay below me. How did I describe it to you before? A world of salt water and stone. Buildings standing in whitewashed spirals, free of coal smoke and grit.

A forest of masts and sails along the coast. It was all still there, and nearly unchanged. (I wonder, now, what the closing of the Doors has meant to the other worlds, not just my own familiar one.)

"Shall we?" I murmured to Bad. He led the way down the craggy hillside, away from the stone archway and raggedy curtain I'd come through, away from the sunbaked bloodstains flaking and cracking on the ground, and down into the City of Nin.

It was fully dusk by the time our feet hit cobbled city street. Honey-colored lamplight oozed from the windows and dinnertime conversations swooped swallowlike through the air above me. The language had a familiar rise-and-fall rhythm to it, a languorous roll that reminded me of my father's voice. The few passersby sort of looked like him, too—reddish-dark, black-eyed, with spirals of ink winding up their forearms. I'd grown up thinking of my father as fundamentally foreign, eccentric, unlike anyone else; now I saw he was just a man very far from home.

Judging from the staring and muttering and hurrying-past people were doing, *I* was still out of place, not quite right. I wondered if I would always be wrong-colored and in-between, no matter where I went, before recalling that I was wearing foreign clothing in a state of considerable disrepair and that Bad I were both limping, dirty, and bleeding.

I wound vaguely north, watching new stars wink mischievously at me in their strange constellations. I didn't, in fact, know where I was going—*a stone house on the high northern hillside* was imprecise, as addresses go—but this seemed a small, surmountable sort of obstacle.

I slumped against a white-stone wall and dug Mr. Ilvane's coppery-green compass out of my sack. I held it tight in my palm and thought of my father. The needle whirled westward, pointing straight out into the calm gray sea. I tried again, picturing instead a golden evening seventeen years ago when I'd lain with my mother on a sun-soaked quilt, when I had a home and a future and parents who loved me. The needle hesitated, jittering beneath the glass, and pointed not-quite-north.

I followed it.

I found a dirt track that seemed to align well with my little copper needle and followed it toward the straw-colored sickle of the moon. It was a well-traveled path but steep, and I paused sometimes to let the pain stomp its feet and yell in my ears, before shushing it and continuing on.

More stars emerged, like shimmering loops of writing in the sky. And then the low, shadowed bulk of a house appeared ahead of us. My heart—and I don't think any heart has ever been so exhausted and wrung-dry in the history of the world—stuttered to life in my chest.

The window lit with flickering light, and two figures stood illuminated: a man, tall but hunched with age, hair sprouting in white tufts around his skull, and an old woman with a kerchief around her hair and arms black to the shoulder with ink.

Neither of them was my father or my mother. Of course. You don't really know how high your hopes have gotten until you watch them plummeting earthward.

A logical person would have turned around then, returned to the city proper and begged or mimed their way into a warm meal and a place to sleep and some medical attention. They certainly wouldn't have staggered onward, tears sliding silently down their cheeks. They wouldn't have stood before the door-that-wasn't-theirs, a graying, salt-preserved slab of wood with an iron hook for a knob, and raised their good hand to knock.

And when an old woman answered, her seamed face tilted questioningly upward, eyes milky and squinting, they wouldn't have burst into tear-slurred speech. "Sorry to bother you, ma'am, it's just I was wondering if you know the man who used to live here. Only I've come a really long way and I wanted—I wanted to see him. Julian was his name. Yule Ian, I mean—"

I saw the old woman's mouth press into a thin line, like a sutured wound. She shook her head. "No." Then, almost angrily, "Who are you, to ask about my Yule, eh? We have not seen him for twenty years, almost."

I wanted to wail at the moon or curl up on the doorstep and weep like a little lost child. My father had never come home and neither had my mother, and what was broken would never be mended; the old woman's words were a final, cruel verdict.

They were also, rather mysteriously, in English.

A dangerous, foolish tingling began in my limbs. How did she know a language from my world? Had someone taught her? And had I gone entirely insane, or did she and I share the same cheekbones, perhaps the same tilt to our shoulders—but then the crowd of questions fell silent.

There was someone else in the little stone house on the hillside. Beside me, Bad's ears stood up straight.

I caught a flash of movement behind the old woman's lamp-lit silhouette—a white-gold glimmer in the darkness, like summer wheat—and then there was another woman standing in the doorway.

Now, with the calming benefit of time and familiarity, I can describe her to you easily: a tired, tough-looking woman with yellow hair gone gray at the temples, skin so freckled and burnt it could almost pass for native, and the sort of strong, unbeautiful features novelists call *arresting*.

But in that moment, standing on the threshold of the home I was born in, with a squeezing in my chest as if someone had reached behind my ribs and seized my heart, I looked at her all out of order. Her hands: thick-fingered, scored and hashed with shiny white scars, with three fingernails missing entirely. Her arms: stringy muscle wrapped in black ink. Her eyes: soft, dreamer's blue. Her nose, her square jaw, her level brows: all just like mine.

She didn't recognize me, of course. It was absurd to wish she did, after nearly seventeen years spent on different planets. I wished it anyway.

"Hello, Adelaide." Should I have called her *Mother* instead? The word sat heavy and unfamiliar on my tongue. I knew her better as a character from my father's book, anyway.

Her eyebrows crimped in the uncertain expression of someone who can't recall your name and doesn't want to offend— her mouth opened to say something like *Pardon me?* or *Have we met?* and I knew it would feel just like being shot again, a burrowing pain that would worsen with time—but then her eyes went wide.

Maybe it was because I'd spoken English, or maybe it was my familiar/foreign clothes that did it, but she began to look at me, *really* look at me, with an avid, desperate hunger in her face. I saw her eyes performing the same frenzied dance mine had a few moments before—my wild bundle of braided hair, my blood-rusted arm, my eyes, nose, chin—

And then she knew me.

I saw the knowing arrive, wonderful and terrible. In my memory she has two entirely different faces at once, like the god she named me for: On one face is riotous joy, blazing at me like the sun itself. On the other is deepest mourning, the keening, marrow-deep ache of someone who has looked for something too long and found it too late.

She reached her hand toward me, and I saw her mouth move. *Jan-u-ary.*

Everything wavered, like the final shaky frames of a film reel, and I remembered how achingly, terribly tired I was, how much I hurt, how many steps I'd taken to arrive at this precise place. I had time to think, *Hello, Mother*, and then I was falling forward into painless darkness.

I cannot be sure, but I thought I felt someone catch me as I fell. I thought I felt strong, wind-scoured arms wrap around me as if they would never let me go again, felt the thrum of someone else's heartbeat against my cheek—felt the jangled, broken thing in the center of me fit itself back together and begin, perhaps, to mend.

And now: I sit at this yellow-wood desk with a pen in my hand and a stack of cotton pages lying in wait, so clean and perfect that every word is a sin, a footstep in fresh-fallen snow. An old, unmarked compass sits on the windowsill, still pointing stubbornly out to sea. Tin-cut stars dangle above me, flashing and twisting in the amber sun slanting through the window. I watch little trails of light dance over the pearled scars on my arm, the neat bandaging at my shoulder, the cushions carefully piled around my hip. It still hurts, a burrowing, spine-deep heat that never quite fades; the doctor—Vert Bonemender, I think they called him—said it always would.

Seems fair, somehow. I think maybe if you write open a Door between worlds and consign your guardian-jailer to the eternal blackness of the Threshold, you shouldn't get to feel precisely the way you did before.

And anyway, Bad and I will match. I can see him now, scrubbing his back against the stony hillside in that ecstatic way of dogs that makes you think maybe you should give it a try. He looks sleek and bronze again, without those jaggedy stitches and lumps all over him, but one leg still doesn't seem to straighten all the way.

Beyond him, I see the sea. Dove-gray, gold-tipped in the sunlight. Adelaide had this room added to the stone house on the hillside years ago; I don't think it's an accident that the windows face the sea, so she can keep her eyes always on the horizon, watching, searching, hoping.

It is the sixteenth day I've been here. My father hasn't come.

I convinced Ade (Ade is still easier to say than *Mother*; she doesn't correct me, but sometimes I see her flinch, as if her name is a stone I've thrown at her) not to load up her boat and sail out into the blue looking for him, mapless and rudderless, but it was a near thing. I reminded her that neither of us knew where his Door came through to the Written, that all sorts of perils might have befallen him in between, that she would feel really stupid if she sailed away from Nin just as Father was sailing toward it. So she stays, but her whole body has become another compass needle leaning seaward.

"It's not so different, really," she told me on the third day. We were in the stone dimness of her bedroom, in the soft, breathing hours before dawn. I was propped on pillows, too fevered and pain-racked to sleep, and she sat on the floor with her back against the bed and Bad's head in her lap. She hadn't moved in three days, as far as I could tell; every time I opened my eyes I saw the square line of her shoulders, the white-streaked tangle of her hair.

"Before, I was always searching for him, questing after him. Now I'm waiting for him." Her voice was tired.

"So you...you did try." I licked my cracked lips. "To find us." I made an effort to keep the bitterness and hurt out of my voice, the *Where have you been all these years* and the *We needed you*—yes, I know it isn't fair to blame my mother for being stuck in another world my entire life, but hearts aren't chessboards and they don't play by the rules—but she heard it anyway.

The firm line of her shoulders flinched, then curved inward. She pressed her palms against her eyes. "Child, I have tried to find you every single damn day for seventeen years."

I didn't say anything. Couldn't, actually.

After a moment, she went on. "When that door closed—when that son of a bitch closed it, according to you—I was left stranded on that little scrap of rock for... days and days. I don't know how long, t'tell the truth. No food, a little water I found floating in the wreckage. My breasts hurting, then leaking, then drying up, and I couldn't get to you, couldn't find my baby—" I heard her swallow. "The sun got at me after a while, and I started to think maybe I could burrow through the stone and find my way through to you. If I tried hard enough. I guess that's how they found me: crazy as a loon, clawing at solid rock, crying."

She curled her hands to her chest, hiding her missing fingernails. That newly mended thing in my chest ached.

"It was a couple of fisherfolk from the City of Plumm who'd seen us sail away, and got worried when we didn't come back. They took me in, fed me, put up with a lot of swearing and screaming. Kept a rope tied around my middle, I guess, so's I wouldn't dive back into the sea. I don't... remember too much of that time."

But she'd gotten better, eventually, or at least better enough to lay plans. She bought passage back to the City of Nin, told Yule Ian's parents what happened—"I told the whole truth, like a fool, but they just figured their son and grandbaby got lost at sea and set about mourning"—earned, begged, and stole sufficient funds to outfit *The Key*, and sailed off in search of another way home.

The first years were lean and frantic. There are still stories told about the mad widow who turned white with grief, who endlessly sails the seas in search of her lost love. She haunts out-of-the-way places—ocean caves and abandoned mines and forgotten ruins—calling out for her baby girl.

She stumbled through dozens of Doors. She saw winged cats

that spoke in riddles, sea dragons with mother-of-pearl scales, green cities that floated high in the clouds, men and women made of granite and alabaster. But she never found the only Door she wanted. She wasn't even sure such a Door existed, or that she would find her husband and daughter on the other side of it. ("I thought maybe you got lost in the in-between—thought maybe I should go diving in after you, sometimes.")

Eventually she took up small-time trading to pay her way around the Written. She earned a reputation as a sailor willing to go very far for very little money or sometimes just for the price of a good story or two, who was sometimes delayed for days or weeks but who often showed up with strange and wondrous goods to sell. She never made much money because she refused to run regular routes to the same places, as any sane trader would, but she didn't go hungry.

And she kept looking. Even after she knew her daughter would be ten, twelve, fifteen—an absolute stranger to her; even after Yule's parents suggested, gently, that she might have another child if she remarried soon. Even after she'd forgotten the precise shape of Yule Ian's hands around his pen, the way he hunched over his work, or the way his shoulders shook when he laughed (had I ever seen him laugh like that?).

"I come back here a few times a year, between jobs, sleep in my own house, remember how to set still. Visit Julian's folks, who moved out here when Tilsa gave up her ink shop. But mostly I just...keep moving."

The sun had risen by then, and a line of lemony light crept across the floor. I felt like something recently taken apart, scrubbed clean, and reassembled, except nothing was quite where it used to be. There was still some bitterness floating around in there, and quite a bit of hurt, but there was also something feather-light and glimmering—forgiveness, maybe, or compassion.

I hadn't spoken in so long my voice creaked a little, like a disused hinge. "I always used to dream about a life like that. Roaming around, free."

My mother blew a sad huff of laughter out her nose. "A natural-born wanderer, like I always said." She stroked Bad's head, scratching his favorite under-the-chin spot. He became a furry bronze puddle in her lap, pawing weakly at the air. "But take it from me: freedom isn't worth a single solitary shit if it isn't shared. I've spent so much time wishing we'd never sailed through that door, January. But at my ugliest, most self-ish moments—I wished it had been me standing in the prow, with you. At least Julian had *you*." Her voice was so soft I could hardly hear it, choked with seventeen years of vicious pain.

I thought of my father. Of how rarely I saw him, and how his face had the same hollowed-out tiredness my mother's did, and how his eyes skimmed across my face as if it might hurt if he looked too long. "I ... Yes, he had me. But I wasn't enough." Odd—that used to make me so angry, but now the anger had gone all runny and soft, like melting wax.

A ragged, furious gasp from my mother. "You damn well *should* have been! Was he—did he—" I knew she was going to ask, *Was he a good father?* and I found I didn't want to answer; it seemed needlessly cruel.

"Would I have been enough for *you*?" I asked instead. "Would you have stopped looking for Father?"

I heard her breath catch, but she didn't answer. She didn't need to. "Here." I wallowed around in my cushions and quilts, found the warm leather cover of *The Ten Thousand Doors*. "I think you ought to read this. So you can"—*forgive him*—"understand him."

She took it.

I still catch her rereading passages, running her fingers over the printed words like they were miracles or magic charms, her lips moving in something very much like prayer. I think it helps. Well, not *helps*, exactly—I think it hurts like hell to reread the narrative of her life, with all its broken promises and lost chances, to read about the man my father became and the choices he made.

But she keeps reading it. It's a kind of proof, I suppose, that he still lives and still loves her, that he's striving to find his way back to her. That what was shattered will be made whole again.

So now there are two of us staring seaward. Waiting. Hoping. Watching ships crest the curve of the horizon, reading the black swirls of blessings stitched into their sails. My mother translates them for me, sometimes: *To many fat fish. To mutually profitable dealings. To safe travels and strong currents.*

Sometimes my grandparents sit with us and watch, too. We don't do a lot of talking, probably because we're busy being mutually stunned at one another's existence, but I like the feel of them sitting near me. Tilsa, my grandmother, often holds my hand, as if she isn't quite convinced I'm real.

Sometimes, when it's just the two of us, my mother and I talk. I told her about Locke House and the Society and the asylum, about Father and Jane and rather a lot about you. I told her about Aunt Lizzie living alone on the Larson farm. ("Lord, I'd like to see her," my mother sighed. I reminded her that the Door was open and she could skip through it any day of the week, and her eyes went wide. But she didn't leave; she kept staring toward the horizon.)

We're mostly quiet now. She mends ripped canvas, rereads my father's book, stands on the hillside with the salt-sweet wind drying the tear tracks on her face.

I write. I wait. I think of you.

There is a sail rising on the horizon now, like a sharp-toothed moon. Its blessings are crooked and rough-looking, as if sewn in a wild hurry by someone unskilled with needle and thread.

It's only as the ship grows larger that I realize: I don't need these blessings translated. I can read them myself, in plainest English: *To home. To true love. To Adelaide.*

I can see—can I? Am I imagining it?—the sun-silhouetted figure of a single sailor standing in the prow. He leans toward the city, toward the stone house on the hillside, toward his heart's desire.

Oh, Father. You're home.

And now: I curl in the belly of *The Key*, writing by the silver-tongued light of the full, foreign moon. The wood smells of cloves and tannin and juniper wine. It smells of sunsets on strange horizons, of nameless constellations and spinning compass needles and the forgotten borderlands at the edge of the world. It can't be entirely coincidental that my mother's ship smells just like my father's book.

Well, I suppose it's not my mother's ship anymore, is it? She gave it to Bad and me. "It deserves a good last run, I figure," she'd said, and smiled in a crookedy, sad sort of way. My father's arm had tightened around her shoulders and the smile had righted itself like a gull pulling up from a dive, soaring sunward.

They'd both looked so young as I sailed away from them.

They'd wanted me to stay, of course, but I couldn't. Partly—and you're forbidden from ever telling them this—it's because standing beside my parents is not dissimilar from standing beside an open blast furnace. When I turn away from them my cheeks feel raw and sunburnt, and my eyes sting as though I've been staring directly at the sun.

It's been like that since the moment my father stepped off his ship. Bad and I were still making our slow, limping way down the stone streets, sweat-sticky in the afternoon heat;

my mother was already on the pier, bare feet *slap-slap-slapp*ing over the boards, hair running like a pennant behind her. A dark figure stumbled toward her wearing a familiar shapeless coat, his arms upraised and his hands wrapped in rough bandaging. They moved as if drawn together by physical law, like two stars hurtling toward collision—and then my father staggered to a halt.

He was feet away from my mother. He leaned toward her, raised one rag-wrapped hand to hover above the curve of her cheek, but did not touch her.

I'd stopped moving, watching them from a hundred yards away, hissing *go-go-go* under my breath.

But my father was for some reason resisting the thing that had kept him in desperate motion for seventeen years, that'd dragged him through ten thousand worlds and finally brought him here, standing in the City of Nin in 1911 by my reckoning, or 6938 by his, looking into his true love's summer-sky eyes. It was as if his own heart had split in two and gone to war against itself.

He curled his hand away from my mother's face. His head bowed forward and his lips moved. I couldn't hear the words, but later my mother told me what he said: *I left her. I left our daughter behind.*

I watched my mother's spine straighten, her head tilt to one side. *Yes,* she told him. *And if you thought you could come crawling back to me without our baby girl and everything would be all right— son, you got another think coming.*

His head fell further, his poor, burnt hands hanging hopeless at his sides.

Then my mother smiled, and I could almost feel the blazing pride of it from where I stood. *Luckily for you,* she said, *our kid took matters into her own hands.*

He didn't understand, of course. But it was at that moment that Bad came limping into view. I saw my father see him, saw him freeze, like a man who has just encountered a mathematical impossibility and is struggling to understand how two plus two is suddenly five. Then he looked up, up—his face lit with luminous, wild hope—

He saw me.

And then he collapsed onto the pier, weeping. My mother knelt beside him, circled his heaving shoulders with the same strong, sunburnt arms she'd wrapped around me that first night, and pressed her forehead against his.

Probably it was only in my head that a silent thunderclap rolled out over the waves, that everyone in the streets of the City of Nin paused in their work and stood, looking toward the shore, and felt their hearts thrum in their chests. Probably.

But it's my story to tell, now, isn't it?

I've gotten sort of good at storytelling, I think. When I finally told my father my own story, he watched me with such intensity he must've forgotten to blink, because tears kept creeping down the side of his nose and dripping, silently, onto the floor.

He didn't say anything when I finished, but only reached out to trace the words carved into my arm. His face, which was still thin and hungry-looking despite days of my mother's awful cooking, was racked with guilt.

"Stop that," I ordered him.

He blinked at me. "Stop—?"

"I *won*, see. I escaped Brattleboro and Havemeyer and Ilvane, I survived Mr. Locke—" My father interrupted with expletives in several languages, and some rather violent-sounding hopes for Locke's eternal afterlife. "Hush, that's not the point. The point is that I was scared and hurt and alone sometimes, but in the end I won. I'm... free. And if that's the price for being free, I'll pay it." I paused, feeling a little dramatic. "And I'd like to go on paying it."

361

My father stared into my face for several inscrutable seconds, then looked past me to my mother. Something annoyingly telepathic slipped between them, and then he said, softly, "I shouldn't be proud, because I did not raise you—but I am." The mended thing in my chest purred.

They didn't try too hard to stop me from leaving, after that. Well, they had their concerns (my father and grandmother begged me to stay and apprentice to a real word-worker, on the grounds that I'd done impossible, powerful things with my words and ought to be properly instructed; I argued that it's much easier to break the rules of reality when you don't know exactly what they are, and anyway I was through with studies and lessons), but they didn't try to lock me up. Instead, they gave me everything I needed to do what I was going to do. Even though it was dangerous, and scary, and perhaps a little mad.

My grandmother gave me several dozen flat honey cakes she baked herself, and offered to hide my scars beneath tattoos, if I liked. I considered it, tracing the raised white lines of the words in my flesh (*SHE WRITES A DOOR OF BLOOD AND SILVER. THE DOOR OPENS JUST FOR HER*), and shook my head. Then I asked if she could tattoo around the scars without covering them up, and now there are wandering tendrils of words sliding up my arm, weaving between the white-cut letters like black vines. *January Wordworker, daughter of Adelaide Lee Larson and Yule Ian Scholar, born in the City of Nin and bound for the In-Between. May she wander but always return home, may all her words be written true, may every door lie open before her.*

My mother gave me *The Key* and three solid weeks of sailing lessons. Father tried briefly to argue that, as the more experienced sailor, he ought to teach me, but my mother just looked at him in this flat, square-jawed way, and said, "Not anymore, Julian," and he went very quiet and did not interrupt again.

My father gave me a book titled *Tales of the Amarico Sea*. It's written in a language I don't speak, with an alphabet I don't recognize, but he seems to think languages are things one just "picks up," like milk at the store. He also gave me his shapeless, patched coat, which used to be my mother's, because it'd kept him warm in faraway places and always seen him safely home, and perhaps it would do the same for me. Besides, he said, he was through with wandering now.

"And, January"—his voice was strained and thin, as if it were coming from a long way away—"I'm sorry. For leaving you all those times, and for leaving you the last time. I t-tried to turn back, at the last, I l-love—" He stopped, tear-choked, his eyes closed in shame.

I didn't say *It's all right*, or *I forgive you*, because I wasn't sure it was or I did. Instead I said simply, "I know."

And I fell into him the way I had as a very small girl when he returned from his trips abroad, the way I hadn't when I was seven. We stayed that way for a while, my face smeared against his chest, his arms tight around me, until I pulled back.

I scrubbed my cheeks. "Anyway, I won't be gone forever. I'll visit. It's your turn to wait."

The rest of my family (see that scrolled *f*, like a leaf unfurling in the sunlight?) together gave me food, fresh water in clay casks, charts of the Amarico, a compass that pointed reliably north, a set of new clothes sewn from sailcloth into very rough approximations of pants and shirts by seamstresses who'd never actually seen them in real life. They're odd, in-between sorts of clothes, a perfect patchwork of two worlds; I think they suit me rather well.

I intend, after all, to spend the rest of my life diving in and out of the wild in-between—finding the thin, overlooked places that connect worlds, following the trail of locked Doors the Society left behind and writing them back open.

Letting all the dangerous, beautiful madness flow freely between worlds again. Forging myself into a living key and opening the Doors, just like my father said.

(This is the second reason I couldn't stay in Nin with my parents, of course.)

You can guess, I bet, which Door I'm opening first: the mountain door my mother sailed through in 1893, that Mr. Locke destroyed in 1895; the Door that shattered my little family into pieces and sent us careening alone into the fearful darkness. It's an old wrong that ought to be righted, and a far enough journey that I might finish this damn book in time. (Who knew writing a story would be so much *work*? I have a newfound respect for all those maligned dime novelists and romance writers.)

You're wondering why I've written it at all. Why I'm here, hunched over a sheaf of moonlit papers with my hand cramping and nothing but my dog and the wide silvery shadow of the ocean for company, writing as if my very soul depends on it. Maybe it's a family compulsion.

Maybe it's simple fear. Fear that I might fail in my lofty purposes and leave no record behind me. The Society, after all, is an organization of very powerful and very dangerous beings who have crept through the cracks in our world, all of whom very much want the Doors to remain closed. And it would be foolish to suppose that our world has been the only one to attract such creatures or ignite such ideas. In my nightmares I'm in an endless carnival hall filled with Havemeyers, reaching their white hands toward me through a thousand mirrors; in my really bad nightmares the mirrors are filled with pale eyes, and I can feel my will unspooling inside me.

It's dangerous, is what I'm saying. So I've written this story as a sort of extended insurance policy in case I screw up.

If you're some stranger who stumbled over this book by

chance—perhaps rotting in some foreign garbage pile or locked in a dusty traveling trunk or published by some small, misguided press and shelved mistakenly under Fiction—I hope to every god you have the guts to do what needs doing. I hope you will find the cracks in the world and wedge them wider, so the light of other suns shines through; I hope you will keep the world unruly, messy, full of strange magics; I hope you will run through every open Door and tell stories when you return.

But that's not really why I wrote this, of course.

I wrote it for you. So that you might read it and remember the things you were told to forget.

You remember me now, don't you? And you remember the offer you made me?

Well. Now at least you can look clear-eyed into your own future, and choose: stay safe and sane at home, as any rational man would—I swear I'll understand—

Or run away with me toward the glimmering, mad horizon. Dance through this eternal green orchard, where ten thousand worlds hang ripe and red for the plucking; wander with me between the trees, tending them, clearing away the weeds, letting in the air.

Opening the Doors.

Epilogue

The Door in the Mist

It is late October. Jagged lines of frost creep and bloom in every windowpane, and steam wisps from the lake; winter in Vermont is an impatient thing.

It is dawn, and a young man is loading sacks of Washington Mills Peerless White Flour into a truck. The truck is glossy black, with curlicued golden lettering painted on the side. The young man is dark and solemn-eyed. He pulls his cap low against the chill, mist pearling against the back of his neck.

He works in the comfortable rhythm of someone familiar with hard work, but there are faint, unhappy lines gathered around his mouth. The lines are fresh-seeming, as if they've only recently arrived and aren't certain how to behave. They age him.

His family attributes the lines to a slow recovery from his illness over the summer. One night at the end of July he simply vanished—after some very odd behavior and an urgent conversation with that African woman from Locke House—and staggered back home nearly two weeks later, disoriented and senseless. He didn't seem to recall where he'd been or why, and the doctor (actually the horse doctor, who prescribed more stringent tonics at half the price) speculated that a bad fever might have boiled his brain, and recommended purgatives and time.

Time has helped, some. The dizzy confusion of July dissipated into a vague uncertainty, a slight cloudiness in his eyes, and a tendency to stare out at the horizon as if he were hoping something or someone might appear there. Even his beloved story papers can't hold his attention for long. His family supposes it will fade, eventually, and Samuel himself hopes the ache in his chest will fade, too, and the nagging sense that he's lost something very dear to him but can't recall what it was.

Three weeks previously something happened that made it worse: A woman had approached him as he made his delivery to Shelburne Inn. She was obviously foreign, black as oil, and far too familiar for someone so strange. She said a lot of things that made no sense to him—or rather, they did but then didn't, as if the words were sagging and sloughing away in his mind, and he could almost hear a voice saying *Forget it all, boy*—and eventually she grew irritated with him.

She had pressed a slip of paper into his hand with an address scrawled in red ink, and whispered, "Just in case."

"In case what, ma'am?" he'd asked.

"In case you remember." She had sighed, and something in the sigh made him wonder if she had a hole in her heart, too. "Or in case you see her again." And she was gone.

Since then he has felt the ache in his chest like an open window in winter.

It is worse on mornings like this one, when he is alone and the crows' cries are brittle and cold. He thinks, for no reason at all, of the gray ponies he drove as a boy, of rattling down the drive to Locke House and looking up at the third-story window hoping to see—he does not recall what he hoped to see. He tries to think only about delivery routes and flour, and how best to position the busted sack so it won't spill.

Movement startles him. Two figures have emerged, rather

suddenly, from the mist at the end of the cobbled alley. A dog, heavy-jawed and deep gold, and a young woman.

She is tall and brownish, and her hair is braided and coiled in a fashion he has never seen before. She is dressed like some combination of vagabond and debutante—a fine blue skirt fastened with pearl buttons, a leather belt slung low over her hips, a shapeless coat that looks several centuries older than she is. She limps, just slightly; so does the dog.

The dog barks at him, joyfully, and Samuel becomes aware that he is staring. He flicks his eyes sternly back to the flour sacks. But there is something about her, isn't there, a sort of glow, like light shining around a closed door—

He imagines her wearing a champagne-colored gown, dripping pearls, surrounded by the bustle and swirl of a fancy party. She looks very unhappy in this imagining, like something caged.

She does not look unhappy now; indeed, she is beaming, her smile shining bonfire-bright and a little wild. It takes him a moment to realize she has stopped walking, and the smile is for him.

"Hello, Samuel," she says, and her voice is like a knock at that closed door.

"Ma'am," he answers. He knows at once it was the wrong thing to say, because her bonfire-smile dims a little. The dog is unconcerned; he shimmies up to Samuel as if they are old friends.

The woman's smile is sad, but her voice is steady. "I have something for you, Mr. Zappia." She produces from her coat a fat bundle of papers tied with what appears to be brown string, a rag, and a strand of fencing wire. "Sorry about the mess—I wasn't patient enough to get it printed and bound."

Samuel takes the pile of paper, because there doesn't seem

to be anything else to do. He notices as he does so that her left wrist is a labyrinth of ink and scars.

"I know this must all seem very strange to you, but please just read it. As a sort of favor to me, although I guess that doesn't mean much anymore." The woman huffs an almost-laugh. "Read it anyway. And when you're done, come find me. You know—you still remember where Locke House is, don't you?"

Samuel wonders if perhaps this young woman is a bit mad. "Yes. But Mr. Locke has been away for months now—the house is empty, the staff have started to leave—there are rumors about his will, about his return—"

The woman flaps an unworried hand. "Oh, he won't be returning. And his will has just recently been, ah, discovered." Her smile is sly, mischievous, with a little curl of vengeance at its edges. "Once the lawyers get done signing things and siphoning off as much money as they can, the house will be mine. I think it'll suit my purposes rather well, once I get rid of his ghastly collections." Samuel tries to picture this wild young woman as the rightful heiress to Locke's fortune, fails, and wonders if perhaps she is mad *and* a criminal. He wonders why this possibility doesn't bother him more. "I'm thinking I ought to return his things to their proper owners, where possible, which will require a great deal of travel to some very strange and surprising places." Her eyes spark and flare at the thought.

"We'll go to East Africa first, of course. We'll need Jane to show us the precise spot, but I imagine she'll turn up—have you seen her, by chance?" She continues before Samuel can answer. "I'll miss her terribly once she goes home, but I might be able to do something about that...There are so many doors in Locke House, after all—who's to say where they lead?"

She squints her eyes like a woman redecorating her parlor. "One to Africa, one to Kentucky, maybe even one to a certain cabin on the north end of the lake, if you like. They'll cost me, but it would be worth the price. And I'm getting stronger, I think."

"Ah," says Samuel.

That summer-bright smile returns, shining at him like a small sun. "Read fast, Samuel. We have work to do." She reaches up, quite fearlessly, and touches his cheek. Her fingers are ember-warm against his cold skin, and she is very close to him now and her eyes are alight and the hole in his heart is howling, chattering, aching—

And he sees her face, just for a moment, peering down at him from the third story of Locke House. *January.* The word is a door creaking open in his chest, pouring light into that terrible absence.

She kisses him—a soft heat, so fleeting he isn't sure whether he imagined it—and turns away. Samuel finds himself entirely unable to speak.

He watches the woman and her dog walk back down the alley. She stops and draws her finger through the air, as if she were writing something on the sky. The mist swirls and snakes around her like a great pale cat. It draws itself into a shape like an archway or a door.

She steps through it, and is gone.

Acknowledgments

Books, like babies, require villages. Through a combination of luck, privilege, and witchcraft, I happen to have the best village in the history of the world. This, I am afraid, is simple math.

I am grateful to my agent, Kate McKean, who answered every email with patience and grace, even the ones with bullet points and color coding and extraneous historical statistics. To Nivia Evans, an editor who knows the difference between doors and Doors, and whose chief business is building more of them for readers to walk through. And to Emily Byron, Ellen Wright, Andy Ball, Amy Schneider, and the entire Orbit/Redhook team, who know how to make those Doors shine on the shelf.

To Jonah Sutton-Morse, Ziv Wities, and Laura Blackwell, the first people to read this book who weren't contractually bound to be kind through either blood or marriage, but who were kind anyway.

To the history departments of Berea College and the University of Vermont, who should not be held accountable for my fanciful use of fact, but who should probably be blamed for the footnotes.

To my mother, for giving us ten thousand worlds for the

choosing—Middle Earth and Narnia, Tortall and Hyrule, Barrayar and Jeep and Pern—and my brothers for wandering through them with me. To my father for believing we could build our own, and for standing beside me in that overgrown hayfield in western Kentucky.

To Finn, who was born in the exact middle of this book, and Felix, who was born at the very end. Neither of them helped in the slightest way, except to trample around in my heart, toppling walls and letting in the light.

And to Nick, first and last and always. Because you can't write your heart out until you've found it.